AN ANDALUSIAN
MURDER MYSTERY

AN ANDALUSIAN MURDER MYSTERY

PETER PEETERS

The Book Guild Ltd

First published in Great Britain in 2018 by
The Book Guild Ltd
9 Priory Business Park
Wistow Road, Kibworth
Leicestershire, LE8 0RX
Freephone: 0800 999 2982
www.bookguild.co.uk
Email: info@bookguild.co.uk
Twitter: @bookguild

This work is entirely fictitious and bears no resemblance to any persons living or dead.

Typeset in Garamond

Printed and bound in Great Britain by CPI Group (UK) Ltd, Croydon, CR0 4YY

ISBN 978 1912083 299

British Library Cataloguing in Publication Data.
A catalogue record for this book is available from the British Library.

PROLOGUE
FEBRUARY 1994

'You want us to go to southern Spain!' exclaimed Julie. 'You're not expecting me to lie on a beach with hundreds of tourists and enjoy it, are you?' Julie was not very tall, but when she objected strongly to something, as she did just now, she seemed to grow in size.

'No, no! We're going to a quiet village inland. It'll be the most peaceful holiday you've ever had,' promised Charles. 'Believe me.'

'You use the word peaceful! And you're asking me to believe you? Remember 1974? We'd just met and to surprise me you took me to Cyprus…'

'But I chose the island specifically because you like history and ruins. And weren't the villages picturesque?'

'They were. But we'd only just arrived when the Turkish army invaded and we had to flee! It wasn't exactly peaceful.'

'That wasn't my fault, was it? How could I have known? I just wanted to surprise you.'

'And surprise me you did!'

'Well… things do happen in the world…'

'Sure, sure… That may be fortunate for your job, but not for unsuspecting people like me,' protested Julie. 'Do you remember that time you took me to Dubrovnik? When was that again…' She put a finger on her lips and started thinking, an expression of intense concentration on her face. 'A few years ago…'

'But I had to go there on a mission and you didn't want to stay behind! That's why I took you. And Dubrovnik is a very beautiful town.'

'Maybe, but while we were there the Serbs, or some people like them, started shelling the town and we had to leave in a hurry. You and your peace missions! Can't you do something else?'

'As if I had the choice! It's fortunate communism collapsed and Eastern Europe fell apart, otherwise they wouldn't have employed me at all in recent years. Even so, I wonder when I will get another assignment. I've been waiting for months now and nothing turns up.'

'And to think I gave up my job for you!' Julie sighed. 'Mind you,' she added as an afterthought, 'it wasn't well paid, and doing fieldwork in the winter rains wasn't very pleasant.'

'But you told me you gave up your job because you liked going to foreign places and seeing ruins and historical things! And then you didn't like some of the places we went to because they were too insecure… that's why I have chosen Spain where everything *is* secure – I thought we might as well spend the rest of the winter in southern Andalusia, rather than wait here in Brussels for a sign that they will consider any of my proposals. And now you don't want to go there!' Charles shook his head.

'Yes, but Spain! I went there before we met… to a place called Marbella. And I didn't like it. There was no war or unrest, but there were policemen in green uniforms everywhere… and there was no culture.'

'That was all a long time ago. Franco died in 1975, and Spain is very different today. And you may not think so judging from what you've seen in Marbella, but the country is actually a treasure chest filled to the brim with history.'

'All right,' agreed Julie. 'But can we at least visit a few interesting places?'

'Well… as we've got all the time in the world we might as well drive down to Andalusia and see plenty of ruins and old towns on our way through France and Spain.'

When she heard this, Julie's eyes brightened and Charles couldn't help thinking how pretty she was. 'You've convinced me!' she exclaimed. 'So once we get there, where are we going to stay?'

'In the house of one of my friends in a small village called Frigiliana. And I can promise you that nothing ever happens there.'

'No invasions… no unrest?'

'Promised,' said Charles.

And two days later they were off.

That was in 1994. And as no foreign troops had invaded Frigiliana during their stay, Julie was keen to return the following year to another uneventful holiday…

PART ONE
SPRING IN ANDALUSIA

1

Charles had just stepped out onto the terrace at the top of the house where they were staying when he heard someone shout in the street below, 'Oh Jack, ain't this quaint!' As he leaned out over the railing he saw an overweight woman struggle up the steps of Calle El Darra, the steep street leading to the top of the old part of Frigiliana. Jack, probably her husband and equally plump, lifted his camera and began taking pictures of the street, of the black metal grilles in front of the windows and of the pots with brightly-coloured flowers that contrasted so vividly with the white-chalked walls. Even Sam, the black curly-haired dog lying fast asleep in the sun in the middle of one of the steps, had his picture taken.

'You're right,' agreed the man who was called Jack. 'I don't think I've ever seen such a picturesque village in my life. Hey Beth, wait for me!' he shouted as he tried to catch up with his wife who was about to disappear into the alleyway that led to the Garden Restaurant higher up. He quickened his pace, puffing with the effort, his camera clicking away as he took a few more photographs, until he too turned into the alleyway and disappeared from view. Americans, reflected Charles as silence returned.

It was getting on for ten but Julie and Charles had arrived late the previous evening and he had only just got up. Agustina must already be there, he thought, because the small wooden donkey was standing outside the souvenir shop that took up the ground floor of the house where they stayed. The donkey was about two feet high, carried a pot of bright-red geraniums on each side and it had long ears, which had been broken a number of times and glued on again – even now it had clamps around its right ear. It was patched up all over the place but it was attractive and children and grown-ups alike loved it. Presently he saw Agustina going in and out of her shop carrying odds and ends such as glazed pots, a mannequin, dresses and woollen blankets, displaying the lot artistically along the outside walls.

The shop's strategic situation at the beginning of El Darra Street which led to the traffic-free upper part of the old village, and the colourful exhibition of goods at the shop front and on the opposite low wall, never failed to attract tourists. The wooden donkey further reduced the passage while Sam, Agustina's dog who was usually sprawled out full length on the step in front of the door, almost filling up the rest of the narrow street, helped in his own, innocent way to slow the pace of passing tourists and divert them into the shop which Agustina had called *Locura* – Madness. It seemed a very appropriate name.

Charles felt pleased with himself and with life in general. They were going to stay here for two whole months with nothing to do but enjoy themselves, visit a few places, eat out every now and then, and meet the friends they had made last year. It was such a relief to be here after Bosnia. And he'd even been sent to Somalia a few months ago! Julie is right, he thought. I should be leading a quieter life. There he was, forty-four and still rushing off to all those dangerous places, risking his life. Was it worth it? He had to admit that it was no fun for Julie who sometimes didn't see him for weeks on end. And when he hadn't got an assignment it was even worse: if he went on being as stressed as he had been last year, waiting for one of his proposals to be accepted, his light-brown hair would soon lose its colour – it was already beginning to grey at the temples. No, nothing could beat the tranquillity of village life. Julie had told him that she was set on buying a house in the village, or maybe a small farmstead with some land around. 'Country life is what we need,' she had said. 'No more problems or insecurity, a small plot of land for vegetables, and a garden with lots of flowers. Healthy outdoor life, blue skies and sunshine… that'll keep us young.'

Just then Charles heard the clatter of mules' hooves on the cobblestone steps of Calle El Darra. A mule was climbing up, a heavy bag sticking out on each side. As usual, the muleteer was hanging on to the tail. Muleteers did this to steer the mule by pulling the tail towards left or right, but Charles half suspected that hanging on to the tail was also an effortless way to get up.

Climbing up was hard work but not very dangerous; it was coming down that was quite a feat. Charles remembered how last year, sitting on the terrace, he had often heard the hooves of descending mules clatter and slide, making him hold his breath, expecting the inevitable fall. But the mules invariably regained their balance and got down the street safely. Humans found this more difficult. The cobblestones had been polished over the years by thousands upon thousands of feet; they shone like mirrors and the steps, each about five feet deep and slightly sloped, were extremely slippery. The local people all knew and walked down carefully so as not to lose their balance, but many an unsuspecting tourist had found him- or herself suddenly sprawled in a most ridiculous position, legs stuck up in the air, sun hat and bag rolling down the steep street. But then, thought Charles, wasn't that all part of the fun of being on holiday?

2

When Julie opened her eyes and realised where she was she felt immensely happy. This was the life she had always longed for: travelling to foreign places slowly, at her own rhythm, while having time to spend a day or two in a beautiful old town or to visit a museum. She liked museums and anything ancient.

As a child she had often dreamt that she would one day excavate the remains of ancient civilisations and in a way, it had come true. After that disastrous holiday in Cyprus, now many years ago, she had gone back to England to study archaeology. The problem had been finding a job afterwards. She had done some fieldwork, but standing up to her knees in the mud while digging for elusive pre-Anglo-Saxon artefacts had been much less fun than she had expected.

It was fortunate that Charles had refused to take 'no' for an answer when she had left him in 1974, and that they had got together again. He was such a wonderful man – kind-hearted and affectionate. Pity about his job though; it forced them to live in Brussels. And they always sent him to dangerous places. If only they could lead a quieter life…

But today all this didn't matter. Nothing mattered. It was only the beginning of March but the sky was blue and the bright sunlight, filtering through the curtains, was shining on Julie's face. She closed her eyes again, savouring the moment, feeling elated. They were going to spend two uneventful months in Frigiliana, far away from the hassle and foul climate of Brussels. Sixty sun-drenched days with nothing to do. What a privilege! What more could anyone dream of?

3

It must have been well past ten by the time Charles heard Julie get up because the bus from Nerja, the holiday resort on the coast, had just arrived. As usual it was full of tourists who came here for the day. In this out-of-season period they were mostly retired people, but they invaded the village like a band of schoolchildren turned loose, chatting excitedly in English, German, French, Dutch, Danish or Swedish.

When Julie and Charles first came to the village a year ago, they too had felt like those tourists. Driving up from Nerja they had rounded a bend of the narrow road and suddenly, in the distance, the bright cluster of Frigiliana spread out in front of their astonished eyes. The old part of the village looked like a jumble of white cubes rising out of the green-brown countryside. It was a harmonious entity of small, intertwined human habitations that had grown over the centuries. The houses seemed to be piled up one on top of the other, all huddled together as if seeking protection in their closeness. Only a few isolated properties, detached from the rest like foam blown off a wave, were scattered towards the flat top of the hill that towered above the village against the background of a purple-blue mountain range, the Sierra Almijara. It was a vision of beauty – a perfection to behold.

As they had entered the village, coming from the grey, miserable northern winter into the sunlight radiating from the houses with the vastness of the azure sky above, they too had succumbed to the enchantment of Frigiliana without an afterthought. They had walked the steps of its narrow streets in excitement, discovering a new, even more extraordinary view at every turn: this was Andalusia at its best. They had soon forgotten the rain and depressing weather of the north and after a few weeks they had taken the sunshine and beauty for granted.

Nothing has changed, thought Charles as he stood looking out from his terrace over the dazzlingly white walls and red-tiled roofs of the village with the rolling hills below, sloping down towards the sea a few miles away. The view is still as breathtaking as it was before. It's exactly as I remember it. This is total peace at last – just what I need.

'Breakfast!' Julie suddenly called out. 'Come on. I've got shopping to do.'

4

An hour or so later Julie was back, her eyes glowing with excitement. 'You won't believe this,' she said dropping her shopping bags on the floor. 'It took me almost half an hour to get to the grocer's shop. Everybody recognised me and wanted to kiss me and have a chat!'

No wonder, thought Charles. Julie did stand out in Frigiliana with her slender figure, her Nordic skin and fair curls framing her pretty heart-shaped face – she was very different from the people over here.

'And look what I found in the grocery.' Julie dug into one of the bags, bringing out a greenish-looking fruit with reticulated skin and holding it up.

'A custard apple! I thought the season had ended by now. How wonderful!' Charles immediately set out for the kitchen and came back a minute later with a knife, teaspoon and a small plate. He cut the custard apple in half and began scooping out the sweet white flesh with the teaspoon, sticking it in his mouth while mumbling ecstatically, 'Yumm…'

'Oh, by the way, we're invited for tea this afternoon.'

'Wheh?' Charles found it difficult to articulate because his mouth was full.

'At Sarah's. Remember Michael and Sarah? I met her at the grocer's shop. So I bought a cake and biscuits.'

'Do I really have to come?' protested Charles after having spat out a few black pips on the plate.

'Of course. They're expecting you.'

'But I just feel like lolling about for a day or two after all this driving.'

He continued eating, 'You know… yumm… just lie in a deckchair and do nothing… yumm.'

Julie cut him short. 'We can't disappoint Sarah. You know how sensitive she is.'

Charles sighed. He remembered feeling comfortable with Michael, but he had found Sarah less accommodating. She seemed perfect in every way but there had been times when he had the impression that maybe a little red devil was hiding underneath her angelic exterior.

'All right… if I have to…'

'Well, it's all been arranged. So you can't back out now.' She looked at him with bright eyes. 'And I'm sure you'll enjoy it.'

Will I? thought Charles.

5

Around five that afternoon Charles and Julie were sitting on the terrace of Michael and Sarah's house. They lived in the top part of the old village and as Julie looked out over its red roofs and white walls shining in the sun, and at the fields and olive groves sloping down to the Mediterranean, she couldn't help exclaiming, 'How magnificent! I wish I could live here. How lucky you are to have this house!'

'That's true enough,' affirmed Sarah who was pouring out the tea, holding the teapot carefully in her white, almost transparent hands. Everything was delicate about Sarah: her slim figure; her slow gestures; even the faded pastel colours of her blouse and matching long skirt. She smiled slightly. 'I wouldn't dream of living anywhere else.'

'This is indeed a really nice village,' agreed Charles. 'And it looks as if it's going to get even better.'

'What do you mean?' asked Sarah somewhat sharply. She stopped pouring out tea and turned towards him.

'Well, aren't they planning to create a green area around here? At least that's what I made out from the billboards I saw at the entrance of the village.'

'Are you talking about those hoardings near the Guardia Civil post?'

'Yes. They are proposing to plant hundreds of hectares with trees. It sounds like the beginning of ecological awareness.'

'Ecological awareness, my foot!' snorted Sarah and her face lost some of its angelic composure. 'There's nothing ecological about it!' She turned rather aggressively towards Charles. 'It's just a screen behind which some promoters plan to ruin Frigiliana for ever!'

'Well… if you say so,' retorted Charles. 'But the words they use on the hoardings seem to come straight out of a Green Manifesto.'

'Let me explain,' intervened Michael trying to avoid a dispute. 'From what I've heard, that so-called green initiative seems to be no more than a cover.' He was sitting upright on a straight-backed Spanish chair in the shade of the reed awning that covered the terrace. Michael was a boisterous, athletic man with a dry sense of humour who had retired from business but was still an active hiker. He was in remarkably good condition for his age in spite of being slightly overweight, and with his white hair and ruddy face he contrasted singularly with the luxuriant growth and bright colours of the flowers that surrounded the terrace. I'm sure he would like a glass of wine instead of the tea he's served, mused Charles, if only Sarah let him. But he has to be constantly on the watch-out not to upset her delicate feelings. Charles couldn't think of two less well assorted people but then, he thought, they say that opposites attract. And obviously she is quite pretty and years younger than him.

'The real aim,' continued Michael, unaware of Charles' musings, 'appears to be to get permission to build housing for two to three thousand people.'

'Three thousand people!' exclaimed Charles. 'But that's ludicrous! That would double the present population of Frigiliana. Surely there is no room for more houses. They have already extended the village along the road to Nerja, and from what I've seen, the new part has literally been built up to the edge of the river canyon; some houses have even been constructed on pillars.'

'That's right, but they plan to develop the area on the other side of the canyon.'

'But isn't that a natural park… a protected area?' countered Julie.

'I always believed it was,' sighed Sarah shaking her head, 'but now I'm not quite so sure…'

'Whom does the land on the other side of the canyon belong to?' Charles wanted to know.

'Most of it seems to be private,' replied Michael. 'Whether the owners want to sell or not, or have sold already I don't know. But they would be able to sell land that otherwise would be worthless. And where money is involved...'

'Has the village Council given the go-ahead?'

'Not yet,' said Michael, 'but there are rumours that there's a lot of pressure on the Council members.'

'Fortunately some are incorruptible,' countered Sarah. 'In particular Sebastian.' She looked up with pride. 'Lucky we have him.'

Michael stuck up a finger. 'Yes, but if the Council approved it, the project would create work for hundreds of people here. It would give a great boost to the local economy. No wonder many people here are in favour.'

Sarah's face darkened. 'There are many others who *don't* like it!'

'I don't see how they could ever get to the other side of the river?' Julie looked sceptical. 'The canyon is quite deep.'

'From what I've heard,' replied Michael, 'they plan to build a bridge over the canyon at the entrance of the new village where the road towards Nerja starts. And the land where the bridge is supposed to be built is privately owned. It belongs to a foreigner – a German.'

'That's bad news,' commented Charles. 'This may be the opportunity the man has been waiting for to make a good profit. Property over here is no more than an investment to most foreigners. He's sure to sell if they offer him enough.'

Sarah who had just got up to make a second pot of tea turned around. 'Not him!' she countered. 'He lives here in the village – in a large property on top of the hill. And... what's his name again...?' She stood there thinking for a few seconds, her brown curls framed against the blue sky.

'Meier, I think,' came Michael's voice.

'That's right... that's his name.' Sarah nodded. 'Well... it seems that he's very environmentally conscious and doesn't want to know about the project. Very fortunate for us!'

'Even so,' objected Michael, 'the promoters may find a way around all these obstacles because a lot of capital is involved. I've heard figures of over a hundred million pounds.'

Charles whistled. 'That's enough to make people's head spin – certainly here in Andalusia. Is it Spanish money?'

'Not really. Apparently, most of it is foreign.'

Julie stood there, a distraught expression on her face as she looked out towards the hills on the other side of the canyon, which could be seen from the terrace. It had taken millions of years for the wind and rain to erode them and give them their present shape. They stood out against a clear blue sky, their lines smooth, perfect – as perfect as nature could make them. Was this varied, quiet, unspoiled beauty going to be turned into one more incongruous, ugly medley of concrete and noise? She sighed. 'How horrible that this should happen to the village.'

'But will there be enough water for all the extra people who are supposed to come and live here?' asked Charles. 'Last year, when we went to visit friends in Almuñecar, they told us that the water from their taps was salty. They could no longer drink it because so much water had been pumped out of the aquifer that seawater had been seeping into it and...'

Sarah, who had made a second pot of tea and was now pouring it into delicate cups, suddenly interrupted him. 'Oh, but that's at the coast. There are problems in many places along the coast, especially in the summer when there are so many tourists that the population of some towns more than doubles. But here in Frigiliana we are lucky.' She looked at Charles as if she found a heathen pleasure in contradicting him. 'You may not know it...' she had a superior expression on her face, 'but the water here comes from eternal springs in the Almijara Mountains.'

'I wonder how eternal they would be if this project went ahead and the population of Frigiliana doubled,' retorted Charles. 'So much of the water that flows down the mountains is already diverted for irrigation and human use that the river is dry most of the time.'

Sarah cut him short. 'Water is not the issue here! I think there is much more to worry about than just water. If this project gets the green light the village will never be the same again. And it has already changed such a lot. It was so nice and rural when we came here eight years ago.' Her face lit up with the memory. 'And cheap. But prices have gone up since. And the mules are disappearing too. Instead, noisy motorbikes and cars are beginning to clutter the street below. Still, we are lucky to live in the upper part of the old village, which can only be reached on foot. But if this project goes ahead we are leaving…' she looked at Michael, '…aren't we?' She put down the teapot and began walking agitatedly to the edge of the terrace and back; the matter seemed to touch her deeply. 'And we're not the only ones,' she added.

Julie nodded. 'Still, I don't understand where they think they're going to find three thousand people to live there. Surely, with the kind of development they propose on that billboard – a health centre, a green park, a water world, a forest – local people will be unable to afford it. And most foreigners prefer to be right on the coast.'

'That's correct,' agreed Charles. 'And there are plenty of apartments for sale in Nerja. Foreigners with money can find anything they fancy along the coast, so who would want to come to this new development? I can't imagine people sitting there the whole day long just looking at the mountains.'

'Well…' Michael reached for one of the biscuits on a flower-pattern Andalusian plate on the table. 'I have heard rumours that retired Japanese would come to live there; mind you, these are only rumours.'

'Retired Japanese!' exclaimed Julie. 'They would have the money of course. And they would probably be quite happy if they could have satellite TV and make Bonzai gardens.'

'But imagine the village being overrun by three thousand Japanese smiling their puzzling oriental smiles at the flabbergasted local people while clicking their cameras at anything that moves,' commented Charles. 'Yes, that would really change Frigiliana beyond recognition!'

6

Julie and Charles were slowly walking up the mule path behind the Garden Restaurant, which zigzagged steeply up the hill past the old *fabrica de miel* – the molasses factory. As they climbed higher and looked back, the *barrio nuevo* – the new village – seemed to lie below their feet; further away they could see the *campo* – the countryside – stretching all the way to Nerja and the sea. In one of the streets down below, maybe two hundred yards away, a lottery-ticket vendor could be heard, calling at the top of his voice, '*Lleva premioooo… lo que me quedaaaa…'* which meant that the tickets he had left would certainly win a prize.

What was called 'the new village' had expanded through the years along the road to Nerja as the population of Frigiliana had grown and people wanted more space and modern amenities instead of living six or seven in a small house above the mule's stables. Now it had even outgrown the old part. It had been constructed in the same Andalusian style and was white-chalked too so that from afar it didn't look very different, but it lacked the charm of the old part with its cobblestones, its stepped streets and authentic centuries-old houses.

As they worked their way up through the green area above the old village, the land seemed to fall behind them in flights of terraces. The birds were singing their hearts out and although it was late morning, the grass in the gardens they passed and the leaves of the fruit trees were still covered in sparkling dewdrops.

'Isn't this enchanting?' Julie looked at Charles with bright eyes. 'It must be wonderful to live here.' She stopped and pointed at a small plot of land studded with a few fig and custard apple trees, spread over three different terraces. 'This is the piece of land I told you about. The one Sarah showed me the other day. Isn't it beautiful? Why don't we buy it?'

'How much do they want for it?'

'Eight million pesetas, I think.'

'Eight million! But that's about fifty thousand pounds sterling! For a small almost inaccessible plot of land! I think money has gone to their heads! Has it got building permission?'

'I don't know. But, surely, that's no objection?'

'That *is* a problem. And a big one too!'

Julie looked peeved. 'But I like it,' she insisted. 'Think of the view. We could build a small house on one of the terraces and keep the other two as a garden. Wouldn't that be wonderful?'

Charles snorted. 'Even if we got permission to build, all the building materials would have to be brought up by mule. And later on all our belongings and our food if we lived here. A nice prospect! I don't even want to think about it.' And he turned and started climbing again, while Julie followed him dragging her feet.

They continued on their way. The path, zigzagging uphill, was bordered by a profusion of wildflowers and the scent of jasmine permeated the air. Then, abruptly, they faced a high wall covered in bougainvillea and honeysuckle, a feast of mauve, yellow, white and red. The mule path turned left in front of the wall and as they followed it they came to a cement road which ended in a garage, its entrance shut off by solid steel doors.

'There's no name,' remarked Charles. 'Just a buzzer. And look at this!' he exclaimed, pointing at a security camera above. 'The proprietor must be very keen on his privacy.'

'Yes... and don't you think it strange to have a road come up so high? It seems to run just below the hill. Shall we follow it?'

'Now that we've got so far, maybe we could climb to the top of the hill?' suggested Charles. 'This is the place where the Moors had their fortress centuries ago. Let's go and have a look.'

They crossed the cement road and started climbing up the hill. When they reached the top and saw the landscape on the other side, they held their breaths.

Below their feet the hill fell abruptly towards an almost dry riverbed which, from where they stood, looked like a white, undulating snake winding its way through a deep canyon, its steep sides covered with small shrubs and isolated trees. On the other side of the canyon lay the Sierra Almijara, a series of jagged mountains which stood out clearly against a pure blue sky, its ridges sharp as if cut with a knife.

The south from which they had come was marked by human habitation and the fields and flower beds humans had created, but to the north there was no sign of human interference – only untamed nature, wild and majestic. They sat there for a while, awed by the grandiose beauty of the landscape. 'This is a different world altogether,' murmured Julie, lowering her voice in reverence.

Somewhere below their feet they heard the bubbling of water. Charles got up to have a look and noticed a narrow irrigation channel – an *acequia* – some ten yards below them, filled to the brim with fast-flowing water. 'I wonder where this leads to?' he said, pulling up Julie. As they followed the *acequia* from above and got to the eastern side of the hilltop, they suddenly looked down upon a high wall; the irrigation channel continued to the edge of the wall and from there the water cascaded down into the canyon. Beyond the wall they saw a large white-chalked house with a red-tiled roof and a wide terrace that gave on to the canyon; the wall surrounded the property in a semi circle, from canyon edge to canyon edge.

'That's the high wall with its garage door entrance we've seen before,' whispered Julie.

'How strange,' remarked Charles. 'It's as if the owners had deliberately turned their backs on the inhabited world.'

'Yes, but what a view they have.'

'I wonder who lives there. They must be rather odd people.'

Julie pondered aloud. 'It wouldn't surprise me if this is the house of that man Michael and Sarah were talking about – that Meier. And if his property is a reflection of his character, I think the people of the housing development scheme will have a hard time with him. I bet you they will not be able to break his resistance.'

'I hope they won't break him instead,' commented Charles.

7

Konrad Meier was sitting on the terrace of his house up on the hill, reclining in a deckchair, his eyes closed, listening to a record. He loved romantic music, and the second symphony of Bruckner perfectly expressed his mood that day. He had been lying there for as long as the record lasted and only when the last notes had died away and silence returned did he open his eyes to look out over the jagged mountains of the Sierra Almijara. Classical music combined with undisturbed nature… sheer perfection, he thought. That's how life should be: beauty and harmony. Then he reflected that he ought to get ready. That young artist had phoned him some time ago and she was due to arrive any minute now.

He hummed the last bars of the symphony as he got up and went inside. He saw few people of interest nowadays. He rarely left his house and was really looking forward to spending an hour or two with that young woman. She was a gifted sculptor and such refreshing company for a man of his age. He liked her. In her presence conversation flowed easily. But why, he wondered, hadn't she come to see him for a whole month when he had asked her to sculpt his bust? He had once phoned to ask her, but she had told him she was extremely busy. This time he would insist that she started his bust to make sure he would see more of her.

Why wasn't his daughter like that young woman? Why didn't she love music and art? Or nature? He had tried but he just couldn't get on with her. If parents were allowed to choose later in life amongst grown-up children instead of being saddled with whatever happened to grow out of the babies they had produced, there would be much more harmony in families, he mused. He would gladly exchange his own daughter for that young artist.

The bell rang even before he had time to freshen up. I can't let her wait, he thought. I'll show her in first, and make her sit down on the terrace.

He went to the door but when he opened it, he was faced by an unknown woman and a tanned-looking man. He immediately regretted that he hadn't bothered to check the camera screen to see who had rung. 'Yes…' There was a defensive ring in his voice.

The woman stepped forward and held out a hand. She looked every inch the efficient businesswoman. 'Christina Eckmann,' she said. 'And this is my colleague, Marc de la Gaillère. We have a proposition for you. Maybe we could discuss it inside?'

Konrad Meier did not move aside to let them in. He disliked the woman at first sight and was displeased at being disturbed by business people when he had expected to see his young artist friend. 'What exactly is it you want?' he asked bluntly.

The woman hesitated. Meier could see that she hated being rushed into having to reveal her intentions, but she had little choice. 'Well… we'd like to talk about the piece of land you own at the entrance of the village. We'll…'

'What! You're the people from that damned project, aren't you!'

'We're willing to make a very good offer, a very…'

'Answer me!' he thundered. 'Aren't you?'

'Well… yes, but…'

'You can never leave anything alone can you! You miserable moneybags! Out!'

The man now stepped forward. 'Please calm down,' he said soothingly. 'You're misjudging our intentions. We want to create a natural park. We're going to improve the area, not destroy it. And you could become an important shareholder if you were willing to collaborate.'

'Over my dead body!' bellowed Meier and he slammed the door in their faces.

8

Next morning Julie was reading one of the health books she relished while Charles was studying Spanish grammar from a course he had bought last year; he had been plunging into it since their arrival. 'Wouldn't it be a good idea if we had Spanish lessons?' he suggested.

'An excellent idea!' There was an unmistakable intonation of irony in Julie's voice. 'I can already see us going down to Nerja two or three evenings a week to sit in a classroom with a few beginners, getting terribly bored.'

'Yes but... what else can we do?'

'I think we just need practice – simple conversation if you see what I mean, not a beginners' course. Why don't we have private tuition here in the house? That would be so much simpler and more enjoyable.'

'And where are we going to find a teacher who's willing to come to our house? We may have to go to Nerja or even Malaga to find one. And he'll probably ask so much that it won't be worth it.'

'Well, let me see what I can do.' Julie's face had that determined expression Charles knew so well. It meant you should never give up without trying. 'I'll go and look around in the village.'

'In the village!' exclaimed Charles, incredulous, but Julie had already gone out.

He picked up his course again and started plodding through some exercises that dealt with the subjunctive. Minutes later he had finally attained a state of mental concentration where he felt that, after all, he might at last be able to master the subjunctive, when he heard steps coming up the stairs to the second floor. Then a voice shouted something like, 'Anyone in?' He sighed in exasperation, put down his book and got up. When he opened the door he found himself face to face with a strongly built, dark-haired middle-aged man.

'Hi there,' said the man. 'So there's someone in after all. I'm Frank

Beruzzi of the Southern Investment Company, Miami.' He grabbed Charles' hand and squeezed it painfully. 'What's your name?'

Charles stood there, flabbergasted. He replied hesitantly, 'I'm Charles. What can I do for you?'

'I think it looks nice,' said the man without so much as attempting to explain his presence. 'Where are the rooms?'

'I beg your pardon?' Charles wasn't often knocked off his feet, but this time he stood there, his face one big question mark.

'I've already had a look at the first floor with the kitchen, living quarters, fireplace and TV. They're OK. Now show me the second floor,' ordered the man.

A light flashed through Charles' mind. 'You mean you want to rent the house?'

'Isn't that what it says above the front door downstairs: **To Let**.' He looked at Charles with a reproachful expression in his dark-brown eyes.

'Yes but it also says to enquire at number six, and that's next door.'

'Come on man. Be serious. If you leave the door open you're in and, what's more, you're inviting people in.'

Julie must have left the door open, thought Charles. 'But they all leave their doors open in the village,' he protested.

The man didn't reply: his eyes were measuring up the second-floor apartment. Next he went to each of the three bedrooms and the bathroom, opened the doors and looked inside; one glance seemed enough for him to take in the essentials. Then he asked, 'How much?'

The man seemed to have a brain-dampening effect on Charles. Somehow he couldn't think what he was talking about. 'How much what?'

'Ha, ha! You're pulling my leg Charlie!'

'Charles is the name!'

'Whatever, my friend. That's of no importance. What's important is that you tell me how much you let it for?'

'But I'm occupying this house myself,' replied Charles, getting more exasperated by the minute.

The man's face suddenly turned unpleasant. 'You can't do that,' he warned. 'I could sue you for that! You cannot offer to let it and then refuse.'

'But I'm renting it myself!'

'Why didn't you say so from the start instead of wasting my time,' grumbled the man. He looked thoroughly put out. 'How long are you here for?'

'Two months...'

'Oh that's OK. I won't need it till after the summer when the project begins in earnest. Good thing you're leaving before that time, otherwise I'd have to buy you out. I want it, you see...' and he added with a smug smile, 'and I always get what I want.'

He turned to leave but paused in the doorway. 'They speak English next door?'

'No, only Spanish.'

'Well, that's okay. I've done a lot of property development in Puerto Rico and I know the essentials of the local lingo.'

He left without shutting the door and as the sound of his footsteps receded in the stairway Charles remained speechless, thinking, property development; a project; he wants to rent this house... He shut the door, went back to his Spanish lesson and tried hard to concentrate, when suddenly the steps came up again and there was a loud knock on the door.

Before he had time to get up the man had already let himself in. 'Stupid woman,' he muttered. 'Impossible to do business with her. She's not the proprietor and says she cannot do anything without the proprietor's consent. She doesn't know her correct name but calls her *Maria de Africa*. I've never heard anything so dumb in my life! And she can't find her address or phone number! She's mislaid it or something like that, would you believe it? Now, what kind of an organisation is this?' He looked extremely displeased.

'But the woman next door is authorised to let the house,' protested Charles, hardly able to suppress his irritation. 'She lets it for weekends and...'

'I don't want it for weekends!' the man interrupted sharply. 'I want it for a year. I'm going to install my office here; so no more weekenders.'

'Well... if you want it for a year, I guess the neighbour is quite right. You'll have to ask Maria.'

'Then, tell me how I can contact her. The stupid woman next door just kept rambling on that this Maria is a friend of yours.'

'Hang on, I'll give you her surname and phone number.'

As Charles handed him the details he suddenly ventured a question. 'I say… are you involved in that project to build houses on the other side of the river?'

'Yeah, great project, ain't it?'

'But I've heard that it's doomed because of the opposition of a German who owns the land where a bridge to the other side is to be built.'

'That guy!' The man snorted. 'He'd better agree or he'll regret it. I am beginning to be fed up with that blockhead and I'm not the only one. To dare oppose us…' And Frank Beruzzi turned on his heel and disappeared, this time slamming the door hard.

9

Julie returned about two hours later looking rather pleased with herself.

'You're not going to tell me that you've located the rare bird we're looking for?' asked Charles.

'Maybe. As I went down the street, the woman who has a clothes' shop was standing outside, and while I was explaining the problem to her another woman walked by. When she heard what it was all about she said I should ask Alejandra, and then she took me to where Alejandra lives with her parents. And we got on very well; look, the mother even gave me a few custard apples for you from their garden.'

'How nice of her. How did she know they're my favourite fruit?'

'Your reputation as a custard apple eater must have spread far and wide last year.' Julie laughed heartily.

'There was a good reason why I ate so many custard apples last year!' Charles spoke defensively. 'I had worried so much about not getting an assignment that I developed gastritis before coming here, remember? And the doctor had ordered me to swallow a thick white liquid after every meal to absorb the acid in my stomach; it wasn't going to cure me, but it would stop me from getting an ulcer. I just hated it. And then I started eating custard apples and within a few weeks I was cured!'

'Yes, yes, I remember. I'm all for natural cures. Anyway, to come back to

Alejandra: she's a young teacher who hasn't got a job for the moment. We had a good chat and in the end she was eager to teach us Spanish.'

'Is she willing to come here then and teach us?' Charles looked interested.

'I think so. All that needed discussing was the price for the tuition.'

'And that's where the problem lies, isn't it?'

'Not really. We agreed to six hundred pesetas per lesson of one or two hours…'

'That's very cheap! How did you manage that?'

'… plus an exchange.'

Knowing Julie's propensity for making the most outlandish arrangements, Charles immediately felt alarmed. 'And what exactly is that exchange?'

'Oh, nothing very special. Alejandra is trying to get her driver's licence. She says she's a bit nervous in a car, so she'll need a lot of practice to get to the point where she'll be able to drive, and the driving school is very expensive. So I've arranged for you to give her driving lessons in our car.'

'What! You must be joking!'

'Of course not! I thought it a marvellous idea.' Julie beamed with satisfaction. 'Everyone seemed pleased with the arrangement.'

'Not me! I think it's mad. I have no legal right to let her drive our car.'

'We did discuss that. Don't worry. It seems they are quite relaxed about such things over here.'

'What if she causes an accident?'

'She won't. She's going to be extremely careful. And anyway, I told her that you're a very good teacher and that she needn't worry about anything. So you'd better not disappoint her.'

'But I've never taught anyone to drive!'

'And you know what else?' went on Julie, ignoring Charles' objections. 'Alejandra's father knows a farmer who wants to sell a piece of land in the *campo* with a view over the sea. Apparently it's very cheap, and there's already a *cortijo* – a farmstead – on it too. Her father is going to see the farmer to make an appointment for us. So it's important that you give these driving lessons. You want a private teacher, and you want to buy some land here in Spain, and now that I've arranged everything you can't back out.'

Charles sighed. Female logic! As if it was he who'd had the idea of wanting a private teacher! As if it was he who wanted to buy a piece of land in Spain, when Julie had been pestering him about it almost from the day they'd arrived! It was high time he put his foot down. 'No,' he said firmly. 'I'm not going to do it.'

10

On the morning Alejandra was due to give her first Spanish lesson she was looking at herself in the mirror, torn by indecision. She had been trying on various outfits since eight that morning and even now, at ten, she still couldn't decide what to wear: trousers or a skirt? What would those people think appropriate? Something serious, for sure, because they're probably not much younger than my parents, she thought. Yet, they look so young – quite unlike people of that age in the village. How was it that foreigners kept so young?

She had never done any private tuition before, and as the hour of departure came nearer she felt more and more nervous. She looked in the mirror again. Her face was so ordinary – really uninteresting – and so, she had to admit, was her life. Why wasn't she attractive like the foreign woman who'd come to her house yesterday? Or like those girls they showed in TV adverts, the sort men admired: girls who played tennis or drove a sports car. But she couldn't even drive!

And now that foreign woman had talked her into accepting driving lessons! The idea had seemed marvellous when the woman had proposed it, but now the thought of sitting behind the wheel, incapable of changing gears correctly and doing all the wrong things, filled her with anxiety. That foreign man would certainly laugh at her, maybe even get angry like the driving-school instructor. Oh, why had she let herself be talked into this? And what was she going to teach? This was much worse than having to take exams.

But she had desperately wanted to meet foreigners – educated people. She had heard that the man had been all over the world. What would he think of her? I do hope he won't think me stupid, she worried.

And Julia, the woman who had come yesterday! She had such self-assurance, even in her broken Spanish. It didn't seem to worry her in the least that she made mistakes. If only I spoke English like she speaks Spanish, reflected Alejandra. I could if I dared. Why am I so inhibited?

She looked once again in the mirror. 'Oh, what am I going to wear?' she murmured in desperation.

11

Resolutions are there to be broken. The first thing Charles did when Alejandra arrived was to agree to give her driving lessons. She seemed eager to learn and showed such trust in him that he simply didn't have the heart to disappoint her.

Alejandra was like many young women here in Andalusia. You wouldn't really notice her if you met her in the street. She had straight dark-brown hair down to the shoulders, a roundish face, thick eyebrows and large brown eyes, and she was a little on the plump side. She was shy too, but she had a simplicity and honesty that went straight to the heart. Charles felt they would get on; Julie had made a good choice. The Spanish lesson went well, and later that morning he took Alejandra down to the car for her first driving lesson, trying to live up to the reputation Julie had cut out for him, and just hoping for the best.

12

The next morning Julie was readying herself to go to Nerja, and as this might take anything from fifteen minutes to half an hour, Charles thought he might as well go for a stroll through the village.

The crooked street that ran from the parking lot at the Guardia Civil past the beginning of Calle El Darra to Church Square was proudly called Calle Real – Royal Street – maybe because it was the only street of the old village open to traffic. It was a one-way street and for a good reason: for most of its length it was only just wide enough for a car to squeeze between the walls of the houses on both sides.

Drivers rarely managed to get through the village from one end to the other without being stopped by some delivery van in the process of unloading. Or else the traffic was held up by people who just left their car in the middle of the street while disappearing into one of the many small shops that lined Calle Real. By the time they were back, three or four other cars had usually piled up behind, creating a miniature traffic jam. The fact that some people were now driving cars hadn't made them more disciplined. They seemed oblivious to traffic rules and to wasting someone else's time, but it never caused any bad feelings. If they had to wait behind another car they would soon be talking to passers-by, or get out and buy something for themselves.

As Charles walked along, he saw a small blue car stop in front of the butcher's. The driver, a woman, got out and disappeared inside the shop, leaving the door of her car wide open and the engine running. The butcher's was the tiniest of shops. It had no window, just a dark-brown door and stairs going down into a semi-dark small room. Through the open door you could see a counter, a scale, and meat hanging up. The woman had been gone no more than a minute when a flashy red Range Rover arrived and the driver began to hoot. Local people sometimes did so when they had to wait a long time but this was different; this was an impatient, aggressive hooting which seemed to mean: how dare you block my way?

The driver now got out. He was a tall, well-built foreigner, good-looking but arrogant, dressed in a casual but fashionable manner, with a mobile phone sticking out of his breast pocket. Without hesitation he went to the entrance of the butcher's shop, leant inside and started shouting at the woman, telling her in no uncertain terms to move on.

Thirty seconds later the woman came rushing out of the shop with a parcel of sausages, looking annoyed. As she got moving, the man in the Range Rover followed her closely as if to edge her on to make up for her misbehaviour, and hooted his horn again.

My goodness, thought Charles, doesn't that man see how offensive his behaviour is? And he felt almost ashamed to be a foreigner.

13

Bob Marvey's nerves were on edge. First there had been that stupid woman who had gone into the butcher's. Next he had been held up by a van that was unloading. And to top it all, when he finally got out of the old village, rushed around the new ring road below it, and was about to enter the *barrio nuevo*, the bus for Nerja had just left and was now in front of him. And as always happens at such times, a lorry had arrived from the opposite side and everything got blocked. He hooted loudly but to no avail, and he started biting his nails in frustration.

He'd been so looking forward to his first date with Amanda but nothing was going according to plan. It seemed as if everything conspired against him this morning. Lesley had been positively horrible and had done all she could to delay him. He had done his best to sound casual, even to be friendly to her, but she had kept pestering him.

'Why do you have to go to Nerja now?' she had enquired. 'The restaurant doesn't open till twelve.'

'I've got lots to do this morning,' he had lied. 'The accounts, you know…'

'You're not going to see that red-haired bar girl, are you?' she had suddenly asked.

He had blushed in spite of himself. 'How could I see her?' he had objected. 'She's not due to come in till twelve.'

'Maybe you're going to meet her somewhere before the restaurant opens?'

Do women have a sixth sense? He had tried so hard not to show his eagerness to be off. How did she guess? And suddenly she had said, 'If you've got so much work to do, I'm going to come and help you. It won't bother you, will it? If you love me you'll want me to come with you, won't you?' And she had put her arms around his neck and had tried to kiss him.

That had been too much – just too much. Lesley's lips on his mouth when he had been dreaming half the night of kissing Amanda; and when she was waiting for him that very moment. He had felt stifled. It was almost physical, like the urge to breathe fresh air in a stuffy room where the windows had remained closed for too long. God, how he wanted to get away from here, from Lesley! He had pushed her away yelling, 'How can you say you love me when you don't even trust me? I'm going!'

She had begun to plead, 'Oh, please, take me with you,' but he hadn't even bothered to listen. He had wasted enough time already.

If only he could get rid of her and keep everything for himself. Start a new life with Amanda. Beautiful Amanda, so young and seductive. But now that he finally had a date he was stuck behind that damned bus, unable to move! He was very late already. She'd probably given up waiting for him by now. And he hit the horn again in frustration.

14

After Bob had left, Lesley sat staring blankly out of the window. Now look what you've done, she thought, scolding herself. Another scene! Maybe all for nothing. Maybe Bob is just tense because business isn't too good? But that bar girl! She hoped there was nothing going on between her and Bob. He was a good-looking man and it was natural that women were attracted to him. In a way she had always liked it; it made her feel good to know that he was hers; that others envied her.

She knew of course that men in their forties often looked at younger women. It had happened to several of their friends, couples she'd known for a long time and had thought of as Jim and Ann, or Tom and Pat. Then, one day, she learned that Jim had gone off with a younger woman and that Ann had been on the bottle ever since. And Tom had left Pat who had been depressed for the last three years and had put on weight. Lesley shuddered when she thought about it. That must never happen to her. But she found the competition with younger women harder every year. The fact that she was seven years older than Bob was beginning to tell.

She'd had a few scares in the past but she didn't think Bob had ever been unfaithful to her. She had given him more than any other woman ever had and it was her he loved. But this time things seemed different. Lately he had become distant, even irritable. He hadn't made love to her for ten days now. That had never happened before.

She had let Bob run the restaurant she had bought – made him the boss so that he would feel important. She had always thought it a good psychological move. She was no longer so sure since he had hired that red-haired girl. She should have objected from the start but, as always, she'd been weak; she hadn't wanted to oppose his choice. If only she could have foreseen where this was going to lead? For the first time she was beginning to feel really scared.

15

When Bob Marvey finally got to Maro, a little fisherman's town just outside Nerja, he was thirty-five minutes late for his rendezvous. He had been driving like a madman, worrying all the way and now his worst foreboding had come true: Amanda wasn't there.

Why had everyone conspired to make him late on this one day? Damned Lesley! Damned Frigiliana bus! Damned everything! He hit the steering wheel with his fist till his anger turned into despair. Finally he dropped his arms on the wheel and let his head fall on them. He remained like that for some time while a torrent of frustration and disappointment surged up through him.

This can't be, he finally decided. I must do something. I'll go to her house. Maybe she'll be there. But he wouldn't have much time; he had to open the restaurant at twelve. 'Damned life!' he exclaimed as he started the Range Rover and drove back to Nerja.

Amanda would probably be very upset, and rightly so. A man of forty-one shouldn't let a beautiful girl of twenty wait for well over half an hour on their first date. She could have anyone she wanted. He had often seen men look at her, not just with interest in their eyes but with lust. God, how attractive she was! Seduction oozed from her.

He parked the car and walked to where she lived in one of the small houses in the old part of Nerja. He had stood there only a few days ago, trying to peep in through the curtains to catch a glimpse of the secret world that lay inside. Would Amanda be in? Would she still want to see him?

He was nervous, he who had always been so sure of himself, of his attraction, who was used to dominate. And now he felt like a teenager, insecure, fearing the kind of reception he would get. He hesitated for a few seconds and then knocked on the door. There was no answer and his heart sank. He was about to turn away when the curtain was pulled back and Amanda's face appeared; then she opened the door.

'A fine way you've got with girls,' was the first thing she said, trying to sound joking, but he felt that she was vexed.

'I'm… I'm so sorry,' he heard himself stutter. 'The car was stuck. Sorry.'

'Well, it doesn't matter.' She forced a smile onto her lips. 'I just thought you couldn't make it. Come in.' And she took him by the hand, pulled him in and shut the door.

He stood there, looking around. The interior was simple but cosy. And Amanda! She wore a light pink top and a printed cotton miniskirt, which left her legs visible to just above the knee. Such beautiful legs! How he longed to move his hands up them, to take off her clothes, kiss her… He had done so a hundred times in his fantasies. He would pass his hands over her breasts, caress her belly and then, slowly, pull down her panties. She would become wildly aroused and he would make love to her as he never had before. And then, when it was over, she would lie in his arms, trembling and whispering, 'I belong to you…'

Amanda looked at him. 'Are you just going to stand there?' she asked rather matter of fact. 'Do sit down. Or…' she said it almost mechanically, '… is there anything you would like to do?'

This is an invitation, thought Bob Marvey. I'm going to do it! And without a word he went towards her, grabbed her by the waist and began to kiss her on her full, warm lips.

'Wait,' she said holding him back, and she took off her miniskirt and pulled off her top. She wore no bra underneath and as he gazed at her firm round breasts and saw how young and supple her body was, he suddenly felt self-conscious. Over-eating, drinking and indulging in anything he fancied had affected him; he was becoming thickset and slightly pot-bellied. She looked at him as he sat there, apparently frozen, unable to make out what was happening. Then she said, trying to sound funny, 'You're not shy or something, are you? Won't you take off your clothes too?'

Almost unwillingly he began to undo his belt, dropped his trousers and underpants and then, slowly, unbuttoned his shirt. She didn't even look at him but took off her panties with a swift movement and lay back on the divan without the slightest embarrassment.

As he lay on her, held her tight, put his hands under her buttocks and started rubbing his body over hers he felt her stiffen, but he kept it up. He knew he had to perform, and quickly too because it was getting on for twelve, but however much he tried he didn't seem able to get an erection. Come on, he thought, do it! But nothing happened. He began to sweat profusely and after a few minutes he let himself roll over by her side and gave up.

She stared at him in surprise. 'Are you all right?' Was there contempt in her voice?

He felt waves of red-hot shame go through his head as he replied hoarsely, 'I don't know. This has never happened before.'

Then, abruptly, he got up and as he began to put on his clothes he heard himself say, 'It's time to go to the restaurant.' He was out of the house in a minute, feeling like someone who had just suffered the most crushing defeat of his life.

16

Charles and Julie were walking through Calle Pintada, one of the many busy shopping streets in Nerja. It was a narrow, winding, one-way street, and like most streets in the old part of the town it was lined with restaurants, travel agencies and colourful shop fronts: shops selling clothes; shoes and leather-ware; post cards and souvenirs; sweets and pastry; in fact anything to tempt the tourist.

The traffic was quite heavy but even so people were walking almost anywhere, not just on the narrow pavements but also in between the cars and all over the street. Motorbikes and cars had to proceed carefully to avoid pedestrians. And there were other obstacles too: a horse-drawn carriage ferrying four elderly tourists passed by, followed by a procession of at least ten cars; it was on its way back to the Balcón de Europa where two or three of these carriages were usually waiting to take tourists on a tour around the old part of Nerja.

Charles and Julie kept weaving in and out of the slowly moving cars without much interest, when they found themselves in front of an ostentatious shop window of a new real estate agent. It had the usual photographs of properties for sale complete with prices underneath, but something else caught Charles' attention: almost half of the window was taken up by a huge colourful impression of a hilltop with hundreds of houses set against a blue sky. Below was written:

Green Park One
A unique development in a prime, unspoiled location in the mountains.
Close proximity to the most beautiful village in Andalusia.
Only six kilometres from the sea.

'Look!' he exclaimed pointing at the sketch.

'Yes?' Julie waited to see if anything more was forthcoming.

'But don't you see? That's the project... the Frigiliana project.'

'You're right!' Suddenly her interest was awakened. 'Let's go in and ask.'

'Do you think we should...' but before Charles could say more, Julie had already opened the door and gone inside.

The interior was very grand. The floor was tiled in marble and long mirrors lined the walls. A receptionist was sitting behind a large wooden desk, bent over a pile of papers; seen from the entrance she seemed no more than a mass of dark curly hair and two hands lying on the papers. Julie walked resolutely up to her.

'Can I help you?' said the woman without even bothering to look up.

'We would like to have some information about this development scheme... what is it called...' Julie turned around to Charles.

'Green Park One.'

The receptionist now looked up, showing a round Spanish face. 'One moment please,' she said. 'I'll call the project specialist.'

She spoke briefly down the phone and less than a minute later a door at the back of the room opened and a well-dressed woman appeared. She wore a smart navy-blue skirt and white blouse, and had short brown hair and regular features. Late thirties, thought Julie. Or maybe just forty? What struck her most were the woman's penetrating blue eyes.

'Yes... what can I do for you?' The woman's manner was amiable and efficient. Her voice had a smooth professional quality, but the slight German accent was unmistakable.

'We're looking for a property in this area and find your Green Park One project rather attractive,' said Julie without so much as blinking an eye.

'That's to say,' interrupted Charles, 'if private people are allowed to buy.'

The woman seemed surprised. 'And why shouldn't private people be allowed to buy?'

Charles feigned embarrassment. 'I've heard rumours that the whole project was reserved for retired Japanese.'

An expression of annoyance passed over the woman's face. 'How such rumours get around is beyond me!' Her voice sounded sharp. 'There have been contacts with a Japanese company but we prefer to sell to private customers.' Then, suddenly, she was her smiling professional self again, as if she had suppressed any personal feelings and had slid back into business mode. She got up and made a welcoming gesture. 'It'll be a pleasure to assist you in your choice. That's what I'm here for.'

She led them into a private room, invited them to sit down on two easy chairs, moved to the other side of her desk and took some brochures out of a glass-fronted cupboard.

'As you see,' she began, opening one of these and pointing at the drawings, 'there will be a choice of both apartments and houses. Which did you have in mind?'

'I don't think we have any fixed idea yet,' replied Julie, 'but we are definitely interested in buying a property in this region.' Then she added, as if it were an afterthought, 'We prefer something inland rather than in the built-up coastal area.'

The woman's eyes showed interest. 'In that case,' she replied, 'Green Park One is exactly what you want.' She pushed a brochure towards Julie. 'It will have all the modern amenities, swimming pools, a theatre, a shopping mall, restaurants and tennis courts, and yet you will find yourself surrounded by trees and beautiful vistas. Houses and apartments will be finished in luxurious materials and will have both air-conditioning and central heating. And all bedrooms will have en-suite bathrooms.'

'That sounds almost too good to be true,' said Julie, trying to look impressed.

'I can assure you that this is the most imaginative project in Andalusia.'

The woman seemed to muster all her power of persuasion. 'You will not find any better.'

'Has the project already started?' Julie's voice sounded as innocent as could be. 'Or is it still to be approved?'

'It's virtually approved and will start soon.'

'So there's no risk? We wouldn't want to sign up and pay and then find out that there were obstacles after all and lose our money.'

'I'm always honest with my customers.' The woman's face was the very image of sincerity. 'There are a few more details to clear up but that won't take much longer. Rest assured. We are almost ready to go ahead.' The woman looked Julie straight in the eye. 'But I must tell you that if you want to buy, you shouldn't delay too long. There's a lot of interest in the project and we are expecting to be sold out shortly.'

'And how much will these properties cost?' asked Charles.

'It depends on what you opt for, of course. Single bedroom apartments start at twenty million pesetas. That may sound a lot but it's cheap considering that this is the top of the range.'

Just then the door opened slightly and a voice shouted, 'Chris, the big boss on the phone!'

Before the woman had time to react, the door opened fully and a deeply tanned man in a white shirt, his sleeves rolled up, barged in. When he noticed the two clients he pulled back, mumbling something like, 'Sorry, I didn't realise.' The woman's face contracted; she got up saying, 'Excuse me for a moment,' took the man by the elbow, went out with him and shut the door.

'Did you hear that?' whispered Charles. 'Starting from twenty million pesetas!'

'Look what they say here in the brochure,' observed Julie. 'They want a down payment of fifty per cent upon signing, the rest on completion.'

'I bet you that fifty per cent represents their real cost. The rest must be pure profit.'

In the meantime an animated discussion was taking place behind the closed door. Charles tried to catch what was being said but he couldn't distinguish a single word. Finally the woman came in again; she seemed disturbed and had lost some of her easy manner.

'Will you excuse me?' she said. 'I have to leave on urgent business.

Here's my card. Please contact me any time you like.' And she held the door of her office wide open, making it clear that the meeting was over.

Back in the street Charles glanced at her name card. It read: Christina Eckmann, Sales Manager, Housing Company, Zürich and it gave the Nerja phone number.

As they strolled back and approached the Balcón de Europa a man came walking towards them at a brisk pace. It was the American who had entered uninvited into their apartment two days before! As he came level with them he recognised Charles and stopped.

'Charlie,' he grumbled, 'I'm really pissed off. I phoned that landlady of yours, that Maria de Africa, and would you believe it! She refuses to let the house.' He looked offended.

Charles was unable to suppress a smile. 'Well… ahem,' he said clearing his throat, 'she must have her reasons.'

'Reasons! What she calls reasons! Says that if she lets it for a year she will not be able to come over herself in the summer. Now what kind of business is that, I ask you? That's monkey play! I'm upset, very upset! And I'm not going to have it.' And with that he was off, as if he had already wasted too much time.

'Follow him discreetly,' Charles motioned to Julie. 'I'll wait at the Balcón.'

He had only just sat down on a bench, gazing absent-mindedly at the tall palm trees that line the Balcón de Europa, when Julie returned.

'Did he go into the estate agent's office?'

'Yes, he did.'

'It wouldn't surprise me if he were the big boss,' concluded Charles.

17

As they returned to Frigiliana in the early afternoon they saw a man sitting on the low wall at the entrance to Calle El Darra; he was leaning on a wooden stick and seemed to be just enjoying the mild sunshine. They were about to pass him when he got up and came towards Charles.

'Germann?' he asked with a strong Spanish accent, taking Charles' hand

and shaking it. 'Ingliss?' He had a round, friendly-looking face and wore a felt hat like so many men here in the village.

'Belgian,' answered Charles.

'*Que bien!*' A big smile now split his face. 'You wouldn't have hundred pesetas for a *bocadillo* would you?' he said in Spanish, looking at Charles with large brown eyes like a dog expecting to be given a bone.

Charles duly dug into his pocket and produced a coin.

'*Muchas gracias* Belgian,' said the man, accepting it.

They had not even reached their front door when he had already set off down the road, walking at a brisk pace.

'He doesn't look particularly hungry to me,' remarked Julie eyeing the man's disappearing bulk. 'I bet you he's going to drink that straight away instead of buying a sandwich!'

'How can you think such a thing?' objected Charles. 'He looked perfectly honest to me.'

Julie just sighed and shook her head. 'How gullible men are,' she said as she began to climb the stairs to their apartment.

18

Bob Marvey had had a really awful day. Time and again the scene of his inability to make love to Amanda had kept flashing through his mind. When he had finally got that far! And then this! His face flushed red-hot each time he thought of it.

He had always prided himself on being such a good performer: he had never even once failed in all his love affairs, and there had been several. Of course, he had always hidden everything carefully from Lesley. Women tend to be jealous and he felt it was better she didn't know anything; he didn't want to risk upsetting the good life she gave him. A few affairs here and there didn't matter anyway; they had never prevented him from having sex with Lesley.

But things were different this time; his attraction to Amanda was affecting his relationship with Lesley. Why then had he failed so abominably with Amanda? Later that day, in the restaurant, she had told him it didn't matter, as if to console him; that it would be all right next time. But would it? He felt profoundly perturbed. She had said it so lightly – as though it was something to be expected in a man of his age. He knew that men lost their sexual drive later in life, but he had always thought that this happened well beyond sixty or seventy. Could it be that he was losing his sexual potency at forty-one? Had he been drinking too much for too many years? The thought made his stomach muscles contract with anxiety. Sex was all-important to him. He couldn't imagine his life without it.

He had often daydreamed that one day he would make a lot of money. And then he would surround himself with young women – gorgeous young women – and he would just pick and choose. How many times had he not fantasised about it, about the life he was going to lead later on? But maybe there wouldn't be any sexual life later on?

Days that start badly often continue badly. The restaurant hadn't been good either. His bad mood had seemed to communicate itself to the personnel and even to the customers. One of them, when he was served stewed rabbit in garlic sauce, denied ever having ordered it and arrogantly told the waiter to take it away, making a flicking gesture with his fingers. As the customer is king, the waiter bit his tongue, but when he brought it back into the kitchen the cook flew into a rage saying he was an ass; that the rabbit's ears should be sewn onto his head so that he would hear better next time. That was too much for the waiter, a proud lean man with shiny black hair, and he had shouted what he thought of the cook, his smelly breath and his filthy habit of passing his finger through pots and pans and then licking it. They had started to throw plates at each other and the row had been heard all over the place, even by the customers. And all this in a four-star restaurant! It was just the sort of publicity they could do without; there were too few customers already.

Later that afternoon a man from the bank came to tell him they were in arrears with the mortgage and that he would have to pay up soon if he wanted to avert problems. But how could he? Something seemed to have gone wrong with the trade. This year they hadn't even made a profit. Lesley said it was his fault because he employed too many people. By too many she meant Amanda, of course. But the girl was good! She attracted customers. He needed a pretty girl like her behind the bar. He had been right to hire her. Amanda was willing; she had style; she had everything. But he was no longer so sure now that *he* had everything.

He closed early that night and as he drove home and approached Frigiliana, his heart sank. What a rotten day! And he was expecting worse to come with Lesley: tears and a scene. God, what a life!

When he reached home he heard soft music coming from the drawing room. Should he go in or would it be better to withdraw to the terrace and pour himself a drink there? I might as well face the music now, he thought, and opened the door.

Inside, the light was dimmed and Lesley was reclining on the divan, her eyes closed. She was wearing a creamy-coloured satin evening gown and he couldn't help thinking that she looked quite attractive. As he came in, she opened her eyes and smiled at him. 'You're all right Bob? Shall I pour you a drink?'

He noticed that everything was ready on the low table in front of the divan, the glass, the whisky and ice-cubes. This was certainly not what he had expected and he breathed a sigh of relief. Maybe there wasn't going to be a row after all. And suddenly he longed for a pleasant, peaceful evening. He'd had more than enough trouble for one day.

Lesley sat up to fix him a whisky on the rocks and as she moved her legs the gown opened, revealing the light-brown nylon stockings she wore. In a flash he saw the flesh of her thighs above the darker rim of the stockings, the white garters and the edge of the whitish satin slip she was wearing. Then, slowly, Lesley drew the gown back over her legs.

Bob Marvey stood there for a moment as if hypnotised. The sight of stockings and sexy underwear invariably stimulated his senses and he felt a flame of lust go through his groin.

When she had prepared his drink she got up to hand him his glass and as she approached, the scent of her perfume penetrated his nostrils. She had put on her best perfume, and she knew how it beguiled him.

He poured the whisky down his throat and felt relaxed now, in the mood. That's how it had always been when their relationship was good: Lesley inviting, not demanding. He needed reassurance tonight and Lesley was reassuring.

He took her into the bedroom, slipped off her satin gown and then made love to her as he had always done. When it was all over he suddenly thought, I'm all right! There's nothing wrong with me. He felt immensely relieved and then his body became limp. Seconds later he was asleep, still lying on top of Lesley.

She listened for a while to his regular breathing, then she brushed his hair away from her face, pushed him over and wrapped her arms around him. He had come back. She felt elated, triumphant! She knew how to keep him. He was hers and she was going to make sure that he remained so.

19

Lesley lay lazily in a warm bath looking at her body. The pores seemed to dilate and her skin to swell and regain a youthful aspect. She passed her hand over her legs: they were soft and smooth. And her flesh felt full and bouncy as she squeezed her arm.

When Bob had lain on top of her last night, his rather rough, dry skin pressing hers, he must have felt this tender warmth of her flesh, this surrender of her whole being. She smiled and a feeling of lightness flowed through her as she stepped out of the bath and caught the reflection of her image in the long mirrors covering the opposite wall. Her breasts were still firm and her waistline was slim. Only her hips had somewhat broadened. It was fortunate she hadn't had any children. Just think what some women looked like after having given birth once or twice! And Bob didn't mind broad hips. 'They stimulate my imagination and kindle my desire,' he had once told her. No, she was altogether lucky to have remained attractive. Then, suddenly, she shuddered when she thought of her age: another two years and she would be fifty! She didn't want to get old; her whole being rejected it.

She had bleached her hair when it had begun to turn grey some years ago. It's fortunate women can do that, she thought as she looked at herself in the mirror. She had been fair as a child but, as it often happens, her hair had gradually darkened. Now that it was fair again she was pleased with the effect. She liked brushing her wavy, silky hair, which fell down to her shoulders without quite touching them – feminine but not too long.

What worried her was her face. Not that it wasn't pretty: it had an almost perfect oval shape and her features were classical. No, it was the wrinkles that worried her, all those little lines that were beginning to appear at the side of her eyes and on the upper lip, especially when she smiled. She had become self-conscious about it to the point that she tried not to smile. Too much sunshine has ruined my face, she reflected. I must do something about it. If I become ugly Bob will look at other women. Maybe I should get a facelift.

She had known Bob for eight years now, but she was still attracted to him as strongly as in the beginning. He had been everything to her. Her mother had died in England just before they met and she had come into quite a lot of money. She had abandoned it all to his fancy, to his lust for spending – to his ambition. She had dreamed of this style of life since she was young, and her inheritance and Bob had made it a reality.

Five years ago they had moved to Frigiliana to be nearer her father and she had bought this house up on the hill. Then she'd found a fancy restaurant in Nerja and bought it too. It was heavily mortgaged but she was sure that wouldn't be a problem. She had wanted it for Bob and had appointed him manager. It linked him to her and gave him something to do. And above all, it gave him status. They had called it *El Jardin de Roberto* – Robert's Garden – after Bob's real first name. But lately problems had arisen.

They had been spending heavily, and the restaurant was not bringing in enough money. She had reproached him for it but now regretted having done so. And then, yesterday... she had felt so insecure. Whom could she turn to? Her mother was dead and her father... had he ever cared for her? For some unknown reason he didn't approve of Bob and had cold-shouldered her. If she lost Bob she would be utterly alone.

She looked again in the mirror. For how much longer, she wondered, will I be able to remain attractive? When her face was made up and the lights were dimmed she could still look very beautiful, but over the last weeks doubts had begun to torment her. She had been frightened since that red-haired girl had come into Bob's life. She had to admit, reluctantly, that the girl was pretty. I'm sure that bitch is trying to take him away from me, she couldn't stop thinking, and the fright had lately turned into a morbid jealousy. It was eating her heart out, gnawing at her day and night. It had made her turn sour and furious against everyone, including Bob! How the hell was she going to compete with a twenty-year-old girl? she thought as she looked at herself in the mirror. How unfair it was to have the disadvantage of age!

But all was not lost. She knew how to handle Bob whilst that girl was just a silly young idiot without any experience or money. Last night she had decided to play it cool and everything had worked out beyond expectation. It had almost been like in the first years of their love-passion. She had felt confident again.

Today everything seemed possible. She would overcome her jealousy; she would stand at Bob's side and back him to the last. I must try to smile like in the past, she told herself. My enigmatic smile was what first attracted him. He felt it as a challenge. I must do it again. Yes, I'll manage.

20

The weather had been overcast for a few days but it hadn't rained. In fact, it hadn't rained for a long time and today it was bright and sunny again. Julie and Charles were having lunch with Sarah and Michael in the Ingenio, a small restaurant which mainly consisted of an outside terrace overlooking the river canyon next to the old *fabrica de miel*. From where they sat the opposite ridge looked quite brown in patches.

'About time it rained,' remarked Julie.

'That's true enough,' replied Michael. 'Do you know that they had a mass said last week imploring the Lord to send rain. I think half the village must have turned up.' He grinned.

'They seem to be pressing the government too,' cut in Charles, 'just to be on the safe side I suppose. I've read in the papers that thousands of farmers from all over Andalusia converged towards Seville the other week, demanding water. As if the government had to provide them with everything, even rain.'

'I know.' Michael shook his head. 'They are talking about building more dams and pumping more water. I wonder where all this is going to end.'

'Haven't they understood that, ultimately, they will need to plant more trees if they want to attract more rain?' observed Charles.

'It's good then what we did a few weeks ago,' said Sarah, a self-congratulatory smile on her face.

'What did you do?' asked Julie while her eyes brightened.

'We went to plant trees along the riverbed.'

'How wonderful!' enthused Julie. 'Many more people ought to follow your example.'

'Oh, but many did! There were at least fifty of us – Spanish and foreigners. We took spades, tins of water and three saplings each. It was all organised by a young man from Sweden who's in the Green Movement. A really nice man...'

'There was a problem, though,' admitted Michael, unable to suppress a grin. 'As you may have noticed, there are still a few goatherds driving their flocks around the countryside...'

'Yes. I've seen some of them.' Julie nodded. 'Such a wonderful sight they are. And the sound of all those tinkling goat bells... I just love goats...'

'Well...' continued Michael unperturbed, 'when some of the people went back two days later to water the saplings, they discovered that the goats had eaten everything down to the last little branch.'

'Such a shame.' Sarah sighed sadly. 'I always thought that people who wander around in the countryside with their animals and live off the land would be the first to respect nature. It's really sad. And to think that we were all so enthusiastic and felt we were really doing something worthwhile to help the planet. Sven – that's the nice young man from Sweden – was extremely upset when he discovered what had happened.'

'Has he been here long?' enquired Julie. 'We didn't meet him last year.'

'He only arrived a month or two ago. It's really lovely to have him here.' Sarah's face lit up. 'He's very keen on nature. I think you should meet him. He's a friend of Charlotte's.'

'Charlotte the sculptor?' Julie looked surprised. 'Is she still here?'

'Oh yes, but she no longer lives in the village. She's living in the *campo*. In fact she and Sven are almost neighbours.'

'Is anything going on between them?' Julie sounded interested.

'Oh no!' Sarah sounded shocked. 'Sven's such a pure young man. But Charlotte does have a friend...'

'Australian, isn't he?' interrupted Michael. 'What was his name again? Edward, I think?'

'Yes. And guess what?' continued Sarah. 'They're thinking of getting married.'

'How exciting!' exclaimed Julie. 'We must go and see her.'

21

The next day they set off towards the *campo* to see if they could find Charlotte. They drove a short distance up the road to Torrox to a spot where a narrow dirt road split off, but seeing that it was not in a very good condition they thought it best to park their car and follow the road on foot. It climbed very slowly, turning around a rocky hill on the right where a new villa had been constructed, while to the left the land fell away to orchards of avocado, loquat and custard apple trees. As they carried on, oleander and red flowery bushes lined the road, and further away there were banana plants and long reeds waving in the wind. After a while they came to a small *cortijo*. It was whitewashed like all the properties around here, and surrounded by a thick growth of bushes. The entrance was on the side away from the road and as they walked around the *cortijo* they came upon a terrace shaded by the bright purple-red flowers of a bougainvillea that grew upon a metal frame overhead. There was a wooden table and a few easy chairs, and some empty boxes were lying in a corner of the terrace.

'This must be it,' concluded Julie. 'This is exactly as Michael described it. It's a perfect place for an artist, charming and very quiet.'

'Are you sure this is Charlotte's *cortijo*? I wouldn't want to intrude upon strangers.'

'We'll know soon enough.' And Julie walked to the bright-blue entrance door and began to knock vigorously. There was no answer and she was about to give up when they heard steps inside, the door was flung open and Charlotte's face appeared.

'Julie! Charles! I don't believe it!' Charlotte gave them both a long, affectionate hug. 'How did you know that I live here?'

'Michael told us yesterday.'

Charlotte tugged them inside saying, 'Come in. Don't just stand there in the doorway.'

Inside, the house was in total disorder. Packets of clay, bottles half-filled with coloured powder, and unfinished heads and busts were lying about all over the place; sketches of models were strewn on chairs and on the table; unwashed cups, plates and cutlery were piled up in the sink, and a chair had fallen down in a corner. Charlotte was an extremely gifted sculptor and ceramist but she had no eye for order.

'You look really happy Charlotte,' said Julie, holding her at arm's length. 'Is it true that you are getting married?'

'You've heard the news then.' Charlotte beamed. 'And I thought that this would never happen to me.'

As Charles looked at Charlotte he couldn't help observing that she might be very attractive if only she made up a bit and dressed properly instead of looking like a sack of potatoes. She was wearing baggy overalls and a worn sweater with a gaping hole in one elbow; her light-brown hair looked as if it hadn't been combed for days, and there was a large smear of grey clay on her face. 'What surprises me is that you have managed to fit a man into your life,' he remarked.

'Oh but he's really nice. Wait! I'll show you his photograph.'

She went to her bedroom and came back, not with one photograph but with a whole pile of colour prints. 'Isn't he handsome,' she couldn't stop saying while pressing one photograph after the other into their hands.

The prints showed Edward on the terrace in the sun; Edward asleep; Edward drinking coffee; Edward in a restaurant; Edward smiling; Edward looking in love; Edward in bed with a teddy bear stuck next to him. 'That's a little teddy bear he gave me.' Charlotte chuckled. 'I like it very much.'

Charles had expected to see one of those tanned, muscular, beach-adorning young Australians, but Edward's hair was greying at the temples and his chin was beginning to sag. He looks like an older movie actor who is used to seducing women, he thought; this is certainly not his first romance. 'He seems much older than you Charlotte,' he remarked.

'Well... yes. He's forty-five but I don't think that matters. Age has its advantages. Older men have more experience. They know what they want and how to get it. They also know how to speak to women and how to treat them. When we're in a restaurant he whispers mad words in my ear: how he loves me, how much he desires me and many other things no one has ever said to me before.' Charlotte closed her eyes and an expression of pure bliss came over her face. 'It just shows that fate exists.' She nodded as if to show that she was in full agreement with what she said.

'Do you think that it's fate then that brought you together?' asked Julie, embarking upon one of her favourite subjects.

'Of course.' Charlotte spoke the last word with a strong German accent, rolling the r which, if anything, added charm to her words. 'How incredible that our paths should have crossed. I feel, no, I'm sure that he came all the way from the other side of the world to Frigiliana so that we should meet.'

'Did he come to Frigiliana a long time ago?'

'Five weeks ago.'

'So you've known him for only five weeks? That's not a very long time,' Charles couldn't help observing but Charlotte continued, carried away as she was by her own enthusiasm. 'Yes, but it was love at first sight.' There was a huge smile on her face. 'Oh! I am so lucky!' she continued, 'Because it might so easily not have happened. He was about to go back to Australia, you see, but unfortunately something went wrong with his credit card and he couldn't take out any money from his account. "Such a nuisance," he said, "that this should happen when I'm on the other side of the globe".'

'What did he do then?'

'He came to live with me and I covered all his expenses. It was the least I could do for him.'

'When are we going to meet the hero then?' Julie's face had the eager expression it always took on when she encountered romance.

'I don't know.'

'What do you mean?' Julie looked puzzled.

'He's gone back to Australia. He left a week ago.'

'But he was going to marry you!' exclaimed Julie.

'He is. But first he had to go back to Sydney for an exhibition that had been planned before he came here. He was really sad about it. So I advanced the money for his return flight – what else could I do? But he'll pay me back when his exhibition finishes. He's a painter, you see. And a musician and writer too.'

'Do we know him?'

'His name is Edward Bear. He told me he's very well known in Australia.'

Julie looked puzzled and maybe a bit sceptical, and to change the subject she asked, 'How is your work getting on?'

'Well, I'm not sure… I seem to be just fiddling about. I haven't produced anything outstanding for a month or so. In fact, I feel quite restless.'

'But this is an ideal place for an artist,' countered Julie. 'If I could create like you I would be thrilled to be here.'

'Oh, I rather liked it in the beginning, but strangely enough I've never managed to get the right inspiration here. I felt better in Frigiliana last year. The vibrations were different there. Anyway, I shall have to leave this *cortijo*. It belongs to German friends who will be coming over very soon.'

'Where are you going to live then?'

'I have no idea…'

'Why don't you come back to Frigiliana?' suggested Julie. 'You could rent the house you had last year; you'd only be a few doors away from us.'

'But it's so dark in there. And the house is too small.'

'Try and find another one then,' insisted Julie, 'but do come back to Frigiliana.'

'Well…' replied Charlotte, 'I'll think about it.'

22

On one of the mornings Charles was giving Alejandra driving lessons along the ring road below the old part of Frigiliana, he noticed Julie in a field talking to a man with a horse. He didn't have much time to look though, because he had to keep all his attention focused on the portion of the road ahead and on Alejandra. She was sitting in a cramped position, clinging to the steering wheel with both hands as they sped along in second gear at twenty miles per hour. It had already taken a couple of lessons to move from first to second gear and Charles dared not, and could not, let her go into a higher gear: there wasn't a straight stretch in the half mile of road below the old village; Alejandra needed all her concentration to keep the car from going off the road; and Charles had to pull constantly on the steering wheel to make sure she kept to the right. And then there were obstacles: an approaching car created a wave of panic; or there was a mule to overtake; or worse, she had to avoid a crossing pedestrian. It seemed pointless to say, 'Relax Alejandra.' Her face was bright red and beads of sweat trickled down her forehead.

'Oh Carlos,' she sighed as they finished for the day. 'I'll never be able to drive.'

'It's all right Alejandra,' said Charles trying to encourage her. 'You've been making a lot of progress.'

In a way he enjoyed teaching Alejandra. She had little talent but was eager to learn. On the other hand he was relieved every time the lesson was over. If ever she had caused an accident they would have been in serious trouble. The risk was limited though, as there was little or no traffic on the ring road in the late morning.

They had only just got back to the house when Julie arrived, bubbling over with enthusiasm. 'I've met a very curious man!'

'Was that the man with the horse?' asked Charles.

'Yes. And he said I could ride it! Wouldn't that be wonderful? He offered to take me on his horse for an excursion in the mountains. I just have to say when.'

'Is he going to pull you along on his horse then?' asked Charles teasingly.

'Of course not! I can ride, didn't you know? And he'll accompany me on his mule.'

'That must have been Fernando Lortez,' intervened Alejandra. 'He tries to take people on excursions. He's always short of money.' There was disapproval in her voice.

'But he seemed a nice man!' objected Julie. 'And he appeared to like his horse.'

'Fernando doesn't *like* his horse,' corrected Alejandra. 'He *loves* his horse! Some in the village say that he prefers his horse to women.'

'I'm sure he likes women,' disagreed Julie.

'*Seguro* that he likes women. But the problem with Fernando is that he likes drinking even more: wine, beer, liquor, anything that contains alcohol. That's why he has never been able to get married. It's really a shame because he has a good heart.'

'It seems to me that married men also drink a lot here in Frigiliana,' cut in Charles. 'I sometimes go for a stroll through the village in the evening before turning in, and I'm surprised to see the bars quite full. And usually there's not a single woman in there.'

'*Sí, sí...*' Alejandra nodded. 'Drink is a serious problem here. Most of the men are bored at home, especially the older ones...'

'And maybe frightened of their wives so that they use any pretext to get away,' interrupted Julie, a twinkle in her eyes.

'Don't defend them, Julia!' reprimanded Alejandra. 'Some of them are really bad cases. They drink up all the money.'

'Like that man you told me about the other day.' Charles smiled. 'The one who lives in a house that belongs to your parents and doesn't pay any rent.'

'You must have misunderstood me,' corrected Alejandra. 'He does pay rent, but not much. Only two thousand pesetas per month...'

'What's that story?' interrupted Julie. 'I haven't heard it.'

'Well... Pépé – that's his name – pays so little because his grandfather and father already rented the house. They paid very little rent in those days and the law has not permitted us to put it up very much.' Suddenly she looked up. 'I've got an idea, Julia. You're looking for a house to buy. Well... here is a unique opportunity. My parents don't know what to do with the house and would sell it cheaply. And it would come with a premium.'

Julie seemed interested. 'What premium?'

'Pépé!' replied Alejandra exploding with laughter. 'He's the *premio gordo* – the big prize. You get him with the house because he cannot be turned out. The Council won't allow it because he is an invalid and lives off a pension.'

'What's wrong with him?'

'Well... he has drunk so much that he can no longer work and the state pays him nineteen thousand pesetas every month so that he can live.'

'Does the state really have to fork out for that?' asked Charles, incredulous.

'Pépé is not such an exceptional case. Many people around here live off state allowances. But that Pépé! The first thing he does when he gets his money is rush to the bars to drink it up.'

'Good heavens!' exclaimed Julie. 'That poor man will drink himself to death.'

AN ANDALUSIAN MURDER MYSTERY

'*Que va*! He has still got many years in him. He's only in his early forties. You may have seen him. He often sits on a wall down in the street here trying to get money out of tourists, only to drink it all up.'

'I think we've had the pleasure of meeting him.' There was a clear ironic note in Julie's voice. 'He has a round, red, jovial face, wears a beige cardigan and leans on a stick, doesn't he?'

'That's him,' confirmed Alejandra.

'Well, well...' Julie turned to Charles. 'What did I tell you? The poor hungry man wanted money for a sandwich, didn't he?'

'How was I to know?' countered Charles, looking away from Julie's sarcastic eyes.

Suddenly Alejandra intervened. 'Let's not waste any more time. We haven't done any Spanish today and that's what I'm here for.'

'But Alejandra,' objected Julie, 'listening to you and talking to you in Spanish is as good as any lesson. And I like your stories.'

But Alejandra was not to be diverted. 'Talking is not studying,' she said and she resolutely opened her books.

23

Charlotte came by later in the afternoon to say that she had been looking for a place to rent. So far, however, she hadn't been able to discover the 'ideal' house.

'Any news from Edward?' enquired Charles.

'You do realise that it takes time for a letter from Australia to get here,' replied Charlotte, sounding slightly pedantic. 'But he's sure to have already written...' she beamed, '...because we were predestined for each other.'

Julie was interested. 'How can you be so sure you were predestined?'

'Because he said so!' She threw out the words. 'Not once but several times!' Then she began to whisper, almost as if she were about to reveal something confidential, 'But there's much more than that.' Her eyes sparkled. 'He is my musician. And I... I'm his guitar.'

'You're a guitar!' exclaimed Charles mockingly. 'I would never have thought so. But maybe you're hiding a few strings under those floating overalls of yours.' And he began to laugh heartily.

Charlotte stared at him with furious eyes. 'You don't know anything!' she blurted out. 'You're totally ignorant.'

'Ahem...' intervened Julie looking at Charles with fixed insistence. 'There's an urgent errand to be done before the shops close. You know... paper and glue. You couldn't just go out and get me some?'

After Charles had taken the hint and left the room, Charlotte said, 'You, at any rate, will understand that a woman's body is like a guitar.'

'Yes...' Julie looked at her encouragingly.

'You see... a musician cannot just grab his guitar and start strumming the strings! If he does, nothing but jarring notes will come out; everything will be out of tune. You follow me?' She stared at Julie and then carried on. 'A woman needs someone who can play her. She is the precious guitar that has to be taken out of the case that covers her... slowly, carefully. First the player has to hold the guitar in his arms, thinking of the music he's going to produce. And the guitar has to be warmed up. The strings have to be touched with care, brought up to the right temperature, tuned one by one. The player too has to get into the mood. Then, hesitantly, the first notes float out while the player listens to the sounds he and the guitar are producing in symbiosis... while he listens appreciatively. He has to find the melody, make the strings resound, bring out the deepest vibrations in the guitar's body. Not everyone can do that. You have to find the right player, someone who caresses the strings with trained fingers... but once you have found your guitarist, the one who makes your strings vibrate like no other, you want to be played. And Edward is my guitarist!'

Julie nodded. 'I see what you mean.'

'Let me give an example,' continued Charlotte. 'You must have listened to Flamenco music here in Andalusia. That's maybe what comes nearest to what I'm trying to explain about a woman and her lover. When the Flamenco player is satisfied that the guitar has been warmed up and the strings been tuned, then, and only then, does he run his fingers over them. Only then does he produce thrills and emotions that pass through the guitar like the gasps of a woman in love. And the guitar longs for his caresses, for the hands of the musician. That's what it is made for, that's its reason for existing. Then, as the player feels the heat of the guitar, he becomes more daring, gets into fiery movements, plucks the strings more wildly while the instrument vibrates ever more strongly. His fingers move faster and faster, the sounds come tumbling out of the guitar, which almost screams with delight. The singer is possessed by madness, his voice rises, becomes almost a wail, the music grows to a crescendo… and then, suddenly, comes the finale: the player throws out an *Olé*, his body crumples over his instrument and he sits there, shaking for a long time while the guitar lies trembling in his arms…' Charlotte looked at Julie. 'That's why, once you've found your guitarist, you never want to let him go.'

24

That morning Bob Marvey looked so dispirited that Lesley couldn't help noticing it.

'Are you all right?' she asked, worried.

He didn't answer but went towards the fridge and poured himself a stiff drink.

Lesley looked at him with all the sympathy she could muster. 'Why don't you tell me?'

He gulped down the contents of his glass and finally said, 'It's the restaurant.'

'The restaurant?'

'It's worrying me.' Suddenly he turned to her, an almost offended look on his face. 'Why can't I have a day off every now and then? Why is it me who's got to go there every single day of the week? Do I always have to be responsible for everything?'

'But Bob, you wanted it that way!'

'Yes, but I need a break sometimes.'

'You know what?' said Lesley. 'I'll go today. You stay at home and have a rest. It'll do you good.'

And he said 'yes,' and even looked rather pleased.

The waiters and cook of the *Jardin de Roberto* were surprised to find her inside when they arrived just before midday because she hadn't been to the restaurant for some time. In fact, she had stopped coming shortly after Bob had hired that new bar girl.

That girl! It was well past twelve already and she hadn't even turned up yet. The cheek of it! thought Lesley as she went to the door to have a look outside. At that very moment she saw Amanda arrive, strolling along as if she had all the time in the world.

Just look at her, thought Lesley in disgust. The way she's dressed. A short miniskirt and no bra under her blouse. You can see her nipples almost push through it. What does Bob want a tart like that for? In our restaurant? And suddenly, upon an impulse, Lesley stepped in front of Amanda, blocking the entrance.

'We no longer need your service,' she said in a cold, haughty voice. 'If service is what one can call it.'

Amanda just stood there, staring at her in astonishment. Then a defiant look came into her eyes. 'I want to speak to Bob,' she said trying to push past Lesley into the restaurant.

Lesley sneered at her. 'You won't find him inside. He sent me especially to get rid of you. There's no place for your sort in here. Your sort works in those clubs along the road to Torre del Mar where they pay women for their services to men… you whore!'

Amanda went crimson. Then she turned around and left without saying a word.

25

For days Bob Marvey hadn't felt his usual self. He had been depressed since his fiasco with Amanda, and had hardly spoken to her in the restaurant. He had even begun to avoid eye contact. And today he hadn't wanted to go down to Nerja at all. Lesley had gone instead.

It was strange to be alone at home. He wasn't used to it – he tended to get bored when he was on his own. He began to do some long-overdue repairs in the house but he couldn't keep his mind on it. His loss of face with Amanda continued to sting him. What was he to do?

Just then the bell rang. He went to the door in a foul mood, annoyed at being interrupted, but when he opened it he felt the blood drain from his face: there was Amanda, standing on the threshold, her reddish curls framing her head, the sun illuminating them.

He motioned her to come in without uttering a word, unable to speak. As they sat on the divan in the living room, he could hardly believe it. How was it possible? Amanda here… with him? Only minutes ago he had felt hurt, he had felt angry with her, but now! She looked so youthful, so innocent, so fresh… she was everything he desired. How could he be angry with her?

Suddenly she gazed at him from under her curved eyelashes, her eyes shy. 'Hello Bob,' she whispered. There was nothing left of her usual cocksureness. She seemed vulnerable, even submissive. Then she held out her hand for him to take, as if offering to be his, her eyes pleading to be friends again. That was the moment he surrendered. His whole being seemed to topple over, he wanted to melt inside her, to become one with her.

He leant forward without even knowing what he was doing, put his hand on one of her smooth legs and pushed back her miniskirt. His hand moved up Amanda's thigh as if it had a will of its own and before he had time to think he had pulled down his trousers and threw himself on her there on the divan. His hands went greedily under her buttocks, pushing her bottom up when his hips moved down. He felt his desire rise, rise, but tried to hold back until all went black in front of his eyes. Then his whole body contracted and all the tension of the previous week shot out of him. It was agony and death, glory and paradise. It felt good, good, good…

He lay there, his eyes closed. A world of colours was whirling behind his eyelids and his whole body was aching with pain and delight. He felt so close to Amanda, to the warmth of her body. This was something new, something strong; this was a feeling he had never had before. This, he thought, must be love.

He opened his eyes after a long time and looked into Amanda's in wonder. Then, to his surprise, he heard himself say, 'Oh baby, you're super, I love you…'

She put a finger on his lips but he went on. 'Stay with me. I need you.'

She took his head between her hands and kissed his lips, his cheeks, his eyelids. Then she freed herself from under his weight, adjusted her clothes, caressed his face once more with her delicate fingers and left the room quietly.

Bob Marvey rolled over on the divan, closed his eyes again and sank at once into a deep sleep. When he woke up, maybe half an hour later, he was surprised to find himself on the divan with his trousers down. Then the memory flowed back. Was it true? Had Amanda really been here or was it all a dream? But the feeling was too vivid. The softness of her skin, the springiness of her flesh, the freshness of her being was imprinted upon his body. And he felt so warm, so tender, so loving. He felt like never before. He was overcome with joy and all the time the thought was with him: a new life is beginning.

26

'Where did you put that tin of cat food we bought yesterday?' asked Julie. 'I just can't find it and the cat is getting frantic.'

Charles looked up from his papers. 'What did you say?'

'Oh you're such a nuisance!'

'What do you mean by that? I haven't done anything!'

'I wasn't talking to you,' said Julie. 'I was talking to Gato. Look how he keeps pestering me! And I can't find that tin we bought yesterday. Where is it?'

Gato was a stray cat that had pressed itself upon them. As he had no name Julie simply called him *Gato* – Spanish for cat. He had his way of getting into the apartment via the roofs and the terrace, and now that he had found a house and people who supplied him with food, he had set his mind on keeping them.

'I've no idea,' replied Charles absent-mindedly. 'Didn't we bring up all the bags last night?'

'Maybe the tin rolled out? The bags were scattered about everywhere as usual with all those bends in the road, remember. You wouldn't like to go down and have a look in the car, would you?'

Charles was cosily installed in a comfortable armchair and didn't really want to go, but he realised that he'd better do it: Gato was running around Julie's legs meowing plaintively and her patience was dwindling by the minute. With regret he left the comfort of his armchair, put on his sandals and walked out.

It was much warmer in the street in the full sunshine than inside the house, which still retained some of the coolness of the morning. The sunlight reverberated from the white walls and Charles squinted not to be blinded by the strong light. By the time he was halfway down he felt hot and was longing to take off his sweater.

When he reached the place where his car was parked he found it sandwiched between the wall and another car. Last night Julie had squashed the passenger's side almost against the wall 'to leave more room for cars to pass,' she had said. And now someone had parked so close alongside that it was impossible to get into his car. 'What a nerve!' grumbled Charles.

With difficulty he squeezed in between the two cars and peered inside his own. From under the back of the passenger's seat he saw the edge of the tin of cat food sticking out, but how could he get at it? He thought of Julie, expecting him to return with the tin, and of Gato, hungry and bothersome. Somehow he would have to retrieve that tin.

He unlocked the driver's door, opened it as far as he could, slipped his arm inside, managed to open the back door till it touched the other car and was able to wind down the rear window. Reaching the tin was a different matter though. He shut the door again, crawled on top of the other car and, hanging down, began to squeeze his head and shoulders inside the open rear window, stretching his arms as far as he could to reach the tin. It was exactly when he found himself in this most awkward position, sweating profusely with the effort, that a loud hoot scared the wits out of him; then he felt the car on which he was lying move away from underneath him, his legs dropped down and he was left hanging through the window of the back door of his car, bent double.

How can anyone behave in such a way? he fumed, and he wriggled himself out of his back door window in an access of fury, ready to give the driver a piece of his mind. By that time the other car had managed to turn around and as it approached he noticed a mass of reddish hair through the windshield. A girl, he thought. In a flash he saw an extremely pretty face lit up by a triumphant smile. Then, as the car passed, the girl blew him a kiss through her open window, burst into impish laughter as if she had thoroughly enjoyed herself and drove away, her eyes sparkling.

Charles stood there speechless, eyeing the car as it disappeared into the *barrio nuevo*. All his anger had dissipated. That girl could get away with anything, he thought, and she knows it. He felt intrigued. Who was she and what had she been doing here in the village?

27

When Lesley got home that evening she felt victorious. She had really enjoyed her day! The reception she had given that red-haired girl when she'd arrived at the restaurant! It made her almost giggle with a childish pleasure. The whole day her thoughts had returned to the scene where she had told that bar girl that her sort did not work in a decent restaurant. You should have seen her face! Crimson it had been! She had turned around and left, just like that. Gone! Out of the restaurant. Out of Lesley's life.

She was so bubbling over with satisfaction when she got home that Bob noticed it.

'You seem to have had a nice day,' he remarked – he looked happy himself.

Should I tell him about the bar girl? she wondered, but she felt so excited that she blurted it all out before she could stop herself. She began to tell him animatedly what she had done and said, and was on the point of bursting out into happy laughter when, unexpectedly, Bob flew into a rage.

'You stupid woman!' he yelled. 'What a damned fool you are!' And suddenly he slapped her face, grabbed the car keys out of her hand, picked up his jacket, turned around and left, slamming the door.

28

Lesley stood there in a state of shock, holding her cheek pulsating with pain. Her hands began to tremble and her throat tightened; then tears streamed out of her eyes and she burst into uncontrollable sobs. She thought she was going to faint and just wanted to curl up, close her eyes and never wake up again, but when she went to lie down on the bed and shut her eyes, her heart was thumping; she felt the beats in her temples, banging in her head till they nearly drove her mad. Tension had been building up in her for days and now she was so taut that she had reached breaking point.

Darkness came and she was exhausted, but she couldn't sleep. Her mind seemed wound up like a clock. Images kept flashing through her head: Bob's angry face; his hand hitting her; the red-haired girl going crimson; Bob rushing to Nerja to make it up with her; and then… Bob going to bed with her! When she imagined him taking that girl in his arms she felt sick. She was unable to get rid of the image and felt hot and cold with shame and horror; her temples ached and she was astonished at the loudness of the throbbing in her ears. She couldn't stand it much longer; something must happen to release her from this unbearable strain.

It was early morning before she finally dropped off into a restless sleep. Hours later she was woken by the sound of the door closing below. She lay there for a few seconds, dazed; then the events of yesterday came back to her and she instinctively touched her cheek where Bob's hand had struck her. Was it true? How could this have happened?

Suddenly the door to the bedroom opened and Bob came in. When he stepped forward she pulled up the satin sheet as if to shield herself.

'You're still in bed? It's two in the afternoon.' He looked at her, not aggressively but with reproach in his eyes.

She didn't answer but turned her head away.

'Oh, come on,' he said, 'stop sulking and listen. I haven't got much time. I've just dropped by to tell you that the bank manager came to see me at the restaurant. If we can come up with some money within a month they're prepared to wait and reschedule the debt, but otherwise it's bankruptcy. And don't look at me like that! Don't tell me it's all my fault. Do something instead of lying there moping. I need your help. I know you can get money if you want. Come on, get us out of this.' And he turned around and shut the door behind him.

After he had left, Lesley lay there for at least half an hour, unable to move. Then she thought, maybe all is not lost. He needs me. He cannot do without me. I'm the only one who can help him.

She sat up mechanically and began to pull herself together. Don't give up, she tried to encourage herself. You know what to do. Go to your father and get the money – a lot of money – and Bob will return to you. Have the courage to do it!

29

It was three in the afternoon, a time when everything was quiet and there was usually nobody around. Charles often went for a walk at that hour and he was advancing at a brisk pace along the ring road below the old village, when the croaking of frogs became audible. He had heard it before, but this time he decided to have a look and began to climb up on one of the small plots of land that lined the village, until he noticed a small water reservoir. He was almost level with it when the croaking suddenly stopped and he heard splashing sounds. He quickly crouched down between the vegetation to see what was going to happen, keeping very quiet, until a few heads popped up from below the greenish water surface. Then more frogs appeared, looking around with suspicious eyes. Finally, gaining confidence, they resumed their activities: chasing each other in the water or hopping onto the sides of the basin. They were tiny, yet the noise they made was tremendous.

After a while he slid down to a clump of banana plants that grew on one of the lower plots. He was just having a close look at a huge purple flower hanging from one of the tall stems when he noticed a car stopping on the road below. Next a man emerged from the fields beneath the ring road, pulling up a mule.

When villagers met they always started a loud conversation, but this was different. Charles could just about hear the driver say something like, 'How many this time?' but he was unable to hear the answer. Next the muleteer picked up some heavy crates which his mule had been carrying, shoved them onto the backseat of the car, shut the door and waited. The driver handed over something, the muleteer looked at it, his hands moving as if he were counting, and nodded. He put whatever it was into his pocket and as he turned, Charles could see him clearly: there was a look of satisfaction on the man's face.

The muleteer immediately trundled down again toward the *campo*, pulling his mule behind him, whilst the car, whose engine had been running all the time, moved off rapidly. The whole scene had lasted no more than a minute or two.

It was so unusual that Charles wondered what had been going on. What had they been doing, behaving almost like conspirators? Then, as he continued his walk, he began to doubt his feelings. Maybe there was nothing unusual about it? Maybe it was all his imagination?

30

Charlotte was sitting in her *cortijo*, feeling extremely excited. She had received a letter from Edward and he told her that he loved her! And he needed her! When he got back to Australia he found out that his finances were low and that he hadn't got enough money to set up his exhibition. Poor Edward, he sounded so desperate. He apologised a thousand times but, please, could she send him some money?

How could she not help him? Of course she would, but there was a big problem: she had already spent a lot on him and there wasn't much left in her account. Where could she get the large amount of money he wanted?

Then she thought of Meier. He was a rich man and it was obvious that he liked her. The last time she had seen him had nevertheless been difficult. He had sounded nicely surprised when she phoned him, but later on, when she got to his house and rang the bell, he had taken a long time to open the door and he had seemed displeased. When she had asked him if he was upset with her he had said, 'No,' but all the same, she felt there was something wrong. 'You haven't come to see me for a whole month,' he finally reproached her. 'What about my bust you promised to sculpt?' She had apologised for not having come for so long, but how could she have gone to see him while Edward was with her? It was no good telling Meier though. She felt that it would just have put him off. How could men think she was there just for them? Anyway, she had tried to be nice to him, and in the end he had quietened down and become pleasant again. He had told her that he looked upon her as his own daughter and that he was going to do a lot for her; so she ought to come and see him more often and especially, he had insisted, start sculpting his bust.

Maybe she should go to him and ask him for an advance? But how was she going to explain why she needed so much money without mentioning Edward?

31

Christina Eckmann of the Green Park One project was nervous. She opened her handbag, took out a little mirror and looked at her face, then picked up her make-up set and applied some eye shadow to her eyelids. As always the touch of the soft brush on her skin had a soothing effect on her. Was it being occupied that calmed her nerves? Or the view in the mirror, which told her that she was still a beautiful woman? She wanted to be beautiful; she had to be.

She looked sideways at Marc who was driving the car. He seemed calm enough; he had the self-assurance that goes with class. He was the master, even when they made love – especially then. She looked at his deeply tanned skin, his clean-shaven, handsome face. Why was she so in love with him? She had always been such a cool businesswoman, but in his arms she felt like jelly; he dominated her completely.

She put her hand on his knee, slid it gently up his leg and felt the muscles tighten under her fingers. He turned his head towards her and in his light-brown eyes was that look of desire she so longed for. She felt reassured: he would make love to her tonight; he would make love to her as long as he admired her, as long as he believed she was strong. She must never show that she was nervous; she must hide her weakness from him – and above all, her dependence on him.

There was no way back now anyway. She had sunk all her money into this project; he had wanted her to do it, and he had done the same. This time she must succeed – they both must. If the project failed, her life would be finished. Don't think of failure, she tried to tell herself. We shall succeed. And then we'll be rich, very rich… and together forever. But as the car approached Frigiliana she became nervous again. They had been unable to convince that German the other day, and the boss had been furious. Tonight they must be successful…

32

That same evening Julie had decided to make spaghetti but as she started preparing supper she noticed that she didn't have the main ingredient: the pasta. 'You couldn't go down and buy me a packet, could you?' she asked turning to Charles. 'Not the ordinary white one but the wholemeal kind.'

'Do you think they have wholemeal spaghetti in the shops here?'

'In the shops maybe not, but possibly in the *supermercado*.'

Frigiliana had a number of small groceries, but only one larger shop; it was situated at the entrance of the *barrio nuevo* and although it proudly called itself 'supermarket' because you could push a trolley around and pay at the exit, it was really only a slightly larger version of a grocer's shop.

Surprisingly, the *supermercado* did have wholemeal spaghetti. After Charles paid he was about to walk back home when he saw a man and a woman near the phone box on the opposite pavement. He might not have noticed them because the phone box was squashed in between a kiosk and the bus shelter, but somehow the woman's figure seemed familiar to him and their furtive manner aroused his suspicion. The sun had just set and their faces were half in the dark, but even so they turned their heads away so as not to be recognised. They entered the phone box and Charles saw the woman pick up the receiver, dial a number and talk for a minute or two. It was no business of his and he ought not to have stayed there, half hiding behind a parked van, but he felt intrigued.

As they came out, their faces turned for a moment towards him and he recognised them. She was the estate agent they had seen in Nerja, and he was the man who had come into her office. What, wondered Charles, were they doing here in Frigiliana? And surely, he thought, people like them must have a mobile phone. So why were they phoning from a public call box?

33

The next morning Fernando Lortez was walking his mule up the hill. It had served him well for many years but now it was getting old. It would last another year or maybe two if he didn't push it too hard, but he would soon have to buy a new mule and take it up with the old one so that it would have time to learn its job. Such a nuisance! Fernando lifted his cap and scratched his scalp. It would be a shame to lose the old one. It had such a sure foothold; it could climb all the way to the top of the hill without him having to pull the tail even once. And how was he going to pay for a new mule?

Fernando was fretting about other things too. Two years ago he had bought a piece of land and had started building a villa on it, doing the work all by himself. It had seemed such a good idea. He was sure to let the villa to tourists; it would give him a regular income, and maybe he would even be able to marry afterwards? He had borrowed to acquire the land, and next had gone back to the bank, asking for another loan to buy building materials. But building the villa had been much more costly than he had thought, and after a year he was in arrears with his monthly payments. The bank had refused to fork out more and he had been forced to stop all building work. How was he ever going to pay back the bank now? Selling his potatoes and vegetables didn't bring in much – and maybe he was spending too much in the bars – although he was loath to admit it. He occasionally did odd jobs such as delivering firewood and tried to take tourists around on his horse to make a bit of extra money. And a year ago he had even agreed to work for that German a few mornings a week, but the man didn't pay much.

He had been thinking about his problems for a long time and had finally struck upon a way to make some additional money. It was risky, though. What if the German found out? But he didn't see any other way out. If only he hadn't started all this. Why had he got himself into this fix? And now he had begun doing things he had to hide.

He had been to his own field down in the *campo* since daybreak to look after his potatoes, had a long chat with his neighbour and then went to fetch the crates of food and drinks that he had to carry up to the German. He would have liked to go into a bar first but he was late already and the German was a stickler for punctuality! As he glanced at his wristwatch a worried look came over his face: it was nine and he was supposed to have been at the big house up on the hill by eight-thirty to deliver the four heavy crates, and to weed and water the garden plots afterwards.

Fernando didn't like the German very much. His Spanish was poor and he was haughty and distant. When he explained something, he didn't so much speak as bark commands! No, he didn't like that man; he was altogether too different from himself.

And now Fernando had to grow vegetables up there, and imagine, the German wanted all the weeding done by hand instead of spraying one of those wonderful new liquids that had come on the market! And he lived alone without any neighbours, think of that! Fernando would never dream of living alone outside the village, but he was Fernando and foreigners were foreigners.

When he reached the entrance of the German's house, to his surprise, Fernando saw that the garage door was half open. That was strange. What was he to do now? He lifted his cap and started scratching his scalp again, but it was getting late and finally he made up his mind. He pushed the door hesitantly and led his mule into the property. He wanted to get rid of those crates.

Minutes later he came running down the hill screaming, '*Por Dios*! *Por Dios!*' all the way to the Guardia Civil post.

34

At nine that same morning Alejandra's father had knocked on the door of the house where Charles and Julie were staying to introduce the farmer who wanted to sell his *cortijo*. The man was lean and no more than five foot three tall like quite a number of farmers around; they looked wiry, yet were very tough, doing all the heavy work in the *campo*. The *cortijo* was several miles away, so they took the farmer in their car, drove along the asphalted road to Torrox and then continued on a dirt road through a valley where a lot of development was taking place.

After a while the farmer motioned to Charles to park and they continued on foot along a narrow path till they finally came upon a small *cortijo*. Inside there were two minute rooms in which the farmer kept some tools, and a small stable which in the past must have housed a mule. There didn't seem to be any water, electricity or sewage system.

Next he took them to the other side of the *cortijo* to what could be considered a small south-facing terrace. 'Look,' he said, 'magnificent view, isn't it?'

The view over the *campo* sloping down to the sea was indeed not bad, but Julie had no eyes for it; she pointed at the *cortijo*, a disappointed look on her face. 'It's rather small. And there's no kitchen or bathroom.'

'No problem,' said the man. 'You can easily transform all this. Just build on a kitchen and a bathroom and it will be perfect.'

'But where would we get the water from?' Charles wanted to know. 'And the electricity?'

'*Ningun problema* – no problem. You can have electricity brought up to here. And as to the water, they are building a large reservoir just below.' And he pointed towards what they now saw were the foundations of a reservoir less than fifty yards away, right in the middle of what was to be their view towards the sea. '*Que buena suerte!*' continued the farmer enthusiastically. 'Really lucky that they are bringing the water so nearby, isn't it?'

'How much do you want for your *cortijo*?' asked Charles, who was not impressed.

The man paused for a minute as if he had never considered that point before. Finally he replied, 'I have no longer any need for it you see, so I want to sell it cheaply.'

'How much is "cheaply"?'

'I think… five million pesetas.'

'And how much land comes with the *cortijo*?'

'Basically…' he looked sideways, 'basically, it's the land on which the *cortijo* stands and the terrace.'

'Doesn't the land around belong to you then?' Julie sounded incredulous.

'It did belong to the family… but it has already been sold you see.'

'Well…' said Charles evasively, 'we'll think about it.' And he began to walk back to where the car was parked.

35

They had just got to the dirt road when a brand-new luxury Chrysler Jeep approached. The moment the driver saw the farmer he stopped and called out, 'Trying to sell your worthless *cortijo* again, hey!'

The farmer became visibly smaller than he already was, and if he could have disappeared altogether he would have.

The driver now got out. He was a tall, corpulent man of maybe fifty and his black leather belt cut tightly into his belly. He wore a printed pink shirt, neatly pressed white trousers, white socks and black moccasins, but the top buttons of his shirt were undone, showing the bushy, greying hairs that covered his chest.

'Don't trust that farmer!' His voice rang out like a tenor's. 'He's trying to cheat you,' he warned them, speaking English with a strong accent. 'There's no access to his *cortijo*. All the land around is mine and he knows I withhold permission to bring water, electricity or anything.' Then he sized them up. 'Are you looking for land?'

'Well… yes,' replied Julie.

He now opened the door of his car. 'Get in,' he commanded. 'I'll show you some really good land.'

'We'll follow you,' suggested Charles. 'We've got our own car.'

'I'll drive you!' It was an order, not an invitation.

As they drove off, leaving the poor farmer behind, the driver introduced himself as Massimo Zizi and began questioning them – where they came from, what they were doing. When he had satisfied his curiosity, he began to talk about himself.

'I used to live in Roma,' he said. 'Those were the good days. But ten years ago I had to move to Spain for business. You can't imagine how boring it is down here. There's no one decent to talk to; no culture. *Mamma mia!*' He sighed. 'Ten years of my life…' His plump, tanned face and his dark-brown eyes expressed annoyance and disgust as he spoke. His hair was still black – or had he dyed it? – but he was getting bald in front and his short, neatly clipped beard was grey in patches.

He took them to see three different plots of about an acre each. 'Now this,' he said waving his arms about, 'is good quality land. Nothing like what the peasants here have to offer.' He looked at them proudly. 'I only deal in the best.'

'How much do you want for it?'

'Oh! I'll have to think about that. Phone me in a day or two. I'll give you a good price.' He looked at his gold Rolex watch. '*Basta!*' he exclaimed. 'Come and have lunch with me.'

They tried to refuse but the man waved their objections aside. He picked up his mobile phone, which was lying on the seat next to him, and phoned home to arrange lunch, all the while manoeuvring his big car with one hand at high speed over the uneven track. Minutes later they drove up to the entrance gate of a large property. Massimo Zizi hooted his horn and a man rushed forward to open the gate. The driveway curved between pine trees and suddenly the house came into view. It was more than a house: it was a sumptuous mansion extending over three levels. On each of these levels was a terrace with French windows and marble balustrades. Wide stairs extended from the lower terrace to a large swimming pool. Emerald-green marble urns decorated each of its rounded corners, and impeccably manicured lawns stretched below.

'My house,' said the man when he had stopped the car. 'Designed by the best Italian architects. It's simply the most magnificent property this side of the Sierra Almijara.'

As they went inside and entered an impressive hall with an ivory-colour marble floor on which oriental rugs were spread, Pavarotti's voice began to resonate from loudspeakers, and Massimo accompanied him enthusiastically, singing loudly, though slightly out of tune. The Italian now took them one floor up into a vast living room and told them to sit down on one of the black leather divans. The walls were lined with huge mirrors set in chrome and gold, but most striking was the view through the wide panoramic windows that surrounded the living room. Towards the east lay the dazzlingly white village of Frigiliana while towards the south they could see the *campo* and the rolling hills, stretching away towards the white buildings of Nerja with the blue Mediterranean in the background.

'What do you think of the view?' asked the man. '*Magnifico*, isn't it? As if a slide was projected in Technicolor.' Then he added, 'But it is always the same; that's what is so annoying. Sometimes, when I see it, I wish I could move on to another slide.'

Their host now began telling them about his recent trip with his wife to New York and Florida, and about how wonderful everything was in America compared to Spain – the hotels first class, the people civilised, the service good, the country well organised.

'What about the food in America?' Julie managed to get in.

'Oh that! No problem. There are top class Italian restaurants if you know where to find them. But of course, if you haven't got the right connections...'

Two servants brought in trays with glasses, cutlery, bread, butter, a choice of pastas, dishes of *carpaccio* – 'specially cured in Italy for me' said their host, 'the very best' – and red Italian wine, and put everything in front of them on low glass-and-chrome tables.

'*Pronto!*' exclaimed their host, and as he began to attack his food with gusto, he added, '*Buon appetito!*'

He had been speaking almost non-stop so far but now that he was eating, Charles was able to divert his attention to the room. The wall opposite the windows was lined with furniture of Italian design, but what attracted his interest most was a large oil painting. It represented a woman of about thirty-five in a white frilly blouse and black velvet trousers. She was sitting in a chair, her legs crossed and her hands folded in her lap, and had blue eyes and fair hair drawn back in a knot.

Massimo Zizi had just stuck a forkful of carpaccio in his mouth when he noticed that Charles was looking at the portrait, and he couldn't help saying proudly, 'My wife. Magnificent, no? She is most beautiful as you can see.'

Beautiful she was indeed, yet Charles couldn't help feeling that dissatisfaction showed up in her face and that her eyes didn't have a kind look.

'She isn't here?' asked Julie.

'No. For the moment she's in Amsterdam where she has a business. She's Dutch.'

They finished their meal and the servants now brought in cappuccino.

The conversation had tapered off and for want of anything better Charles said, 'It was good of you to show us the land you have for sale.'

'Oh!' exclaimed the Italian, almost laughing. 'Don't call that the land I have for sale. Those plots are mere crumbs. I only showed them because they're the right size for you. But I'm about to sell land many, many times that size. I bought it ten years ago when it wasn't worth anything.' The man, whose face had begun to look bored, brightened up visibly. 'As I always say: just let it sleep and one day it will be worth a fortune. And that day has come.'

'Where is it situated?' asked Charles, just to say something.

'Near Frigiliana on the other side of the river. Have you not heard of the magnificent development project there?'

'I have.' Suddenly Charles' interest was aroused. 'But aren't there problems?' he ventured. 'It seems that a rich German who owns quite a lot of land too is opposed to the project.'

'That German, pfft…' The Italian waved his hand in derision. Suddenly he looked at his gold Rolex and exclaimed, 'So late already and I still have much to do! I'll have to ask one of my boys to see you back to your car.' He got up precipitously and was almost out of the door when he turned around, shouting a final, '*Ciao*!'

36

It was well past three by the time they got back to Frigiliana. Usually the village was quiet by then; people were either lunching – which started after 2p.m. when work stopped and shops closed – or they had already finished their meal and were at their siesta. But as Charles and Julie arrived at the Guardia Civil post they found the parking lot full of people. There were also several police cars and an ambulance.

'Maybe there's been an accident,' ventured Julie. 'Stop a second, I'll get out here.'

Charles stopped the car to let her get out and then continued until he found a place where he could park. When he returned to the Guardia Civil post it took him some time to pick out Julie amongst the crowd that had gathered there.

'What's going on?'

'It's all a bit confusing but if I understand correctly, someone has been murdered.'

'Someone from the village?'

'No. A foreigner, but I couldn't make out who.'

Just then Charles noticed the woman who let Maria's house for weekends and he turned to her asking, 'Is it true that someone has been killed?'

'He was killed all right,' affirmed the woman, an excited look in her eyes. 'His head was bashed in.'

'Who is it?'

'It's that man who lived on the top of the hill... that German. Not that I knew him; I don't think many in the village knew him.'

'The German!' exclaimed Charles. 'You don't say? Where is he now? I mean... his corpse.'

'Oh, there.' She pointed at the ambulance. 'They've just brought him down.'

At that moment an officer came out of the Guardia Civil post followed by someone who was probably a doctor. At once the crowd moved forward, but two policemen motioned the people to stand back and make way for the police officer, the doctor and several other officials. Soon the police cars and ambulance left through the narrow street of the *barrio nuevo* with howling sirens, and gradually the crowd began to disperse.

'How terrible the German has been killed,' said Julie as they walked home. 'This is really going to affect the village.'

PART TWO
THE CURSE OF THE MOORS

1

Contrary to what Julie and Charles had expected, the people in the village didn't seem to be at all affected by the murder. They went by on their daily errands just as usual, greeting each other with a joyful '*Hola*!' or stopping for a chat. It was uncanny.

'Maybe we can ask Alejandra about it?' proposed Julie as they sat waiting for their Spanish lesson.

Just then there was a knock on the door and Alejandra came in. She was dressed very neatly: she wore a black cardigan over a flowery blouse with a large collar; a grey miniskirt; dark tights and black leather low-heeled shoes. Her face too was made up nicely with rouge on her cheeks, and there was just a hint of eye shadow and lipstick. She looked much more confident than when she first came.

She had only just sat down and put her books on the table in front of her, when Julie asked, 'What do you think of the murder?'

The Spanish teacher paused a second as if pondering whether to say anything or not. Then she let out, 'I happen to know a lot about it.' There was a conspiratorial look in her eyes. 'My cousin told me everything last night.'

'Why would your cousin know about it?'

'Because her husband is a police inspector and...' she looked up proudly to see the effect her words were going to have, '...they have put him in charge of the investigation of the murder!'

'How exciting Alejandra!' exclaimed Julie with great enthusiasm. 'Tell us all about it!'

Alejandra suddenly hesitated. 'I don't know if...' When she saw Julie's disappointed face she explained, almost excusing herself, 'You understand... my cousin was not really supposed to tell me anything... and I promised her to keep it secret...'

Alejandra seemed to have made up her mind not to say anything, yet Charles felt that if she could just say the first word, all the rest would follow.

'I wonder how the German's body was discovered?' He turned to Alejandra. 'But maybe you don't know that.'

'*Que va*! Of course I do!' she protested. 'Fernando Lortez...' Then she stopped.

'Oh, that nice man with the horse!' Julie smiled encouragingly. 'What has he got to do with it?'

'Well... it was like this,' Alejandra began hesitantly. 'Fernando Lortez did errands and gardening for that big house up on the hill, you see, and when he arrived at the house two mornings ago with his mule carrying provisions, he found the door wide open...'

'The front door was open?' interrupted Charles. 'How can that be?'

'Well, it was!' Alejandra continued, slightly perturbed. 'Fernando hesitated to go in but finally he did, calling out, "*Señor*!" As there was no answer Fernando thought that maybe the German had fallen ill and he stepped inside the house, all the while calling, "*Señor*!" There was a large living room to the left and as he looked inside he noticed a pair of legs sticking out from behind a low table: the German was lying on his stomach on the floor! The first thing Fernando thought was that he'd had a heart attack and he rushed forward, but when he got close to the body he stopped dead in his tracks. The back of the German's head was bashed in! It had become an ugly mess of grey hair and dark blood clotted together. Fernando said he stood there for maybe ten seconds staring at the deep gash in the head as if hypnotised. Then he was seized by a wave of panic. This surely was the work of the Devil himself! And he turned around and ran out of the house.'

'Is this Fernando Lortez to be trusted?' enquired Charles.

'Of course he is!'

'Are you sure? Maybe he's hiding something and the German discovered it? Maybe Fernando himself killed the German.'

Alejandra seemed shocked. 'Carlos,' she replied in a voice that tolerated no opposition, 'don't say such things. Fernando is from the village. He's one of us!'

'Do you know how the German was killed?' asked Julie to defuse the tense situation. 'But maybe your cousin hasn't told you?'

'Of course I know.' Alejandra's voice was still tense. 'He was hit on the back of the head with a poker. It was lying not far from the body and had a lot of blood on it.'

'How awful!' exclaimed Julie. 'The poor man! I do hope the police will find out who did it. But they will if your cousin's husband is in charge. I'm sure he is very good, isn't he?' She looked encouragingly at Alejandra.

Their Spanish teacher brightened up visibly. 'Yes, he is,' she confirmed. 'We're very proud of him in the family.'

'Maybe the police have already solved the murder?' ventured Charles.

'Carlos,' said Alejandra as if reprimanding a naughty pupil, 'it's not that simple. There were no fingerprints on the poker or anywhere else. And unfortunately, the rest of the search has been unsuccessful too.'

'Then the police haven't really been able to find out much.' Julie sounded as if she were very disappointed.

'But they have!' protested Alejandra. 'They were able to fix the time of the murder. It must have happened between eight o'clock and midnight the evening before the body was discovered.'

'Still, that isn't much,' remarked Charles. 'I would have expected the police to have interrogated everyone by now. Or someone might at least have seen a suspicious figure go up the hill that evening or heard something.'

'Of course the police have interrogated everyone! They know how to do their job.' Alejandra seemed upset. 'And a couple who live up the hill and were out for their evening walk declared that they heard a quarrel. They were unable to tell the exact time but they think that it was around ten o'clock.'

'Did they say how many voices they heard? And were these men's voices? Or was there a woman as well?'

'They seemed to be pretty certain they heard a man's voice, but that was all.'

'Can they be trusted?'

'I don't think there's any reason not to trust them. They're an English couple who own a restaurant in Nerja.'

'Were they on good terms with the German?'

'They said they hardly knew him and never spoke to him.'

'Maybe they're hiding something,' surmised Julie. 'They might even have done it themselves.'

'That's for the police to find out,' said Alejandra defensively. 'And it's high time to start the lesson…' she looked at her watch, '… because I have to leave within an hour.'

2

Charles bought a local newspaper at the stationery shop to see whether it would tell him anything more. The murder had made front-page news, as was to be expected. Murders were rare here. There had been an attempted murder last year and another apparently still unsolved case several years ago, but that was all.

The newspaper carried all the details of how Fernando had found the German. The reporters had also interviewed the English neighbours and the doctor who had examined the body, but Charles didn't learn much more than what he already knew. There was some information about the German too. His name was Konrad Meier, and he had been living in Frigiliana for the last ten years.

They haven't found much, thought Charles. If they continue like this they may well end up with another unsolved murder case. It wouldn't surprise me.

Then, as he turned to page three, there was a photograph of Fernando Lortez standing up straight with his arms held stiffly against his sides, smiling proudly. But… but… I'm sure that's the man I saw down the road a few days ago, thought Charles as he looked more closely. The one with the mule who was talking furtively to someone in a car!

3

Around five in the afternoon Julie and Charles were strolling along Calle Real, the main street, when they noticed Iago, one of their friends. He was standing on the steps of a narrow dead-end street, arranging a few carvings outside his house, which was also his workshop and showroom. Iago had given up his secure office job in a big town to follow his dream: to live in a small village in the south and create objects in wood. His showroom was filled with photo-frames, lamp-stands, small tables, cupboards with sculptured doors, artistically designed mirror frames into which he worked the shape of trees or clouds… it was an artist's dream-world, each piece an original creation in honey-coloured pine. The only problem was that Iago was rather too shy to sell his own work well.

Julie suffered from no such inhibitions. She was a born saleswoman and after they had said 'Hello,' she immediately began trying to sell some of Iago's work to a couple of foreigners who, led by their curiosity to see what was inside his small shop, had innocently entered its wide-open doors.

Sometimes Charles joked that Julie could sell anything to people, from stale bread to broken chairs if she wanted to. Some years ago, after she had come to live with him in Brussels, she had decided to do antique fairs, and had developed a special selling technique. In the morning she would go around her stall looking around the exhibited pieces of furniture to decide what she wanted to sell that day. Then she put her hands on each of the chosen pieces, concentrating her mind and putting what she called 'power' into them. However unscientific – even totally irrational – it appeared to Charles, he had to admit that her success rate was considerably higher than the laws of probability allowed for.

As he had nothing much to do while Julie was helping Iago with his customers, Charles went to sit down on the outside steps. The sun flooded the street, life seemed as pleasant as it could be, and he was looking absent-mindedly at the mass of mauve bougainvillea that covered the façade of Carmen's souvenir shop opposite, when Lola came out. When she saw him she smiled and sat down next to him.

Lola had blue-green eyes, which was exceptional in Andalusia, and she was an extremely pretty girl too; no wonder she attracted so many young men. She liked their company but, fortunately, she liked her studies even more, and helped in Carmen's shop during holidays and weekends to earn some money to pay for the last year of her secondary school.

Whenever she saw Charles she tried to practice her English on him.

'There are no customers in the shop. It is very quiet today.' Lola looked at him questioningly. 'Is that how you say it?'

'That's correct. By the way,' Charles asked in Spanish, 'have you heard about the murder of that German from up on the hill?'

Lola laughed. 'You live in a big city and may have murders every week, but we don't. The whole village knew about it less than an hour after Fernando had discovered the body.'

'We only heard about it in the afternoon. When we came back to Frigiliana we noticed that there was quite a commotion in front of the Guardia Civil post.'

'Did you go to visit friends?'

'No, not really. We had gone to the *campo* to see a *cortijo* and ended up having lunch with a very rich man. He had a really magnificent property with a beautiful marble swimming pool.'

'That must have been the house of that Italian!' exclaimed Lola. There was a look of disapproval on her face. 'He's a bad man!'

'Well, he's a pompous ass but that doesn't make him a bad man.'

'But that man hides many things. In the village it is whispered that there is a lot more going on in his house than... how do you say that in English... encounters the eye?'

'...than *meets* the eye,' corrected Charles. 'Anyway, you mustn't believe everything people say, Lola.'

'But I know what I'm talking about!' she protested. 'A few weeks ago that man gave a party. I had been asked to help with serving the guests and cleaning up afterwards, and I can tell you that there were some strange people there.'

'What do you mean by "strange"?'

'Well... how can I explain it? Gangster types... men I wouldn't fancy being left alone with.'

'Don't judge people from the way they look,' said Charles trying to sound fatherly. 'The fact that some of the guests looked like gangsters doesn't make the Italian a bad man.'

'But he *is* a bad man!' insisted Lola. 'Some young men have run after me and that's quite natural because isn't that what girls like? But married men should leave young girls alone. I may seem daring but... how do you say it in English... I trace the line there?'

'I *draw* the line there. And Lola, married men sometimes cannot help feeling attracted to pretty young girls.'

'But that's horrible!' A deep frown appeared on her forehead. Suddenly she looked at him. 'Can I trust you?'

'Are you going to tell me something personal then?'

'Yes. But you must keep it secret.'

Charles nodded, and she began hesitantly. 'That Italian asked me to come back a few days later. When I got there and he let me in, I realised that I was alone with him. "Where is the party?" I asked, worried. He grinned. "The party is going to happen here between us." Then he locked the door from the inside and turned towards me with a creepy smile. "You'd better do what I say, because otherwise you're going to regret it. Take your clothes off!" And he began to undo his belt, that fat man!'

'God, that's terrible!' exclaimed Charles, shocked. 'What did you do?'

'I wasn't going to obey! I ran to the other side of a big table and faced him, but as I saw him advance with a threatening look on his horrid face, I dashed to the far side of the room. He followed me closely, holding on to his trousers, but I quickly picked up one of the low glass side tables that lined the wall, and threw it in front of his feet. He stumbled over it and fell heavily on the floor. After that he was enraged and began to swear like a madman; I can tell you that I was very scared. In panic I tried the handles of a few doors but they were all locked. I was trapped like a bird in a cage! By now the man had got back on his feet, hissing, "I'll teach you a lesson, you little bitch!" and he went for me again, limping heavily. As I fled I suddenly noticed that he had left the key in the door he'd locked a moment ago. I ran towards it like lightning, unlocked it and flung it open. He was just about to lay his hands on me when I rushed out onto the terrace and nearly ran into the swimming pool.'

'What happened next?'

'He was close on my heels and almost caught me but I managed to duck away at the very last moment. As he tried to grab me with both hands his trousers dropped to his feet, he tripped, fell into the pool with a loud splash and disappeared under the water.'

'Served him right! That must have cooled him down.'

'Not very much. When he resurfaced, coughing up water – he must have swallowed a lot of it – he was very, very angry and began to hit the water. Then he swore at me, sticking up his fist, and shouted, "You'll pay for this!"'

'I hope he didn't catch you!'

'No. I didn't wait for him to get out of the pool but ran away as fast as I could.'

'Did you report what happened to the police?'

'No,' replied Lola. 'What would be the good of that? There was no one to see it, and who would have believed me? That man is very powerful.'

'But you told your parents?'

'I thought it better not to. They might blame me and then they would no longer allow me to go out.'

'Be careful!' said Charles as he saw Julie come out of Iago's shop and got up. 'I wouldn't like anything awful to happen to a nice girl like you.'

4

Charles was standing under the shower all soaped up, his hair full of shampoo, when the flow of water suddenly decreased. Within seconds it became no more than a trickle and then it stopped altogether. The hot water had created an illusion of warmth and comfort but now, with the water evaporating from his skin, he felt cold and began to shiver. And the shampoo began to run into his eyes, pricking them and blinding him.

He called for Julie but there was no answer. As he stepped out of the shower tub feeling for the towel, he walked straight into the edge of the half-open bathroom door, banging his head painfully. He didn't normally swear, but if ever there was a time to do so, it was now. He found a towel, rubbed his eyes dry and began to think. They must have cut off the water somewhere in the street he deduced, feeling very irritated. How am I going to rinse the shampoo out of my hair? If only I had known, I would have kept some water in reserve but no, they cut it off without warning, leaving maybe half the people in the village with shampoo on their heads!

Then he remembered that there was mineral water in the fridge. It was a shame to waste it on rinsing his hair but there are times when one has to make a sacrifice. He grabbed two bottles from the fridge, went back to the bath and poured them over his head. The water was of course icy cold and he swore again. He had just finished rubbing himself down, got into fresh clothes and was beginning to think about breakfast when he heard footsteps rushing up the stairs, and Julie came in urging, 'Quick! I've heard that they're going to cut off the water. Quick! Fill up the kettle and a few pots.'

'Too late! They've already cut it off.'

'And I've just invited Sarah and Michael over for mid-morning tea! They'll be here in a quarter of an hour.' She sighed. 'We'll have to use our bottled water then.' And Julie went to the fridge and opened the door.

'But there's only one bottle left!' she exclaimed in surprise. 'I was certain that we had at least two or three bottles.' She looked accusingly at Charles.

'I can assure you that I haven't drunk them,' retorted Charles. He was in a grumpy mood.

'Well… I don't understand how this could have happened.' She shook her head. 'We'll have to make do with this bottle, then. That'll be just enough to make tea for Sarah and Michael. Listen. When they're here I'll pour you half a cup, and you then pretend that you've just had breakfast and don't want any more tea.'

'But I haven't had breakfast and I want at least three cups of tea!' protested Charles, feeling grumpier by the minute.

'There are times when one has to make a sacrifice,' said Julie, 'and half a cup is all you're going to get.'

By the time Michael and Sarah arrived, tea was ready.

'Imagine!' Charles couldn't help complaining. 'They cut off the water supply this morning while I was having a shower!'

'They do that every now and then to clean the pipes that bring the water down from the mountains, or to do repairs,' explained Michael, 'but the water board gives warning beforehand. Anyway, most people in the village have already been up several hours by now and taken their showers well in advance. They're not going to be caught under the shower all soaped up! They're not as stupid as that.' He grinned while Charles looked away.

'Tea!' exclaimed Julie walking in, and she began pouring it out. Then, as she sat down, she turned to Sarah. 'How terrible, that murder! Who is going to stop the project now that the German has been killed?'

'The village Council will,' replied Sarah. Her voice was soft but she had a firm look in her eyes. 'They are divided, and Sebastian will never agree to the project.'

'Well... I always say, wait and see...' remarked Charles.

'He's incorruptible!' There was a note of clear self-righteousness in Sarah's voice.

'Anyway, seeing what's happened to the German, he might be well advised not to oppose the project,' advanced Charles.

Sarah looked at him as if to say, how dare you suggest such a thing?

'I wonder who killed Meier?' said Julie, ready as always to deflect a tense situation.

'The project people, of course! Who else had any interest in doing away with him?' Sarah looked at her husband for support.

'Well...' replied Michael, nodding, 'it's true that they're the ones who gain most from his death. They must have wanted him out of the way.'

'But how to prove they did it?' argued Charles.

'Didn't you tell me that you saw that Swiss woman of the project and her partner in Frigiliana the evening of the murder?' intervened Julie, turning to Charles.

'See!' exclaimed Sarah.

'Maybe they just came to offer money to members of the Council,' countered Charles, '...such as your Sebastian,' he added gleefully.

Sarah stared at him with disapproval. Then she went on stubbornly, 'I'm sure it's those project people.' She sat there for a while cradling her cup, sighing deeply. 'We must stop them. If only we could prove they committed the murder.' Suddenly she looked hard at Charles. 'Why don't you do something about this? You walk around a lot and have time on your hands.'

'What! *Me?*' Charles snorted. 'What can *I* do? And frankly, it's dangerous to oppose those project people... if it *is* them. The other day an American just walked in here, imagine! I believe he's one of the top people in the project and he was quite frank about the German; said he'd better watch out. And now he's dead. I don't want to end up like him! After all, this murder is none of my business.'

'But it is!' Sarah nodded several times as if doing so strengthened her argument. 'It affects us all. If you care for the village – and I always believed you did – you must do something about it. Search! Don't you want to find out?'

Charles was getting very hungry by now and he was feeling extremely grumpy. He was about to say, 'All I want is my breakfast,' but convention got the upper hand and he said instead, 'That's a job for the police. I'm just here on holiday.' And he added, 'And nothing proves that the project people did it.'

'But those people are bad!' Sarah began to argue. 'They…'

Julie cut her short. 'Would you like another cup of tea Sarah?' She held the teapot invitingly over Sarah's cup.

'Oh yes, thank you. Your tea is really delicious.' She looked at Julie with an angelic face. 'I would never have thought of serving tea with a squeeze of fresh orange juice. I wonder why we English always stick to milk.'

Michael got a second cup too while Charles declined, pretending to take another sip from his empty cup.

Sarah and Michael were sipping their tea, looking out over the terrace, when suddenly Julie remarked, 'No one seems to have known that murdered German. That's really amazing, considering that it's almost impossible to live in this village without everyone knowing all about you.'

'Yes, but he lived outside the village and he kept pretty much to himself,' explained Michael. 'We didn't know him either. All I can say is that he was a tall man because I once saw him at an exhibition. But I never talked to him. No one really knew much about him, whether he received people up there or had any relatives.'

Julie looked up. 'I wonder whether he had something to hide. Why else would he have lived such a secluded life?'

Suddenly Sarah sighed. 'I never thought about him while he was alive. I was hardly aware of his presence in the village, though he must have been up there all the time.' She was silent for a moment. Then she continued. 'But you know what's so strange? Now that he has been killed I somehow feel that this village has become very vulnerable.'

'What exactly do you mean by that?' asked Julie.

'How can I explain this? It may sound exaggerated but it is as if his death has woken up a dormant evil, a power over which we have no control and which, once in motion, will engulf us all. I'm worried about what's going to happen to us.'

5

The next morning Julie had decided to go to Nerja, but putting the last touches to her appearance took time. Charles had always been amazed at how women can start off in a certain outfit, look at themselves in the mirror, decide it's not what they wish to look like, try something else, change again, to finally put on the clothes they started off with and this time feel quite pleased with themselves. It is one of the mysteries of life for which there seems to be no logical explanation. Maybe men should not ask questions but simply accept women as they are.

He thought he might as well go down and spend his time waiting in the street. Agustina had already opened *Locura*; she had just put the donkey out and now reappeared, her arms loaded with clothes she was about to hang out in front of her shop window. As she kissed Charles affectionately, he asked if he could give her a helping hand.

'I'm an independent woman and I'm used to doing everything alone,' she said with a large smile, 'but I don't want to disappoint gentlemen.' And she pressed the load of colourful dresses she had been carrying into Charles' arms and showed him where to attach them to the iron grille in front of the shop window. Then she began to pile multicoloured woollen carpets and blankets onto the low wall on the opposite side of the street and afterwards brought out the female mannequin made of flat board, which she called '*La Maripili*'. It was dressed up in the colourful clothes Agustina sold and it wore necklaces. La Maripili had to be attached to hooks in the wall with string, lest she toppled over or was blown away.

'Sam isn't here this morning?'

'Oh, he rushed down one of the side alleys. One never knows what he has on his mind. He will eventually turn up when he feels like it.'

'By the way, I read an interesting story the other day. Murder is not as new to Frigiliana as I thought. It seems that a man attempted to kill his wife some time ago, and that he's still in jail.'

'*Sí!*' exclaimed Agustina. 'I was there when it happened. I remember very well. I was sitting in my shop reading a book because there were no customers...' and she went to her desk and sat on her chair pretending to read, 'when suddenly I heard the most horrible screams higher up in the street. I rushed to the door to see what had happened and saw a man running past my door, holding up his hand dripping with blood. Then, not a minute later, another man came running down, looking white as a sheet. When he saw me he pushed into the shop and, heavily panting, dropped into my chair, shrieking, "He has killed Manuela! Help! Phone for an ambulance!"'

'It appeared that the man with the bloodstained hand was Manuela's husband. He had lived in Malaga for some time, separated from his wife. Then he met another woman and wanted to set up house with her but he had no money and so, that Saturday, he had come back by bus to press his wife, who still had a farmstead and some land, to sell it and give him the money.'

'You mean to say that he wanted his wife to sell her land so that he could live with his mistress? That's unheard of!'

'Anyway, the wife refused and seeing that her husband had drunk quite a lot, and sensing he was becoming violent, she backed to the door with him following closely. She had been sewing, there was a pair of pointed scissors lying on the table, and as she stepped inside the husband grabbed the scissors and stabbed her in the back. She began to shriek and ran out into the street but he was so enraged that he just shouted abuse and kept stabbing her till she collapsed on the cobblestones. At that point a neighbour – the man who rushed into my shop – came out and grabbed his arm, making him drop the scissors, but the husband pulled himself free and ran down the street and past my shop as I told you…'

'Did he escape?'

'No! He ran straight to the Guardia Civil post to give himself up for the murder of his wife. Just think of that!'

'That was an easy murder case to solve then. The murder was committed before a witness, and the murderer ran to the authorities and pleaded guilty with the blood still on his hands.'

'Yes, it wasn't much of a mystery. Nothing like the present murder case.'

'And what happened to the wife?'

'They found her lying in a pool of blood in front of her house in the upper part of Calle El Darra. She had several wounds in her back and there was little hope that she would survive, but eventually she pulled through after spending weeks in hospital.'

'Did she recover completely?'

'I'm afraid the event has left scars on her body, but especially on her soul. The poor thing has never been the same since. She is frightened to go out in the street although her husband is still in jail, and she locks herself up inside. When anyone knocks on the door she will only open when she's quite sure who it is.'

'And I thought Frigiliana such a peaceful place.'

'Andalusia wouldn't be Andalusia without passion, would it?' Agustina's face expressed excitement.

'Well… well…' mumbled Charles, trying to take in that the interplay of passion, wine and hatred could make men cross the borderline between life and death, even in so small a village as Frigiliana. Then he went to the door and called out to see how far Julie had got.

'I'm coming!' he heard her voice from upstairs. And indeed, it took her no more than a minute or two after that to appear on the doorstep, checking her bag and talking to herself, enumerating the names of all the things she was going to buy and do.

'I haven't forgotten anything have I?' she asked turning to Charles, as if he were to know what was on the mind of that charming, but sometimes totally muddle-headed woman.

6

'A fire!' exclaimed Alejandra when she came in to teach Spanish the next morning. 'What a nice surprise!' She drew her chair nearer to the hearth and held her hands towards the flames.

It had been surprisingly cold that morning and Julie had asked Charles to make a fire in the open hearth.

'I love wood fires,' commented Julie. 'They remind me of my childhood in England.' Her eyes shone with the memory. 'Wood fires create a world of their own. They add an extra dimension to life, unlike modern heating systems which lack the scent, the feeling of cosiness, the sounds of the wood crackling and of the flames singing. Fires create more than just warmth.'

'Yeah,' said Charles. 'They produce smoke too. And there was a lot of it this morning. I had a hard time lighting that fire.'

'How unromantic you can be,' sighed Julie. 'What's a little discomfort against the wonder of an open fire?'

'Nothing I suppose, unless you happen to be the one who has to light it.'

They began their Spanish lesson, all three sitting close together. Their lessons had turned into friendly, unconventional gatherings. At the beginning Alejandra had thought that she was expected to give them a course; she had been shy too, but she felt more at ease now and had begun to adapt to their ways of learning and living. And she had become used to them consulting her about anything that went on in the village; she was in fact quite pleased to talk about it now.

'By the way, has anything new turned up in the murder case?' asked Julie.

'Not much. Miguel – the police inspector in charge who is my cousin's husband – says that all the suspects have alibis.'

'Does he include the people of the Green Park One project among the suspects? You know... the ones who have an office in Nerja.'

'Of course he does!' retorted Alejandra. 'Miguel has interrogated them. The woman who is running it – she's Swiss it seems – and her partner who appears to be a French businessman, swear that they spent the whole evening in their office working on the project until nearly midnight...'

'But Alejandra, that's not right at all!' interrupted Julie. 'Charles saw the two project people the very evening of the murder here in Frigiliana.' She turned to him. 'What time did you say it was?'

'It must have been half past eight. I told you that they acted in a suspicious way. They were phoning from the public call box in the *barrio nuevo*.'

Julie turned to Alejandra. 'Now why would they do that when estate agents like them are sure to have mobile phones?'

'Well, isn't that obvious?' explained Charles. 'If they had used their mobile phones, the police would have been able to establish a link between them and the person they were contacting – probably someone in the village. It just shows that they were about to do something illegal. Why else would they take such care to avoid the call being traced back to them?'

'I wouldn't know,' replied Alejandra somewhat offhand. 'Anyway… there is also an American businessman who was around at that time. Unfortunately he left for America the morning after the murder and no one knows exactly who he is or where he is now…'

'But we know who he is!' exclaimed Julie. 'The American businessman is in with those estate agents. We have reasons to believe that he may even be the boss of the Green Park One project.'

'That is very interesting Julia. I think that you are making an important contribution to this case.' Alejandra sounded like a schoolmistress handing out good marks, and her round face looked very serious. 'I must tell Miguel.'

'Are there any more suspects?' Charles wanted to know. 'Who else has been interviewed by the police?'

'Well, there are those people who live in a house below that of the German.'

'The English couple who heard the quarrel on the night of the murder?'

'Yes. They have been interrogated again. They seem to be a nice, normal couple. Miguel doesn't think they have anything to hide. The man says he was with his wife the whole evening and she confirms it. They say they just went for their usual evening walk around the hill; otherwise they didn't leave their house.'

'But we only have their word to go by?'

'Yes.'

'Anyone else?' asked Charles.

'I think that's all.'

'What about that very rich Italian who lives towards Torrox? He may have had good reasons to do away with the German because he had a lot of land for sale on the other side of the canyon.'

'I had forgotten!' Alejandra held up her right forefinger. 'The police have interrogated him too. He says he was at home with his wife the evening of the murder, watching TV.'

'How strange,' remarked Julie. 'We happened to see him the morning after the murder. In fact, he invited us in and his wife wasn't there. He told us she was in Holland.'

'It looks as if the police will have to check up on these alibis,' concluded Charles. And seeing Alejandra's discomfited face, he couldn't help adding,

'Tell your cousin's husband that he has to do his homework better next time.'

Alejandra turned away with a gesture of annoyance. Then she resolutely opened her course and started to explain the meaning of a few verbs. As her voice droned along, Charles' attention wandered. He was thinking of the murder case when suddenly he heard Alejandra say, '... verb *tirar* Carlos?'

'Sorry! What?'

Alejandra repeated her question. 'Could you make me another sentence with the verb *tirar*?'

Charles sat there looking sheepish, unable to answer.

'*Tirar algo a la basura* – to throw something into the dustbin,' Julie answered for him. 'That wasn't difficult. Why couldn't you think of it?'

'I don't know. I was dreaming. I suppose it's this murder business that keeps returning to my mind.'

He tried to be attentive, but after a few minutes his attention wandered again and he began to stare into the fire while Alejandra's voice went on in the background. The flames seemed to hypnotise him. Emanating from the deep red glow of the embers, they kept moving and flickering like burning tongues, blue at the base and yellow at the top, licking the logs, consuming them, turning hard reality into smoke. A tree, a life of maybe seventy years, would be gone in a matter of hours with only some ashes to testify that it had existed, and these ashes to be dispersed afterwards. Was that not what happened to life? he thought. So vibrant and seemingly endless when we are young, so fleeting when we get old. So it had happened to Konrad Meier. So it would happen to us all.

7

That afternoon Charles wanted to go for a stroll in the countryside but Julie wasn't very keen. Only when he suggested that they were sure to find a few properties for sale during the walk did she become interested and made no further objections.

They were trudging up a dirt road just outside the village when they came to a large ruined building. 'Shall we have a look inside?' Julie looked at Charles with eager eyes. 'You know how much I like ruins.'

They went through an open door into what must once have been a hall, but the roof had fallen down and was lying on the floor in big chunks overgrown by weeds. A large opening led into a room where there was nothing apart from the remains of an open hearth, and from there, stepping through wide arches over a lot of rubble, they came upon a maze of other rooms. Some of the walls had collapsed, most of the wooden beams that had supported the roof had rotted, and what remained of the roof was hanging down. As they passed through an opening, to their surprise, they found an old man sitting with his back against a wall, smoking a cigarette.

'Excuse us,' apologised Charles. 'We didn't want to intrude.'

'It doesn't matter.' The man smiled invitingly.

'We were just passing by and thought we'd have a look,' explained Julie, looking embarrassed.

To their surprise, the man got up and held out his hand to shake theirs. 'You are interested in buying? Or maybe you have friends who are?'

'I don't know,' replied Charles noncommittally.

'I see you're interested,' nodded the man, looking at Julie. 'Follow me. The part of the building where we are belongs to me. I'll show you. Come!' The man pointed to a breach in the wall and stepped through it. 'This is where my part of the property begins.' Then he led them along a narrow path that ran between the outside wall and a dense, impenetrable growth of prickly pear cacti, until he came to where the building had completely collapsed. 'And this is where my part ends,' he said. 'From here on everything belongs to my cousin. He lives in Nerja, but he and I have agreed to sell our parts of the building.'

'What's that new construction at the end of your cousin's part?'

'It's a small farmstead he built for himself. But he only comes here at weekends.'

A loud cackle came out of the farmstead.

'What's that?' asked Charles, startled.

'Oh, that's nothing. He keeps a few chickens in there. For the eggs you know.'

'I see,' said Charles shaking his head. He turned around. 'Your part of the building seems to be in the middle. What about the side through which we came in? Does that also belong to your cousin?'

'No. It belongs to three brothers, but that's not really important. It is only the beginning of the building. Come along.' And he made a sign to follow him down a narrow path perpendicular to the outside wall; it led straight into the outside cactus forest.

Julie declined but Charles followed the man hesitantly, looking warily at the long prickly thorns sticking out from all sides. The downward slope was steep, there seemed hardly any decent foothold for the loose sandals he was wearing, and he didn't feel like having to grab one of the spiky blades of those cacti in case he slipped. 'Ahem...' he said after a few yards, 'I think I'm going to stop here.'

'But all this belongs to my part of the property,' protested the man, 'right down to the bottom of the valley. I want to show it to you.'

'Sorry,' said Charles turning resolutely back, and as he began to move cautiously upwards again amongst the cacti, the man followed him with obvious regret.

The top edges of the blades of the prickly pear cacti were lined with yellow flowers, and some were bearing red fruit, juicy and nice to eat, but Charles knew how treacherous these fruits were: they looked very attractive but they were covered with tiny hairs. If you had never been told, as had happened to Charles in Bosnia a year ago, and picked one of the fruits with your bare hands, dozens of those prickly hairs would get lodged into your skin. They were almost impossible to remove and you would be in agony for days.

When Charles got back into the building he found Julie bubbling with enthusiasm. 'I've found something very interesting!' she exclaimed, taking him by the hand and leading him to an old granulated conical stone. 'What do you think this is?'

Charles turned to the old man who had just come in.

'Oh that? That's the stone which they used to crush the olives.'

'So this was a factory where they pressed olives?'

'Yes... all the land around here as far as you can see used to be planted with olive trees.' He made a sweeping gesture with his arm. 'It all belonged to my great-grandfather... but that's a long time ago.'

'When did they stop using the factory?'

'Some thirty years ago.'

'And why did they stop pressing olives here?'

'Because everything was done manually and labourers were becoming too expensive. It was impossible to compete with factories where the work was done by machines.' The man raised his arms. 'So you see… this press fell into disuse.'

'Not many olive trees left around here now,' observed Charles.

'No.' The man explained that the land had been divided amongst the children, the grandchildren and then the great-grandchildren; parts had already been sold off to build new houses, and on the rest they had planted avocado trees. 'Avocadoes bring in much more money than olives, you see,' he commented.

'And the building has been divided up among the heirs as well.'

'Yes.' The man sighed deeply. Then he turned to Julie. 'The *señora* likes it here, yes?' He offered Julie a cigarette, which she refused. 'You can easily build another floor and then you will have a beautiful view. I remember that, as a child, I often climbed up on the roof. You could see the Mediterranean from there.'

'Not much left of the roof now,' remarked Charles dryly.

'No…' The man sighed again.

'How much does this ruin cost?'

'I shall have to consult my cousin, but it will be a good price.'

'Can you give me at least an idea?' insisted Charles, but the man seemed unwilling to let the cat out of the bag. They finally left and continued slowly along the track.

8

'How is the murder investigation getting on?' asked Julie after Alejandra had finished her Spanish lesson the next morning. 'Have they interrogated the project people again?'

'They have. The Swiss woman of the real estate agency and her partner have admitted that they went to Frigiliana that evening.' Alejandra shook her forefinger. 'They'd forgotten to mention it because it was so unimportant; they just went to check the project's hoardings in Frigiliana, but returned to Nerja immediately after.'

'Do the police believe them?'

'No, but they can't get anything more out of them. However, they were seen shortly before nine o'clock that evening going into the house of one of the members of the village Council.'

'I see.' Charles sniggered. 'Trying to buy him off! Wasn't the Council going to have a first meeting about the project within a few days.'

'I don't know.' Alejandra did her best to sound non-committal.

'Even if they went to see a member of the village Council first,' Charles persisted, 'they would still have had ample time to sneak up to the German's house around ten o'clock. So that doesn't free them from suspicion.' He looked pointedly at Alejandra and saw her face tense up.

Julie thought it was time to intervene. 'We went to the *campo* yesterday and saw a nice old building I quite liked. One of the owners was there but unfortunately he didn't know how much it cost. Maybe you could help me to find out?' It was a very obvious attempt to change the subject but it worked because Alejandra asked, 'Where is it situated?'

'It's the old olive press below the road to Torrox.'

'Oh I know how much they want for it: nine million pesetas.'

'That's a ridiculous amount of money for what it is!' exclaimed Charles. 'There's no water, no electricity... only broken walls and collapsed roofs. And the rest of the land is useless. It's all steep slopes full of prickly pear cacti. How do they set their price?'

'I think the three brothers who own the first third want a million pesetas each because, they say, what can one do nowadays with less than a million pesetas? So that's three million for their part. And so the other two owners want no less for each of their respective parts.'

'Do they really believe someone will pay nine million for their ruin? It's ludicrous.'

'It's all the foreigners' fault...' Alejandra looked upset, '...because they have been paying any price people have been asking. Only last year a foreigner bought a small house in the village for eight million pesetas, and now everyone here thinks that they can sell any property for eight million or even more. They no longer want to sell to local people who wouldn't dream of paying even a quarter of that. They all want to sell to foreigners now. The foreigners have ruined the property market!'

Julie was not to be discouraged. 'There was a small *cortijo* further along that I liked as well,' she said, 'but I don't know whether it's for sale.'

'You must be careful Julia!' Alejandra's voice had the warning ring of the country girl who would never be induced to spend a single peseta on worthless ruins. 'Maybe I should go with you for a walk in the *campo* to show you what to look out for.'

9

Towards eight-thirty that night, the time the few grocer's shops in Frigiliana began to close, there was suddenly loud noise in the street below. A car drove along with old pots and pans attached to it, banging on the cobblestones. A quarter of an hour later a group of youngsters passed by, kicking an empty drum along and banging spoons on pots and pans, making a deafening racket.

As this was their second holiday in Andalusia, Charles was acquainted with the Spanish love for noise. He remembered having seen small children run towards a metal plate covering a part of the pavement that was being redone, leap *bang*! onto it with shouts of joy, and keep jumping up and down. They all did it, even mere toddlers, and it seemed to give them a great kick.

But this cacophony of pots and pans was something of a different order. It was a huge indulgence in an unbelievably loud noise, an orgy of ear-shattering sound rolling through the village like a peal of thunder. Charles had to block his ears, but the young people themselves didn't in the least seem affected by it.

The procession next streamed into the *barrio nuevo*, the youngsters' lanterns lighting up the dark streets as they passed, and came to a halt in front of a house with a balcony where they began to sing mock love songs. Shouts of '*Al balcón*!' followed, but nobody appeared on the balcony. The crowd didn't give up though and started a new round of noise. They all burst out in loud laughter when a few voices shouted, 'Come on Dolores, show us your young lover!'

Finally, around 10p.m., one of the upstairs windows opened hesitantly amidst cheers from the gathered people and as the much called-for Dolores stuck her head out they all began to chant a love song. Suddenly Dolores decided that she couldn't face the crowd after all; she withdrew rapidly and shut the window. The cacophony of banging and shouting immediately took off again and even grew in intensity, but Dolores seemed determined to remain hidden. The noise went on till well after eleven, and only petered out gradually.

10

'There was a lot of noise in the village last night,' said Charles after Alejandra had arrived the next day. 'Do you know what it was all about?'

'Oh that!' she replied. 'It's a tradition here. When a widow and a widower remarry, the people put on a mock celebration. But last night was rather unusual. Dolores and her man, Jésus, are no longer young. They're both in their sixties and don't really want to marry again.'

'Why not?' asked Julie. 'Lots of people now remarry when they're in their sixties.'

'Yes, but you see… Dolores gets a pension for her late husband, and Jésus also draws some money because his late wife worked. And they would lose these incomes if they remarried. So she and Jésus are now living together without being married, and that was why there was such a great fuss in the village last night.'

'So it's a question of money?'

'Well, a lot here is a question of money. Much more than you would think. Take Paco for example – Dolores' eldest son. He threatened her recently.'

'What do you mean by threatened?' Charles wanted to know.

'A week or so ago he came to her house and started banging on the door shouting that, if she remarried, he would kill her. Dolores was so frightened that she refused to let him in.'

'I don't see why his mother's marriage is any business of his,' intervened Julie, indignant.

'Well, he's afraid that Jésus will try to get Dolores' land for his own children,' explained Alejandra. 'The following night Paco brought a hatchet with him and started hacking at his mother's front door – the neighbours saw it all. Dolores has had a steel grid put in front of her door since, and hardly dares go out.'

'Can't the police do anything about it?' wondered Julie. 'I mean, he's threatened his mother! And there are witnesses!'

'How do you expect the police to act if Dolores doesn't file a complaint? So, until something actually happens, the police can't do anything. Anyway,' said Alejandra looking ostentatiously at her watch, 'it's time we started our Spanish lesson.'

That morning they were studying the many meanings of the verb *Echar*. Apparently it didn't just signify: to throw, but it had a whole list of meanings, which their teacher now began to explain.

Charles was only vaguely listening, because suddenly he had an idea. 'Do you know if Dolores ever sold land to the murdered German?' he interrupted.

Alejandra frowned. 'I have no idea but I can ask my parents. They'll know. Now: *Echar de menos.*'

'That sounds to me like: to throw away less, or something like that,' said Julie. 'What exactly does it mean?'

'It's the Spanish way of saying: to miss. I miss you is: *Te echo de menos.*'

'Isn't that funny Charles?' Julie looked at him, but Charles was only half listening. A hatchet and a violent temper? he was pondering. He should try to find out more about that Paco.

11

That night Charles slept badly. He had a sequence of muddled dreams as often happened when something was worrying him. He was sitting on the top of the hill above Frigiliana when a huge dog came running towards him, barking ferociously. Suddenly it stood up on its hind legs and turned into an enormous man brandishing a hatchet: Paco! It frightened the wits out of Charles and he tried to run down the hill, but his legs seemed to be made of lead, so he hid behind a bush along the cement road that led to the German's garage but Paco, who had again become a dog, kept searching for him, and now the Paco-dog came down the cement road on a motorbike! Charles heard the pitched roar of the engine becoming louder... Paco would soon get him... and then he woke up with a start, sweating, his heart pounding in his chest.

It was already broad daylight and the village was full of sounds: people talking; a dog barking; a motorbike passing by. Charles did not usually have nightmares but then, dreams emanate from the subconscious; maybe he had been thinking too much about the murder. It's all Sarah's fault, he mused. She planted this in my mind. Why did she have to insist that I find out?

Julie was still peacefully asleep. Only a little tuft of fair hair stuck out from under the sheet as Charles got up quietly, washed, dressed and set off for the bakery. It was already ten o'clock and he would be lucky if there was any brown bread left by now. The baker made two varieties of bread: a large quantity of white loaves, and a small number of what he called *pan negro* – black bread – which was in reality only a slightly darker variety of the white bread. For some unknown reason the baker thought that white bread was what everyone should eat and he had only recently, and grudgingly, begun to produce his "black" bread because foreigners had kept asking for it.

Charles was lucky that day. There were two *pan negro* loaves left and he was so pleased that he bought them both. As he left the bakery a woman greeted him saying, '*Vaya con Dios* – Go with God'. He had been lost in thought, hardly noticing her, and before he could think of what to answer she had already passed along. Spanish still came to him slowly in the morning; only after breakfast did he become more fluent, like an engine that needed warming up.

He didn't know the woman or, maybe, he knew her but hadn't recognised her. She was dressed in black, like so many older women in the village. They all looked a bit alike to him as they sat on chairs alongside the façades of their houses, two or three together, chatting to each other, or as they came tottering through the village street on bent legs, steadying themselves on sticks. Some were quite old and small and looked like little black witches out of a fairytale world. They had shrill voices and when they spoke together Charles usually didn't understand a word of what they were saying but only noticed the rapid cadence of their words.

The village looked normal enough that morning in the bright sunshine. The murder seemed almost imaginary, or in any case totally irrelevant. Doesn't life go on, even after the worst tragedies? Charles reflected.

12

'How did you know?' asked Alejandra as she was accompanying Charles to where his car was parked.

'How did I know what?'

'That Dolores did sell a big piece of land below the hill to the German. He wanted it to build a road around the hill and take it all the way along to his house. He had to offer her a good price for it because she refused to sell otherwise. Even so it seems that Paco, her eldest son, was furious about it.'

'Why should he be? Had it not been for Meier wanting it for his road, she probably wouldn't have been able to sell that land, would she?'

'True enough, but what good is that to the son? His mother will now spend all the money on her new man, Jésus, and the son will see nothing of it. So Paco tried to stop the sale. He said that he would destroy the road; it seems he even threatened the German, but that man didn't take any notice of Paco. The sale of the land went through and the road was built.'

'Would it be possible for your cousin's husband to find out where this Paco was on the evening the German was murdered?'

'You don't think…' Alejandra put her hand in front of her mouth and stared at Charles with wide-open eyes.

'I don't think anything definite for the moment, but I believe that his alibi ought to be checked. So, please, would you tell your cousin to ask her husband, the famous inspector, to do so?'

Just then they reached the car and as Charles opened the driver's door for Alejandra and let her get in he thought, here we go again for one of these adrenaline-heightening driving lessons!

13

The next day Alejandra took them for a walk in the *campo* as she had promised. As they passed the old olive press Julie wanted to stop, but Alejandra carried on, not thinking it worth so much as a look. The dirt road now climbed steeply, turning to reach the top of the ridge opposite the ruin. From where they stood they could see the old olive press below with its collapsed roof and thick walls, sitting ochre-coloured above the green wilderness of prickly pear cacti.

'Doesn't it look beautiful?' Julie's face showed the almost child-like pleasure that the sight of ruins of any sort invariably stirred up in her.

'Julia,' reprimanded Alejandra, 'you must keep your head cool. It's just rubble.'

The dirt road continued along the top of the ridge with the land sloping down on either side. On the left they could see the valley that led from Frigiliana down to the sea. Close to the village most of the land was divided into small terraced plots which the farmers still cultivated, but further towards the sea and Nerja a lot of development had already taken place: red-roofed villas, some large and with a swimming pool, dotted the landscape. The valley on the right hand side of the ridge was much drier, and here the traditional olive culture had largely survived. The olive trees looked like rows upon rows of green dots running along the slopes.

Presently they came to a small, very awkward-looking farmhouse. The right half was all redone, well kept and whitewashed whilst the left half was old, decaying and yellow. Julie stopped in front of it. 'This is the *cortijo* I like,' she said. 'Look what a marvellous view you have from here. And there is quite a flat area around, enough in fact to extend the house. Do you know who this belongs to Alejandra?'

'Yes. The right half belongs to Tomate. The left to his sister Manuela.'

'What a strange name for a man,' remarked Charles. 'Do they call him Tomate because he looks like a tomato?'

'Well... as a matter of fact, he has got quite a red, round face, but everyone calls him Tomate because he loves growing tomatoes. He has tomato fields all over the place.'

'And why is Tomate's half so well kept while his sister's is decaying?'

'The problem is Manuela's husband. He is a *borracho* – a drunkard. He drank all the family money and then he wanted his wife to sell her part of this *cortijo* here so that he could have the money, but the sons forbade their mother to do so. He finally left her, but you know what? One day he came back to Frigiliana, completely drunk, to tell his wife that she must sell her half of the *cortijo* and the land that went with it. When Manuela refused the husband was so furious that he wanted to kill her, but he was too drunk and only wounded her. Now he's in jail.'

'I've heard that story!' exclaimed Charles. 'Agustina told me.'

'In case you're interested Julia, I have to disappoint you,' continued Alejandra. 'Manuela does not want to sell her *cortijo* because she wants to leave it to her sons so that they will at least inherit something.'

'Considering the rate at which it is decaying, they will not inherit much,' remarked Charles dryly.

'Why do they cut all property up into small pieces here?' asked Julie. 'If a man has two children and four plots of land with a *cortijo* on each, why doesn't one child inherit two plots and the other one the other two?'

'That's not how it works here,' objected Alejandra. 'You see, one piece of land is not like another. One may have olive trees whilst the other one may have avocado trees, or a greenhouse where they grow strawberries. One may have good water, the other not. My father too has several plots of land in different places. I've been to all of them when I was a child; they're all different and I like them all. Later my sister and I will cut each piece of land in half and inherit a bit of everything.'

'And the *cortijos* on it will be cut in half as well?'

'The *cortijos* will be cut in half.' Alejandra had a stubborn expression on her face.

'Lucky you're only two. What happens if there are more children?'

'Further down there's quite a big farmhouse. It was inherited by five brothers and so they cut it up into five. Three of them want to sell their part, but the other two don't. And these three cannot do anything with what they've got because there is a law that you cannot make any alteration within a certain distance of someone else's property – I believe it's ten or twenty metres – without the consent of the proprietor. So the farm cannot be sold and is just decaying.'

'It's a nutty system,' commented Julie.

'Well... anyway, that's why you have to be very careful when you buy something over here.'

They continued between hedges of prickly pear cacti that lined the dirt road; some looked as if great bites had been taken out of them.

'How did this happen?' Charles was curious to know.

'The goats eat them,' replied Alejandra.

'But look at those long prickly thorns!'

'The thorns don't seem to bother them.'

Alejandra now turned to Julie. 'There's a piece of land nearby which my mother sold two years ago. We can go and see it if you like.'

They left the dirt road and climbed on to a large flat piece of land. At the end of it, on the south side which overlooked the sea, they saw a house under construction. The terrace and part of the lower walls had already been built, but the rest of the land lay unkempt. It was covered in wildflowers, a mixture of yellow, blue, mauve, pink and red amidst the low brown-green grass swaying in the wind, a thick tapestry woven by nature.

'Oh how beautiful!' exclaimed Julie. 'What a lovely place.'

'This is it,' said Alejandra. 'This is the *terreno* sold by my mother.'

'What a pity,' sighed Julie. 'What a pity it's been sold.'

'How much was it sold for?' Charles enquired.

'Two million pesetas.'

'But that's cheap!'

'A few years ago any land was cheap,' said Alejandra.

'I see they're building a house on it.'

'Not they. He!'

'Who is *he*?'

'You know the man who bought it: Fernando Lortez.'

'The nice man who wanted to take me on his horse?'

'Yes – and also the one who found the dead German. He began to build this house two years ago, but it was all too much for him, first having to buy the land, and then the building materials. He's run out of money and all building has been stopped for at least a year.'

'When he realises that he hasn't got the money to continue, maybe he will want to sell?' hinted Julie.

Alejandra shook her head. 'That's very unlikely.'

'But why did he undertake all this when he didn't have enough money?' asked Charles.

'People here see everything on a grand scale. When they start they always think they will be able to make their wildest dreams come true, but they often run out of money well before they have finished what they are building. Then they go to the bank…'

'You mean that they don't plan properly?' interrupted Charles.

'Plan? People live from day to day here! And if things don't work out as they thought, they just leave everything as it is.' She pointed at Fernando's half-finished construction. 'It may stay like that for a year, for five years, or for ten. Who knows?' She looked at Charles apologetically. 'That's the way it is over here.'

Charles looked at the unfinished walls, at the rusty iron spikes sticking out of the corners, at the rough cement terrace as yet unprotected by tiles, at the concrete mixer that had been left behind and was rusting, at the piles of rubbish that hadn't been cleared. In what state would all this be in ten years' time?

14

Some fifty yards further on, behind the plot where Fernando Lortez had started building, the land rose to form a small hilltop. The hill was surrounded by a high wall and they could see the tops of several tall trees growing inside.

'What a strange construction,' remarked Charles. 'It looks like a medieval fortress.'

'Or a bunker,' suggested Julie, pointing at the thick concrete walls and the narrow vertical slits here and there. 'You almost expect someone to be sitting behind with a gun to defend the approaches!' She turned to Alejandra. 'Who would want to build something like that?'

'It belonged to the German who was murdered,' commented Alejandra with an even face.

'You don't say!' Charles was unable to suppress his excitement. 'But why did that man want another property in Frigiliana when he already had one here in the countryside?'

Alejandra seemed to hesitate, as if she knew something but was unwilling to tell them. Finally she said, 'Well... as far as I know he bought this land when he first came, which was some ten years ago. But after a while he stopped building here and bought that house up on the hill behind Frigiliana.'

'That doesn't answer my question. Why did he move to the village after having gone through all the expense of building here?'

Alejandra turned away. It was awkward. Why didn't she want to speak?

'Look over there!' exclaimed Julie, unaware of the tense atmosphere. She pointed at a spot where a branch of one of the tall trees inside stuck out over the wall. Just underneath lay a big boulder. 'I'm sure we can get up via the boulder and that branch! Shall we give it a try?' Julie's eyes sparkled. 'I've always loved climbing trees.'

Alejandra was definitely not keen. 'I think I will stay where I am,' she said. 'I'll wait for you here.' Charles looked at her miniskirt, black tights and low-heeled leather shoes. She was certainly not dressed for climbing trees, but there seemed to be more to her refusal than just that.

He leaned his back against the boulder, Julie put a foot in his clasped hands, climbed on to his shoulders and then clambered up the boulder. Next she grasped the overhanging branch and swung herself upon it. 'Careful now!' warned Charles, 'you're no longer a schoolgirl,' but Julie didn't listen. She crawled along the branch till she was above the wall. Then she lowered herself down and sat astride on it.

'Tell me what you see.'

'Just a lot of unfinished construction. There's the beginning of a ground floor and a large patio. And a box-like structure which I suppose was to be the garage.'

'Is that all?' Charles seemed disappointed.

'There isn't really much else.'

'Don't you have any special feeling up there?'

'Well... it feels quite windy.'

'There's nothing then that strikes you? And I don't mean the wind!'

'I don't sense why the German wanted to live here, if that's what you mean. Maybe he came here because of the view. If he had built another floor, as I imagine he was going to do, he would have had a fabulous view over Frigiliana and the mountain range behind towards the north, and over Nerja and the sea towards the south.'

Julie had a good last look around and then slid down the wall, lowering herself into Charles' arms. 'Why this need to surround himself with thick walls?' he wondered aloud. 'And I just can't think why he decided to move to Frigiliana.' He turned to Alejandra. 'Do you mind if I ask you again: why did he abandon this construction when he had already built so much?'

Alejandra didn't answer. Instead she suggested, 'Maybe we should go back now. It's already lunchtime and we are four kilometres away from Frigiliana.'

They went back in a pensive mood. The wind had become stronger and was lifting dust off the track, whirling it away into the fields like mist streaming off a cliff. Every now and then they had to screen their eyes against the millions of fine particles that pricked the skin of their faces.

Suddenly Charles had an idea. 'Was there already a lot of development in the valley towards Nerja when Meier bought this hilltop?' he asked Alejandra.

'I don't think so,' she replied. 'The rapid expansion of Nerja and the development of the stretch of *campo* from the hilltop to Nerja began just after the time the German started this construction.'

'Maybe that's why he abandoned his bunker? He probably hadn't expected all these people to build so close to his eagle's nest. Remember how in Frigiliana he literally turned his back on the world?'

'Who knows?' remarked Julie as they continued descending towards Frigiliana at a brisk pace, the wind now blowing on their backs, pushing them along.

15

More than a week had already gone by since Meier's death and the murder was now hardly ever mentioned in the village. People are interested in what happens for only a short while. Then their attention turns to the many other competing events, from a football match to a local wedding, while previous headline-catching news recedes into the background. Even Charles and Julie no longer talked about Meier, and not even about Massimo Zizi, whom they had suspected of having connections with the Mafia or even the drug trade with Morocco. They had settled down to holiday routine.

One of the problems this created, though, was that once away from home Julie's mind refused to be preoccupied by such bothersome trivialities as thinking of meals. She just lived for the day and maybe that is what a real holiday is all about. That particular morning she was totally absorbed in reading one of her books and as Charles enquired what they were going to have for lunch she didn't even look up but mumbled something like, 'How about you going to the grocer's and choosing something?'

He went down the stairs dragging his feet. As he got to the front door, he found it blocked by a number of children and almost had to push his way through a crowd of some thirty fourteen-to-sixteen-year-old boys and girls, probably on a school excursion. They were sitting on the bottom steps of Calle El Darra; on the low wall opposite where Agustina had laid out her woollen blankets; and even on Agustina's doorstep. They were dressed in coloured tracksuits, which seemed to have become the standard outfit for schoolchildren here in the south of Spain. A few boys were showing off and the girls were giggling and pushing each other. There were children inside the shop too, and he saw Agustina showing them how to blow little ceramic whistles shaped like birds, of which she had a whole basket. Agustina has her hands full with these children, he thought. I hope they won't damage the donkey.

Maria's small grocer's shop was no more than a stone's throw down from *Locura*. Usually there were several village women around, choosing amongst the vegetables displayed outside the shop or awaiting their turn sitting on overturned empty crates inside while chatting away about all that had recently happened in the village. Buying anything at Maria's required patience: you might have to wait any time between five minutes and a quarter of an hour before being served. Efficiency and the notion that time is money didn't yet seem to have penetrated the minds of the people of

Andalusia's more remote villages. Everything was still done in a slow, time-consuming way.

That morning there were no more than three women, all dressed in black, but instead of the usual choosing and picking of two apples, ten potatoes, four carrots or whatever they wanted from the crates, and instead of the regular high-pitched chatting, they were just standing close together, almost like conspirators, talking in hushed voices to Maria who was sitting like a black mass on a chair on the other side of the counter. Something strange seemed to be going on.

Charles waited for a while but as none of the women appeared to be interested in being served he began to pick up a lettuce, a few tomatoes, some avocados and a nice-looking, fat mango. While doing so he thought he heard the words 'killed German,' and at once his curiosity was awakened. He pricked up his ears trying to listen to what the women were saying and caught a few more words, but these sounded so surreal that he wondered whether he had heard correctly: they seemed to be talking about a treasure and a Curse of the Moors!

When he finally put his acquisitions on the counter, Maria weighed everything almost mechanically without paying any real attention to what she was doing, and calculated the price. As he paid he drew closer to the three women but they stared at him as if he were an intruder and stopped talking. It was awkward, and he felt relieved to get his change and be able to leave the shop.

He felt so intrigued that he thought he must ask Agustina whether she knew what was going on. Then he remembered those schoolchildren and realised that she would be too busy, but as luck would have it, just as he came out of Maria's shop, a mule began to climb up Calle El Darra. The event created a great commotion amongst the children who all squashed themselves against the walls on both sides to make room for the mule while shouting excitedly. The mule seemed to act like a magnet; once it had passed, followed by the muleteer who hung on to the tail, it drew the whole group of schoolchildren with it. Those who had been inside Agustina's shop now rushed out to follow the others, and suddenly the lower part of the street was empty.

As he reached the shop Agustina came out looking upset. 'Terrible, these schoolchildren,' she muttered. 'They push forward, touch everything and you never know what they're going to do.' Then she saw the bag Charles was carrying. 'Have you been shopping?'

'Just some vegetables and a mango.'

'A mango! I love mangos. They remind me of the tropics.'

'The one I've got is a very ripe, juicy one.' He dug it out of the bag. 'Have it.'

'But I have already eaten a sandwich and a yoghurt, and it's not even twelve o'clock. I can't go on eating like this. I must watch my weight.'

Agustina was on the plump side, but certainly not overweight. 'Nothing wrong with your weight,' said Charles. 'And your eyes tell me you want the mango.'

'*Muchas gracias.*' She took it. 'I can never resist nice things.'

'By the way, have you any idea what's going on? In Maria's shop they were talking about a treasure and a "Curse of the Moors". And all this seems to have something to do with the murder of that German.'

'They were already talking about it this morning when I went for my sandwich and yoghurt. It seems to be a very serious matter; or at least the people here take it very seriously. I understand that it has something to do with the Moorish rebellion.'

'You mean the history that is depicted on the plaques in the streets here?'

'Yes, but I have no idea what it's all about. The village people are keeping it to themselves.'

'Don't they share their secrets with you then?'

'No way! To them I am a *guiri*: I'm from Madrid and that's not much better than being a foreigner here. Anyway, don't bother. This will blow over, like everything else.' And she took a knife and plate out of a drawer and began to cut up the mango, her eyes shining with anticipation.

16

When Charles came out of Agustina's shop he bumped into Charlotte the sculptor. A tall, slim young man was accompanying her.

'I have found it!' she exclaimed enthusiastically.

Charles was used to Charlotte speaking in riddles, but this one was beyond him.

'You have found what?'

'The house! The ideal house.'

'Where is it?'

'On top of the village at the left end of Calle Chorrera.'

'Wonderful Charlotte!'

'It's pure perfection… it's got a top terrace where I can work in the full sun. And you should see the view: the village with the *campo* below and the blue Mediterranean far away. So inspiring!' She was bubbling with enthusiasm. 'I can feel when something is right. I'm so certain of it that I have paid two months' rent in advance! I'm really going to enjoy myself up there.' She was not to be stopped. 'I'm going to move in tomorrow!' she carried on. 'And Sven is going to help me. Oh,' she suddenly said pointing to the young man who had been standing shyly at her side, 'this is Sven.'

Charles shook hands and invited them up, but Charlotte declined. 'No time. I must go back to my *cortijo*. I still have such a lot to do.' And she rushed off, motioning to Sven to follow her.

17

'What's all this about a Curse hanging over the village?' Charles asked Alejandra the next morning. She had been talking animatedly until then but now she suddenly fell silent.

'I don't know,' she replied evasively.

'But Alejandra, you always know everything that's going on in the village.' Julie sounded disappointed. 'Is it that you aren't allowed to tell us?'

Alejandra blushed and looked away towards the hills outside. Then she spoke. 'Julia, this is a serious matter. We cannot talk about it lightly.'

'Is it really so serious?'

'Yes. The people in the village say all this has happened because foreigners can never leave anything alone. They are very upset with them.'

'Are you upset with us, Alejandra?' asked Julie.

'*Que va*! Of course not! You are different. I think of you as my friends.'

'By foreigners the villagers mean the murdered German, don't they?' intervened Charles.

'Please don't say it so loudly.' Alejandra had lowered her voice to a whisper.

'Was the German killed because of the Curse then?'

Alejandra opened her mouth, ready to speak, and then hesitated again, but Julie felt that she might let the secret out and was maybe even eager to do so; after all, secrets spread because those who know them are often all too willing to reveal them. Alejandra needed just one more little prod and Julie, to whom many secrets had been revealed through the years, gave it. 'Oh Alejandra!' she exclaimed, 'it's so exciting that you know about these things. I would love to hear about them from you.'

It was all Alejandra needed to yield. 'All right,' she said. 'But you must promise to keep it a secret.'

Julie nodded agreement.

'It all began at the time of the Moorish rebellion – you have seen the plaques that depict it in the village. When the leader of the Moors here in Frigiliana was captured, he prophesied that one day the Curse of the Moors would fall upon the descendants of the Christians.'

'Did he specify how this would happen?' asked Charles.

'Not him! He was unwilling to reveal any more even though he was tortured, but some of the other men did talk: before they were defeated, the Moors managed to hide their treasure on the hill above Frigiliana and...'

'You mean gold and silver?'

'That's not known. But what seems to be known is that it consisted of sacred objects.'

'And what has this treasure got to do with the Curse?'

'That's what I was about to explain. The Curse would be unleashed if a descendant of the Christians were to discover the treasure. And the one who found it would be the first to suffer.'

'So that's what happened!' Julie looked thrilled. 'The German found the treasure and was killed.'

Alejandra nodded agreement. 'And now everyone is frightened because they don't know what's going to happen next.'

'The story doesn't say anything more explicit about the Curse?' asked Charles.

'No. Only that it will be terrible.'

'And how do they know the German was looking for the treasure?'

'Why else would he suddenly have moved to the hill above Frigiliana after he had already started that first construction we saw in the *campo*? And why else would he have built a high wall around his property? Certainly so as not to be seen while searching for the treasure.'

'But why was this German allowed to build near the top of the hill then? And how is he supposed to have known about the treasure if it was a secret?'

'The older people knew that there was a... what do you call it... a taboo?'

'Yes, that's the word.'

'Children were not allowed near the top and no one was ever to dig there. This taboo was observed for centuries, but over the last twenty years or so people have begun to neglect the strict observance of old ways. Foreigners were allowed to build higher and higher towards the hilltop and, who knows, someone may have spoken to the German.'

'But that's all allegation. I'm not convinced,' said Charles firmly. 'No one knows for sure whether the German ever dug for that treasure or found it! And now all foreigners seem to be accused of putting the village in peril.'

'Carlos,' reprimanded Alejandra in a stern voice, 'it is not what has happened that counts. It is what people believe.'

18

The four-mile stretch from Nerja, at the sea, to Frigiliana, a thousand feet above sea level, was a narrow, winding, second-gear road, but the views were stunning. If you drove up from Nerja in the early evening, as Julie and Charles were doing, the mauve-blue hills around Frigiliana stood out crystal-clear against a sky turning red – a wonder to behold.

As their car wound its way up towards the village, they came to the hamlet of La Molineta. There was a small café-restaurant, almost on the road, and as they passed by they noticed a man slumped on one of the chairs outside.

'That's Fernando Lortez!' exclaimed Julie who was driving.

'The one who discovered the body of the German?'

'Yes. But what's more to the point, he's that nice man with the horse.' And she immediately stopped and called out to him.

Fernando seemed to wake up from a deep stupor. When he realised that a car had stopped for him he rose with difficulty and came towards them, his body swaying slightly. He had shaved and wore a clean white shirt and dark-blue sweater, but his dark hair was dishevelled and his eyes hazy.

'*Hola, señora!*' He had recognised Julie.

'Can I give you a lift Fernando?'

He looked at Julie like a dog that's getting a nice bone. 'I come with you,' he said firmly and got in.

When Julie started the car he leaned forward, putting an elbow on the back of each of the front seats. 'No one stopped for me,' he complained speaking almost in Charles' face, and his breath smelled so strongly of alcohol that Charles had to turn away. 'I did not know how I would get back to Frigiliana. And now the *señora* drives me. That is good. No, it's more than good. It is superb!'

'We'll take you home Fernando,' said Charles. 'Don't worry.'

'What is your name *señor*?'

'Charles.'

Charles was of course a foreign name, which Fernando didn't seem to know, and he stared inquiringly at Charles who translated, 'Carlos.'

'Ah! Carlos...' He put his hand on Charles' shoulder. 'I have got a horse and I can take you for walks into the mountains.' His voice sounded thick and he spoke with difficulty. 'I shall not charge you anything for it. Tell me whenever you want to go.'

'But how will the *señora* go if I ride the horse?' asked Charles.

'*No hay problema* – there is no problem. I have a mule too. Do not worry Carlos. I have taken *señoras* for walks before. If you come to my house I will show you a photograph.'

They had reached the village by now and Julie needed all her attention to steer the car through the *barrio nuevo*. Cars were parked left and right wherever the drivers had decided to stop; people were talking, standing in the middle of the street; a fully loaded mule trod along slowly and a dog suddenly crossed. Next the car in front of them stopped abruptly: the driver had noticed someone he knew and called out to him. The other man crossed over, bent towards the open window and the two began a conversation. Then a huge lorry came down the other way, hooting, and all traffic was blocked. Julie and the other drivers going into the village had to back up quite a way to where the street was wide enough for the lorry to pass.

'It would be nice if they could finish the bypass below the *barrio nuevo*,' sighed Julie.

Work on the bypass road had begun a year ago. In fact, the new road was nearly completed; it only needed its surface asphalted, which required a few weeks at most. Yet, for the last half year nothing had happened. So the unfinished bypass, which cut through the fields like a dusty strip below, was just used as a parking lot and people continued to wriggle their way in and out of Frigiliana through the narrow street of the *barrio nuevo*.

At last they reached the parking lot near the Guardia Civil post at the entrance of the old part of the village, and Julie turned towards Fernando. 'I'm afraid that's as far as I'm going. I hope it was nice being driven.'

'Not nice *señora*,' he corrected. 'It was divine.'

They had been home about twenty minutes when there was a knock on the front door. Julie went out on the terrace and leaned over the railing to look at the street below. 'It's Fernando!' she called out. 'He says he wants to speak to you.'

Charles went down and when he opened the door Fernando stood there with one hand behind his back and a finger against his lips going, 'Shht…'

Suddenly he produced a large bunch of white sweet-scented freshly cut mock-orange flowers from behind his back saying, 'This is for the *señora*.' His voice was a low whisper and he had a conspiratorial look in his eyes.

'Come up then and give them to the *señora*.'

He looked shocked. 'I cannot give these to her.'

'Why not?'

110

'But Carlos, the *señora* is married! You are the husband. You must give them. That is becoming.'

Charles smiled and took the bunch, thinking that there was probably not a flower left on the bush outside Fernando's house. 'That's very kind of you,' he said. 'Most thoughtful. I can assure you that the *señora* will be very touched.'

Fernando's face beamed, and as he turned and walked away Charles thought, here at least is a man who doesn't seem to be affected by the Curse.

19

Julie was reading one of her favourite books the next morning and Charles thought he might as well go for a walk. When he reached Calle Alta at the top of the village he suddenly remembered that Charlotte lived close-by now and started climbing the steep Calle Chorrera. It was a short sloping street with lanterns and flowerpots lining both sides; in places it was no more than four feet wide because the raised steps to the houses reduced its width. The street turned a sharp left after only thirty yards. Looking up from below, however, you got the impression that it ended at this turn. It seemed to be blocked by the white-chalked house at the corner. The front wall of the house was decorated with pots of geraniums of all colours, and behind it the hill of Frigiliana rose abruptly, golden yellow in the light of the sun. It all looked so picturesque, so innocent.

He had nearly reached the top end of the street when a stout, heavy-breasted older woman appeared in the doorway of the house above. When she noticed Charles, she stared hard at him from under a mop of dark, undulating hair. It was a scrutinising look, and as he stopped and knocked on Charlotte's door, the look in her eyes turned into an unwelcome, hostile glare and she screamed something unintelligible at him in a high-pitched voice.

After a while the door opened an inch or two and Charlotte's face appeared, looking out guardedly.

'Come in quickly,' she said opening the door. She sounded nervous.

'What's the matter Charlotte? What's happening?'

'I can't stay here,' she blurted out. 'I just can't. I'm leaving.'

'But you've only been here a few days! When I last saw you, you told me you were so certain you liked the house that you paid two months' rent in advance.'

'I know, but I'm leaving all the same.' She looked like a stubborn, upset child. 'I hope the owner will pay me back.' Her mouth twitched nervously.

'Come on girl.' Charles took her by the hand and made her sit down. 'Take it easy. Tell me what's going on.'

'It's that woman,' she whispered. 'The one who just screamed at you. I'm… I'm afraid of her. She's a witch.'

'She did look unfriendly but why bother about her? She's probably just a grumpy old woman. Forget her and think of the wonderful views you have from your terrace, and about all you're going to create here.'

'I can't go up on the terrace.' Charlotte's hands trembled. 'When I did on the first day she stood at her front door. She can look out over my terrace from there, and she stared at me fixedly till I felt surrounded by evil vibrations. I could no longer concentrate, I couldn't think… I… I was only aware of her presence.'

Charles was about to say that maybe that was just imagination, but then he thought that Charlotte was an artist and therefore probably much more sensitive than he was. If she said she felt evil vibrations, he had to accept that.

'The day before yesterday I went out in the morning,' she continued, 'and you know, I'm not used to locking my door here in the village. Nobody does it. And would you believe it?' Her mouth twitched nervously. 'She came into the house during my absence to look through my things! She was still inside when I came back. In my kitchen! I was shocked and remained speechless. She didn't even excuse herself but went out saying something about cursed foreigners!'

'But that's really horrible!'

'In the afternoon Sven came to visit me – you've met him: the Swede who was with me a few days ago. And that same evening, when I went shopping, I heard from Pilar that she had been telling the whole neighbourhood that I receive men alone in the house and that I'm a whore!'

'I imagine that my visit will give her more to talk about then. She stared at me from the moment she came out till I went into your house. She is probably incapable of thinking that men come for anything other than sex.' Charles grinned. 'Maybe she's just jealous because you're young and good-looking whilst she's old and ugly?'

'I feel... no I'm sure there's more than that. She has got at least a dozen cats and does nothing but mumble strange words. And she seems to be speaking all the time about a curse. She's a witch!' Charlotte shivered. 'I'm afraid to go out. Yesterday I shut myself in the whole day.'

Charles looked around. The only window in the room gave on to the courtyard where a big fig tree and the wall of the house next door blocked the view. A large bust of a man, half finished, lay on the floor, and several crates with clay and colours stood there, unopened. Charlotte, who had such a need for space, had been made a prisoner in her own house and was utterly dispirited. 'We'll have to get you out of here,' Charles said. 'And quickly.'

20

In the late afternoon Charles went up El Darra Street to have a look at the ceramic plaques that depicted the rebellion of the Moors. They were quite large but were actually made up of a number of smaller tiles. Every fifty yards or so along Calle El Darra and up Calle Alta, the top street of the old village, plaques had been set into the walls. Charles had of course seen them before because they were a picturesque attraction, and he had stopped in front of some to look at the drawings like most tourists did, but this time he decided to follow the whole sequence and to read the accompanying texts.

The sequence of scenes looked like a comic strip. They showed Moorish figures working the fields; the Moors being treated unjustly; some men raising a green and crimson banner, inciting the others to rebellion; people on donkeys fleeing to a hilltop above Frigiliana; the landing of the Spanish fleet; the siege of the fortified hilltop; the Moors defending themselves valiantly, throwing huge stones down at the Christians, the Moorish women helping in the defence; then the defeat of the Moors, bodies lying around everywhere, and a long line of people being led away into captivity.

Even though it was depicted in simple, almost childish drawings, it was a poignant story of injustice and merciless killing. By putting up the plaques and by naming a street after Hernando El Darra, the leader of the Moorish rebellion in Frigiliana, it was as if the village had wanted to make amends for the past – as if it had tried to redeem its guilt over so much bloodshed.

But the rebellion had happened long ago, and though many bones probably still lay buried in the hill above, Charles failed to understand what had brought about this sudden fear of the past. Did the people in the village really believe that the dead were going to rise after more than four centuries and haunt them at night?

After he had looked at the last plaque he went down Calle Al Garra, the very steep street at the western end of the village which the locals called *La Caída* – The Fall – because so many people had slipped down there before they put in steps. It was lined with potted plants and flowers, a veritable garden flanking the walls of the narrow street. Patches of strong sunlight brightened the façades and out of one of the houses came the sound of Flamenco music.

Surely, he thought, such a profusion of life ought to be far stronger than all the dead of long-forgotten ages?

21

On the way towards his house Charles caught up with Lola, the pretty girl with the beautiful blue-green eyes. She had just shut the souvenir shop where she worked and was walking slowly down Calle Real.

'Hello Lola!' exclaimed Charles, kissing her on both cheeks. 'Are you going home?'

'I don't know…' She looked dispirited.

'What's the matter?'

'Oh... nothing,' she replied evasively.

'Is it the Italian man, that Massimo Zizi? He hasn't been bothering you again, has he?'

'No... nothing to do with him. It's... it's my parents.'

'Your parents?'

'Yes. I'm fed up with them. I don't want to live with them any longer. They quarrel all the time.'

'Maybe they have their reasons?'

'No!' She spoke decidedly. 'They've been quarrelling ever since I was a small child. And from what I've heard, even before they married.'

Charles shook his head. 'If that's so, why did they marry?'

'They shouldn't have, but in those days tradition required that a man married the first girl he courted.'

'So they got married because of tradition?'

'Not quite. My father was from another village, and when he came to court my mother at her parents' house he came on his motorbike. Few young men had a motorbike in those days, and it made him very special. He had been courting my mother for a while but somehow he seemed unwilling to bring up the subject of marriage, and apparently she was becoming very anxious. Then, one day when my mother's parents weren't in, he tried to kiss her but she refused unless he first promised to marry her. They had a terrible row and he left in a fury, slamming the door. As he started up his motorbike and set off she came rushing out with his helmet which he had forgotten, and threw it after him shouting, "Take this with you. I never want to see you again!"'

Charles grinned imagining the scene, while Lola continued. 'But as fate would have it the helmet hit him straight on the back of his head, the motorbike crashed into the wall opposite and my father lay there sprawled in the street, apparently lifeless. When she saw what she had done my mother ran towards him, threw herself on his body screaming, "I've killed him!" and began to cover his face with kisses, all the time wailing, "My Juan, my Juan, I love you, I love you. Don't die." Suddenly my father opened his eyes and whispered, "I'll marry you." Was it her kisses and the tears he felt on his face that had done it? No one knew, but three weeks later they were married.'

'That's really extraordinary!' Charles laughed.

'In a way, yes, because otherwise I wouldn't have been here. But they've quarrelled ever since.' Lola sighed despondently. 'And I so want to live in a place where I feel in peace.'

22

After leaving Lola Charles decided to carry on down the lower ring road, which ran between the old village above and the *campo* below. He liked walking; he wanted to keep lean and was always looking forward to some good exercise. As he marched along at a brisk pace he caught up with what seemed to be a huge load of cut grass with two legs beneath. When he had overtaken the slowly moving load and turned around he recognised the man who was bent double underneath.

'Hello Fernando,' he said. 'You're not going to eat all that, are you?'

Fernando twisted his head upwards and recognised him. 'No Carlos, it's for my horse.' And he gave him a large grin from under the load of grass.

Charles walked on, looking at the *campo* below Frigiliana. The sloping hillsides had been converted into terraces many centuries ago and these narrow strips of land continued to be cultivated intensively. Day after day peasants went out there with their mules. From this distance the men who were weeding, irrigating, digging up potatoes or pulling out lettuces and other crops, looked like miniature doubled-up figures. On one of the nearby fields a man was at work with a span of oxen, ploughing the land. He was a hefty, muscular fellow, and he needed to be strong because he had to lift the plough out of the earth and force the oxen to turn at the end of each furrow. Charles stood there for a while, looking at the two black beasts pulling the plough back and forth along the strip of land and admiring the precision of the farmer's work: the furrows were neatly spaced out in a regular geometrical pattern, following the contour lines of the hill. Only years of experience could produce such a perfect result in such a seemingly effortless way.

Further along a mule was tied up against a tree, waiting patiently for its master and for the next chore. Suddenly it began to bray, a forlorn sound which felt like a long drawn-out, heart-rending sob that went straight to the heart. To Charles the braying of the mules expressed all the sadness of a life of ceaseless toil, especially towards the end of the day. Like the Moors under Spanish rule, the mules were exploited and pushed to the extreme. And like them they had no hope of anything better to come.

23

That night Charles just couldn't go to sleep. He felt slightly on edge. Was it the north wind, which had been blowing steadily for the last two days rattling doors and windows? But that evening it had stopped as suddenly as it had started. In the dark he heard Julie's breathing, deep and regular. How she did it was a mystery to him, but the very moment she pulled the blanket over her ears she was fast asleep.

Charles was in a pensive mood. Over these last days something had begun to change in the village. At first he had thought it was all his own imagination. You couldn't really point to anything tangible, but the atmosphere had become less carefree. People seemed reluctant to say 'Hello' to foreigners now and behaved as if they wanted to avoid contact. And all because of that Curse, he thought. Can people really go on believing this nonsense about a treasure and a Curse? The strong wind that has cleared the skies surely ought to clear their minds too?

I might as well go for a walk, he thought, slipping out of bed and pulling on his clothes and a warm sweater. He had always loved walking alone at night when the world around was asleep and nothing stirred. The village streets were dimly lit by a few lampposts, but as he set out on the narrow path that led to the few large properties up on the hill everything around him was clouded in darkness. There was no moon and the stars seemed to shine more brilliantly than he had ever known. The dry north wind had blown the clouds out of the sky and cleared the air, and stars were visible even low over the Mediterranean where the humidity usually absorbed their light.

Bright Sirius hung low above the western horizon, but as his eyes grew accustomed to the darkness he began to see thousands upon thousands of much fainter stars. And from Sagittarius to Cassiopeia, in a wide sweep over the eastern sky, stretched the Milky Way, its billions of stars like a whitish, meandering river that wound its way across the heavens. He sat down on a low wall, gazing in awe at the star-spangled sky and at the galaxy of which we are but an insignificant part. The starlight was uplifting, peace-inspiring. It pervaded the senses with a feeling of the vanity of all our strife and endeavour.

In our modern world the glare of the city lights blocks the much fainter light of the stars but here, tonight, in the darkness of the hill, there was nothing to rival the starlight. This is the way the ancient Greeks must have seen the sky at night, Charles mused. No wonder they invented the constellations. The stars were important to them. This could no longer happen today. What do people nowadays care about the constellations? Or about the position of those bright wandering stars, the planets?

Castor and Pollux of Gemini were about to set while Leo was still almost straight overhead. One particular star, yellow-red, outshone all others in that constellation. That must be planet Mars, he thought. Towards the east beautiful Scorpio stood well above the horizon, its curved tail like diamonds in the sky, and the brightest of all, majestic Jupiter, was just rising.

Only the far-away croaking of the frogs in one of the water reservoirs at the foot of the village and the chirruping of a few crickets reminded Charles that there was life on planet Earth. Then he perceived a faint movement at his side and felt the rugged head of Gato rub against his hand. He was surprised to see Gato so far up on the hill but then, cats go out at night in search of food.

With a swift movement Gato jumped onto his lap and as Charles started stroking the cat's head and scratching its neck, Gato began to tremble softly as if overcome by some strong emotion. Then the cat stood up on its two hind legs, put its paws against Charles' throat and its nose against his face, and began to purr softly.

'All right, Gato,' he whispered. 'You know I love you but do sit down.' And he put the cat back on his lap.

It's nice to know that there is life in the cosmos, he thought, feeling the warmth of Gato's body on his knees. It would be dreadful to be alone somewhere out there on an uninhabited planet. And Gato purred loudly as if to show agreement.

Suddenly the silence of the starry night was shattered by shouting. A door to the terrace of the big house somewhat higher up was flung open, a beam of light shone through the night, and the voices became much clearer. There is no fixed time for human tragedies. Great and small, they are played out at all times of the day and night, but this one sounded particularly bitter. The voices were English, a man's and a woman's. His had a biting quality without a trace of concession; it sounded like the voice of a man whose patience had been totally worn out and whose only intention now was to hurt. Hers seemed to alternate between pleading and threatening.

Spanish voices carry far. Charles had heard farmers having a conversation from one hilltop to another, at least a hundred yards apart. English voices do not have the same dagger-like thrust and clarity. From afar they seem to melt into a whisper of soft sounds, but in the stillness of the night the ear distinguishes words it would not catch in the daytime. The house was at least fifty yards away but when one of the two people turned in Charles' direction he could hear some of what was said.

'... always turning around that... can't keep your hands off...'

'... fed up with your insinuations...'

'... send her away!'

'... shut up... old bitch!'

A sound as of an exploding grenade followed. She must have thrown a glass at him, but had obviously missed. She yelled with frustration and ran inside. Then Charles saw the man in silhouette against the dim yellow light of the open door and heard the clang of a bottle against a glass. He was standing up, his arm lifted, pouring a drink down his throat. It reminded Charles of those Indonesian shadow plays where you see the shadow of puppets moved by some invisible hand, playing a drama in which they are driven by forces much more powerful than themselves.

Presently the woman reappeared on the terrace, sobbing. For a while there was nothing but the sound of those sobs, which seemed to come from very deep down, and the clanging sound of another drink being poured out. In the background the frogs went on croaking their ageless love songs, the vast expanse of the sky continued to turn imperceptibly towards the west, and Gato was fast asleep on Charles' lap.

The conversation started again, falteringly, in lower tones, and went on for a minute, maybe more. Then the voices picked up again.

'... where's the money you promised?'

'... your fault... waste money...'

'... go and... yourself!'

She screamed like a wounded animal, rushed inside and slammed the door hard. The man remained alone in the dark and the only sound Charles heard afterwards was the occasional clang of bottle on glass. Suddenly he felt half frozen and shivered. Leo was already turning westwards and Sagittarius had risen well above the eastern horizon, with bright Jupiter directly below. He picked up Gato who, roused from his sleep, wondered what was happening, and put him on the ground.

'I can't stay here all night,' he whispered to Gato who was looking at him in the dark with sleepy eyes. He stroked the cat's rugged head. 'Tomorrow morning you'll get something tasty for breakfast.' And he turned and went back home.

24

As Julie and Charles walked up towards the Balcón de Europa in Nerja the next day, the north wind was blowing again and there were few people around. The Balcón, a paved promontory lined with palm trees, was a favourite spot for tourists because it looked exactly how people imagined a promenade on the southern coast to be. And the view of the coastline stretching along for many miles with the mountains plunging into the Mediterranean was indeed magnificent.

The beach to the west was private. It was not accessible from the Balcón but belonged to the smart hotel situated on that side, with the result that only richer – and usually older – people occupied the deckchairs thoughtfully placed near the water's edge. But the eastern part, which could be reached from the Balcón via a stairway, was a free for all. The cliffs on that side were covered in semi-tropical plants creating a coastline of lush green vegetation, ochre-brown rocks and bright sandy beaches; and the small coves were both prettier and more sheltered from the prevailing western winds than the private beach on the western side, proving that money doesn't always buy the best.

However, the beaches and coves, which on sunny days were full of sunbathers, now lay empty. Up in Frigiliana the wind had been less strong but here, at the sea in Nerja, Julie and Charles felt its full force. The pale blue-green Mediterranean was covered with whitecaps and the tall palm trees on the Balcón de Europa were swaying in the wind. One was so bent that it looked as if it was about to break.

A man was sitting on the terrace of the Café Mediterraneo, braving the chilly weather in a thick Scottish lamb's wool sweater and drawing comfort from a cup of hot coffee. As they walked past he called out, 'Hello Charles! Come and join me. Can I offer you a coffee?' It was Howard, someone they had met the year before.

'Why don't you sit with Howard while I do my shopping?' suggested Julie. And off she went without waiting.

Howard's table was sheltered from the wind by a big square pillar and it did feel relatively comfortable on the terrace. Charles had been rather looking forward to a cup of coffee, something he rarely got at home – Julie had the absurd idea that coffee wasn't good for his health – and gratefully accepted the *café con leche* he was offered.

Howard hadn't changed much since last year. He still wore the same brown jacket and trousers; he was just as skinny; his brown curly hair was as unwieldy as ever; and he never stopped talking about astrology. 'Uranus has now moved into Aquarius,' he explained while picking up his curved pipe, 'and that's beginning to affect the way people are behaving...'

A minute ago Charles would never have imagined that he was going to be enlightened about the effects of distant celestial bodies but then, life is an eternal surprise. He wasn't really interested in the whereabouts of Uranus, Neptune and Pluto and their influence on humankind, but Howard was very enthusiastic about it and was not to be discouraged. He felt very strongly about cosmic energy. He had left America for the south of Spain because it seemed that the cosmic energy was much more powerful there, and to capture that energy he would take up the most extraordinary positions. Charles had been told that Howard had a favourite wild fig tree in the river canyon below Frigiliana from which he would sometimes hang upside down to meditate and capture energy.

'... and with four of the outer planets in such an exceptional position, energy is flowing back into the world. This part of Spain is very special because it is on a crossroad of lines of positive energy...'

Just then a girl and a man passed within less than ten yards from where Charles was sitting. She was an attractive girl with dark, wavy hair, whilst the man, thin and of medium height, was gesticulating as if he was trying to convince her of something. They paused for a moment and as the girl turned, Charles saw her face and recognised her: it was Lola, the pretty girl from Frigiliana. What was she doing here with that man? He wore tight blue jeans and a dark sweatshirt, his hair was short-shaven and he had Arabic features, a scar on his left cheek, and hard, pitiless eyes. Charles was sure he had seen him before, but when and where?

They disappeared from view while Howard carried on between two puffs from his small curved pipe, '... and we all need to restore our energy. Life takes too much out of us and if we're not careful we will upset our energy balance. We must fill up with cosmic energy.' But Charles was only half listening; he was consulting the archives of his brain and searching for a dark Arabic face, a moustache drooping at the sides of the mouth; a scar on the left cheek; a sloping forehead, and shifty eyes.

25

'Anyone in?' a voice called from the staircase.

'Oh Sarah, it's you!' exclaimed Julie who had gone to look. 'What a pleasant surprise. Do come in.' A moment later Sarah appeared, slightly out of breath.

'Climbing two flights of stairs should be child's play for you,' commented Charles with barely hidden amusement. 'You're used to climbing to the top street of the village every day.'

Sarah didn't seem to like his comment. 'That's not the same. Your stairs are much steeper and… and I do find it harder every year to carry my shopping bags all the way up to my house.'

'Then, why don't you let Michael carry the bags?' Charles replied jokingly. 'Isn't he a keen hiker?'

'He's from the Lake District,' came Sarah's peeved voice. 'That's why he likes going uphill.'

'Isn't that where you both met? On a hiking tour?'

'That was a long time ago and…'

'I was about to make tea,' interrupted Julie. 'Would you like to have a cup with us?'

'But I didn't come for tea,' Sarah excused herself. 'I was only passing by and just popped in to see how you were.'

'Yes, but now that you're here you can't refuse.' And without waiting for Sarah's answer Julie left to prepare tea.

'You look worried,' observed Charles as Sarah sat down on the divan.

'Well… yes. I keep worrying about what will happen to the village if that project goes ahead.' She sighed and just sat there, not speaking.

'By the way,' asked Charles after a while, 'do you know the English people who live in the house below that of the murdered German? They had a terrible quarrel on their terrace two nights ago.'

'Well… these things happen.' Sarah looked up. 'That must be the couple who own a restaurant in Nerja. Bob and Lesley Marvey. I've never liked those people. They're real upstarts. You should see them drive about in their Range Rover. They behave almost as if they were royalty.'

'A Range Rover!' exclaimed Charles. 'But then I saw that man some time ago. I remember how he hooted his horn arrogantly when he was stuck behind another car in the village.'

'That doesn't surprise me,' replied Sarah. 'I met them once at a party and while I was explaining a problem I had with some Spanish people in the village he sneered, "You should have reminded them that you are English."'

'You mean that he thinks the English a cut above the local people?'

'Yes. I can't understand why foreigners would want to live in a village like this if they are going to look down upon the locals. Obviously the villagers are not rich, and many of the older people and especially the women are illiterate, but I'd rather have them for neighbours than those Marveys.'

'So the Marveys despise the villagers?'

'They do and they show it. And the people here have their ways of paying them back.'

26

'How about seeing if we can find out something about the Curse?' proposed Julie later in the day.

'You surely don't believe in such nonsense, do you?'

'Why not? Isn't it better to take such things seriously?'

'And how do you intend to find out about it?'

'Well… by going to the hilltop. Up there I might feel some vibrations.' She looked at Charles encouragingly. He shrugged his shoulders but then he thought, it's a nice walk anyway, and off they went, climbing up behind the Garden restaurant and alongside the stylish properties that had been built on the eastern side of the hill.

When they reached the cement road they realised they weren't the only ones to have come for a look. Three men were talking together: one was sitting on a low boulder next to the road, another had a foot upon the boulder and his hands in his pockets, and a third man who wore a straw hat was leaning on a stick. Ten yards further stood two women, dressed in black, and higher up there were a few more people from the village. They were all staring at the wall that surrounded the murdered man's property and at the closed garage door as if something might appear if they waited long enough.

'No good hanging around here,' said Charles. He smiled. 'I don't think the Curse is going to manifest itself just to satisfy the curiosity of all those people. Let's carry on.'

As they climbed higher the whole mountain range to the north appeared. Then, when they reached the other side of the hill and looked down at the canyon, they saw the riverbed. Nowadays the river contained no more than a mere trickle of water at the best of times, but in the distant past, maybe millions of years ago, it must have been extremely powerful to be able to erode the rocks and finally cut a deep gorge into the landscape.

'This is absolute, perfect beauty,' whispered Julie as they sat down and looked out over the canyon. 'There is nothing but peace here…'

Yes, everything is still so unspoilt, thought Charles. Yet soon maybe they will start building on the other side. The death of Herr Meier could well change the whole aspect of Frigiliana as Sarah feared.

Suddenly a goat appeared higher up, peering apprehensively at them.

'Let's climb as high as we can,' suggested Charles, pulling Julie up. 'To the very top.'

The hilltop was like a rounded skull, a hundred and fifty yards long by fifty yards wide. Boulders, pieces of broken rock and small pebbles were strewn over it, and here and there the bare rock showed between coarse grass, scented herbs and small, drought-resistant flowers.

Some fifty goats were grazing, scattered over the hilltop. Then Julie and Charles noticed a goatherd sitting on one of the larger boulders, leaning on his staff. As they approached they said hello, but he only uttered incoherent sounds and gave them a large, crooked smile.

'I think he's simple-minded,' concluded Julie. There was compassion in her voice and her face had that unmistakable expression of sadness it always showed when she saw a wounded animal or a handicapped person.

'That man must have seen many things from his vantage point,' remarked Charles. 'I bet you he knows a lot about Meier – about whom he met or knew.' He sighed. 'And to think he cannot speak!'

They decided to return along the winding mule track that led to the upper part of the village. As they went down the steep track they met a couple of tourists walking up slowly. Judging from their appearance and the stiff-legged way they walked, they must have been well in their sixties. The woman wore a blue flowery dress that left her bare shoulders fully exposed to the sun; they were already bright red. The man had taken off his shirt and was sweating profusely; his face, forearms and neck were tanned, but his torso was burned just as much as his wife's shoulders.

'The poor things,' observed Julie when they had passed.

'Wasn't the Curse going to be unleashed on foreigners?' Charles had a twinkle in his eyes. 'Look, it has already struck them. They're red.'

Julie shrugged her shoulders. 'They must be real fools to get terrible sunstroke at their age! Can't people ever be sensible?' And she continued her way downhill muttering to herself.

27

Charles was just coming out of a local grocer's shop the next morning when he bumped into Howard, his eternal pipe stuck in his mouth. The pattern of encounters is strange. Sometimes you do not meet certain people for weeks on end, but the moment you have come across them once, they keep turning up. 'What are you doing in Frigiliana?' asked Charles.

'I had to get out of Nerja.' Howard sighed. 'I need to load up with cosmic energy.'

Just then two youngsters who didn't look a day older than sixteen passed by on motorbikes, the engines screaming, the high-pitched sound reverberating from the walls; it was painful to the ears.

'I can't understand why these motorbikes are so noisy,' said Charles. 'And I'm not the only one who's bothered by them. I remember a retired American who rented a house in the village last year. He was so infuriated by the ear-shattering noise that he told me he wanted to sneak up to the parked motorbikes in the middle of the night and stick potatoes up their exhaust pipes.'

'I have a theory that motorbikes in Spain differ from those in other countries,' replied Howard sticking up a forefinger. 'They have been conceived to produce more noise than movement.' He took the pipe out of his mouth and continued, 'You have to get used to noise if you live in Spain. It's everywhere.'

'Of course!' Charles laughed. 'You know what you're talking about. Are you still living in the same apartment as last year?'

'Hell no! It was cheap but... do you remember where it was situated?' Charles nodded while Howard carried on. 'There were lots of bars around, and the mixture of music blaring from so many different bars and discos till three or four every morning was more than my nerves could take. I couldn't sleep at night, and couldn't work because I kept dozing off in the daytime. One summer was enough for me.'

'I don't know how people over here can stand it. I've often wondered whether the noise to which their ears are exposed from birth doesn't make them gradually deaf over the years.'

'Very likely. You go to any restaurant and you'll find the TV blaring, as well as loud music on. And the customers are screaming to each other to make themselves understood above the background noise.'

'That's why I hesitate to go to restaurants.'

Howard grinned. 'I have thought of a particular form of torture for the youngsters here. They should be put in the middle of a large room with walls lined with TV sets and radios all tuned to different channels and blasting away at maximum level. And to top it all, noisy motorbikes should be racing around them. Maybe that would teach them?'

'I'm not so sure. They might well enjoy it and be shouting to each other throughout the whole cacophony.'

'Perhaps you're right.' Howard shook his head.

'Where are you living now?'

'I've moved to a building on the other side of Nerja where there are no bars or discos. Mind you, it's not ideal. The walls are paper-thin – so thin that if someone farts in an apartment at the other end of the building you hear it! And people have their TVs on at full blast. And they don't go to bed till one o'clock!'

'Spain *is* a noisy country.' Charles nodded. 'According to *El País* it's the second noisiest country in the world.'

'I don't believe that!' retorted Howard. 'I can't think of any country that's noisier.' He sighed. 'And I so love silence and peace.'

'So do I.'

'If you're a peace-lover I can take you to a wonderful spot not far from Frigiliana,' suggested Howard. 'It's up in the hills and it's one of two spots around here full of Uranian energy.'

'All right. Whenever you like.'

'Tomorrow would be a good time.' He looked up. 'I'll be here around two. I'll come on my motorbike.'

'Not one of those noisy things?'

'You won't hear me arrive,' replied Howard, taking a puff from his pipe. 'My bike is old and doesn't go fast but it's very, very quiet.'

28

'What time did Howard say he was coming?' asked Julie. She was standing on the terrace of their house, looking out over the street.

'Around two o'clock,' replied Charles. 'And it's two now.'

'How's he going to get here?'

'Oh! On his motorbike.'

'I didn't know he had a motorbike.' Julie seemed surprised. 'I've always thought of him as of someone without any worldly possessions.'

'That just goes to show that materialism has corrupted even the most worthy amongst us.' Charles grinned.

'I can't possibly imagine Howard on a flashy motorbike.'

'Well... if you ask me, I don't think he's going to come. Look at the sky.' Big black threatening clouds were rolling in from the west and the wind was beginning to blow in sudden gusts.

Charles had hardly spoken when an old motorbike drove up the street, its engine purring softly. The skinny driver, sandals, dark-blue jeans and beige corduroy jacket, helmet slung around his arm instead of on his head, and pipe in his mouth, was unmistakably Howard. He parked his bike and when he noticed them up on the terrace he called out, 'Shall we go?'

'How far is your favoured Uranus spot?' asked Charles as they joined Howard.

'Some three miles from here.'

'In that case let's take the car,' suggested Julie, looking at the sky.

'That's not a bad idea,' agreed Howard. 'I have to be back by four thirty.'

The car was parked near the Guardia Civil post and as they passed under the Seville orange trees that lined the street below, the wind shook the leaves and the first big drops began to fall. There was a flash of lightning followed by a resounding thunderclap that reverberated against the mountains and took some time to die. Seconds later the rain began pouring down, forcing them to run for shelter into the nearby café-bar *Virtudes*.

Virtudes was a small, local affair which had its name written in homemade white characters on a black background. The inscription *Vinos* above the entrance of the wine shop next door looked professional in comparison. It was executed artistically on old tiles, the characters a pretty faded blue and yellow on a creamy-white background, the whole finished off with a blue frame. But today no one had an eye for such details. Several people rushed into Virtudes after them to seek shelter from the pelting rain. The downpour was so heavy that from the bar it looked like a grey curtain. It was as if the skies were coming down, and thunder rumbled almost without interruption.

Next to Charles stood a couple of English tourists, carrying bags crammed with souvenirs. The man wore a light sweatshirt and his white hat was so small that it was perched above his red face like a crumpled eggshell, while the woman's shorts were so tiny that they left far too much of her bulging buttocks visible. They both looked cold and miserable. This was certainly not what they had come to Spain for.

'Not what you expected, I imagine,' observed Charles.

'This is just like England,' muttered the man with a look of disgust in his eyes. 'Even worse.'

When it rained in Frigiliana, the water just flowed down the sloping streets until it eventually ran off into the surrounding *campo*, but the village was not built to cope with such a heavy downpour. The water, gushing over the cobblestones outside Virtudes, looked like a real stream a few inches deep.

Presently Iago, the woodcarver, came rushing in dripping with water, followed by Sam, Agustina's dog, and as the dog sat down a puddle formed around him on the floor where the water ran out of his black coat.

There were a few unoccupied stools at the bar and they all sat down and ordered coffee. 'Who wants something to eat?' proposed Charles. The bar offered a choice of stews, salads and sausages which could be seen behind the counter, and from the ceiling above hung two large dried hams against a background of bottles of brandy.

Howard and Julie declined, saying they were not really hungry, while

Iago ordered a large *bocadillo* – a ham sandwich – for himself, and a piece of sausage for Sam who was getting dry by now.

Presently Charles turned to Howard. 'It looks as if we'll have to call off our drive to your favoured Uranus spot.'

'I should have known.' There was a despondent expression on Howard's face. 'Jupiter has just gone retrograde and that's upsetting all the signs. But the moon is waxing. That should create a strong positive flow. I'll come back on Tuesday afternoon to take you. It'll boost up your energy, you'll see.'

'We promised to help a friend who's moving on Tuesday,' Julie excused herself. 'Sorry.'

Iago turned to Howard. 'I'll come if you like. It's time I boosted up my energy. I feel very low at the moment.'

'But Iago, you create such beautiful things!' Julie's eyes expressed disbelief. 'Every time I pass by I find you in your workshop, producing one marvel after another. You never stop.'

'That may be so but I've just been repeating myself, producing the same sort of things over and over again. It no longer satisfies me. I need new inspiration.'

'Come with me then and sit under the trees.' Howard sucked his pipe vigorously. 'Sometimes I feel so shattered by the negative energy that emanates from people in town that I retreat there. Then, when all the strong Earth energy has flowed into me, I feel reborn and can face this wretched life again.' He looked at Iago with great intensity. 'It's a very, very strong spot. Several lines of Earth energy meet there…'

But Iago wasn't listening. His sandwich had just been brought and he took a large bite from it saying, 'Ouf, I was hungry…'

29

Suddenly the English tourist who was standing next to Charles asked, 'Excuse me. Isn't this the village where that German was murdered?'

'That's right,' confirmed Charles. His face must have shown displeasure because the man began to mumble apologetically, 'Well… we thought… the wife thought… that we might have a look at the place where it happened.'

'Yes, and maybe take a photograph or two,' added the woman. Her face expressed eager interest; she seemed unaware of the looks of disapproval around her. 'They say he was clubbed on the head by his mistress. They had an argument or some such.'

'That wasn't the way it happened Val,' interrupted the man. 'He was murdered because of a treasure. It's in the papers you know.'

Suddenly Julie cut in. 'I'm afraid you've got it all wrong.'

The couple turned around and looked in surprise at Julie.

'I'm sure it was a love affair,' repeated the woman called Val, her eyes full of expectation, like a child eager for a story.

'Wait,' said Julie, 'I know the story, let me see… how did it go exactly?' She put her forefinger to her lips and her eyes turned inwards as if searching for inspiration. Then she began.

'About a year ago the house just below that of the German was bought by a foreign businessman – I think he was Danish – and with him came his beautiful thirty-year-old wife. The German invited them over once or twice and they returned his hospitality. Now, the businessman often had to go abroad, leaving his wife alone, sometimes for days, sometimes even for a week or two. She had little to do, was bored stiff and often just lay in the garden sunning herself, at times completely naked, believing nobody could see her. But the German could see her from a small window at the top of his house!

'He had been alone for several years, quite contented to be so, when these new neighbours interrupted the ordered rhythm of his life. Seeing a young woman move around seductively in her garden or lie on her deckchair, offering her golden-brown naked body to the sun, had a shattering effect on him. He began to long for her, and as the weeks passed by, he became obsessed with her…'

'That's exactly how men are!' interrupted the woman called Val shooting a stern glance at her husband. 'They can never keep their eyes off other people's wives. And what happened next? Did he get her?' Her breath came fast.

'Well, he was the sort who, once he'd put his mind to something, didn't give up easily. He sent her flowers, gave her presents when her husband was away, and kept offering to take her out for dinner, which she often accepted because she was utterly bored. Then, one night, she drank too much and let him make love to her. From that day on they were lovers.'

'I knew it! I knew it!' exclaimed the Englishwoman. 'That's exactly how these things happen.'

Encouraged by the success she was having, Julie began to wax melodramatic. 'Oh, those endless days when the husband was there. The German would turn around in circles in his house and then climb up to the top room to see if he could catch a glimpse of her in the garden. Every moment without her was torture. Worst of all were the evenings. He suffered agonies when he imagined her in bed with her husband. And when the husband finally went off again, the relief of holding her in his arms, but also the jealousy and the probing questions, becoming more pressing every time. "Had she slept with her husband? Had he forced her to make love to him?" And when she gave evasive answers, he felt flames of jealousy consume him.'

'That's men for you!' interrupted the woman called Val.

'Then, one day when the husband had again gone on a business trip, the German took her to one of the restaurants in Nerja where she liked to dine. There was a new waiter and as there were few customers, the man paid extra attention to them. He brought the dishes along as if they were special presents while turning around their table with the agility and grace of a Flamenco dancer. The woman was amused and remarked how slim, yet muscular he was. The German was not amused and replied that he thought him just a primitive gypsy. All through the evening the waiter was attentive to the woman, moving forward to refill her wineglass, looking at her with fiery eyes while the woman smiled at him, followed him with her eyes and hardly listened to the German's conversation. In the end the German became so enraged that he called the waiter an insolent beggar, paid and took the woman home.'

'And quite right too!' commented the Englishman.

'The next day the woman told the German that she had a migraine and wanted to be alone. The day after, it was an aunt of her husband's who had phoned and was due to arrive any minute. And the aunt was going to stay till her husband returned! When the German asked if he could have coffee with them in the afternoon, she said, "No!" The aunt was very suspicious and he'd better stay away. That evening he went to the top room to look at the garden in which he had so often seen the woman, aching to possess her, when he suddenly noticed a dark shadow appear at the garden wall, climb over it like a cat and disappear inside. It had all happened so quickly that, when he looked again at the empty garden, he thought he must have imagined it. Then, suddenly, he realised: a thief! My lover is in danger! And he rushed down to warn her.'

'Gosh!' The woman called Val put her hand in front of her mouth, her eyes wide with fear.

'He rang the bell frantically but there was no answer. He was about to turn back in order to call the police when he heard steps inside. A moment later the woman opened the door, her face tense. When he told her he had seen a thief she shouted, "Leave me alone!" and slammed the door in his face. He spent a miserable night and was awake when the sun rose. As he looked out from his top room, pondering over the inexplicable events of the last few days, a man sneaked out of the house next door, slipped quickly through the garden and crawled onto the top of the wall. As he let himself down on the far side his face turned for an instant towards the German: it was the waiter from the restaurant!'

'Hell!' exclaimed the Englishman. 'Trust a woman!' whereupon his wife planted her elbow in his ribs hissing, 'Don't interrupt!'

'The next days were probably the worst in the German's life,' continued Julie, now quite carried away by her own story. 'He felt paralysed, his mood swinging between depression and rage. He went to see the woman, pleading, promising to give her everything he possessed, but she just mocked him, shouting that she had found passion and that he had no idea what passion was. He began to drink heavily, and one evening he even went to her door threatening to tell her husband everything, but to no avail: she refused to open. It was all the fault of that gypsy beggar! He had bewitched her. Then, a plan emerged in his drunken brain. If only the waiter disappeared, everything would be all right again. He went to the restaurant and asked the waiter to come to his house that night. The man refused at first, but the German insisted, saying that he had to tell him something very important about the woman, and at long last the waiter agreed. When he finally arrived, the German offered him money if he would disappear without ever seeing the woman again, but the waiter proudly refused to be bought off. The German just couldn't believe it: a penniless beggar! And he raised the stakes, in the end offering a fortune, when suddenly the young man spat on the floor in front of the German's feet, turned haughtily around and moved towards the door. The German was seized with rage. How dared he, a gypsy, a miserable good-for-nothing! He picked up a poker from the chimney and rushed after him, but the young man, like a toreador avoiding a wild bull, jumped aside and gave his attacker a push. The German was carried away by his own momentum, stumbled and banged his head hard on the corner of a heavy metal chest. It fractured his skull and that's how he died!'

Julie stopped and gazed around her with a look of satisfaction in her eyes. The two English tourists had lapped up every word she had spoken and one could see from their faces that they regretted that the story was over.

'How thrilling!' exclaimed the woman. She turned to her husband. 'And to think, Mike, that we're hearing the story almost first hand!' Her cheeks were pink with excitement. 'What happened to the waiter?' she enquired, breathlessly.

'He disappeared,' replied Julie, 'and to this very day they have found no trace of him.'

'Could we go to the house and see it?' the man asked, his eyes round with curiosity.

'That's easy enough.' It had stopped raining by now and Julie went outside and pointed up the hill. 'Look, you climb as high as you can. It's the last house. But I don't know whether you'll be able to go in.'

'Come on Val,' said the man motioning to his wife. 'Let's go and see,' and his eyes widened with anticipation, '... the place of the crime.' And off they went over the wet cobblestones that sparkled like diamonds in the light of the sun which had just come out again.

30

When Julie returned to the bar Charles kept muttering, 'How could you?' shaking his head.

'Wasn't it an exciting story?' she replied. 'I'm quite pleased with it to tell you the truth.'

'How can you utter the word truth after telling such a pack of lies?'

Howard too was shaking his head. 'Tomorrow it'll probably be in the newspapers. And people will believe it.'

'But it might have happened that way,' objected Julie. 'And at least, the story I told is more romantic than the gruesome murder stories you read about in the papers nowadays.'

'Romantic! That German must have been at least seventy years old!' retorted Charles.

'There's no age limit to love.' Julie had an offended look on her face. 'I think it is always so touching when I see two old people walking hand in hand.'

'Anyway, for your story to be possible you will have to conjure up a beautiful Danish woman and her businessman husband,' remarked Charles dryly. 'And there is no such couple up on the hill. That's a fact.'

'You with your facts! Why can't we have dreams and imagination instead? And the German may have been a drunkard.'

'Maybe that's why he was murdered!' exclaimed Charles sarcastically.

Howard turned towards them drawing smoke from his pipe. 'If being a drunkard were a reason for being murdered, quite a lot of men in this village would be in danger.'

'And first of all Fernando!' suggested Iago. 'You know… the one with the horse. He'd be dead many times over.'

'But he's a nice man!' protested Julie. 'He certainly isn't always drunk.'

'Being under influence is his natural state,' affirmed Iago. 'But he has moments when he is sober.' He laughed. 'I believe that he doesn't drink on feast days. Let me tell you a story: I once saw him come up pulling his horse along the village street. The horse was so used to him always going straight into the first bar and having to wait there for him to empty a glass or two that it stopped automatically in front of the door. But this was one of Fernando's rare dry days and there he was, trying to pull the horse along, shouting, "No stupid, not today!" and the horse refusing to budge until he first disappeared into the bar.'

'He does have a very well-trained horse,' agreed Howard. 'Once, walking down to the river canyon to my favourite fig tree, I found him sleeping off his bout of drunkenness in the middle of a small field holding his horse's reins in his hand; and the horse was standing at his side, waiting patiently for him to wake up!'

'Why does he drink so much?' asked Julie. 'Is it because he's alone and unhappy?'

'I wouldn't say that,' replied Iago. 'He's not alone. He's got two or three friends; and more in particular, he's got his horse. No, he's quite a cheerful fellow. He probably just likes the bottle and he seems to be quite contented that way. He doesn't ask much from life.'

'Why doesn't he have more friends?' Charles enquired. 'Does the village reject him because he's so often drunk?'

'That's not it,' replied Howard taking his pipe out of his mouth. 'Being a drunkard is not considered such a terrible thing here. And I don't think he's actually rejected.' He looked at Iago for support. 'No, I would say that he's tolerated. The problem is that he's an independent person, and he happens to have stepped outside the usual pattern. If you're born in this village you are expected to live by its rules, but he doesn't care about what they think of him; he just does what he likes, but he has thereby forfeited the right to have a say in local matters.'

'It isn't as bad as that,' objected Iago. 'A few years ago he was so drunk that he fell off the steep edge of an alleyway and broke his leg. They've put up a rail since. And it seems that the village Council is going to give him a new front door.'

'Why is that?' asked Julie, surprised. 'Hasn't he got a front door?'

'Well… he had one until a winter or two ago…'

'I don't see how a front door can disappear?'

'Normally, front doors don't, but this was Fernando's front door you see… Let me explain. One day it was very cold and Fernando could think of nothing better than to cut up his front door and burn it. It kept him warm for a couple of days.'

'I don't believe it!' exclaimed Julie. 'The poor man! How does he manage to keep the drafts out?'

'He has pinned an old blanket over the entrance.' Iago chuckled. 'It has hung there for more than a year now and the Council feels that it spoils the picturesque look of the village. They have discussed his case several times and have come to the conclusion that there is nothing else to do but to give him a new door.'

Suddenly Howard glanced at the clock on the wall. 'Good heavens,' he exclaimed, 'it's four already. I'll have to return to Nerja.' He looked at Iago. 'I'll see you next Tuesday at two in the afternoon then, OK?' Then he turned to Julie and Charles. 'I hope I'll be able to take you to the Uranus spot another time.' And he left on his sandaled feet without hurry, clouds of smoke coming out of his pipe.

PART THREE
SECOND MURDER

1

As Charles had nothing much to do on Monday morning he went down the stairs and turned into *Locura*. There were no customers and Agustina was sitting behind her desk, so absorbed in reading a book that she didn't even notice his presence. A cassette recorder was playing oriental music, which fitted the atmosphere perfectly: the shop was a world of deep scents and vivid colours, of warmth and vibrating life, almost like an oriental bazaar. You felt you had suddenly stepped into one of the mysterious back alleys of Marrakech with a touch of Bali, Vera Cruz and Kathmandu thrown in. There were sand-roses from the Sahara, colourful jars from Andalusia, leather-ware from Morocco, scented boxes made of sandalwood, and jewellery from India. This was more than a shop: it was the entrance gate to a dream-world, a treasure chest, and Agustina, who had the looks of a gypsy, seemed to be a natural part of this cave of Ali Baba.

Suddenly Agustina looked up from her book; she had perceived a movement. When she saw it was Charles, her red lips broke into a full smile and her large brown eyes sparkled. She got up to kiss him on each cheek, as was the Spanish fashion, and then hugged him. Her embrace was as warm as the Spanish sun.

'How are you?' asked Charles looking at her smiling face. Then he hastened to add, 'Sorry to disturb you. You seemed very absorbed. What are you reading?'

'Poetry,' she said, handing him the book.

'Who reads poetry nowadays?'

'*I* do. And many other people too I hope. Poetry is the essence of life. Look what our world is becoming without it.'

Charles had to agree there.

'Don't you sometimes get bored in your shop?'

'Never. When there are visitors I help them, and if there are none I read. I really love being in the shop. Do you realise that I've read nearly a thousand books in the seven or eight years the shop's been open!'

'That's incredible!'

'Why do you think so? I like reading, so why shouldn't I?' Her eyes shone. 'Isn't life what you make of it?'

'Well… that may be so, but you work a lot too. I see that you've unloaded your van.' Agustina had arrived late at night a week ago, her mini-van so stuffed with goods that there had been just enough room for her to squeeze behind the steering wheel. She had left it below in the street. It was parked, or rather squashed, against the bright-yellow mailbox at the bottom of El Darra Street, leaving just enough space for other cars to pass by.

'I didn't unload the van.'

'But it's nearly empty!'

Agustina laughed heartily. 'I've sold most of the contents.'

'How do you mean?'

'Well… only yesterday I sold ten camelhair blankets straight from the van. It was easier than having to drag them all up here. Anyway, there was no room in the shop for all that stuff. But I did bring in a few smaller objects.'

'So you have an extension of your shop out in the street?' Charles shook his head in disbelief. 'Not bad!' He now began to admire some of the boxes she had brought in. They were a lovely mottled light-and-dark-brown colour and the wood was polished and shone like a mirror. He picked up a slightly larger one with a curved lid. It had a smooth, pleasant touch.

'Open it,' said Agustina who stood beside him, her hand touching his elbow.

He opened the lid with some difficulty. The inside had not been polished and the wood had retained its natural scent and colour.

'Now smell it.'

He held the box close to his nose.

'What does it remind you of?'

Charles knew the scent but couldn't quite place it. 'Aren't these boxes made of sandal wood?'

'No, of cedar wood. They're actually made of the roots of cedar trees,' explained Agustina. 'That's why they are so mottled. But their scent takes me straight back to my childhood.' She took the box out of his hands and leaned forward. As she did so her hair fell over it and the box disappeared in a mass of dark ringlets. Then she lifted up her face with an expression of pure delight; her eyes were closed and her voice seemed to come from far away. 'You know… when I was a child and I sharpened pencils and held the freshly sharpened wood to my nose, that's exactly how it smelled!'

'You're right. That's the scent.'

Suddenly it occurred to Charles that he hadn't seen Sam for several days.

'Where's Sam?' he asked. 'He hasn't disappeared I hope.'

'Isn't he out in the street? He was there some time ago.' Agustina went to the door and looked out. 'No, he's gone. He disappears quite often these days. It wouldn't surprise me if he is off again with that lady friend of his.'

'Do you know that the other day I surprised him with what you call "that lady friend"? He was standing on top of her in the middle of the street, in full action! I called him but he was much too busy to listen.'

Agustina's face lit up. 'How nice for Sammy. That's why he's been so tired lately. Sometimes he comes home late at night, laps up a bowl of water and drops asleep on the floor before he has even half finished his supper.'

Just then the local vendor of lottery tickets walked by, calling out that he was about to sell the winning number.

'Do you ever buy lottery tickets?'

'No one has ever won a prize in Frigiliana,' replied Agustina. 'It's not worthwhile buying a ticket.'

Charles was about to say that he fully agreed, when a customer came in and he quietly left the shop.

2

In Spain jobs such as selling lottery tickets were reserved for handicapped people and the vendor, who had a pronounced limp, took a long time to pass by. As Charles' eyes followed him, waiting for him to disappear behind the bend of the street, he saw Sven appear at the top end of Calle El Darra, carrying two suitcases.

'Sven!' he exclaimed running up the street. 'What's happening?'

'I'm moving Charlotte's things,' replied Sven almost apologetically.

'No! I thought she was moving tomorrow! And we were going to help...'

'Sorry. It's all finished. I... well... Charlotte was so unhappy there... she couldn't stay an hour longer.' He stopped in front of the house Charlotte had occupied last year. 'I do hope she'll be all right in here.' His voice sounded worried.

Charles took one of the suitcases out of his hands and carried it inside; he found Charlotte busily unpacking her things. 'How come you're back here?' he asked. 'You said you didn't like this house because it was much too dark!'

She kissed him. 'Oh, did I? Well... it doesn't matter. I feel so relieved!' Then she turned to Sven. 'Just carry the suitcases up to my room, will you?'

Sven took the suitcases up obediently, came down again and sat on a chair, looking at Charlotte as if he were waiting for further orders.

Charles turned to Charlotte. 'When did you two meet?'

'Oh! I don't quite remember. Maybe a month or two ago?'

'On the fourteenth of February,' said Sven, his grey eyes brightening for a moment while Charlotte continued to unpack several half-finished heads and began placing them around the room.

'Any news from Edward?' asked Charles.

'Well, yes... he wrote me a letter asking for help but... but I've had to disappoint him... I hope he hasn't taken it too badly. I've written him several times since but there's been no reply.'

'Maybe he doesn't like writing,' replied Charles diplomatically. 'Some people are much better at saying things than at writing them down.'

'Not him!' She lifted her head defiantly. 'He's a famous writer, so he is quite capable of writing a letter.'

Charles suddenly felt annoyed with her. 'That's right. You've told us: he's that famous Bear, isn't he? But now that I think of it, you can't possibly marry him, Charlotte.'

'Why not?' asked Charlotte, looking slightly alarmed.

Sven sounded interested. 'Is anything wrong with him?'

'Yes. Most definitely.'

'Some hidden disease?' There was a flicker of hope in Sven's eyes.

'It's his name,' replied Charles.

Charlotte stared at him defiantly. 'What's wrong with being called Edward Bear?'

'A lot! People will call him Teddy Bear. And you would be Mrs Teddy Bear.' Charles laughed heartily.

'Well, I happen to like teddy bears,' retorted Charlotte, sticking out her chin.

'Even as a husband?'

'Especially as a husband.'

'Of course, this opens up a whole range of possibilities,' continued Charles.

'Such as...' There was suspicion in her voice.

'When you have a daughter you could give her a typical Australian name such as Koala.'

'That's not funny!' Charlotte turned away and resumed her unpacking. 'Anyway,' she said, 'he'll hear from me when he gets back.'

'When will that be?' asked Sven.

'When he left he said he would be back in a month or so.'

'You won't have to wait long then,' concluded Charles.

'No,' sighed Sven, a rather unhappy expression on his face, but Charlotte didn't notice it and just continued to sort out her things.

3

Now that she was back in her old house in Calle El Darra, Charlotte thought it was fine. 'It's so restful,' she said. 'So peaceful.' And she started to work on the terrace there like she had done the year before, listening to one or another of her Spanish neighbours as they swept their terraces while singing age-old songs. Life seemed pleasant again. She even thought the house large enough to throw a party for her birthday!

Julie had insisted on helping with the preparations and had told Charlotte that she would drive to Nerja to buy the drinks. Once there, however, she immediately disappeared into a shop where they sold candles and small presents, leaving Charles with a long list of drinks to buy. There was nothing else for him to do but set off for one of the supermarkets that had a particularly large selection of beers, wines, aperitifs, liquors, brandies, vodkas, rums – everything under the sun that could quench the tourists' thirst for alcohol.

As he pushed his trolley along while checking the list for what he had to buy, he almost bumped into a young woman who was loading another bottle of some kind of spirit in her already full trolley. Fortunately he looked up in the last split second and just managed to avoid a collision.

The girl was utterly striking. Her dark-blue tightly-fitting mini-dress moulded her attractive figure suggestively, drawing attention to the provocative shape of her buttocks; the mini-dress left almost more of her thighs visible than decency permitted, and she had the sort of legs that made men dream and women turn away with envy: long, slim and golden brown. She wore dark-blue matching shoes with high heels and walked with a studied grace, her shoulders drawn back and her head held up proudly. Her arms and shoulders were bare and her reddish hair was tied up in a chignon. She was the personification of the gracious body, and if men had been dogs she would have been followed by a string of admirers; but men have been taught to suppress their instincts and here, in the supermarket, trailing behind their wives and pushing the trolleys, the most they risked was a furtive glance or two.

By the time Charles had finished paying, the young woman had already left and somehow he felt disappointed; he had wanted to see her face. When he got to the parking lot with two full shopping bags, a small car came rushing out and nearly ran him over. As he saw the girl's red hair and very pretty face flashing by, he almost dropped one of his bags in surprise and stood there gaping: it was the girl who had boxed in his car some time ago in Frigiliana!

4

How bothersome life is lately, thought Amanda as she was driving back from the supermarket to the restaurant in Nerja. This whole affair was running out of control. It had been amusing for a while, especially when she had taught that Lesley woman a good lesson. She wasn't going to let herself be done in by a jealous old bitch! And Bob had been so apologetic afterwards. He had given her more responsibilities, such as shopping for drinks. 'Choose whatever you like,' he had said. 'You know best what the customers want.' And he had even doubled her pay.

She didn't mind having fun, and it had been fun in the beginning, but now everything was turning into one long drag. Bob was becoming very possessive. God, how jealous he could be! And what a pompous bore he was! Even shopping for drinks no longer amused her.

What a girl has to put up with nowadays to keep her job, she reflected bitterly. And I don't trust that Lesley woman. It wouldn't surprise me if she had a few more dirty tricks up her sleeve. The look in her eyes when I saw her the other day! If looks could kill, I'd be dead by now. I think I'd do well to prepare an exit, just in case.

5

Charlotte had invited lots of friends, and friends of friends, but not all had been willing to come. Howard, for one, had declined the invitation. With Mars in Leo and Jupiter having gone retrograde, the cosmic energy was too violent; and the vibrations of so many people of different signs together in one house would be too disturbing. But most of those who had been invited had no such objections or, most probably, were unaware that they were mixing opposing cosmic energies.

Julie had already gone ahead two hours earlier to help with the preparations and by the time Charles arrived, the house was quite full and he had to push his way through the people who were standing around a table in the small dining room below. He said hello to some he knew, but most were too busy helping themselves from a variety of cold dishes – avocado salads, tortillas, lots of different cheeses, artichokes, olives…

He poured himself a glass of wine and paused to listen to the conversation. The guests had split up in small groups of two, three or four, and a cacophony of languages struck his ears: Spanish, German, English, French, Swedish... it felt like the European Union in miniature, with the same communication problems.

Conversations in a party are usually of the "Where are you from? What are you doing? How do you like it here?"-type. Tonight Charles somehow just couldn't rake up the courage to show interest in these superficial, trivial exchanges and he worked his way up the narrow staircase to the top floor where Charlotte had her workshop.

When he had last seen it, the small workshop had been taken up by a muddle of unfinished busts and by the sketches she made as a preparation for her sculptures. Tonight these had all been removed, the room was lit by candles, creating a feeling of cosiness, and a table with drinks occupied the middle. Several people were sitting around it – Julie amongst them – and an animated conversation was going on in Spanish.

Charlotte got up, calling out, 'Hello Charles! You've finally arrived.'

'Happy birthday Charlotte.' He kissed her on both cheeks.

'I *am* having a very happy birthday. Look, tonight I'm surrounded by friends.' She waved her hand around her while Charles looked at the faces in the semi-darkness – at the eyes that were sparkling in the flickering light.

'Sit down Charles,' said Julie. 'We were just going to try out the pendulum.'

'Shall I do it?' proposed Charlotte looking very eager. She took the pendulum out of Julie's hand and held it by the chain. 'What do I do now? Do I close my eyes and think of a question? And will the pendulum then begin to move?'

'You first have to define what's yes and what's no,' stated Julie. 'Ask a question to which the answer must obviously be yes.'

'Let's ask whether two plus two makes four,' suggested Charles. 'That's a sure yes.'

'How dull and unromantic!' protested Julie.

'I've thought of something,' announced Charlotte. 'All right! Silence everybody.' She closed her eyes and spoke in a solemn voice, 'Are we in Frigiliana?' The pendulum hung motionless from her right hand and refused to move, even after a minute.

'You're no good,' concluded Agustina. 'You have no psychic powers.'

'But I want to!' Charlotte looked distraught.

'Whether you want to or not is neither here nor there,' said Iago. 'Either you have them or you don't. And you don't.'

Charlotte looked upset.

'Shall I try?' suggested Angeles. She was a Mexican girl who had a rather plump figure and a high-pitched voice, but she seemed to be eternally smiling and good-humoured. She held the chain of the pendulum in her right hand while Julie steadied the weight.

'Are we in Frigiliana?' she asked.

The pendulum vibrated slightly and then began to move from left to right with increasing amplitude.

'It works!' exclaimed Julie.

'So left to right means yes,' concluded Iago.

'I knew I had psychic powers!' Angeles almost stuttered with excitement. 'I'm sure I was a witch in a previous life in the Middle Ages. I sometimes feel it very strongly. Has it ever happened to you that you enter a street or a house where you have never been and that you know, but clearly know, that you have been there before, a long time ago? That you recognise it? It happened to me regularly in the old parts of Cadiz and Seville when I first came to Spain two years ago.'

'Why don't you ask the pendulum if you've been a witch in the Middle Ages?' suggested Iago.

'Good idea,' agreed Sven.

Angeles closed her eyes, Julie steadied the pendulum, and everyone became silent.

'Have I been a witch in the Middle Ages?'

The pendulum at once began to swing from left to right and everyone went 'Ooh!' and 'Aah!'

'Wait, wait!' exclaimed Angeles. She closed her eyes again and asked, almost in a whisper, 'Was I a bad witch?'

The pendulum started to move from left to right again, first slowly then more rapidly.

'Ooh...' Angeles' face contracted with fright. 'I knew it!' she shrieked. Her voice was even more highly-pitched than usual. 'I have always felt that I was burned at the stake.'

'Maybe the pendulum always says yes,' interrupted Charles sceptically.

'Well… let's ask a question to which the answer must be no,' suggested Sven.

'We should have done that from the beginning,' insisted Charles. 'We must approach this with a critical mind.'

'You sound like one of those unbelieving scientists,' remarked Julie. 'All right! Just to be sure, let's ask whether we are in Nerja.'

Angeles closed her eyes. 'Are we in Nerja?'

The pendulum began to swing backwards and forwards giving a clear *no* answer.

'See!' Julie looked triumphant.

'Are you still a witch today, or have you become normal?' asked Angeles' boyfriend who was looking rather nervous by now.

'I don't want to ask.' Angeles' throat seemed dry. 'I prefer not to know.'

'Oh, do be a sport Angeles,' pleaded Charlotte. 'We want to know.'

'Hold my other hand,' whispered Angeles turning to her boyfriend. She closed her eyes while everyone fell silent in the flickering candlelight. The door to the terrace was open and the light of the waxing moon shone mysteriously on the floor of the room. The scene might have come straight out of the Middle Ages.

'Am I still a witch?' Angeles' voice trembled as she spoke. The pendulum made a few small circles and then distinctly said *yes*.

'How frightening!' exclaimed Agustina.

'Ssht,' motioned Julie, 'I think she wants to ask another question.'

Angeles' face looked quite white now and her voice quivered. 'Am I still a bad witch?' The pendulum, after some hesitation, began to move backwards and forwards.

The blood flowed back into Angeles' face, and her boyfriend looked relieved.

'Can you ask a question for me now?' interrupted Charlotte.

'Put your right hand on Angeles' left hand while you ask the question,' said Julie.

Their two hands touching, Charlotte asked, 'Is there a man who loves me?'

The pendulum made a few small hesitant circles.

'It doesn't work.' Charlotte's face sunk.

'Your energy is too disturbing Charlotte. That's why it doesn't work,' said Angeles. 'Hold your hand a bit above mine but don't touch it.'

'Let's make a test first,' suggested Iago, 'because Charlotte seems to create problems.'

'All right.' Charlotte held her hand an inch above Angeles' and then asked, 'Am I an artist?'

The pendulum began to move and after a few seconds gave a strong *yes* answer.

'No doubt there. And from the movements of the pendulum it's obvious that you're no small artist either,' deduced Julie.

'Good, let me ask again: is there a man who loves me?'

Charlotte's eyes were fixed on the pendulum while it described a few small circles. Then it began to move strongly from left to right. 'Hurrah!' exclaimed Charlotte. 'Somebody loves me!' She spread out her arms while a large smile split her face.

'But who is he?' Agustina wanted to know.

'I'll ask.' Charlotte closed her eyes. 'Is it…?' She whispered a name, so softly that no one understood. The pendulum, after a while, began to move backwards and forwards. Charlotte looked disappointed.

'Hey, that's no fun!' exclaimed Agustina. 'We do not even know who he is, and if we have to go through all the men you know we'll be here till tomorrow morning.'

'Let's ask something else,' suggested Julie. 'Let's try to find out who committed the murder.'

Charlotte looked annoyed. 'No,' she said. 'No. I still have many other questions.'

'Yes, let's find out about the murder,' agreed Iago. 'That's much more interesting.'

'Why should we want to know?' protested Charlotte trying to steady her voice.

'Of course we want to know,' intervened Charles. 'Let's ask if the murderer lives outside the village.'

Everyone was silent now. The flames of the candles flickered uncertainly. A cloud moved in front of the moon and it became suddenly darker as if the moonlight had been switched off.

Angeles' hand trembled. She went white in the face as she spoke with an uncertain voice, 'Does the murderer of the German live outside the village?'

All eyes were fixed on the pendulum. It made a few hesitant movements and then began to swing backwards and forwards.

'So he lives in Frigiliana!' exclaimed Charles.

'Who says it's a man?' objected Julie. 'It might just as well be a woman.'

'Let's ask,' came Sven's voice.

'No please,' pleaded Charlotte. 'Let's stop this. It's enough... I'm frightened.'

'Go ahead Angeles,' pressed Agustina.

Angeles closed her eyes but hesitated; then she said slowly, 'Is the murderer a woman?'

Suddenly the door burst open and the guests from downstairs all pressed into the room behind a large birthday cake covered with small, lit candles, singing, 'Happy birthday to you...'

A great muddle ensued. Charlotte had to blow out the candles and cut up the cake and everyone had to eat a piece. Suddenly Angeles' boyfriend looked at his watch. 'Good Lord!' he exclaimed. 'It's past midnight already and I have to work early tomorrow morning. Come on Angeles, we must be getting back to Nerja.' They said goodbye and left the room in a hurry.

'A shame,' murmured Julie. 'Just when we were going to find out about the murder.'

6

Next morning Charles and Julie decided to have a lazy day. They planned to drive to Torrox and from there on follow the coastal road, sit for a while on a quiet beach, and carry on to Nerja to have lunch afterwards. As they reached the spot where their car was parked they heard a woman's voice call, 'Vicente!' The name was pronounced with a strong English accent. Several older men were sitting on the low wall that lined the pavement while others were standing near a stall where a woman sold soft drinks and sweets. The village men had a propensity to spend hours like that, talking while standing up or sitting under the orange trees in the early spring sunshine, and they would comment on anything that went on around them, but strangely enough, none of them seemed to take any notice of the woman.

'Vicente!' she repeated, her face contorted with anger.

There was a small local garage at the end of the parking lot and the Vicente who was called for finally stuck his head out of his workshop. When he noticed the woman he seemed in no great hurry to go to her.

'Vicente! Come here and see what they've done this time!' commanded the woman. Vicente blinked and seemed to be gathering his courage together. He had a pleasant, olive-coloured face and his thick curly hair was still black although he must have been in his fifties. But for his dark-blue overalls he looked like so many Spanish men of his age. The woman now came forward, grabbed him by the elbow and pushed him along the row of parked cars. 'Just look at this!' she shouted pointing with her other hand at a flashy red Range Rover, which was parked next to Charles' car. One of the rear lights had been smashed.

'I'm sorry, *señora*,' said the garage man.

'Sorry! You say you're sorry! None of you in this village are sorry!'

By now Charles and Julie had arrived at their car and as he unlocked the door the woman turned to them. 'Look what they've done!' Her lips trembled.

'Ahem…' replied Charles politely, 'maybe another car bashed into your light while turning?'

'No!' she screamed. 'They do it on purpose! A few days ago they slashed a tyre with a knife. And now this! It's just too much! Bandits they are! All of them! They hate foreigners. You'd better watch out too!' The woman's sun-tanned face was a distorted grimace, making her look ugly.

As they drove off, Charles turned to Julie. 'That's the Range Rover of the English people who live in the house below that of the murdered German,' stated Charles while manoeuvring to avoid a crossing pedestrian. 'I've seen the man before; that must be his wife. Sarah mentioned her name. What was she called again? Lesley? Maybe they just ran over something pointed and found the tyre flat the next morning?' he ventured. He refused to believe that the village people would do anything like bashing in lights or slashing tyres. Once last year, when he got to his car, he noticed that he had forgotten to lock it. It had been standing like that for three days with a lot of bags inside, and nothing had been disturbed! On another occasion they had come back from Nerja after sunset and had been home for no more than fifteen minutes when a man he didn't know had knocked on the door to tell Charles that he had left the lights of his car on. 'You have to be careful *señor*,' the man had said. 'If you don't switch off your lights, *la batería* will be flat in the morning.' The village was a small world, and although Charles didn't know very many people, the villagers obviously knew all the foreigners.

The atmosphere had changed since people had begun to talk about the Curse but even so, why would they pick out that Range Rover for revenge? Was it the villagers' way of paying those English people back for looking down upon them, as Sarah had suggested? No, he thought, they probably just attract bad luck.

He turned towards Julie. 'She had a quarrel with her husband the other night...'

'Well...' remarked Julie, 'she's got a problem. Did you see her face?'

'Yes, it looked quite horrible.'

'That's not what I meant. You can see that she was beautiful once. Take off twenty years – or even ten – and she could have been a film star. But her beauty is fading; her face is full of wrinkles and lines. She's had too much sunshine and has probably been living too fast. And she is aware of it. Aging doesn't matter so much to men...'

'That's what you say!'

'...but for some women, and especially for women who have been beautiful, it's a tragedy. And she's probably on a diet too, trying desperately to keep her body young and attractive.'

'Feminine intuition eh,' commented Charles, swerving to avoid a dog that was running straight down the middle of the road.

But Julie didn't seem to hear him; she was absorbed in thoughts. 'It wouldn't surprise me if her husband were looking at younger women,' she mused. 'I can see the whole story: she trying to do what she can to keep him; he, fickle, like so many men – maybe even unfaithful. She must be very unhappy.'

'That eternal romantic streak in you,' observed Charles shaking his head. 'I wonder whether it will ever fade.'

7

They were driving slowly along the road to Torrox when a bright-red car came up from behind, going much too fast for the kind of tortuous road they were on. It caught up with them in a difficult section where the road had narrowed and was full of potholes. Even so the driver tried to overtake them, but had to pull back when a car appeared opposite. After the third or fourth hairpin bend he became very edgy. He advanced to within a yard and hooted his horn repeatedly.

'What an idiot!' exclaimed Charles.

Julie turned around to look at the man. 'He seems in a hurry,' she said. 'Why don't you let him pass?'

'Why should I?' Charles felt annoyed. 'He can jolly well wait. Who does he think he is?'

They came to a straight section of the road and the other car suddenly accelerated and began to overtake them. As it drew alongside Charles looked at the driver.

'But that's... that's that Frank-what's-his-name!' he exclaimed. 'The big boss of the project.'

'Are you sure? I thought he'd gone back to America.'

Charles had only seen his profile for a split second, but he was reasonably certain it was him.

The red car, which by now was already a hundred yards ahead, suddenly turned off into a dirt road.

'Isn't that the road we took to see that farmer's *cortijo*?' asked Julie.

'Yes. I wonder where that Frank is going.'

'Shall we follow him?'

'No. I've got a better idea. Further along there's a viewpoint from where you can see the whole area.'

When they got to the viewpoint there was no red car to be seen, maybe because only parts of the dirt road were visible from where they were standing. Or maybe the car had already reached its destination? Suddenly they saw a fast-moving red spot about half a mile away. Then it disappeared again, to reappear after a while in the driveway of a big property where it stopped next to a large swimming pool. The man had gone to visit the Italian with the most beautiful house this side of the Sierra Almijara!

8

Two hours later they were walking past the church in Nerja to a square lined with plane trees. On the side of the square where the old buildings had been preserved was a bar-restaurant called *El Jardin de Roberto*. Its façade was olive green, and its black wooden windows were framed in white. 'That looks tasteful,' remarked Julie.

'Yes,' agreed Charles, 'it looks very fashionable... and very expensive.'

Just as they were considering whether or not to go in, a young woman crossed the square. Charles recognised her instantly with her red hair and saucy look on her face. This time she wore a tight, long, dark-blue skirt; it was split in front, in turn revealing the inside of each leg up to the thigh as she walked towards them. She passed by without taking any notice of them, her head held high.

Charles turned to Julie. 'That's the girl I told you about. The one who boxed in my car in Frigiliana and nearly ran me over yesterday when I went shopping in a supermarket here. Let's follow her.'

The girl stepped straight into the *Jardin de Roberto* and as she entered the restaurant a waiter with black shiny hair gave her a flashy smile saying, 'Here comes *la guapa* – the pretty one.' Then, half in jest, half serious, he added, 'Give me a chance, just one,' but she stuck up her chin and passed him. She was about to sit down behind the bar when she noticed a man at one of the nearby tables, making a sign to her. He looked about forty and was well dressed and clean-shaven. She went over to his table, her high heels clicking on the tiles, and gave him a seductive smile.

'You didn't keep our date,' the man said. He tried to be amiable but one could see that he was vexed. She bent forward, put a finger on her lips and Charles and Julie, who were about to sit down at the next table, heard her say something like, 'Shht... be patient... there will be other times.'

Suddenly they noticed the silhouette of a man in a half-open door at the back, watching the scene. Then the door was flung open and the man stepped out yelling in an angry voice, 'Get over here! Now!' It was the Range Rover man! The girl turned around slowly and walked to the back of the room without the slightest hurry. As she got there he snatched her wrist and pulled her inside.

Seconds later she came out holding her hand against her left cheek, her face a mask of pain, and as she seated herself behind the bar, they noticed that her eyes were burning with anger.

Charles felt Julie touch his arm. 'I don't want to have lunch here,' she whispered. 'Let's go somewhere else.'

9

Every now and then – all too rarely for his liking – did Charles manage to convince Julie to go for a walk down the track that started behind the Guardia Civil post and led to the bottom of the canyon. She didn't really mind going down; it was climbing up afterwards she didn't fancy. Charles usually had to pull her along all the way up, but even so she would sit down every hundred yards or so to rest.

As they came out of their house they saw Agustina. Sam was there too with another dog the same size as him but light brown, and they were busy playing about and chasing each other.

'Going off to Nerja?' enquired Agustina.

'No. We're going down to the riverbed for a walk.'

'Why don't you take Sam and his friend with you? They're a real nuisance today, running around my legs all the time. I think a walk would do Sammy a lot of good; and it would keep him out of mischief in the village.'

'Do you think he'll want to come with us?' asked Julie.

'*Seguro*! He knows you quite well and likes you a lot.' A look of tenderness came into Agustina's eyes.

Julie still seemed hesitant. 'What if we lose him?'

'You won't; he'll wait for you. He really is a good boy. Shall I tell you a story?' And without waiting for a "yes" she began. 'Some weeks ago I went to wash Sam in the waterfall a few miles from Nerja – he loves the waterfall because he can splash in the pool below to his heart's content. On the way back I stopped at the petrol station in Nerja to fill up; Sam was lying asleep in the back of the car, I had left the window open to give him some air, and when I started off again I forgot to check whether he was still there because I was thinking of all the things I still had to do. It was only when I parked the car in Frigiliana and wanted to let Sam out that I discovered he'd gone. I rushed back to the petrol station in Nerja in a panic and there he was, a bit anxious maybe, but waiting and looking out for my car. When I appeared he was so overjoyed that he jumped up and nearly knocked me over.'

'What a clever dog you are Sammy,' said Julie, patting him on the head while Agustina beamed with pride.

'All right then,' agreed Charles. 'If you're sure the dogs will not run away we'll be delighted to take them.'

'Wait,' said Agustina. 'I'll tell Sam to behave.'

'Do you think he'll understand?'

'Of course! He always does what I tell him.' And she bent over and whispered something into the dog's ear. Sam immediately went towards Julie and Charles and looked at them from under his fringe of black hair, wagging his tail. He seemed innocence personified, and they all set off.

They had only just begun the descent when Sam suddenly ran down the slope, followed by his friend.

'Sam!' called Charles as the dogs rushed at top speed towards the edge of the canyon. 'Sam! Stop!'

'They're going to fall off the cliff!' screamed Julie, but inches before the edge the dogs turned a sharp left and carried on racing further down the track into the riverbed.

A sigh of relief escaped from Charles' lips. 'We'll just have to go down and hope for the best,' he said.

As they began the descent, the world changed. The noise that accompanies people – the sound of engines and the music coming out of houses and bars – gradually faded. By the time they reached the riverbed, the white houses of the village, still just visible high above them at the edge of the steep cliff, seemed small – almost insignificant. The modern world was receding rapidly and the moment they had rounded the first bend of the canyon, the village and the man-made noises that came from it had disappeared altogether.

Most of the riverbed was dry, making it easy to walk; only in the very middle was there a foot or two of water. As they followed the canyon winding its way through the mountain range, they could only see as far as the next bend. In places the bottom was no wider than ten yards and the view was limited to the steep slopes on both sides and the bright-blue sky above. They were in a world wholly different from the one they had left behind – a world of buzzing insects, humming bees, and birds singing their hearts out. Scents changed too; as they walked along, the scent of herbs, of rosemary and thyme grew more intense.

The sides of the gorge were covered in small bushes and dark-green pine trees, but rocks showed up here and there in grey and ochre patches. 'Look there!' exclaimed Julie, pointing at some miniature flowers in between the rocks. 'Aren't these beautiful?' You hardly noticed the flowers unless you looked carefully, but they were everywhere, tiny coloured specks, white, yellow, mauve, pink and blue, and very fragrant. This was nature without the interference of man where nothing was pre-arranged; where shrubs and flowers grew wherever the seeds happened to fall; where pines and Mediterranean palms belonged as much as the birds and bees.

As they advanced slowly, the crunching noise of their feet on the loose gravel and white pebbles seemed loud, almost irreverent. They saw a lizard hurrying away from them and began to walk cautiously so as not to disturb any small creatures. 'How peaceful the world is,' remarked Julie smiling happily.

They came to a clump of eucalyptus trees. The trunks had been carved with names, inscriptions and hearts. Some were recent and clear: Marcos loves Laura, or, Manuela and Sergio surrounded by a heart. But other pledges of eternal love had become almost illegible with age. Carved many years ago, at a time when the ones who had written these words of love had been young, they had faded, maybe like their love.

Some boulders were strewn through the river nearby the eucalyptus trees and the water looked inviting in the hot afternoon. 'I'm going to sit here for a while,' decided Julie.

'But the dogs?' objected Charles. There was still no sign of them.

'Oh, they'll come back,' she replied without the slightest concern while taking off her sandals. Then she rolled up her trousers and dipped her feet in the cool water with an expression of pure bliss on her face. Charles sighed and resigned himself to walking on alone.

Beyond the next bend there was a well-trodden path running alongside an open irrigation channel through which water streamed. As Charles stepped on to the concrete edge of the channel a frightened frog jumped off and plunged into the water with a great splash, leaving extending rings of ripples where it had disappeared. Charles carried on and came to a narrow waterfall, which cascaded down almost vertically like a sparkling moving curtain and ended up in the irrigation channel, filling it to overflow. Most of the waterfall was hidden from sight by a dense green growth of bushes and low trees, but here and there the water was visible.

Charles continued past the thundering noise to the next bend where the gorge widened and the slopes were less steep. He noticed several caves up in the cliffs. What erosion can do! he marvelled. It had maybe taken millions of years, but the water seeping through the rocks had eventually dissolved the limestone underneath and dug out those caves. They would make ideal hiding places, he thought, and began climbing to have a closer look.

He picked his way carefully among loose stones and prickly vegetation, crawling around several big boulders that had broken off the cliffs and lay in precarious equilibrium on the slopes. As he looked back the view was breathtaking. The riverbed stretched below him, the pebbles and whitish stones making it seem like a bright path amongst the dark-green pine trees that lined it. Higher up, the steep rocky slopes were only sparsely covered by bushes, and the contours of the canyon stood out sharply against the cloudless sky.

Everything was quiet except for the bubbling of the water below and for the shrill, repeated note a bird made in one of the bushes above. Then Charles heard a sound. Below, from behind a bend in the riverbed, the two dogs came into view: Sam was chasing his friend in and out of the river. The dogs were jumping and splashing, stopping every now and then to shake the water from their coats; they behaved like two naughty boys just let out of school.

'Sam!' called Charles. 'Come here!'

Sam at once came running up the slope, stopped within a foot and began to shake himself vigorously, wetting Charles' trousers completely.

'You pig!' yelled Charles. 'I'll get you!'

But Sam wasn't going to let himself be caught. He rushed further up the slope as if he had guessed Charles' intentions, stopped and turned as if to say, 'Well, come on then and get me.' Suddenly he stuck his nose up in the air and disappeared into one of the caves.

'Hey Sam, come back!' ordered Charles, but the dog didn't come back. I hope he hasn't fallen into a hole, he worried. If anything happened to him Agustina would never forgive me. There was nothing to do but climb up after Sam. With a great effort Charles finally reached the opening of the cave, and when his eyes had got accustomed to the darkness he noticed the dog, digging away at something.

'What's that Sam?' he asked stepping forward. 'What have you found?' He cleared away some loose twigs and there, to his surprise, lay a dozen long-necked wine bottles.

How strange, he thought, picking up a few bottles. They were full, and he took them to the entrance to have a look at them in the daylight: they were made of green glass and the labels clearly stated that they contained top-quality white wines from Rhine and Mosel!

When Charles returned inside he noticed that Sam was sniffing around in a corner of the cave. Then the dog picked up something and ran outside where he stopped, turning to see if Charles followed him. He stood there, a blue woollen piece of clothing hanging from his jaws, his front paws flat on the ground and his back end sticking up, clearly indicating that he wanted to play.

'What have you got there?' Charles called out, moving toward the dog but Sam immediately ran higher up the slope and then waited in anticipation, wagging his tail.

'Sam, come down and give it to me!' commanded Charles, but the dog seemed unwilling to let go of his new plaything and ran higher up the slope.

Charles shouted a rude word and went after him. He had got close to Sam when he noticed that he had stepped onto a clear-cut path that started from there. He hadn't seen it until he had literally put his feet upon it; someone had hidden the approach carefully. It seemed to run towards the hilltop and he stood there, wondering why there was a path so high up and pondering whether he should follow it, when the dog suddenly shot past him, the blue piece of clothing still dangling from his jaws, and rushed down the slope toward the riverbed.

Just then Charles heard a long drawn-out call, 'Owee... owee...' The sound reverberated off the cliff sides, echoing back and forth: it was Julie calling from behind the bend; she was probably wondering where he was. He slid down the slope and finally got back to where Julie was sitting on a nice flat rock, her feet still dangling in the water.

'Where have you been? I was getting worried.'

'Imagine what I found in a cave?' said Charles, bubbling with excitement. 'A dozen bottles of wine!' And he explained how Sam had made the discovery. 'I wonder how those bottles got there.'

'Maybe some sect is holding wine orgies in that cave?' ventured Julie jokingly. 'The world is full of all sorts of cranky people. Think of Howard!' She smiled at her suggestion.

Charles shrugged his shoulders. 'This wasn't just ordinary wine. It was top-quality German white wine.'

'Does that make a difference?'

'Well... yes... there is probably only one person liable to have had a cellar full of expensive German wines around here, and that was Herr Meier.'

'You don't mean to say that he went down to that cave to drink his wine. That's ridiculous.'

'No. It obviously wasn't him bringing the bottles down. Someone else must have done so. But then... they were stolen!'

'Another mystery,' sighed Julie.

The part of the canyon where they were sitting, which had been in the full sun only an hour ago, was by now in the shade and it was getting chilly. 'Where are the dogs?' asked Julie.

Just at that moment the two dogs came trailing towards them. Sam, who was still carrying the dark-blue piece of clothing in his jaws, went towards Julie and deposited it in front of her feet as if he wanted to make her an offering. She picked it up and shook it out. 'It's a man's sweater!' she exclaimed, surprised. 'Where does this come from?'

'From the cave where I found the bottles. I suppose our wine sampler must have forgotten it there.'

The two dogs were lying down by now, their tongues hanging out of their mouths; they looked exhausted. 'I think they've had enough,' said Charles. 'Let's go home.' And this time Sam played no more pranks but followed them meekly all the way up.

10

'Shouldn't Edward be back by now?' asked Charles the next morning. 'And come to think of it, we haven't seen Charlotte since her birthday, have we?'

'True enough. I wonder what's happened. It's troubling. Let's go and see her.'

'Do you think we ought to?' Charles hesitated. 'Maybe Edward is already back and celebrating his return in Charlotte's new love nest. What if we find them in bed?'

Julie cut him short. 'You don't seem to know anything about women! If he had arrived, Charlotte would have wasted no time in showing him off.'

They went to her house and found the front door closed but not locked.

'Charlotte!' Julie called out as they went inside the dark house. 'Are you there?'

There was no answer and she called again. Presently they heard sounds upstairs and then steps coming down slowly.

'See, I told you,' whispered Charles. 'We shouldn't have come. They *were* in bed.'

Finally Charlotte appeared, looking dishevelled; her hair was an untidy tangle and her eyes were red and swollen.

'Charlotte!' exclaimed Julie. 'What's happened? You look wretched.'

'He's written.' Her voice was almost inaudible. 'He's not coming back.'

'It's not true... but why?'

'He says his exhibition didn't go well... he didn't have enough money to organise it... it's all my fault...'

'Maybe it's all a lie,' cut in Charles.

'Why should he lie? He loves me. And now we'll never see each other again. I no longer know what to do...'

Julie stepped forward and put her arms around Charlotte. 'Have you eaten anything?' she asked.

'I haven't eaten or slept since I received that letter.'

'When was that?'

'Yesterday morning.'

'Come with us,' Julie said resolutely. 'I'll cook you something nice. I'm not going to let you sit here alone, pining away in the dark.'

11

'Strange how the houses all interlock here,' remarked Julie as she stood on the terrace of Sarah's and Michael's house later in the afternoon.

'You have no idea,' replied Michael. 'It took us quite a time to figure out who lived left and right of us, and especially below us. The houses in the old part of Frigiliana are like an intricate puzzle. But Fernando's house tops it all – you know... the man who found the murdered German.'

'In fact,' cut in Sarah, 'we are neighbours. Our drawing room is situated above his stables.'

'How can that be?' objected Julie. 'Isn't the entrance to his house – the door opening with the blanket pinned over it – on the little square around the corner? That's several houses away from here.'

'You can best describe his house as a long, irregular tunnel of rooms running below several other houses. And his stables are at the end of that tunnel, right below our drawing room.' Michael grinned. 'You want to see them? If you lean out from our terrace you look straight into them.'

'But how does he get his horse and mule in there?' Charles wanted to know.

'He leaves his mule out in a shelter in the *campo*, but his horse... yes... he puts it in there,' affirmed Michael.

'You don't mean to say that he walks the horse every day through all his rooms, including his own bedroom?' Charles found this hard to believe.

164

'He does. And I don't think he minds. He adores his horse. It wouldn't surprise me if they slept together.' Michael laughed out loud.

'Michael!' Sarah was shocked. 'Don't say such things.'

'I can understand that he likes his horse, but the flies that come with it!' Michael shuddered. 'They're all over the place! Our house is always full of them.'

'Yes, those flies… they are terrible.' Sarah nodded her delicate head in agreement.

'Does he have any friends?' asked Charles. 'I've heard that he's quite a lonely man.'

'He does have a few friends,' replied Michael. 'I often see him in the bar below with some other men.'

'What does he do for a living?'

'He has his own plot of land where he grows food; he also does odd jobs for people like cutting wood or transporting things; and sometimes he takes tourists for a ride on his horse.' Michael took a sip from his tea. 'But let me continue. His best friend is that fellow who always tries to get money out of tourists – and then he goes straight to the nearest bar and wastes it all on drinks. What's his name again?'

'Pépé,' replied Sarah. She turned to Julie. 'You may not know him.'

'Oh but we do. He often hangs around in our street, and he's managed to get money out of Charles too. For a sandwich, wasn't it?' Julie looked at Charles with an ironic smile.

'Well… many men over here drink,' intervened Michael diplomatically. 'But the worst, by far, is Fernando.'

'He probably has his reasons, darling,' interrupted Sarah. 'We mustn't judge other people. And he is never nasty when he's drunk. Still, it's a shame… such a nice man.' She had looked sad before, but when she said that he was a nice man her eyes, which were of the palest blue, brightened up and she smiled. She didn't often smile because her two front teeth were quite big and she was self-conscious about it. She once told Julie that it made her look like a rabbit. Charles thought that, at moments like these, her slightly bunny-like smile gave a particular attraction to what would otherwise have been a too angelic face.

'But what a handful he can be when he is drunk,' continued Michael. 'And that's all too often.'

'Yes but he sometimes looks so helpless that you'd do anything for him.' Sarah's eyes filled with compassion.

'Helpless, yes... but he's quite a character.' Michael turned to his visitors. 'Let me tell you a story. Last year we took him to the hospital in Vélez-Málaga where he had to go for a small operation. As it happened we had to stop on the way to buy something at the chemist in Torre del Mar. When we parked the van Fernando was fast asleep in the back, completely drunk, so imagine our surprise when we returned: he had gone... disappeared!'

'Yes, we had to hunt all over the place,' said Sarah. 'Finally we found him in a bar!'

Michael carried on. 'We left him at the hospital where they operated on him and kept him under observation for a few days. When we visited him later, we found him lying in a large communal room. A doctor who was checking his condition asked us whether we were related to him. We said we weren't but that we were good friends.

'"Then you must watch over him!" said the doctor in a stern voice. "I have forbidden him to drink ever again. His liver is in a terrible state and if he doesn't stop he'll become a permanent invalid."

'Just at that moment the doctor was called away for an emergency and we asked Fernando how he felt.

'"Bad," he said. "I need to smoke a cigarette. You couldn't lend me a bit of money, could you?"

'I dug into my pocket and came up with a five hundred-peseta coin.

'"Thank you," he said, snatching the coin from my hand. And he hopped out of bed and disappeared through the door before I even had time to react!

'When we rushed to the door and looked down the corridor, he was nowhere to be seen. I remember Sarah saying, "There's a cafeteria on the ground floor. He'll be in there," but he was not in the cafeteria and she began to worry, "We'll never find him. The doctor is going to be furious."

'But I had an idea where he might be. I had noticed a couple of bars in the street not far from the entrance of the hospital and sure enough, we found him in one of these, standing against the counter in his pyjamas, gulping down his third or fourth drink. The five hundred pesetas were gone. We led him back to the hospital, and he let himself be put into bed without any fuss and lay down with a large, contented smile on his face. Minutes later the doctor reappeared. "Let's see... where were we? Ah, yes," and he bent down over his patient. Then we saw his nose twitch and he stared at Fernando's beaming face in disbelief. "It's not possible!" he exclaimed. He looked shocked. "My God! He's drunk!'"

12

Charles was reading a newspaper on the terrace the next morning when Julie came up.

'Guess who I saw when I went to the grocer's,' she said.

'How would I know? It could have been anyone from the village.'

'He's not living in the village. He was passing by in his car.'

'The American project leader?'

'You're close. But the man I saw would not be seen dead in an ordinary car. His car would be a *most magnificent one.*'

'That rich Italian, Mister *Magnifico*! Was his wife with him this time?'

'No. But he had two men with him. Not the sort of people you usually see around here. How shall I describe the impression they made? Well... Mister *Magnifico* looked like a Mafiosi boss accompanied by his two heavies.'

'Maybe they were on their way to intimidate the shopkeepers and grocers in the village,' joked Charles. 'Isn't that what the Mafia does?'

Julie shrugged her shoulders. 'Let me continue. I also saw the Swiss woman from the project and her French partner.'

'I wonder what's going on? Just recently the American project leader went to see that rich Italian and now Mister *Magnifico* and the project people are all converging on the village. I wonder what they're up to?'

'I have found out why they're all here. The village Council is meeting tonight to discuss the project.'

'I see... Now that Meier has been eliminated, all the project people need is a yes from the Council. So they have come out in strength to put pressure on the members of the Council. I have a feeling that a lot of money will be dangled in front of their eyes. That sounds like bad news for the village.'

'I'm afraid so,' sighed Julie.

13

When Charles came out of their house the next day he found Agustina busily arranging the front of her shop.

'You're making everything look very attractive,' he commented. 'What's happening?'

'It's *Semana Santa* next week, didn't you know?'

'I completely forgot it's going to be Holy Week. I tend to lose all notion of time on holiday.'

'And you know what? I'm going to drive to Morocco afterwards to buy a load of new goods.'

'Are you going to close the shop then?' asked Charles, surprised.

'Of course not! A friend from Nerja will keep the shop for me.'

'I can't imagine the shop without you, Agustina.'

'Oh, but you'll like her. She's really nice. She is English but don't worry, she speaks Spanish very well.'

Charles laughed. 'I do speak English, you know. And I don't mind English girls at all. But it won't be easy getting used to another person in your shop. What's her name?'

'Peggy. And you had better get used to her because she'll carry on working with me afterwards.'

'How long are you going to stay in Morocco?'

'It depends on what I find. Maybe a week, maybe longer.'

'We may be gone if you stay away a long time.'

'Oh, but you'll come back next year.'

'*Ojalá*,' said Charles, stepping aside to make room for Julie who was just coming out of the house carrying a paperback in her hand. Charles recognised it as the one she had been absorbed in ever since she had found it in a second-hand bookshop in Nerja.

'Let me have a look at your face,' she said to Agustina.

'Why Julia? Is anything wrong with it?'

'No, no. I just want to practice. I'm learning to analyse faces. Look, I've found a very interesting book.' She held it up. 'It teaches how to infer someone's personality from his or her features. I can even tell whether you're going to be successful in business or not.'

Agustina seemed very interested. 'Tell me then what you can read in my face,' she said, coming forward and smiling as if she were posing for a photograph.

'Let me see... your face is more round than oval.' Julie consulted her book. 'Now, that would indicate that you like action... but also that you judge rapidly, are impatient to finish what you set out to do and are often careless. Your precipitation and lack of preparation may get you into trouble. And you're also outspoken and tend to dominate.'

'Is that me?' Agustina sounded disappointed.

'Well, anyway, that's what the book says, but wait! This is just according to the general shape. Everything is modified by the other features. Your mouth, for instance, is... well... large, and your lips are full, even thick.' She flipped through the pages. 'This shows that you are expansive, sensitive and affectionate.' She looked up. 'Does that sound right? You like life but don't worry about tomorrow. Now... your eyebrows are high and rounded... which means that you're a superior businesswoman and an efficient organiser. You're altogether very astute, and always come out the winner in any transaction.'

'I like that much better!' exclaimed Agustina.

Just then Charlotte came out of her house higher up the street, and seeing the others stand in front of the shop she drew nearer. She looked rather dispirited, but after they had said hello the others took no further notice of her. Agustina turned again to Julie. 'Does your book say anything about love? Can you read that in the face too?'

'Oh yes! Let me see... your face shows that your nature is altogether romantic. You are sensual and given to impulsive passion. And you love to move around and meet people. A person with your features enjoys being surrounded by admirers.'

Charles thought of Salvador, her present companion. 'Poor Salvador,' he joked, 'always finding you surrounded by a court.'

Agustina shot him one of her radiant smiles. 'He should count himself lucky to have me.'

'Can you analyse me too?' interrupted Charlotte, who was becoming interested.

'I will,' agreed Julie, 'but let me first finish with Agustina. You're a seducer,' she continued. 'You have a way of pleasing but you highly value your own independence. You seem to be naïve, but you know very well what you want and are capable of turning any situation to your advantage.'

'That's quite natural,' commented Agustina. 'We women have had to survive for so many centuries in a male-dominated society here in Spain, that we've had to develop our own indirect ways of achieving our goals.'

At that moment two customers went into the shop and Agustina followed them inside.

'How do you know all that?' asked Charlotte who had brightened up somewhat.

Julie explained about the book she had found.

'Can you tell the future too?'

'That's more difficult,' replied Julie evasively.

'But I want to know what's going to happen to me,' insisted Charlotte. 'I want to be lucky in love.' Her eyes seemed to say: please don't disappoint me; I have suffered enough already.

'But last year you told me you wanted to become famous!'

'Yes... and I want to be rich too.'

'Love, fame and money! Which one do you value most?'

Charlotte hesitated. 'I don't know. I want all three.'

'Well... that's a lot. Let me see.' Julie looked at Charlotte with deep interest. 'Your face has some really outstanding features. Most striking is your large domed forehead.'

'What does that indicate? Is it good or bad for me?'

'Wait... it shows that you're certainly not weak. It indicates a strong character and a sense of adventure – an ability to make adjustments in life.'

'So you believe that I shall be able to get over this?' Suddenly tears filled her eyes and her lower lip trembled. 'I don't know. I've received another letter.'

'What does it say?'

'It confirms what the first letter said.'

'What do you mean by: it confirms?' asked Charles.

'It's a photocopy of the first letter.'

Julie couldn't believe her ears. 'Are you saying that Edward sent you a photocopy of his previous letter? I've never heard anything more ludicrous in my life! What's the use of that?'

'It probably serves a well-determined purpose,' hinted Charles. 'He wanted to make sure that you got his message in case the original letter didn't reach you. It corroborates what I thought from the beginning. How you ever believed his story – that something had gone wrong with his credit card so that he was unable to draw any money – is beyond me! He has just abused you. Forget him Charlotte.'

Charlotte hid her face in her hands. 'But he looked so honest.'

'He isn't. He's a liar and a worthless profiteer!'

Charlotte burst out in tears. Then they heard her whisper, 'I don't want to be alone.'

'But you're not alone,' objected Julie. 'There is Sven.'

'Sven?' She sounded as if she had never considered such a thing.

'Why not? I find him quite handsome. I'm sure you would get on well. He likes you.'

'More than that,' corrected Charles. 'He worships you. I think you should marry Sven.'

'You're just laughing at me,' said Charlotte looking cross. 'Nobody loves me.' And she turned around and went back to her house, her shoulders drooping.

Just then Sarah passed along the street further down.

'Have you heard the news?' she called out. She seemed very excited.

'Which news?'

'About the meeting of the village Council last night.'

'No. Has the project been accepted?'

'Not at all! There's a faction within the ruling party that is led by Sebastian. It seems that he kept delaying the vote by proposing amendments and asking all sorts of clarifications about details. By midnight the Council gave up. The voting has been adjourned for a fortnight!'

'How extraordinary!' exclaimed Julie. 'He will go down in the history of Frigiliana as Sebastian the incorruptible.'

'I do hope he won't have to pay for his bravery.' Charles looked worried. 'He might well become the next one to be eliminated.'

14

At first Charles had been surprised to find out how little Konrad Meier's death seemed to have affected the people here; he might as well have been killed in Malaga or Madrid for all it mattered, but finally he understood: Meier was not one of the villagers; he was a foreigner; he didn't belong to their world. They had talked about the murder for a couple of days because it had taken place in their village, but it was altogether of little concern to them. They were much more interested in the many small events that happened to other people here than in the murder of a foreigner they had hardly known.

Matters had changed dramatically though since they had begun to talk about the Curse. Few men now went out after sunset and people locked their doors early. Fear seemed to hang in the streets at night – fear of the unknown; fear of the Curse.

Charles had been trying to find out more about the treasure but had drawn a blank. People became silent or just turned away if he brought up the subject, and the more he tried, the more he had the impression that they avoided him – even that he was no longer welcome.

On Friday he had been to the village library to borrow a *Historia de Andalucia*, and also a history of Frigiliana, hoping to learn something about the Treasure of the Moors. So far he hadn't felt in the mood to start reading though. Then, on Sunday, the moment had come to open the books.

It was surprising how fast the weather changed in April. A week ago the wind had been blowing and it had been raining, but in the last few days the sun had been shining and by Sunday it was so hot that people just wanted to sit in the shade. Charles decided that this was the time for a quiet read, and after lunch he settled down with a drink in the front room near the balcony and began to flip through the books.

They repeated what he already knew from the ceramic plaques in the upper part of the old village: in 1492 Boabdil, the last Moorish ruler, surrendered Granada to the Catholic Kings without a fight on condition that those who chose to stay would be allowed to keep their traditions and way of life. However, shortly after Boabdil had left for Morocco with most of his people, the Christians began to break their promises. An ever-growing pressure was exerted on those Moors who had remained behind, and within years they became the target of the Inquisition. When finally, after decades of unfair treatment and injustice, an edict was published banning the use of Arabic, Arab names, customs, dress and music, the Moors rebelled.

One of the last great battles between the Spanish army and the rebels took place in Frigiliana in June 1569. The Moors had dug themselves in on the hilltop above the village and resisted desperately, even hurling rocks at the assailants. When all was lost some Moorish women, who had fought like men, threw themselves down from the hilltop with their children, preferring to die rather than fall into the hands of the Christians. Two thousand Moors and three hundred Christians perished in the battle, and the three thousand surviving Moors were marched off into slavery. Many amongst these were badly wounded and died on the road. It was a gruesome, pitiless tale and Charles could well believe that some Christians had a bad conscience about it to this day. But nowhere was there any mention of a treasure, and less even of a Curse.

He continued reading about the rebellion in other parts of Andalusia before the final stand in Frigiliana. The worst of it had taken place in the Alpujarras, the mountainous region south of Granada and the Sierra Nevada. Aben Humeya, a youngster, had been crowned King of the Moriscos there under an olive tree, but he was killed by a traitor ten months later and his treasure, known as 'the golden fleece of the Alpujarras', had never been found.

At last, thought Charles, a treasure! It was said to have been hidden in a cave in the Alpujarras some sixty miles away from here but who knows, maybe it had ended up on the hill in Frigiliana?

15

Just then Charles heard the sound of Flamenco music coming through the open balcony door. Probably a Flamenco festival on TV, he thought going to the balcony, but as he looked out he noticed that the music came from higher up in the street where an older man was sitting on a chair playing the guitar while another one was singing. Several people were standing or sitting around them. It looked like an after-lunch meeting outside one of the houses: bottles of wine and glasses had been brought out and the people were fully enjoying themselves. A woman and a tanned, tawny man, both well in their fifties, were dancing, their feet following the rhythmical melody. She was holding up her skirt with one hand while her other arm was moving above her head like an outstretched snake; he held both arms up in the air. Their movements were amazingly swift for their age.

The singer's wailing voice seemed to convey the age-old curses of Andalusia: the heat – too heavy; the faith – too absolute; the heart – too burning; the love – too fiery; the passion – too extreme; the jealousy and hatred – too unforgiving. It expressed so well the history of this land, the massacre of the Moors, the fanaticism and intolerance. The Spanish had destroyed the local Moorish culture and had imported people from other parts of the country to dilute the Moorish blood but even so, Andalusia had never become like the rest of Spain; it had remained a world apart.

And yet change was in the air, a change so radical that it could well leave Andalusia without a soul. Those who were playing, singing and dancing out in the street were older people. A few young children, girls in their frilly Sunday dresses, were trying to imitate the dancers but children from ten upwards seemed to be missing. They were attracted, not by traditional Flamenco music but by pop music. Young people preferred to go to the discos whose blaring music could be heard at night in all the towns along the coast. Even the *barrio nuevo* in Frigiliana had its own disco bar. How long before Flamenco became folklore, to be performed no longer spontaneously by village people but solely for the benefit of tourists in a few specialised places?

16

Charles and Julie were sitting on a terrace at the Balcón de Europa in Nerja when he suddenly exclaimed, 'Look over there! That's the English couple from Frigiliana… you know, the people with the Range Rover who've got that restaurant here in Nerja. What's their name again? Barley or something?'

'Don't ask me,' replied Julie. 'You know what I'm like with names. I just think of them as the R.R. people. It seems to suit them too.'

The English couple were occupying a table not very far away. They weren't speaking much. She was smoking a cigarette and having a cup of coffee, while he was reclining in his chair, a large glass of beer in his hand. In the full sunshine their age difference was obvious.

'I don't think he loves her,' remarked Julie. 'It wouldn't surprise me if he'd married her for her money.'

'How you know that sort of thing is beyond me.'

'Well, just look at their faces.'

Charles thought that she looked tired and tense, as if something was troubling her. If so, it didn't seem to affect him. He was clean-shaven, had wavy dark-brown hair down to his neck, and a self-satisfied smirk on his face, but this didn't tell Charles anything about their relationship. He turned to Julie. 'I don't see how you can deduce what they do or don't feel from their faces.'

Julie shrugged her shoulders, gave the R.R. people a scrutinising look, dug into her handbag and brought out the face-features paperback.

'Don't tell me that you're carrying this around with you everywhere!'

'Why shouldn't I? Don't you see how interesting it is? Even you are beginning to ask me to analyse faces.' And without further ado she began to flip through the pages.

'Right,' she said. 'His face is very easy. He's the square-faced type. Such people are generally envious of the wealth of others and seek to further their own advantage. That man wants money, and he wants to show others that he has got it; he wants to splash it out. You can see that he has a taste for the good things of life and probably a large sexual appetite too. But he has no delicacy of feelings or tenderness of heart. He's the dominating male, not to be opposed.'

'If he is like you describe him, he must be an awful man. And in that case I fail to understand what she can possibly see in him.'

'Well… some women like to be dominated. She may be hooked on him – physically I mean; he's the strong macho type. But he has his weak points:

these types are ruled by their senses and given to violent passions, which make them reckless.'

'When I saw him in his car in Frigiliana he didn't appear very pleasant to me, and the other day in the restaurant he slapped that red-haired girl. Still, your description of him sounds pretty ghastly. And what do you make of her face?'

Julie studied the woman for some time with keen interest. Her hair was dyed fair, probably because it had started turning grey; her oval-shaped face was still beautiful but was beginning to be disfigured by many small wrinkles, especially around the eyes and above the upper lip; and her mouth, which must have been charming once, now had a downward turn, indicating deep dissatisfaction.

'She really has quite a lot in common with her husband,' said Julie after a while. 'Like him she thinks nothing of those she considers her inferiors; she despises them. She is self-centred and wilful, although less blunt than he is; she is probably a schemer. But there's a basic weakness in her: she is extremely susceptible and in great need of affection and admiration.' She consulted her book. 'And... yes... she is unstable; I would say that she might be given to loss of self-control and outbursts of anger. Now... let me see... what else?' Julie looked again at the woman. 'It's clear that she wants money and status. In this the two must get on very well as a couple. And the outward signs of riches mean a lot to her too. Just look at the rings she is wearing, and the pearl necklace.'

The woman had been fiddling with her gold cigarette lighter, picking it up from the table and next putting it back, while every now and then she looked at the man as if she wanted to talk about something but couldn't bring herself to speak. The man didn't even notice and kept looking at what was going on around him without much interest. Just then a stunningly pretty girl walked by. Everything about her was conceived to attract: her perfectly tanned slim legs; her tight, dazzlingly white shorts drawing attention to her full buttocks as they moved; her faded top accentuating her voluptuous breasts, and her light-brown hair that moved slightly up and down with every step. The man's face, which had been sullen, abruptly brightened and his eyes followed the girl's every movement as her shapely figure passed by.

'Look,' whispered Julie, 'look how it upsets the R.R. woman.'

The woman's face had contracted. Suddenly she turned towards the man and as her hand shot forward to touch his arm, she knocked her lighter off the table. She bent down with a brusque movement to pick it up and as she straightened herself, her necklace caught on the arm of the white plastic chair on which she was sitting and snapped, scattering the pearls in all directions.

'My pearls!' she shrieked, jumping up so abruptly that she overturned the table. Her coffee cup crashed onto the terrace and broke to pieces but she had no eye for that. She was running about wildly, picking up pearls wherever she saw them and upsetting people at the tables around. A waiter came rushing out of the café and bent down to help her but she yelled at him, 'Keep your hands off my pearls! Don't you dare touch them!'

When there were no more pearls to be seen, she sat down and began to count them, her hands trembling. The waiter who, after having been ticked off, had been standing back with an offended expression on his face, now stepped forward to put the table on its legs again and clean up the broken cup, but he made no comment. After a while the English woman calmed down and the excitement subsided. She sat there, staring straight in front of herself as if lost in thought.

'Good heavens,' commented Charles. 'What a show! It seems to confirm what you deduced from her face. Incredible.'

'Yes, but there's much more. There is a dark side to her character. She may be the sort that can't forget or forgive those who have opposed or offended her, and wants revenge for the injustices done to her. She will defend tooth and nail what she considers hers – and that includes possessions and people. She can't stand being opposed in what are, to her, vital matters.'

'A nasty bit of goods altogether,' summarised Charles.

'And ageing hasn't helped. It hasn't softened her character as it often does in people. In her case it is more likely to have brought out her worst traits.'

'Why do you think so?'

'That's obvious, isn't it? Because she's losing her beauty! For women that's the really important thing: their beauty, their appearance. They want to be attractive.' Julie turned to Charles. 'And that's all because of *you*, men.'

'Why do you look at me when you say, "You, men?" I have nothing to do with that!'

'Oh yes you have. You're just the same. If a pretty young woman passes by you look at her.'

'What's wrong with that? I can't close my eyes every time a pretty woman passes by, can I?'

'No, but what's so unfair is that women can be intelligent, well educated or good-hearted, but if they're not pretty, men just won't fall for them. That's why beauty is the first thing they're interested in. If only men looked more at their inner value than at their appearance, women would be so much happier.'

Charles laughed. 'That may be true, but it's difficult to look at the inner value of a woman passing by – unless, of course, one reads faces like you do.'

The couple on the other terrace had got up by now. He wore blue jeans with a light-brown belt that cut tightly into his belly, and a navy-blue tee shirt with short sleeves, showing his tanned, muscular arms. He was a strongly built man with a heavy chin, still looking young but already showing signs of becoming corpulent.

'Another five years and he'll be fat,' remarked Julie. 'Probably too much beer, too much food and not enough exercise.'

The man had a self-assured, slow way of walking with his shoulders pulled back and his head held high so that his broad chest stood out. She was a full head smaller and walked behind him, elegantly dressed in a white silk blouse and salmon-coloured cotton trousers, a brown leather bag slung over her shoulder.

'Well,' said Julie as she observed them walking away, 'it's clear that he's the master. Do you remember what I told you when we saw her in the parking lot in Frigiliana? I'm certain now. She is a very unhappy woman. She's hooked on him and is frightened that he might go off with someone else. Just look at him: he thinks himself irresistible. I wouldn't trust him for a minute with any young, attractive girl.'

'Well, you may be right but then, what do we really know about them?' commented Charles getting up. 'Come on, it's time to return to Frigiliana.'

17

When Julie went up to Charlotte's house that afternoon to see how she was, she found Sven sitting on a chair, looking dispirited. Charlotte came out of the small room which was her workshop and the first thing she blurted out, even before Julie had time to say hello, was, 'I'm going to Australia.'

'But Charlotte,' protested Julie, 'that's… that's madness. Why?'

'I want to find out exactly what's happened since Edward left. Something must have happened. Maybe a woman he knew before in Australia is trying to win him back? Or maybe he is worrying about not having enough money to marry me and doesn't want to admit it?'

'You aren't really thinking of going to Australia?'

'I'm going. Nothing will stop me. If I don't go, some rich woman will catch him and I'll lose him for ever.' She straightened herself, as if she had decided to fight it out. 'I know how to win him back. He thinks I'm poor, but I'm not, you see.' She stared at Julie with a self-important look in her eyes. 'I'm going to come into a lot of money. And then I'll marry him and offer him half of my money so that he can continue his art.'

Julie shook her head and turned, ready to leave. Sven who had remained mute throughout the whole conversation got up too and left with her.

'How are you Sven?' asked Julie when they were out in the street. 'What are you going to do?'

'If she goes to Australia,' he said, his voice almost inaudible, 'I'll return to Sweden. There'll be nothing left for me to do here.' And he walked slowly down Calle El Darra, his back bent as if he were carrying the disillusion of a broken life on his shoulders.

18

It was about six when Charles and Julie descended into the river canyon behind the Guardia Civil post. It had been a particularly hot day and only now did the heat subside somewhat. The sun had already moved far to the west and part of the riverbed was in the shade.

Suddenly they heard the bleating of goats and the sound of bells, a metallic ringing echoing between the walls of the gorge: a goatherd appeared above them on the eastern slope of the canyon, followed by maybe a hundred goats. The low bushes came alive like a moving sea as the goats passed through them, tearing at whatever was nearest – grass, leaves, flowers or small branches. A few goats were higher up on the rocks, stretching their necks to reach some tender shoots below them.

'Look how they are perched on the slopes!' exclaimed Julie. 'I can't understand how they don't fall off.'

Some goats came rushing down, throwing up clouds of dust or jumping from boulder to boulder like accomplished mountaineers while dislodging small stones which thundered into the canyon. There were lots of kids too, standing on legs much longer than their bodies. They seemed to catapult themselves down on four straight legs while making a high-pitched *mèhèhè* sound, their little tails stuck straight up in the air as they ran after their mothers.

Charles now saw where they were heading for. There was an overhanging rock forming a natural cave in the side of the cliff, and an enclosure of branches and thorn bushes, which shut off most of the entrance. Slowly, almost unwillingly, the goats gave up their grazing, and as they followed the goatherd and vanished behind the enclosure, the bleating and bell-sounds gradually quietened down.

When the last goat had disappeared, Julie and Charles carried on. After some time they reached the clump of tall eucalyptus trees in which lovers had carved their names and soon they perceived the waterfall thundering down.

Julie stood there for a few minutes, looking pensively at it. Then she turned to Charles. 'Remember the irrigation channel we saw that time we went up the hill? Its water cascaded down just next to the wall around Meier's property. I'm sure that's the waterfall we're looking at. And so his property must be right above the spot where we are.'

Charles nodded. 'I suppose so, but how can we be sure? We can only see the bottom of the cliff from here.'

'That's because we're too near.' Julie turned around. 'The slope on the side of the canyon behind us isn't very steep. If we climb up there we may be able to get a complete view of the opposite cliff wall.'

'But that means crossing the river! How do you suggest we do that? Wade through it? I don't want to get my feet wet. Let's just continue.'

'Come on! It's easy. Look!' And Julie hopped lightly on to a boulder that stuck out just above the surface of the water in the middle of the river, and from there to the other side. But when Charles in turn tried to jump on to the boulder, his foot slipped and he landed full length in the water.

When Julie saw him lying in the cold water and looked at his astonished face, she burst out in hysterical laughter, and it took her quite a time before she managed to calm down.

Charles shot a furious look at her, crawled out of the river and began shaking himself like a wet dog.

'Now that you've successfully crossed the river,' said Julie trying hard not to laugh again, 'let's climb up.'

'I don't want to!' grumbled Charles who had begun to wring out his trousers, but finally he followed her up till they were high enough to see the opposite side of the canyon right to the top.

They were just about able to make out the edge of a white wall towards the left and another edge on the right, where the waterfall began. 'Look!' Julie lifted up a finger. 'Those are the ends of the high wall that surrounds Meier's property. And please, note that there's no wall between the property and the cliff.' She spoke like a schoolteacher trying to convince a dumb pupil. It made Charles feel even grumpier than he already was. 'So what?' he countered. 'We knew that already.'

'But don't you see? It's not possible to enter Meier's property from Frigiliana because of the high wall that surrounds it in a semicircle from cliff edge to cliff edge, but maybe we could climb up from the riverbed and enter the property that way?'

'You must be joking! How you think we can climb that steep cliff is beyond me!'

'See that ridge running up there.' Julie pointed to a barely visible line that ran up at a forty-five degree angle. 'Maybe we could follow it?'

Charles shook his head. 'There are lots of rocks in the way. You have to be a trained mountaineer to climb them. And furthermore you need to have all the necessary equipment.'

'But I'd like to have a look at the property!' protested Julie.

There are times when a man has to put his foot down, and this was such a time. 'No!' said Charles firmly. 'Don't even think about it.' And he began to slide back to the riverbed while Julie followed him unwillingly.

He ostentatiously waded through the shallow river while Julie hopped again on to the boulder, and he was about to return to the village when he felt Julie pulling his sleeve. 'Please,' she pleaded, 'if you won't help me, who will?'

Charles stopped and sighed. Men tend to be weak when women appeal to their chivalry, even if they know jolly well that what's demanded of them is not reasonable, and he was no different. 'All right,' he said at last. 'Maybe there's another way up. Remember the cave I told you about the other day? The one where I discovered those wine bottles? There's a path starting above that cave and I had the impression that it was running towards the hilltop. Do you want to give it a try?'

'Oh yes!' Julie's eyes sparkled.

'Well... in that case...' And Charles took her by the hand and reluctantly started the slow climb to the cave.

'Let me show you the bottles first,' he said when they finally got there. The cave was on the shadowy side of the gorge and it took them a while to get accustomed to the semi-darkness, but Charles ended by discovering the spot where the wine bottles had been hidden. They were gone!

'That's strange...' whispered Charles. 'Someone has taken them! I don't like that... Maybe we'd better turn back. Anyway, it's getting late...'

'But you said we were going to climb up!' protested Julie. 'Where's that path?'

'It starts above the cave...'

'Let's go and find it then.' Julie's voice was firm.

They found it and began to climb up in the setting darkness. The path was just wide enough for one person but it ran up gently, zigzagging back and forth.

'Look at this!' exclaimed Julie. 'Someone has cut bits off this rock to make it easier to pass.' The path had in fact been improved all the way, indicating that it must have been used quite often.

As they kept climbing, the sound of water became louder and after a while they entered the dense vegetation that surrounded the waterfall. The transition from dry rock and low, scattered, scented shrub to the humid green world of pine trees, long grass, flowers and lush vegetation was abrupt; close to the fall everything was wet with fine droplets which the wind blew off the falling water. A large dragonfly flew up and sailed away. Suddenly they were facing the waterfall. 'We're stuck!' shouted Charles over the thundering noise.

'How about going through it?' Julie cried out. 'We must be nearly there.'

Charles shook his head. 'Don't be daft! Wade through a waterfall! Who's ever heard of that? Let's turn back. The sun has already set and we're a long way from home.'

'Come on, be a sport! We can't give up now that we're this far!' And Julie resolutely pushed forward.

'Julie!' cried Charles. 'Stop!' But she had already disappeared under the water. 'Come back!' he shouted, but there was no sign of her and he began to panic: she's been carried away by the water; she's been killed!

Suddenly he heard a barely audible 'Coo-ee... coo-ee...' and he breathed a sigh of relief. 'Where are you?' he called out. Then he noticed an arm sticking out from behind the curtain of water, and finally the rest of Julie appeared. As he hugged her, she explained. 'It's really quite simple. If you stand very close to the cliff you can see a narrow space between the sheet of water rushing down and the cliff wall. Slide in there sideways and you can walk under the water and come out on the other side without getting your precious self wet.' She giggled. 'And hold on to the branches when you reach the other side. It's very slippery there. Just follow me. I'll show you.'

Charles did as he was told and was about to disappear behind the moving curtain when a sudden gust of wind blew the water in his face and soaked him thoroughly.

'But you're all wet!' exclaimed Julie when he emerged next to her between the bushes on the other side. 'Really! I just turn my back for a moment and you manage to soak yourself again!'

'Let's not talk about it,' retorted Charles, vexed.

The patch above them was covered in small shrubs and they began pulling themselves up holding on to these when suddenly they emerged into vegetable gardens and saw a large tiled terrace only yards away. They had reached Herr Meier's property.

19

Nothing seemed to have been touched since the murder. The terrace lay deserted except for two upturned chairs and a small table. Night had fallen by now and the house loomed dark and almost gloomy in front of them. As he stared at it, Charles felt a pull at his sleeve. 'It's spooky here,' he heard Julie whisper behind him. She had lowered her voice as if she were afraid of speaking aloud. 'What if it's true about the Curse?'

'Curse or no Curse,' said Charles, 'now that we've got this far we should at least try to see what we can find out. Maybe we'll be able to get into the house?' And he went forward with Julie clinging on to him. When they reached the front of the house, to their surprise, they saw that the main entrance door was half open.

'I don't like this...' whispered Julie in a shaky voice.

Charles was about to step inside when he stopped in his tracks and turned towards Julie, putting a finger on his lips and making a sign to be dead silent. He had glimpsed the flickering of a faint light inside!

He moved on tiptoes towards one of the windows and as he peered in he noticed a dark figure stooping over a desk, holding a torch while rummaging through a drawer! Charles' heart began to beat fast and he drew back, taking Julie by the hand and pulling her very quietly to the end of the terrace where they hid behind a bush.

'There's a man inside,' he whispered in Julie's ear.

They waited for what seemed ages, trying to steady their nerves. Finally they heard steps and someone came out of the house, pulling the front door shut. The intruder walked stealthily towards the high wall that surrounded the property, pressed something there and, slowly, a metal door opened. The figure disappeared and moments later the door began to close with a grinding sound. Then there was silence.

It was some time before they dared move, as if they feared that the intruder might return or that an accomplice was still around. Finally Charles spoke. 'That man seemed to know the place pretty well. A pity it's so dark. I would have been curious to see his face.' Then he continued. 'He wasn't very tall. Maybe he's one of the local men. Someone like... well... like Fernando.'

'I don't think it was a man.' Julie whispered as if some unseen presence might overhear her. 'It was a woman, and I have a good idea who she was.' She paused a moment. 'She walked exactly like that Swiss project woman whom we saw in Nerja.'

'How you can identify anyone in this darkness is beyond me.'

'But I'm quite sure. Only a woman would walk like that.'

Charles remained unconvinced.

'Anyway…' asked Julie after a pause. 'Were you able to see what she – or he if you like – was doing inside?'

'He seemed to be looking for a document, or who knows what? Shall we get out of here now? We could leave through the door in the wall like the intruder. That would be by far the easiest.'

'I don't think that's a good idea. What if there's still someone around? Or if she – or he – decided to come back just when we're opening the door? Or if someone sees us leaving the property? I think it's safer to go back down the cliff.'

Charles was about to say that they couldn't possibly go down in the dark when the full moon rose above the other side of the canyon, illuminating the scene with its bright silvery light. They quietly returned to the passage behind the waterfall, slipped through it and started their descent to the river.

By the time they reached the riverbed, the moon, which had risen further, lit up the canyon with a milky-white light. As they walked back hand in hand there was no sound other than that made by their feet as they stepped on pebbles, and the splashing of the waterfall, which was becoming fainter as they left it further behind. They were moving in a fairytale world of bright moonlit patches alternating with semi-shadows, and the edges of the canyon were much softer than in the blinding sunlight. The mysterious night world had an intangible quality of half-dream and half-reality that held them strangely captivated. Only when they began the climb out of the canyon and entered the lamp-lit world of the village with its voices and human noise was the spell broken.

'So someone is inspecting Meier's house,' remarked Charles when they finally emerged next to the Guardia Civil post.

'Yes. I think it was that Swiss woman. Maybe she was looking for a paper incriminating the project people.'

'That sounds very unlikely to me. Why should the German have possessed such a document? And why do you persist in saying it was a woman?'

'But it was a woman! I'm sure of it. Maybe it was… Oh!' Julie suddenly held a hand in front of her mouth. 'What if it was Charlotte? She said she was going to come into a lot of money. Maybe she was looking for his will?'

'Well… we'll see about that later,' replied Charles evasively. 'What I'd like to do right now is eat something. I'm ravenous.'

20

The next morning Fernando was striding back and forth from one end of his tunnel-like house to the other. Three times already he had stood in front of his horse, stroking its muzzle tenderly, murmuring, 'I can't. I just cannot do it. My horse!' And he turned around, looking very agitated.

Not my horse, he thought as he sat down. Anything, but not my horse. I don't want to lose it. And he sat there pondering for a long time. Suddenly he got up, slapped his right fist into the palm of his left hand, and said aloud, 'I'll risk it. Yes… I'm going to risk it.' And he grabbed his hat, pulled aside the blanket that was pinned over the entrance to his house and went out. But he needed a stiff drink first; that would give him courage.

21

Late that afternoon Julie and Charles were sitting on their terrace, looking at the setting sun colouring the western sky and talking quietly about the events of the previous days. When finally they went inside and Charles flipped the switch, the lights didn't come on.

'We must have blown a fuse,' he said, slightly irritated.

He went back to the terrace and it was only then that he realised that there were no lights anywhere in the village. He had been so absorbed by the sight of the glowing sky and of the first stars which had begun to appear, that he had failed to notice that the streetlights hadn't come on.

'It must be a general breakdown,' he concluded. 'Do we have any candles?'

They went back inside, feeling their way in the dark until they got into the kitchen, found a box of matches, and Julie lit up one of the hobs of the gas cooker. It gave enough light to start hunting for candles, but they didn't find any.

'There's a shop further along the main street where they sell odds and ends. They might sell candles,' suggested Julie. 'Shall we give it a try?'

They felt their way down the dark staircase and went out. It was pitch dark by now. The moon had not yet risen and the sky in between the houses shone with stars; only the outline of the narrow, winding street was vaguely visible. The façades seemed slightly less dark than the doors of the houses and the entrances to the covered alleyways.

'This is how it must have been at the time of the Moors,' whispered Julie, holding tightly on to Charles' arm.

As they progressed slowly through the street they noticed faint, flickering lights inside most of the houses. 'They've all lit their candles,' remarked Charles. 'Why can't they leave their doors open so that the street gets some light?'

'It's because of the Curse.' Julie spoke softly and drew a little closer to him. 'I'm sure their doors are not only closed but locked as well. And those who have curtains have even drawn them.'

When they finally got to the odds-and-ends shop they found it closed and had to turn back. In the stillness of the night their steps resounded loudly on the cobblestones – almost too loudly – and instinctively they began to walk on tiptoes.

'How spooky…' Julie's voice was hardly audible. 'And all those people hiding inside, afraid of the forces of darkness…'

Suddenly they heard steps coming towards them but they could not see who or what was coming. As the sound grew louder, Julie drew very close to Charles and they stopped and pulled back inside an alleyway. They now saw a large shadow come towards them, but it was so dark that it was impossible to distinguish any movement of legs or even to tell for sure whether it was a man or not. Then the shadow came abreast with them and they held their breaths. Had it seen them? But it moved on without uttering a word.

'If that had been the Curse personified it couldn't have been more scary,' whispered Julie after it had disappeared. She sounded frightened.

'Yes. And if ever there was a perfect night for a crime, this certainly is the night.'

Charles was not a superstitious man but he felt relieved when they got back to the safety of their house. And this time he not only bolted the street door, but locked the door to their apartment as well.

22

Next morning they were woken up by the sound of voices outside. The street below was never without sounds: from early morning onward people would chat to each other or say hello as they met. These sounds always had a familiar, friendly ring, but today everything was very different. The voices were loud, upset, and there were angry shouts.

'Something has happened,' said Julie. 'Let's go and see.'

They washed, dressed quickly and went down.

People were standing on their doorsteps or in small groups in the middle of the street, discussing and gesticulating. Charles and Julie were about to ask what was happening when their neighbour came out of his house. Whenever Charles and Julie met him, a large smile usually split his jovial face and he made witty comments, but today his face looked grim.

'What's going on?' asked Charles.

'Someone has been killed!'

'Not again! Another foreigner?'

'No. Someone from the village.'

'I knew it would happen!' exclaimed Julie. 'Is it Sebastian of the Council?'

'Sebastian? No *señora*. Fernando Lortez has been killed.'

'But that doesn't make sense!' Charles refused to believe it. 'Are you sure it's him?'

'Sure as hell! They found him this morning on the slope below the hill.'

'Maybe it was an accident?'

'An accident! *Hombre*! He had his head bashed in. And you can see the traces in the grass where someone dragged him to the edge of the precipice. No!' The man shook his bald head. 'That hill is cursed. They won't catch *me* going up there.'

PART FOUR
APPOINTMENT WITH DEATH

1

In the afternoon Charles and Julie saw Pépé – or *Premio Gordo* as they called him since Alejandra had told them his story – sitting on the low wall at the beginning of El Darra Street. He was trying to take advantage of the tourists who had been arriving in droves these days, and whenever a couple of unsuspecting foreigners passed by he would give them a wide grin. Then, pretending to be hungry, he would ask them for money for a *bocadillo* while holding out his hand.

Suddenly Charles had an idea. He turned to Julie. 'Where did you put that sweater we found in the canyon?'

'Oh! In a cupboard.'

'You couldn't go and fetch it?'

For once Julie asked no questions but went to get the sweater. Charles took it out of her hands, went down with it and walked up to Pépé.

'Do you recognise this Pépé?' he asked showing him the dark-blue sweater.

The man stared in surprise at Charles and then at the sweater.

'What is it you want, *caballero* (sir)?' he asked, half smiling.

Charles held the sweater in front of his eyes.

'Look well, Pépé. I think you know whom this belongs to.'

Suddenly the colour went out of Pépé's face. He got up, looking as if he had seen a ghost and moved a step away, but Charles kept pressing him. 'This sweater belonged to Fernando, didn't it?'

'Where… where did you find this?' stuttered Pépé.

'In a cave in the canyon below the German's house. There were lots of bottles of white wine in the cave too. Fernando stole them from the German, didn't he?'

Pépé drew back another step and pinched his lips.

'Fernando must have told you some of the things he saw and heard up at the German's house. I'm convinced that he was killed because of what he knew.'

Pépé remained silent but Charles insisted, 'Pépé, please, tell me what you know. You must help to avenge Fernando. He was your friend.'

Pépé hesitated. Then he made up his mind and looked defiantly at Charles. 'I know nothing.'

'I don't believe that. Why won't you tell me?'

'*Caballero*,' replied Pépé slowly, 'I'm not ready for the next world yet. I want to empty a few more glasses first.' And he turned on his heel and abruptly walked away.

2

Charles was standing on the terrace of their house, it was just past six, and the sun was about to disappear behind the roofs of the houses. This was the most peaceful time of the day when the heat of the afternoon began to diminish and the temperature became very pleasant; when women appeared on their roof terraces to take in the washing; and when old people came out into the streets to discuss the ills of their age. Swallows were swooping over the rooftops chasing insects. One moment they were high up, the rays of the setting sun illuminating their tummies; the next they dropped into the shade and it was as if a bright orange light underneath their tiny bodies had abruptly been switched off. Sometimes they flew almost into his face, turning away with only inches to spare.

The evening seemed serene enough, yet Charles was profoundly disturbed. Something sinister had happened. He was aware that a dark force was at work, destroying without pity; that a malevolent being was at large somewhere in this village, ready to act again, free to kill.

The swallows were still at play. Six or seven of them were chasing each other while making a high-pitched *tcheee… tcheee…* sound. Suddenly they plunged down, flying between the façades of the houses at top speed, their shrill note echoing between the walls, to emerge from the narrow confines of the street further along and shoot straight up towards the sky.

Charles leaned over the rail of the terrace and looked down. Agustina's shop was still open and Sam lay sprawled out as usual, occupying as wide a space as he could. He was entirely unaware of what had happened. The problems humans create, their efforts to stand out and be someone, their desires and hatred did not enter his world. His dreams, if he had any, were simple: a nice bone to chew on, or a little female to chase. In his way he is much happier than human beings could ever be, mused Charles. He didn't suffer from stress, nor did he desire any of the money or material riches humans work for, or are even ready to kill for. His day was not cut up in hours and minutes; he lay down where he happened to be, slept if he felt like it, and went off into the countryside if he wanted to. He may not be aware of the wide world around him, thought Charles, but I'm sure he's happy. When humans made the long transition from roaming the bush to rushing to the office they had certainly gained a lot but, looking at Sam, Charles thought they had lost a lot too.

An old woman emerged onto the roof terrace of a house further up, carrying a large empty basket. Washing lines were strung over it as everywhere in Frigiliana, and she started unpegging the clothes, which had been drying in the sun the whole day. As she did so she began to sing. When she was alone, sweeping the terrace or hanging up or taking down the washing, she often sang – not modern songs, she knew none of these – but old ballads she had learned as a child from her mother who had learned them in turn from her mother, and so on. These were songs from past ages, from long before the twentieth century: stories of young lovers who killed themselves because their love was forbidden; of family feuds; of a child born out of impure love, dying without being christened. Each song lasted ten, sometimes twenty minutes, and the old woman sang them with a clear, melodious voice, remembering every word and holding the tone unfalteringly. She had sung these same ballads for maybe sixty or seventy years, but when she died they would die with her: her daughters would not carry on.

She had known the Civil War and the hard times afterwards, and had married late. Then, in the nineteen fifties when her daughters were born, the world had begun to change. The village had a school by then, the heads of the children were being crammed full with knowledge and there was no longer any room for oral tradition – for the ballads of long ago. And now television had come and there was so much to keep people busy. Who was interested nowadays in songs from a bygone era? So the old woman sang her ballads to herself when she was alone.

Today the song was about a sombre murder out of spite and revenge. As the woman sang how the murderer came to an untimely end, falling off a cliff while he was being pursued, Charles thought that there was little difference between then and now. Crimes were still committed for the same motives: people went on killing others out of hatred or jealousy; because they coveted someone else's possessions; or because they wanted to eliminate obstacles in their quest for power and money.

Why had the German been murdered? wondered Charles. Was it because someone had hated him? Or had it been for his money? Or what seemed more likely, had he been eliminated because he had been an obstacle? From what Charles had learned, Meier had stood in the way of many people, and he could think of several who'd had both the motive to kill him and had been around on the night of the murder. If any of these had done it, they would not hesitate to eliminate lesser obstacles such as people who stuck their noses into this unsavoury affair. Maybe that's what had happened to Fernando. His death brought home the fact that it was not safe to meddle in this murky matter.

The sun had set, it had grown dark, the temperature dropped notably and suddenly Charles shivered. He had been nosing around a lot these days – maybe too much. Somewhere around was a ruthless killer who would strike again if he felt threatened. I don't want to see my days end abruptly before reaching a well-earned retirement, thought Charles. After all, why should I bother? It's none of my business. I ought to let the police continue their investigations and keep well away from these murders. And he hoped his activities had not already attracted the attention of the killer.

3

It was between three and four in the afternoon, an ideal moment for walking because the village was usually very quiet at that time. People were at their siesta or, what was happening ever more today, watching the afternoon TV shows. Many people around, and especially the older ones, had their TVs on the whole day, and as they all seemed slightly deaf they were in the habit of turning up the sound. And when it was hot they kept their front doors open, with the result that the noise streamed out into the street.

As Charles set off for a walk and passed in front of the neighbour, he heard the sound of his TV blaring out from the open door. The neighbour was a great TV addict, but unlike other people he didn't sit with his back toward the street. Instead, his TV set was placed next to the open front door with the screen facing inside while he was sitting at the end of the room, maybe because that way he also saw who was passing by. And that wasn't all. He was not sitting on his chair in the normal way either; it was turned back to front, his arms were folded on the back of the chair and his chin was resting on his forearms. To anyone passing along in the street he looked a strange sight. In the dim light inside you just saw his legs from the knees down on each side of the back of the chair; the man's heavy face above, lying on his arms with an intent gaze; and the balding, slightly shiny head crowning it all.

Charles carried on, and as he didn't meet anyone, he climbed slowly to Calle Alta and went up Calle Chorrera. He looked at the house with the geraniums where he had seen that screaming woman when he had gone to visit Charlotte some time ago. Lately the woman had begun to cover the geraniums. Charles had been told that she did this to discourage tourists from taking photographs, and the pink sheet certainly spoiled the picturesque view.

The woman was nowhere to be seen though her door was open, and Charles turned left in front of her house. After a short distance the narrow street petered out and turned into a path zigzagging up the hill. He hesitated. Should he go to see where Fernando had died? He stood there for a few seconds, undecided, torn between reason and curiosity, looking at the path. No, he thought, stick to the resolution you made last night and keep out of this. Then his curiosity got the better of him. There was no one in sight; it wouldn't take long, and he wanted to see those traces in the grass! And maybe he would find other clues?

He began to climb the narrow path, taking care where he put his feet. He passed a lonely goat on a small patch of grass; it was tied to one of the branches of a low tree and stared at him with dim, uninterested eyes, chewing on. The path now became steeper and the gravel and loose stones sometimes gave way under his sandals.

As he climbed higher, the whole village spread below his feet. Clothes were hanging from the lines on a few terraces like distinctive colourful blotches, but otherwise the village seemed to be an uninterrupted jumble of white walls and red-tiled roofs. Only the tall, square church tower stood out clearly; he could see the bells up in the tower. Beyond stretched the *campo* with small patches of avocado trees and olive groves around scattered farmhouses, and much further away, in the far distance, he saw the blue of the Mediterranean and the hazy line of the horizon.

Suddenly a sound startled him: there was someone above! He heard heavy steps coming down and then, from around a bend of the zigzagging path, a man appeared. He had the broad shoulders, biceps and build of a champion wrestler and his trousers were pulled tight over his muscular legs. His shirt buttons were open to the waist, showing his powerful chest covered with curly dark hair. Charles vaguely recognised him. He had seen him once in the village unloading a mule and carrying a heavy bag of potatoes as if it had been a toy.

Charles pressed himself against the rocky wall to make room, but the man stopped a step or two away and stared at him. He had hard, dark, pitiless eyes and kept staring, a defiant, stubborn look on his rough red face, until Charles began to feel very uncomfortable.

'So it is you…' he finally said, speaking slowly. 'You're that feller who's been inquiring after me, aren't you?' The tone of his voice was menacing.

In a flash it dawned on Charles who that man was: he must be Dolores' son Paco, the man with the hatchet!

Charles was completely cornered. He felt caught like a fly in a spider's web. He was wearing loose sandals on his feet; if he tried to run away he would slip and fall down onto the rocks below – a sheer drop of ten yards.

The man came a step nearer. His hands looked like huge shovels, used to killing animals with one swift stroke, used to crushing the life out of living beings. He could push Charles down the cliff if he wished and then walk off, and when people found him later, lying amongst those prickly pear cacti down below with a broken neck, they would think it had been an accident.

The sun felt unbearably hot, Charles' throat was dry and sweat started to break out on his forehead. His heart banged inside his chest like a high-speed train as the man took another step forward and stood in front of him. With a brusque movement he grabbed Charles' shirt underneath the chin. 'Sticking your nose in what's none of your business hey!' His fiery dark eyes stared into Charles' from under thick eyebrows and his breath, heavy with the acrid smell of stale wine, struck Charles' nostrils, making him shudder.

The man suddenly hissed between his teeth, 'If I hear from you again, feller...' And he put his two closed fists one above the other and made a wringing movement. Then he pushed Charles to the ground and continued on his way down, shaking with laughter as if he had really enjoyed himself.

Minutes after the sound of his steps had died away Charles was still unable to move; his legs felt like jelly and his head was spinning. In the silence of the afternoon the whole event seemed surreal. Soon, he thought, the body of Konrad Meier will float in the sky with that man sitting cross-legged on it, laughing loudly. And next the sun will become green and the village will turn upside down. But the village stayed where it was, looking more picturesque than ever. Charles gradually recovered his senses, got up and, slowly, started to walk back.

4

When Charles got back home he sat down almost mechanically and began to think. This was worse than a mission to Bosnia! This was a well-aimed, direct attack upon his own person. It was time, more than time, to get out of Frigiliana before that Paco killed him!

He looked at Julie who was absorbed in one of her books. She had a pronounced aversion to insecure places, so she certainly wouldn't want to stay.

'Julie...'

She looked up from her book. 'Yes?'

'Wouldn't it be safer for us to leave Frigiliana? I've been thinking and... I wouldn't want anything to happen to you. You see... it has become very dangerous here… what with the Curse and all those murders… You surely don't want to stay under these circumstances, do you?'

She seemed surprised. 'You want to go?'

'No… not me… but I'm worrying about your safety. Knowing how much you've always hated insecure places I suddenly thought that… well… you probably want to go home?' He looked expectantly at Julie.

'But I'm enjoying myself! You don't want us to leave before these murders have been solved, do you? I want to know how it all happened.' Her eyes shone with excitement.

'So you don't want to go?'

'No way! You promised me a two-month holiday and I intend to stay a full two months.' And she resumed reading her book with a contented smile on her lips.

5

'Why not go to a restaurant?' suggested Julie the next evening. 'I don't think I can face peeling potatoes and standing in front of a cooker just now.'

'But there must be at least a thousand tourists in the village,' objected Charles. 'Good Friday is not a day to eat out. We'll be lucky if we find a free table anywhere tonight.'

But Julie had made up her mind and was determined to go out. 'I'm sure there won't be many people at Eliza's.' Her voice was firm. 'You almost have to stand in front of the entrance to notice it's a restaurant.'

Eliza was a German woman and El Boquetillo, her restaurant, was indeed an inconspicuous small place. Julie liked it because it was reasonably cheap and the food was homemade. 'Well…' sighed Charles, 'if you really don't want to cook, there's nothing to do about it. We'll have to risk it.'

When they opened the door of El Boquetillo Charles knew at once that his worst forebodings had come true: the restaurant was packed. 'Look, there's no room,' he said. 'We'd do better to return home and open a tin of something rather than waste our time here.' Unfortunately, just at that moment a couple got up from a table in a corner and Julie resolutely pushed forward to occupy it in front of two people who had followed her in.

After some time a local girl of maybe sixteen came to take away the dishes left on the table and to put on a new paper cloth, but she didn't bring the menu or take orders. 'She's probably just here to help on busy days,' suggested Julie.

The regular girl was there too. She was a few years older and quite plump. All the same, she usually squashed herself into tiny miniskirts, but because this was Good Friday she wore trousers, which however were so tight that they seemed ready to burst at the seams. Her most striking feature, though, was her hugely oversized bosom. She was sitting behind the counter, a concentrated expression on her dark Andalusian face, preparing the bill for a couple of people who had finished and were standing in front of her, waiting. It took her quite a time before she had made up the bill. Next the customers studied it scrupulously, and when finally they put a five thousand-peseta note on top of it, the girl picked up everything and walked upstairs.

'She probably has to give the money to Eliza,' hinted Julie. Eliza was doing all the cooking in a small kitchen upstairs, helped by a girl who also did the washing up. Julie imagined Eliza stirring a sauce with one hand while looking at the bill the waitress showed her, and digging with the other hand into her purse for the change.

By the time the girl reappeared with the change some five minutes later, other people had got up and were asking for their bill.

'I don't think we're going to be served very soon,' remarked Charles. 'We haven't even seen the menu yet. Are you very hungry?'

'Fortunately not.'

A number of the customers in the restaurant were German tourists, but the local girl spoke only Spanish and a few words of English. The Germans did their best but confusion reigned. The young waitress had just brought the dishes for a table of six people when one of the women protested in English with a strong German accent, 'I want not fish. I ordered the meat of a pig!'

'If only I could have the fish,' sighed Julie, but it went to someone else at another table.

'I can't think why there are so many Germans here,' Charles wondered.

'It's probably the bush telephone,' suggested Julie. 'They must have given each other the word that this is the *German* restaurant of Frigiliana.'

'Shht.' Charles suddenly put a finger on his lips motioning to Julie to keep silent. He had heard the name of Konrad Meier pronounced at the table behind him and leaned backwards, pricking up his ears.

'Yes and Dietrich knows… met him some years after the war when he came back from…'

There was too much noise and loud conversation around and however much Charles tried, he was unable to catch more than a few scattered bits of the conversation.

'… good time to buy then… property was dirt-cheap. But where did… money from? No one had any money in those days in Germany. And you say… prisoner of war?'

'… married a very rich widow.'

'He knew… right investments… considerable fortune.'

'… who inherits?'

'… know if he had children. His wife… never came to Germany.'

Then the conversation moved on to other subjects and finally the party of Germans finished their supper. As they got up to pay their bill at the counter, Charles had a good look at them. There were three men and three women, probably all in their sixties or seventies. He was about to get up and ask them what they knew about Konrad Meier but convention got the better of him and he stayed were he was, cursing himself for his cowardice while the German party left.

6

It was late by the time they had finished their meal. The men's procession which had started from the church at 10p.m. had already reached El Darra Street. The men, dressed in dark purple – the colour of mourning in the Catholic tradition – wore long gowns, and a long piece of cloth was added to the bottom of these gowns, trailing behind, sweeping over the pavement. In their left hand they carried a lighted wax candle and with their right hand they held a cloth in front of their faces. It had two round openings but the eyes were not visible in the darkness. The men in the procession could see and recognise bystanders but could not be identified.

There were literally hundreds of men shuffling along in two parallel lines, one on each side of the narrow street. Towering over these two long lines of silent, mysterious, purple-clad figures and flickering candle flames were two heavy floats, the *pasos* – huge wooden frames carried by twelve men each. The men visibly strained under their loads, and the procession moved forward very slowly, stopping every few minutes to allow the men bearing the *pasos* on their shoulders to rest. The carriers all held a long iron stave in one of their hands. When they moved forward they used these staves to push themselves along, making a thudding noise on the cobblestones, and when they stopped they supported the wooden frame on the flat part in which these iron staves ended so that the float remained at shoulder height.

On the first *paso* lay an effigy of the dead Christ inside a glass coffin. It was followed by eleven figures dressed in pink robes. They represented the twelve apostles – minus Judas of course – and all wore masks with long beards and an abundance of dark hair, but the immobile features of these masks looked bizarre.

Last year the procession had been animated and Charles remembered that a stray cat had suddenly rushed down the street and bumped into an apostle who stumbled and nearly fell because he could not sufficiently see what was happening through the two holes in his mask. In a panic the cat shot down the line of candle bearers, upsetting a few more men, and all the spectators, and the younger candle bearers too, had started laughing. It took minutes before the older men managed to regain control of the situation and impose silence again.

But this year a heavy oppression seemed to hang over the procession. There was apprehension in the air, and the spectators lining the walls of the street were as silent as the men shuffling by. There were no girls giggling because they imagined they had recognised one of the younger men in the procession; and none of the men shuffling by with covered faces whispering, 'Hello José,' to one of the spectators, the José in question asking, 'Who are you?' and the unknown man answering, 'It's me.'

The second float now appeared along the bend of the narrow street, carrying a huge statue of the Virgin Mary dressed in a light-blue velvet mantle. She was standing erect, her hands folded together in prayer, and the heavy wooden *paso* on which the statue stood was covered with white flowers. The face of the Virgin – pure, beautiful – was radiating sorrow; tears could be seen running down her face. As the statue rounded a corner, the bearers stopped in front of a house. On the balcony of the first floor stood a *Saeta* singer, level with the Virgin Mary, and as he stretched out his arms towards the Virgin he suddenly burst out in song in the plaintive way of the Flamenco singers.

'Those who do bad deeds will suffer eternally…' He drew out each vowel, ending each sentence with *aya ha ha ha hayayay*… then pausing to draw breath. This was more than singing: it was a spontaneous outburst of faith, the singer making up each line as he went along. 'They killed your innocent son, *aya ha ha ha hayayay*…'

The man was speaking to the living Virgin, he was consoling her, he felt her pain and suffering as if he himself had been deprived of a beloved being, and the sadness of the melody filled the silence of the night with sorrow. In the light of the street lamps and the faint, flickering candlelight the face of the Virgin seemed to be really crying, and everyone knew that she was crying not only because she had lost her beloved son, but also because a son of the village had been killed.

The procession of the women, which was planned to start at half past midnight, set off with at least a half-hour delay. The lights of the village were switched off as the women set out in two long undulating lines on each side of the street, all dressed in black, carrying a candle in their left hand. The semi-darkness and the flickering candlelight created a mysterious effect of togetherness, and as the faces of young girls and women passed, one after the other, no more than a foot away from Charles, he wondered what was lying behind those shining eyes reflecting the flames of the candle; behind the intimacy of those faces lifted up towards the sky; behind those lips singing, 'Forgive us for all our sins, forgive us…' And the song seemed to implore protection from the fearful forces of darkness, from the Curse that hung heavily over the village that night.

7

Towards five o'clock on Saturday afternoon Charles went to say hello to Agustina. She had been very busy and it was the first time he entered her shop that week. They talked for a while about the events of the last days. 'Bad business that murder,' said Agustina.

Charles agreed. 'It's not exactly what the village needed. By the way, the streets seem deserted today. What's happening?'

'Fernando is going to be buried. Half the village must have gone to his brother's house where the corpse is lying.'

'Where's that?'

'In the *barrio nuevo*.'

'I'll go and have a look,' decided Charles, and waving goodbye he left the shop.

When he got halfway through the *barrio nuevo* he saw the procession come towards him. It was headed by the local funeral car and through the glass top one could see the coffin covered with wreaths and flowers. The close relatives who walked just behind the car were all dressed in black. Then followed a seemingly endless line of men. They did not walk two by two or in groups, but in a single file, one behind the other. Almost all the men of the village must have turned up and they kept passing by in silence, their faces grim, their feet shuffling on the cobblestones as they accompanied Fernando on his last journey.

The sadness on some of the faces, the consternation on others was real. Had Fernando died a natural death, few people would have turned up, but he had been murdered on the hill and this called as much for a show of sympathy to the deceased as a rallying against the perpetrator of such a godless deed.

The killing of Meier had left the villagers indifferent. They had hardly known him. He was a foreigner and therefore irrelevant to their world. But the killing of Fernando affected them deeply; after all, he was a son of this village and his death was an outrage, a slap in everyone's face.

The procession passed the Guardia Civil post and proceeded along the tortuous Calle Real towards the church in the old part of the village. There the women were waiting. When the procession arrived and the coffin was lifted out of the car everyone made the sign of the cross. The coffin was carried up the steps that led to the church and as it disappeared inside, the people streamed up the stairs and began to fill the church.

Charles hesitated. Should he follow them inside the church too? But the events decided for him. The church was so full that the last women who tried to enter had to stand on the steps outside the large wooden entrance door, and he decided instead to go for a stroll to think about what had happened.

8

As Julie looked down from the balcony that evening, Agustina was just about to close her shop. 'Come on,' she motioned to Charles, 'let's help her.'

They went down and Julie began to carry in the multicoloured hand-woven blankets that were lying on the low wall opposite the shop, while Charles picked up the donkey. It was heavier than he had expected.

'How do you manage to do this all alone?' he asked. 'You must be quite a strong woman. I'd better keep on your good side.'

'It isn't really so bad. One gets used to it,' laughed Agustina while she began to unhook the clothes that were hanging on the grille in front of the window and piled them up in her arms. Suddenly she turned towards them. 'Have you heard the news?'

'What news?'

'The police have solved the murder case.'

'What!' Charles stood there, gaping, while Julie nearly dropped a blanket.

'They know who killed Meier?'

'No, not Meier. Fernando Lortez. Three men from Torrox have just been arrested and charged with his murder.'

'Are the police sure?'

'They must know what they're doing.'

'So nothing new has come up concerning the murder of the German?'

'Not that I know of. Anyway, the case of the German no longer seems to matter very much. What matters is that there's a general feeling of relief in the village tonight. Strange as it may seem, I have the impression that everything is returning to normal.'

Charles felt disappointed by the turn the events had taken. Somehow he had the feeling that nothing had been resolved and that the murder of Herr Meier mattered a lot, even if the villagers didn't seem to care.

9

On Easter Sunday, shortly before noon, small groups of people were moving through the village. The procession was due to start after the "high mass" ended, and all those who were going to participate in it, young and old, were hurrying towards the church. They were already dressed for the occasion in green and white garments and as they rushed forward between the white-chalked walls of the houses, they looked like exotic flowers.

Hundreds of spectators had gathered in Church Square and the feeling of hope was almost tangible. Crowds are living entities: they have their moods and emotional reactions. On Friday night the sky had been covered and the ambience subdued. Sadness – worse even, fear – had pervaded everything. But today the clouds had lifted and there was excitement in the air.

The green-and-white-clad participants, wearing white masks, had already lined up in front of the church and the village band was standing at the ready in the square. Suddenly the band began to play, the church doors swung open and a float with the statue of the Virgin Mary was carried out. Her face was no longer sad but radiant, jubilant. The statue of the Virgin was followed by that of Christ, standing up on his float, his right hand poised to give a blessing.

The two floats now stood side by side, swinging rhythmically to the tune of the music on the shoulders of the bearers. Then, at a sign from a man standing in front, the bearers lifted the floats up in the air on outstretched arms, a voice shouted, 'Resurrection!' and the tightly packed crowd cheered. The bearers kept up the effort for a full minute, swinging the floats slowly to left and right on outstretched arms, straining under the effort. Then the floats came down again on their shoulders and the bearers began to move, followed by a long line of green-and-white-clad participants.

The band brought up the rear, its music dominated by the joyful sound of trumpets and copper instruments. As it left the square the crowd pressed into the narrow street, carried away by this mass movement of uplifting euphoria; eyes were shining, faces exultant. As the statues passed through Calle Real, people threw handfuls of purple or white bougainvillea petals on to them from the balconies. The fear of the previous days had dissolved; Christ had redeemed the sins of the believers and the Curse had been vanquished.

The people who are supposed to have killed Fernando have been arrested, thought Charles who was looking on. But did they really do it? And the murder of Herr Meier was still a mystery.

But that didn't seem to matter. Confidence had returned and life was good again. Today was a radiant day, the sky was a bright light blue, the sun was shining, and it was Easter Sunday. What more could you ask for in Andalusia?

10

After the procession had gone, Charles and Julie decided to spend a pleasant hour on the terrace of La Bodeguilla in Calle Al Garra, the street that goes up steeply on the west side of the church, but when they got there they discovered that they were not the only ones to have had the idea; all the tables were occupied. They were about to turn back when they noticed Michael and Sarah making signs to join them. They sat down at their table ordering *vino de Frigiliana* – the local wine which is sweet and goes down easily but is treacherous because of its high alcohol content – and chatted for a while about the procession and the wonderful weather, as people do who have escaped the foul northern climate. Then the conversation turned to the latest developments in Fernando's murder case.

'How odd that they have arrested three men from Torrox,' remarked Charles. 'Why would those three men have killed Fernando? Somehow it doesn't feel right.'

'Sarah knows the whole story.' Michael put his hand on Sarah's arm, beaming. 'She heard it first hand.'

'You exaggerate Michael. I didn't hear anything. It was the woman who lives in the house next to Fernando's who heard everything.'

'Tell me...' Julie drew her chair nearer Sarah's.

'Late one night the woman heard voices in the little square outside her house, and when she looked out of the window she saw Fernando and three other men. She recognised two of them: they were from Torrox.'

'When did that happen?' asked Julie.

'Almost a week ago... on Monday night. The woman told me that the men were pressing Fernando to supply the wine he had promised for their restaurant, or something like that, but Fernando was protesting that he could no longer do so.' Sarah turned to Charles. 'I don't really understand what it was all about. Anyway,' she continued, 'after this the discussion heated up and they all began to shout, carrying on like that for at least ten minutes.'

'What were they discussing?' asked Julie.

'Well... it seemed that the men from Torrox had advanced a large sum of money to Fernando and that he was unable to pay them back; he claimed to have used it to pay his arrears at the bank. In the end the three men insisted that Fernando was to give them his horse as reimbursement.'

'How horrible!' exclaimed Charles. 'Not his horse!'

'Yes! He refused but when they threatened him he finally gave in. He spat in his right hand and then slapped the right palms of the other men as a sign of agreement.'

'Did they walk off with his horse then?' asked Julie.

'No. He had to take it to Torrox last Wednesday, but it's still in his stables. He was killed on Tuesday night!'

11

When Charles went to the bakery the next morning, he found some six or seven people inside, all talking excitedly.

'Yes,' said an older woman, her voice trembling so much she was almost unable to speak. 'And Emilio too has won.'

'How much?' enquired a man who was leaning on a stick.

'Heaps of money.' The woman lifted up her arms. 'Ten or fifteen million pesetas!'

The others went 'Oh!' and '*Dios mio!*' and one woman said, shaking her head, 'He's a rich man now, our Emilio.'

'He's been lucky,' said another woman, 'but my neighbour, she is heart-broken. She had all the digits right except the last which was just one off. And she won nothing!'

So great was the excitement that Charles didn't manage to buy a loaf of bread for quite a time. He finally secured a loaf of *pan negro*, and as he went back home past the little shops, people seemed to be talking about nothing else but the lottery and the millions that had been won. Apparently several other people in the village had won the main prize too, although Charles failed to understand how this could be possible.

When he returned he found Agustina's shop open. A few Spanish customers were inside and a young woman was talking to them; she had wavy light-brown hair hanging lightly to her shoulders and a pretty, tanned face. Of course, thought Charles. Agustina told me she was going off to Morocco. This must be the young woman from Nerja who's replacing her. He waited at the entrance till the customers had left and then went in. 'You must be Peggy,' he said. As she stared at him, perplexed, he excused himself. 'I was just curious to see who would replace Agustina.'

A large engaging smile suddenly split her face. 'I know who you are! Agustina told me about you. You must be Charles from the upstairs apartment.'

'That's right. By the way, I listened to your Spanish while you were talking to your customers. It's amazing! How come you speak it so well?'

'No secret there.' She laughed. 'I married a Spaniard.'

'I see. I've been told that the best way to learn a language is to marry someone who speaks it.' Then he added with a twinkle in his eyes, 'But what if you want to learn three or four different languages?'

'Is that a problem? Marriages last no more than a few years nowadays. I separated from my husband four years after marrying him,' she said, almost with pride.

'Why did you stay in Spain, then?'

'Can you give me one good reason to go back to cold, depressing London? Where people save up for a whole year just to spend two weeks in the south. And I'm here all the year round, think of that! Where could I find a better place to live? In case you didn't know, this is the warmest spot in continental Europe.'

She was about to elaborate further on her good luck when a couple of tourists came into the shop and began ferreting around.

'I'd better leave you,' said Charles. 'Have a nice day.'

'You too,' she replied, smiling contentedly.

12

Alejandra had been too occupied during the *Semana Santa* to give Spanish lessons, but today was Easter Monday and she was back, dressed in a flowery blouse and pink trousers. Spring had definitely come, not only to Andalusia, but also to Alejandra.

When she had first come to teach, Alejandra hadn't known how to go about it and had behaved rather like a stiff schoolmistress. She had gradually become more relaxed but now, after not having seen Julie and Charles for a week, it felt like meeting old friends again. And instead of starting her Spanish lessons without wasting a moment, as she would have done at the beginning, she began to chat about everything she'd been doing. She had participated in the women's procession; the whole family had been reunited on Easter Sunday; and everything had been wonderful.

'It would have been even more wonderful if you'd won at the lottery,' remarked Charles.

'We didn't buy tickets this time. A real shame.' A shadow seemed to slip over Alejandra's round face as she spoke. Then she brightened up again. 'But isn't it extraordinary that the top ticket was sold here? Of all the vendors in the whole of Spain, our vendor had the series with the winning number! Until today no one ever won in Frigiliana and now ten families have become rich in one go! Can you imagine that?'

'I don't understand how ten families can have had the winning number?'

'Because a complete ticket is too expensive. People usually buy a tenth of a ticket here. So now we have ten millionaires in one go!'

'I see. No wonder everyone is happy.'

'Are they no longer worrying about the Curse then?' enquired Julie.

'No. People say the Curse was vanquished by the prayers on Good Friday. And aren't the lottery results proof of it?'

'So no more Curse eh?' Charles sounded cynical. 'Is your cousin's husband – the famous police inspector – making any progress?'

'Haven't you heard the news?'

'About those three men who've been arrested?'

'Yes.' Alexandra looked proud.

'But what about the murder of the German?'

'Miguel hasn't had time for that. He has been extremely busy.' There was a defensive ring in her voice. 'He has been interrogating one of the members of the Council. There may be a case of corruption in the village.'

Julie laughed. 'Only one case? I thought that there was only one member of the village Council above suspicion: a certain Sebastian.'

'But it's Sebastian they have been interrogating!'

Julie shook her head. 'That sounds all wrong. Why him?'

'Because he's just bought a brand-new luxury car, something far above his means.'

'Has he explained where he got the money from?'

'He says he's been saving up for a long time, and that he had the money stuffed away in his house.'

'In an old sock, no doubt,' suggested Charles with unmistakable irony in his voice. 'Or under the mattress! Sebastian the incorruptible! Think of that!'

13

The lesson had only just finished when they heard someone come up the stairs; then there was a hesitant knock on the door. It was Sven, shy as ever but looking very worried.

'Sorry to interrupt,' he said apologetically, 'but have you seen Charlotte lately?'

'Now that you mention it… no.' Charles turned to Julie. 'When did we last see her?'

'It must have been several days ago.' Julie bit her lower lip, concentrating. 'I don't recall having seen her since… in fact since the day Fernando was murdered. But then, with everything that's been going on here, the Semana Santa, and all the tourists in the village, I haven't really paid much attention.'

'I have,' said Sven. 'I've been to her house every day since Tuesday – sometimes twice a day – and always found her door locked.'

'Maybe she's gone off to Australia?' suggested Charles. 'She said she was going there.'

'But in that case she would have come to say goodbye to us first,' objected Julie.

'She must be somewhere around.' Sven's hands trembled and he looked as if he hadn't been sleeping much lately.

'Why?' asked Charles.

'Because her car is parked at the bottom of the village. It hasn't moved for a week.'

'Something must have happened!' exclaimed Julie. 'I hope that she hasn't been… Alejandra… quick! You know the police here. Can you go and ask them to come at once please?'

'All right! It's lucky that Miguel is at the Guardia Civil in Frigiliana this morning. I'll go down and get him.'

'And I know who's got a spare key,' Charles hastened to say. 'Charlotte's neighbour. She's probably in her shop.' He rushed out followed by Sven, located the neighbour and accompanied her to her house where she found the spare key.

'Please open,' urged Sven when he saw the woman come out with the key in her hand.

'No.' The woman's voice was firm. 'Not until the police are here *muchacho* – young man.'

Charles thought Sven was going to wrench the key out of her hand, but he just managed to control himself, although he bared his teeth and his fists were opening and shutting. By the time Alejandra arrived with Miguel and another policeman he was nearly frantic.

The police inspector didn't seem to be in any great hurry and he began by asking Sven what was happening in a studied, official voice. This was just too much for the poor young man; he could hardly utter a word and kept pointing at the locked door. Julie, who had come up too, had to explain everything.

'All right,' said the police inspector. 'The police will go in first. You can come in after us but you're not to touch anything.' Then he turned to the woman ordering, 'Open this door.'

The neighbour did as she was told and stood back to let the two policemen pass, but before they had time to do so Sven rushed inside.

'*Muchacho*!' shouted the police inspector. 'You can't do that! Come back!' But Sven had already disappeared upstairs.

Everyone now pressed in and the policemen were about to go up after Sven when he reappeared at the top of the stairs. He stood there for a moment, his face blank while they all stared at him.

'Sven!' exclaimed Julie. 'Is she…' Julie didn't dare utter the word.

The young man began to walk down slowly, almost like a zombie. At last he spoke. 'I don't understand. She isn't here.'

The police inspector now shot into action. '*Muchacho*,' he said in a severe tone, turning to Sven, 'will you leave immediately please? You are disrupting our work.' And this time Sven followed his orders and went out meekly, shaking his head while mumbling incoherent words.

After he had left, the two policemen began to search the house, going methodically through the kitchen and living room, but they found nothing of any significance. They then moved upstairs to Charlotte's room and stayed there for maybe five minutes. Presently the inspector reappeared with a pile of photographs.

'Do you know this man?' he asked putting several photographs on the table in front of Charles. 'He looks a bit dodgy to me.'

Charles held his hand over his mouth so as not to burst out laughing. These were the photographs of Edward, which Charlotte had shown them so proudly some time ago.

'Inspector,' he said, 'you are a fine psychologist. This man is definitely not to be trusted.' He noticed a glimmer of satisfaction in the policeman's eyes while he spoke. 'Unfortunately,' he continued, 'he left for Australia several weeks ago.'

The inspector pulled a long face, and said, 'Come Antonio,' motioning to the other policeman. 'Let's go. There's nothing of interest for us here.'

'But we haven't yet looked at those drawings over there,' protested Antonio, pointing at a pile lying on a small side table.

'As you wish,' replied the inspector stiffly.

It was always a pleasure to look at Charlotte's work and Julie and Charles drew nearer as the policeman began to turn over the drawings without much interest; most were studies for the busts or heads Charlotte was working on. The policeman had nearly reached the bottom of the pile and was about to turn over a sketch of a man's head when the inspector suddenly woke up from the torpor into which he seemed to have sunk and put his hand on the drawing, holding it back. 'But... but...' he stammered. His eyes seemed to bulge out of his head. 'But that's the German who was murdered.' He looked as if he had seen a ghost.

This was so unexpected that they all stood in silence, staring at the drawing. Charlotte was an exceptional draughtswoman and her subjects always seemed to come alive on paper. Charles had never seen the murdered man and had thought of him more as 'the German', which was totally impersonal, than as Konrad Meier. And all of a sudden there he was, a very real person peering at them from the paper with something like a twinkle in his eyes. Charles had somehow imagined him to be a hefty, uncouth, stubborn man but his face was pleasant, refined – the face of a man of culture. And although he looked about seventy, it was obvious that he had been very handsome.

He stared at the sketch for a long time, intrigued. He had never seen Meier and yet the face seemed familiar. Maybe he had seen someone who resembled him... but when and where?

After a while they all left the house and they were ready to go home when Alejandra, who had kept herself in the background, turned to Charles and Julie.

'So that friend of yours, that Charlotte, knew the German,' she said, nodding her head with a look of disapproval on her face. 'What do you think of that?'

They had absolutely no idea what to think about it.

'And you know what?' continued Alejandra. 'She knew Fernando Lortez as well.' As Julie stared at her in disbelief, she explained, 'I know it from

Miguel's wife – my cousin. When the police searched his belongings, they found a photograph of her on Fernando's horse!'

14

Julie and Charles went back to their house in a depressed mood. 'Charlotte,' Julie kept sighing while shaking her head. 'Who would have believed it?'

Down in the street Pépé – or *Premio Gordo* – was sitting next to the bright-yellow mailbox. Should I try my luck again? thought Charles. But if Pépé hadn't wanted to talk last week, why should he now? However, the whole atmosphere had changed since Easter Sunday.

Charles went up to him. 'Hello, Pépé,' he said in a casual voice. 'How are you?'

'Very well *caballero*. Just a bit hungry.' He stuck out his hand. 'You wouldn't have hundred pesetas for a *bocadillo*?'

Charles dug into his pocket and came up with a thousand-peseta note. When he saw it, Pépé's eyes brightened visibly and he was ready to grab the banknote, when Charles withdrew it as if he had changed his mind and put it back into his pocket.

'You didn't want to help me last week when I asked you about Fernando,' said Charles, pretending to look hurt. 'So why should I help you now?'

Pépé stood there for a couple of seconds, at a loss as to what to do. His face looked like a balance weighing the drinks he could get for a thousand pesetas against the risks of parting with the information Charles wanted. Then Charles saw the balance tilt – the drinks came out winner.

'But *caballero*...' Pépé spoke apologetically. 'Last week was different. Then there was the Curse. And those who killed Fernando had not yet been arrested. But now I can speak.'

'Tell me then: Fernando pinched wine bottles from the German, didn't he?'

'He did,' confirmed Pépé. 'Very good wine too. I tasted a bottle once.'

'What did he do with them?'

'He sold them to people who had a restaurant in Torrox. For their German customers, you see…'

'So that's what he did! By the way, did he ever tell you that he heard or saw something important when he was up at the German's house?'

Pépé hesitated for a while. Then he looked at Charles with the eyes of a conspirator. 'I believe the German found something…'

'What did he find?'

Pépé drew nearer till his mouth almost touched Charles' ear. 'The treasure,' he whispered.

Charles was surprised. 'Are you sure?'

'Well… yes. Last week, that's to say the morning before he was killed, I saw Fernando, very agitated. Then, later in the afternoon, I was down in the bar when he came to me terribly relieved, saying, "Pépé, I won't have to give up my horse." And when I asked him why not, he replied, "Because I know a secret. And I'm going to get a lot of money for it."'

'So he didn't tell you explicitly that the German found the treasure.'

'But *hombre*! What other secret is there up on the hill worth a lot of money?' Pépé held the palms of his hands upwards and turned his eyes towards the sky with a look that clearly showed: those foreigners, they never understand anything.

'Well… thanks,' said Charles handing him the thousand-peseta note. 'And have a nice *bocadillo*.'

'I shall.' *Premio Gordo* beamed. 'And more than one too.' And he rushed off to the nearest bar, wasting no further time.

15

An hour later Charles went for a stroll through the village and as he passed along *La Alegria*, the bar where *Premio Gordo* was often to be found, he looked in to see if he was enjoying his "*bocadillo*". There were five or six men, all visibly under the weather, but Pépé wasn't among them. He was about to continue when one of the men called out, '*Hombre*, come in! Have a glass of wine!'

Charles was surprised. Then he recognised the man who was offering him a drink and abruptly drew back. At the bar, not three yards away, looking at him with drunken eyes, stood Paco. Charles didn't at all feel like having a glass of wine, and certainly not with Paco. Then he reflected that maybe it was safer not to offend the man, and he stepped reluctantly inside.

'Only one glass,' he said. 'I still have a lot to do.'

'Those foreigners,' remarked one of the men as Charles sat down next to Paco. 'Always busy.'

'Yeah! Busy sticking their noses into other people's affairs,' sneered Paco. 'I can't stand Nosy Parkers! But it no longer matters.' And he turned towards Charles sticking out his hairy chest. 'I'm a millionaire now.'

'Congratulations,' said Charles, lifting up his glass to Paco's and putting it to his lips. As he did so, Paco suddenly gave him a slap on the back which nearly made Charles swallow his glass.

'I gave you a good scare the other day, didn't I.' He burst out laughing and began to tell the others how he had met Charles on the hillside and then mimicked how frightened he had looked. The impersonation was greeted with roars of laughter. As Paco started his performance all over again, Charles slipped out saying goodbye, but the men seemed far too absorbed in the story to take any notice of him.

16

At the time Charles was facing Paco in the bar, the project people were holding a meeting in their office in Calle Pintada in Nerja.

'Can anyone think of any more obstacles?' asked Massimo Zizi – the man whom Charles called Mister *Magnifico*.

'The German is dead, which is a good thing,' said a man, 'but we still don't know who inherits from him – or at least I don't. Can anyone enlighten me?' He looked around.

'You're right to draw the attention to that point. We must try to find out who inherits,' agreed Mister *Magnifico*. 'I've left this to Christina. She's good at such things.' He turned to her. 'How far have you got?'

Christina Eckmann moved uncomfortably in her chair. 'I haven't found out so far, but I will soon. I promise.'

'Well...' continued the Italian, 'the one who inherits must sell to us. Persuading him will no doubt be an easy task compared to dealing with that German.' He paused for a moment. 'What's more important right now is that there's a meeting of the Frigiliana Council within a few days, and that the project will be on the agenda once again. And this time I want no more dilly-dallying. This time they must vote *yes*.'

'But Massimo, nothing can go wrong now,' objected Marc de la Gaillère. 'You know that we finally managed to convince Sebastian... that councillor.'

'How much did that cost?' enquired Mister *Magnifico*.

'Four million pesetas...'

'That Green fellow!' grumbled Mister *Magnifico*. 'It's fortunate that we've got enough money. Not everyone could afford to deal with Green people. We're lucky most members of the Council don't need convincing. So... now that this German blockhead has been eliminated and the village Council is going to vote yes, I don't see any more obstacles. And that's just as well. I had a phone call from America last night – from Frank – and he told me that our overseas investors are becoming very impatient. It's high time we started the building works.'

17

Charles was sitting on a wooden bench in Church Square in Frigiliana, thinking about yesterday's events, watching absent-mindedly how a Siamese tomcat with very blue eyes was trying to make friends with a little female tortoise-shell cat that was lying in the afternoon sun, when he saw Julie appear, carrying two shopping bags. She was accompanied by a local girl and they were talking animatedly. The girl was wearing black ribbed velvet trousers and a light-grey sweatshirt, and had her dark-brown hair drawn back in a ponytail. At first Charles thought he didn't know her, but then he remembered: she was a friend of Lola's. Suddenly it struck him that he hadn't seen Lola for a long time, in fact not since that day she had passed by on the Balcón de Europa with the strange man with Arabic features.

Julie continued the animated discussion for a while until the girl left. Then she came over and sat down next to Charles, lost in thought.

'Anything the matter?'

'Yes. Do you remember Lola?'

'Of course! Is she in trouble? It's not that Mister *Magnifico* I hope!'

'I don't know. I've just been talking to her best friend; she says Lola hasn't been home for two nights now.'

'Has she ever done that before?'

'No. And her parents are becoming very worried.'

'Well… she told me she wanted to get away from them. Does she have a boyfriend?'

'It seems so. Do you think she's moved in with him without telling her parents?'

Charles made a non-committal gesture.

Presently Julie got up. 'Maybe Carmen knows more? Could you take these home?' she said handing him the shopping bags. 'I'm going to walk up to Carmen's shop and see what I can find out.'

18

When she returned half an hour later she found Charles talking to Peggy in front of *Locura*.

'Well… did you find out why Lola disappeared?' he asked.

'That depends. It seems she's had an unhappy love affair.'

'Now that's something in your line. I bet you enjoyed your conversation with Carmen.'

'Don't laugh at it. A broken heart is a serious thing, especially when it's a first romance.'

'First romance! Such a charming, attractive girl is sure to have had a few boyfriends before. Doesn't she go out dancing a lot?'

Julie cut him short. 'That doesn't mean she's flighty!'

'Quite right,' intervened Peggy. 'Men always accuse us women of being flighty when they are constantly running after girls. Just look at this one,' she said, pointing at a balding, middle-aged man who was just coming out of his door a few houses higher up. 'He's the living example of what I said.'

The man indeed liked women. He was often hanging about in the street attempting to strike up conversation with any single young foreign woman who happened to pass by and, on occasion, trying to put his arm playfully around her waist. He didn't speak a word of English but all the same, he understood that Peggy was talking about him and stopped in front of her.

'This young one here is a very bad woman,' he said, sticking his finger almost into Peggy's face while turning toward Charles. 'She says she does not love me; she doesn't even want to kiss me, I, the most handsome man in the village!' And he pushed out his chest. Even so, he remained round and short whilst Peggy, who was standing on the doorstep of the shop looking extremely pretty and girlish in her black short dress with a white long-sleeved blouse underneath, seemed to tower above his balding, shining head.

'I don't want you because you're no longer the most handsome man in the village,' she mocked, lifting up her head and making a move as if she were turning her back on him.

'No!' exclaimed the man. 'That cannot be!' He looked like a donkey that had just been refused a tempting carrot.

'Yes,' countered Peggy. 'You've lost your first place since this gentleman here has arrived.' And she gave Charles a kiss on his cheek. 'See... you're only second now.' A large smile brightened her naughty face. She obviously enjoyed teasing the man.

A sad, hurt expression came into his eyes. 'And I expected so much of you.' He wagged his finger in front of Peggy. 'I had such high hopes and now you betray me... with a foreigner!' He turned to Charles. 'This young one is very bad... very bad,' he repeated, 'and very silly. She cannot appreciate a real man.' And he stomped off, clearly offended.

'You've ruffled his feathers, Peggy,' said Charles.

'All the better. He was asking for it.'

Charles now turned to Julie who had been standing there, just shaking her head. 'What's happened to Lola and her boyfriend?'

'Carmen told me that, about six months ago, Lola met a young man from

Nerja. She fell madly in love with him and they began going out together, seeing each other twice or even three times a week. He was almost five years older than she was, and after a while he tried to persuade her that they should become lovers, but you know how it is in the villages here: Lola refused; she drew the line there. Her boyfriend was not happy with the situation and kept telling her that she was cruel; that her refusal showed that she didn't trust him. In the end, not wanting to hurt him any longer, she gave in.'

'Maybe she thought of moving in with him,' suggested Charles, 'and this was a sure way.'

Julie shook her head. 'You, men, don't understand anything. She loved him! They were going to be together forever, so it didn't matter.'

'And were they together forever?' asked Peggy.

'I'm afraid not. A few weeks ago her boyfriend told her that he had met a girl from Torrox whom his parents approved of. She was shy and inexperienced and they thought that she would make a perfect wife and mother for his children.'

'My God!' exclaimed Peggy.

'Indeed! Lola couldn't believe her ears. And their eternal love he had so often professed? The boyfriend told her that nothing was decided yet but Lola was deeply shocked. She said he was to tell his parents immediately that he loved her and not that stupid girl they had chosen for him. And why, she wanted to know, had he never explicitly asked her to marry him?'

'Not very clever that,' interrupted Charles. 'Men hate being pushed into marriage.'

'Anyway,' continued Julie, 'he hesitated a week or two and then, last weekend, he told Lola that he had decided to marry the other girl. "How could I trust you?" he asked, "a girl who goes to bed with a man without being married! If I married you and went to work, how could I be sure you would not dishonour me? With the other girl at least my honour will be safe. She is a virgin, and she will make a good wife and mother for my children. But you, Lola, have passion; you're a great lover and I enjoy making love to you. So I don't want to lose you. I want to continue seeing you even after I'm married."'

'What a bastard!' exclaimed Peggy. 'He ought to be beaten up.'

'And how did Lola react to that?' asked Charles.

'She flew into a rage and started hitting him, but he was much too strong for her and held her back. Then she screamed that she never wanted to see him again and ran away.'

'Where did she go?'

'To Carmen. She told me that Lola was with her the whole evening, crying her heart out. And she has not been seen since!'

'To lose your virginity and then not marry is a terrible thing here,' said Peggy. 'I'm sure she hasn't dared tell her parents. Maybe she has killed herself?'

Julie looked extremely upset. 'Let's hope she hasn't done anything so terrible.'

Suddenly Charles thought of the strange man he had seen with Lola a few weeks ago at the Balcón de Europa, and he felt greatly perturbed.

19

They had gone upstairs and Charles had picked up a book, but however much he tried, he was unable to concentrate on what he was reading. Too many disturbing events had happened lately. First the disappearance of Charlotte, and now Lola! He tried hard not to think about it but Lola's face kept popping up from one of the recesses of his mind, nagging him, urging him to do something.

He didn't believe in a sixth sense or that ideas could be transmitted, but exactly at that moment Julie said, 'I feel that Lola is in danger. We must do something.'

He put his book down and tried to think what he could do. Alert the police? They might begin to act in two weeks' time and then follow the wrong trail. If only he could remember where he had seen that strange fellow with Arabic features. Suddenly he had an idea. Maybe Howard could help? He had lived in Nerja for several years and probably knew most people there.

'You know what?' he said. 'I'm going to ask Howard.'

'What's the good of that?' Julie seemed sceptical. 'Are you going to ask him to read the stars?'

'Who knows?' replied Charles and he got up and left the house.

20

Calle Hernando de Carabeo starts off as a narrow street close to the Balcón de Europa in Nerja. Then, running eastwards, it widens after you come to *El Gato Negro*. Charles had dined there last year on an ordinary weekday and had found the restaurant nearly full. This year it had spread beyond its entrance door. Chairs and tables filled up a large part of the street opposite the restaurant, making it difficult for cars to pass.

The apartment block somewhat further in Carabeo, where Howard lived, was an inconspicuous place. After the bright sunshine in the street it seemed dark inside. Charles went up to the second floor, found the door to Howard's apartment and rang the bell, but nothing happened.

Maybe the bell doesn't work, he thought, knocking hard on the door, and this time he heard steps.

'What a surprise!' exclaimed Howard when he saw Charles. 'Come in. Let's go to the terrace… it's rather dark in here.'

As they passed through the narrow hall and drawing room and stepped outside, suddenly they were in a different world. Inside it had been so dark that Charles had bumped into a chair, but here on the terrace they were in the full sun and the contrast was so great that Charles had to shut his eyes. When he opened them, slowly, he saw the sea.

The view from Howard's terrace was spectacular. To the right the rocky promontory of the Balcón de Europa was jutting out into the sea. It was crowded with people who, from where he stood, seemed no more than small, moving puppets. To the left the coast stretched for many miles, with the mountains plunging abruptly into the Mediterranean.

Howard was about to show his latest books on astrology when Charles told him why he had come, explaining the curious circumstances under which he had seen Lola with a strange man on the Balcón de Europa a few weeks ago – in fact, on the day when they'd had coffee together in Café Mediterraneo. Then he began to describe the man.

'An Arabic face,' repeated Howard. 'And a sloping forehead you say. Hard eyes and a hawkish nose. A rather skinny guy, medium height, dressed in blue jeans. Well… I don't know. There are several people like him.'

'Wait! He's got a very striking mark: a scar on his left cheek.'

'Oh, but then I know him!' exclaimed Howard. 'He's always hanging around the Balcón de Europa, approaching people who are alone. He has bothered me a couple of times. He's a drug dealer.'

In a flash the memory came back to Charles. The man had approached him too a year ago, walking up to him in a casual manner and, as he came alongside, he had whispered under his breath, 'Hash?' But when Charles had seen him with Lola the matter seemed to be much more serious than selling a few ounces of hashish.

'Do you think the police know him?'

'I would think so. But he's just small fry. They're probably not interested in him.'

'Thank you,' said Charles shaking Howard's hand, ready to leave. 'You've been most helpful.'

'But the astrology books...'

'Another day when I have more time...' and Charles quickly left before Howard could hold him back.

For a minute he stood outside the apartment block wondering what to do while gazing absent-mindedly at a small white dog that was sitting in the middle of the street, scratching itself energetically. Then he made up his mind, fetched his car and drove to Torrox.

He was lucky. When he got to the Torrox police station Miguel, the inspector, was in. He didn't seem to have much to do and listened to Charles' explanations politely but absent-mindedly.

'We know she has disappeared,' he said. He sounded bored. 'Her parents have already informed the police, but I don't think this is a matter for us. It seems that she was not altogether...' he gave Charles a glance full of insinuation, '... a serious girl.'

When Charles next told him about the drug dealer in Nerja, he didn't look too pleased.

'But *hombre*,' he objected. 'How do we know that man has anything to do with the disappearance? There's absolutely no proof. My colleagues in Nerja will think this preposterous.'

Charles saw that he was getting nowhere. He had to make up something and quickly, but what? Then he had an idea. He drew nearer and, cupping his hands around his mouth, he whispered in the police inspector's ear,

'There's more but…' he stopped a second or two, '…I don't know whether I ought to tell anyone.'

The inspector looked up, interested. 'You can always tell the police. Rest assured, we keep everything strictly confidential.' And this time he smiled and looked encouragingly at Charles.

'Well… it's just that…' Charles pretended to hesitate, '…you see, someone I know who takes drugs has recently bought from him not hashish but…' he hesitated again, '… heroin.'

'Now that *is* an interesting piece of information!' exclaimed the inspector. 'Can you tell me who this person is?'

'I don't think I could do that,' replied Charles evasively. 'It would put him in a very difficult position. But there's something I can tell you…'

'Yes…' The inspector nodded encouragingly.

'He had the impression that a lot of heroin had arrived.'

'Well… well…' The inspector rubbed his hands. 'I think that we would do well to pay our little friend the drug dealer a visit. My colleagues in Nerja will be delighted.'

'Should you really do that?' Charles tried to make his voice sound as reluctant as possible. 'Nothing is certain. This might just be a false alarm. I wouldn't want to send the police on a wild goose chase.'

'That's for the police to decide,' the inspector replied, a firm expression on his face. And showing Charles the door he said, 'Sorry but I have to go now.'

21

'I'm afraid I may have got myself into trouble with the police,' Charles told Peggy next morning when he went down to the shop. She was polishing a large, round brass tabletop with a piece of cloth and copper polish; her hands were black but the brass shone like a mirror.

He explained what had happened and then hazarded, 'You don't by any chance know anyone in Nerja who takes drugs and would be willing to play the part of the informant?'

'No. And if I did I wouldn't give him away because the poor man would be sure to spend a most uncomfortable time in the police station.' She chuckled. 'I'm afraid you're going to be in for a caning.'

Just at that moment the flashy Range Rover of the English couple who owned a restaurant in Nerja drove by. The man was alone, but he was having an animated conversation on his mobile phone.

'There's that pompous fellow again,' remarked Charles.

'Oh, I know him,' said Peggy. 'I've often seen him in Nerja. And not always alone.'

'Obviously. He's married.'

'But not to the one I have seen him with,' riposted Peggy. 'You don't go and kiss your wife passionately in dark corners when you've been married for a long time.' She sighed. 'Which is really a pity.'

'You mean that he's having an affair?'

'Yes. With a girl with reddish hair. She's about my height and pretty. In fact she looks very much like me.' Peggy drew herself up. 'Only not as pretty as I am of course.'

'But that's the girl who serves in his bar!' exclaimed Charles. 'She's very pretty indeed.'

'Now, now… don't tell me that she's prettier than me.'

'Well… I'm not quite sure…' and seeing her face fall he added, 'But you're the nicest by far, there's no doubt about it.'

'Am I?' Her eyebrows shot up. 'Good.' She gave him a beaming smile and continued her polishing.

22

When Alejandra arrived around noon for her Spanish lesson she looked terribly excited. She began to speak even before she'd had time to sit down.

'My cousin's husband made the most remarkable arrest,' she blurted out, looking at them with undisguised pride in her eyes as if part of the glory of the inspector's deeds rubbed off on her.

'Yes…' Julie and Charles spoke almost simultaneously. They had been wondering the whole of last evening about Lola and about what the police might have been doing.

'He has arrested that very rich Italian who lives in a luxurious property towards Torrox.'

It wasn't at all what Charles had expected and he remained tongue-tied, but Julie managed to exclaim, 'Well, that *is* extraordinary!'

'Yes, isn't it,' agreed Alejandra. 'My cousin's husband is extremely good. Let me tell you the story.' She waited a few seconds, visibly enjoying the show. 'Yesterday afternoon he gave orders to shadow a certain drug dealer in Nerja.'

'Now why did he do that?' asked Charles as innocently as possible.

'Oh, I suppose he had the intuition. Policemen feel that sort of thing, you know. That's what distinguishes them from ordinary people.' Alejandra looked pleased with her reply. 'But let me continue. When the dealer returned to his house later in the afternoon they arrested him just as he was putting his key in the door. And guess what they found in his house?' Her brown eyes were like two question marks under her thick eyebrows, and she paused to make a greater effect on her audience.

'A girl from Frigiliana called Lola?' ventured Charles.

Alejandra's face sagged and her mouth fell open. She looked as if Charles had stolen her show. 'How did you know that?'

'It must be intuition.' Charles chuckled. 'But rest reassured. The police are much better at this sort of thing. Tell me, was Lola pleased to be saved?'

'No,' replied Alejandra continuing her story, but she had lost some of her cocksureness. 'As a matter of fact, she was very upset when the police wanted to take her home. She said she was going to Holland and never wanted to return to Spain. The drug dealer had found her a wonderful job in Amsterdam and they were coming to fetch her that same evening. But the police smelled a rat and decided to wait inside. Finally, around eight o'clock, someone rang the bell and he was quite surprised when the police opened the door and handcuffed him. It was obviously not what the man – a Dutchman from Amsterdam – had expected. He was immediately taken to the police station with the others to be interrogated and at midnight the drug dealer broke down.'

'So quickly?'

'I suppose the police have their ways of convincing suspects to talk,' stated Alejandra looking as innocent as possible. 'Anyway, once the dealer had confessed, the Dutchman – a tall fellow with long blond hair and earrings – caved in too and the police were able to put the whole story together. It turned out that the drug dealer worked for that rich Italian. About four weeks ago the man had ordered the dealer to approach Lola to try and befriend her; she was often in Nerja because she studied at the Institute there. The dealer had done what he had been told and, gradually, he had begun to inform her about wonderful opportunities abroad as a top model; about the fortunes she could earn, and the sort of life she could lead. She had the right figure – he had noticed it immediately – and it would be a pity to miss the chance of a lifetime. But she was not to tell anyone because the selection committee didn't want the public to know before the right candidate had been chosen.'

'And what was the job in reality?' Julie wanted to know.

'She was going to be taken to a nightclub in Amsterdam where she would have to strip and join the customers afterwards. The club was run by the wife of the Italian.'

Charles whistled and turned to Julie. 'So Mister *Magnifico* nearly had his revenge for the bitter defeat Lola inflicted on him.'

'It seems that she wasn't his first victim either,' continued Alejandra. 'And that Italian was dealing in drugs as well.'

'Did he have anything to do with the murder of the German?' enquired Charles.

'The police did interrogate the drug dealer about the murder, but he categorically denied. He said his boss had nothing to do with that.'

'Where is Lola now?' asked Julie.

'She's been taken back to her parents in a terribly depressed state.'

'Poor thing!' exclaimed Julie. 'I must go and see her.'

23

As Charles stepped out of the house in the afternoon he was nearly knocked over by Sam jumping straight up at him, trying to lick his face. Agustina's van was parked close to the yellow mailbox at the entrance of the steps to Calle El Darra and she was carrying up a pile of coloured blankets on outstretched arms, steadying the load with her chin. After she had put them down inside the shop she came out again to give Charles an affectionate hug.

'How nice you're still here,' she said. 'I feared that you might already have left.'

'You seem well.' Charles held her at arm's length and looked into her brown sparkling eyes. 'Travelling suits you.'

'I love it. That's when I live most intensely.'

'I didn't see Sam while you were in Morocco. Did you take him with you?'

'Of course. I take him with me wherever I go.' She said it as if it were the most natural thing in the world. 'He's an excellent traveller. He sleeps in the car until I stop and when I get out, he walks the streets of Tangiers or Marrakech without a leash as if he had done so all his life.' Agustina looked at Sam with pride. 'He likes to discover new places. A strange town is a world full of unknown dogs; and full of new smells. You know… he doesn't experience towns the way we do. For him they are a world of scents.'

'Are you saying that he goes off on his own? It's incredible that you've never lost him.'

'If I lose track of him in a strange town, he goes back to the spot where he was last with me and waits there patiently until I return to pick him up.'

'And he never gets into trouble?'

'Well, sometimes he does… This time he killed two hens in a small town where I had stopped. It wasn't really his fault that those stupid chickens started running away in fright, cackling loudly when Sam stumbled upon them.' There was a defensive look in her eyes. 'Obviously, you should never run away from a dog because that excites him. He thinks it's all fun and games, you see. But the owner of the hens was furious and said it was my fault because Sam was not on a leash.'

Charles glanced at Sam who had spread himself out on the street full length, looking the image of innocence. 'How did you get out of that fix?'

'It was a bit difficult. Before we had time to escape, Sam and I were surrounded by half a dozen angry men and a great discussion ensued. I had to pay up and, of course, the owner profited from the occasion to make me pay the highest price possible. He kept saying these were his best hens that laid lots of eggs every day. But it all ended well. After I had paid, they cooked the chickens for us and we had a nice meal, especially Sam who was quite hungry by the time everything was settled.'

'By the way, is Peggy going to leave now that you're back?'

'Didn't I tell you before? I'll do the mornings and she takes over at three in the afternoon to do the rest of the day. It's nice for me to have her here. But I must carry on,' said Agustina. 'I haven't unloaded even half the van yet.'

24

'Go away Gato!' shouted Julie. She was trying to prepare lunch – not something she really enjoyed during her holidays – and it was just too much that the cat was bothering her while she was forcing herself to cook. 'Leave me alone! What a nuisance he is. Throw him out Charles!'

Charles looked up from his notepad. 'Can't you see he's hungry, the poor thing. Just give him something to eat.'

'He has already eaten this morning, and now he wants food again! He's greedy, that's what he is. When we arrived he was pleased to have anything to eat at all but now, just look!'

'That's because he's become attached to us. He wants to eat when we are eating. I think he looks very human.'

'You're besotted with that silly Gato.' Julie had a reproving look in her eyes. 'All right… all right!' She fetched a bag of cat biscuits and put some on a saucer with oil from a tin of sardines. When Gato understood that he was going to get some food, he began meowing frantically and stood up on his back legs, stretching himself so much that his paws almost touched the sink. Then, as Julie picked up the saucer to put it on the terrace, he rushed in between her legs, making her stumble and nearly fall.

'That's enough!' she shouted. 'You won't get any more food if you don't learn to behave!' But Gato didn't pay any attention to Julie's threat. He was gobbling up his biscuits with visible delight and afterwards licked his saucer clean till the last trace of oil had disappeared. Then he walked towards a sunny corner of the terrace and began to wash himself, going elaborately over every patch of his coarse light-grey fur and passing his paws repeatedly over his funny miniature lion's face.

Charles had begun to write again, sitting in an easy chair, when suddenly Gato jumped onto his lap right on top of his notepad and stuck his nose straight into Charles' face.

'Gato, get down!' He tried to push the cat away but Gato clung on, dug his claws into Charles' shirt and began to purr loudly.

'Leave me alone! Can't you see I'm writing?'

Julie grinned. 'He just wants a bit of warmth, the poor thing. He has been missing it so much. You mustn't be unkind to him. Look how much he likes you.'

'I think he's much heavier than when he arrived.'

'No wonder,' replied Julie. 'With all the food we give him.'

Gato had by now settled cosily on Charles' lap. His eyelids drooped and he was ready to fall asleep. The ballpoint pen had fallen on the floor and the writing pad was stuck underneath Gato's body. Charles sighed and gave up.

With nothing else to do he began to think about the events of the last few days. What had happened to Charlotte? Was she still alive? The police hadn't even begun looking for her. Would they ever find her? It was unlikely, considering that they still had no clue about the murder of Meier several weeks after his death. The murder remained as much a mystery today as it had been on the day he had been killed. And at that time at least, there had been several obvious suspects. But now, one by one, they were losing them: the rich Italian was no longer a possibility and neither, Charles felt, was Paco.

He had never considered the German's English neighbours serious candidates. They were awful, even vicious people embroiled in their own world of lies and betrayal, but that didn't make them murderers. So who remained?

And Fernando. Who had killed him? Charles found it hard to believe that those three men from Torrox had committed the murder.

'Of course!' Charles exclaimed suddenly, moving so brusquely that

Gato nearly rolled off his lap. The cat looked at him, visibly offended, and then settled down again.

'Of course what?' asked Julie who was stirring an elaborate sauce.

'These three men from Torrox didn't kill Fernando. I knew it intuitively all along but now I'm sure. It's so obvious.'

'I don't see it,' said Julie. 'Why do you think so?'

'Because they would have lifted up Fernando's body to carry him to the side of the cliff instead of dragging him through the grass and leaving traces.'

'How evident! Why didn't we think of it before? But who murdered Fernando then?'

'It must be the same person who killed Meier. We know that Fernando worked for the German and pinched his wine bottles. He may have sneaked up on the night Meier was killed to take down some wine bottles he had hidden around the house, and may have seen the murderer. Remember what *Premio Gordo* said? That he knew a secret worth a lot of money.'

'You think Fernando tried to blackmail the murderer?'

'Probably. He may not even have asked for a lot of money, only just enough not to have to give up his horse, but the murderer obviously wasn't going to take any risks. He must have told Fernando that he would give him the money up on the hill at night. And then he killed the poor man.'

'So who do you think killed Meier and Fernando?'

'Well... let me see...' Charles put a finger in front of his lips, '...the murderer must have been alone and he cannot have been a strong man, otherwise he would have been able to carry the body. We therefore have to look out for someone relatively weak... a skinny person such as... well, such as Howard for example.'

'You don't mean to say that you suspect Howard? That's ridiculous!'

'Well... we must consider every possibility.' Charles tried to sound serious but there was a broad grin on his face. 'Considering that he works for an international organisation, he may have had connections with the project people and acted for them? You never know.'

Julie began to laugh. 'I can't see him doing anything of the sort. At the last moment Jupiter would have moved out of Leo; or the moon would be full, or heavens knows what, stopping him from going ahead.'

'I was only joking. Can you see Howard premeditating a murder hanging upside down from a tree? I hope you have a better suggestion.'

'I think so. Isn't it obvious who the murderer is?'

'To me nothing seems obvious in this murder case. Who is it then?'

'A woman.'

Charles sat there for a while without speaking. Why had he always thought of the murderer as a man? 'I think you may be right,' he said at last.

'Remember the intruder we saw that night in the German's house. I told you it was a woman.'

Suddenly Charles had a strange premonition. 'You're not thinking of Charlotte?'

'No. I'm thinking of the Swiss woman from the project.'

'But that's not logical. Why would she have acted alone? Every time we saw her she was accompanied by her French partner. And that Frenchman is strong. He and the Swiss woman together would have had no need to drag Fernando's body along. No. It must have been another woman.'

'All right. If you say so…' Julie's eyes twinkled. 'I think it was that red-haired girl from Nerja.'

'How can you suspect her? I don't believe she would ever do such a thing!'

'Why not? Do you think her innocent just because she's attractive? You would make a fine member of a jury! Maybe she killed the German because the project people paid her to do so. Anything is possible.'

'Yes.' Charles sighed. 'Unfortunately, anything is possible.'

25

Charles was looking down from the balcony later in the day when he saw the bald man from higher up come out of his house. The man stopped in front of Peggy who was standing on the doorstep of *Locura*, and looked up at her with a flicker in his bulging eyes.

'Instead of liking tall, slim foreigners, why don't you find yourself a short, round, local man with experience, hey!' he blurted out.

Charles heard her laugh. 'Yes, but is there such a god-like figure in this village? I haven't seen anyone as perfect as you describe him. I'm afraid I shall have to content myself with tall, slim foreigners.'

'Bad, bad...' mumbled the man, shaking his heavy head while going away. 'How can she be so bad?'

Presently a young woman came up the street, carrying a small bag. Although she was still some fifty yards away her figure seemed familiar to Charles, but somehow he failed to recognise her. He was still laughing at the conversation he had overheard and it was not until she had got quite close that he realised who it was: it was Charlotte! She was alive! Charles felt so relieved that he stood there for a few seconds, unable to speak. Then he called out, 'Charlotte!' and rushed downstairs. He ran up to her, put his arms around her and held her tight.

There was no reaction on her part. She seemed cold, distant.

Charles had wanted to dance about with joy, to ask her a thousand questions... and now he didn't know what to say. She might have been a stranger and he a man who had just made a fool of himself, having hugged a woman he had mistaken for another.

'What's the matter?' she finally said in an expressionless voice.

'But... but, we were so worried. Where have you been?'

'In Malaga.' Her voice sounded evasive.

'Why didn't you tell us?'

'Why should I?' Then she said, 'I'm going to pack. I'm leaving tomorrow.'

'You're leaving? Just like that?'

'I've had enough of Spain.'

'Oh... wait! You don't know, but the police have searched your house.'

Charlotte looked very upset. 'What did they do that for?'

'We thought something had happened to you...'

'Ridiculous.' She shrugged her shoulders, went up the street without so much as a goodbye and soon disappeared inside her house.

26

'I don't understand,' replied Julie when Charles told her about Charlotte's strange behaviour. 'I'll go and see her.' Charles was about to object that it was time to start supper but before he could do so much as open his mouth Julie had already rushed off.

She found the door of Charlotte's house closed but it was not locked and she resolutely went in. There was nobody on the ground floor, but strange sounds seemed to come from above. As Julie crept up the stairs, the sounds became stronger and then she knew what they were: someone was crying in the bedroom.

'Charlotte!' exclaimed Julie as she went inside and found the girl curled up on her bed, sobbing. She sat down beside her and touched her arm, but Charlotte didn't react. She just lay there while her body was shaking piteously. The sorrow of many endless, sleepless nights seemed to be bursting from her in floods of tears that welled up from deep inside her. Julie resolutely pulled her up and put an arm around her. For a moment Charlotte looked at Julie through hazy eyes. Then she stammered, 'I don't want to go on living.'

'Is it Edward?'

When Charlotte heard his name, she threw herself back on the bed and hid her face.

'Has he written?'

Charlotte shook her head.

'What is it then? Tell me what's happened,' insisted Julie, pulling her up again.

Finally Charlotte began. 'A... a friend came to see me a week ago and... and I accompanied her when she drove back to Malaga. And then I met an artist friend at an exhibition and... and she told me she knew Edward.' Charlotte began to cry again.

'Why should that upset you?'

'He met her before me and... he lived with her for a whole month... she paid for everything because his credit card didn't work and... and... he said that she was the love of his life...' She burst out in tears.

'What!' Julie felt so cross that she began to shake Charlotte. 'How could he!'

'... and... and... he gave her a little teddy bear and promised to marry her!' There was another outburst of tears before Charlotte managed to continue, '...but first he had to go back to Australia for an exhibition... so she gave him the money for his return ticket... and after that he met me...' Charlotte threw herself on her bed in a fit of despair.

'What a bastard!' exclaimed Julie. 'Poor Charlotte! Have you eaten anything? I'll go and cook you some food.' And she ran out to prepare a meal in her own house.

27

Later in the evening Charlotte was sitting in her studio in a gloomy mood. I ought to be packing, she thought, but she just couldn't bring herself to do it. Instead, she began to look absentmindedly through a pile of drawings that was lying on a table till she came to the sketch of Meier. When she saw him smile at her from the page, she had to turn away. How could she have treated him so despicably? And now he was dead! It was all Edward's fault. That cheat, that liar! She went to a cupboard, took out Edward's photographs, threw them on the ground and stamped her foot on them in disgust.

Just then there was a rap on the front door below, making her jump in surprise. She went down, and as she opened the door Charlotte looked into the eyes of a woman she had seen a couple of times at Meier's before she had met Edward. The woman was well dressed in a fashionable outfit and wore a string of pearls. She stood there, not moving, a fixed smile on her face.

'Yes?' asked Charlotte, astonished to see her.

'I think we know each other.' The woman's voice sounded apprehensive. As Charlotte nodded she carried on, 'I've heard that you are a very gifted sculptor and... well... would you take on a commission for a marble bust?'

Charlotte stood there, unable to think clearly. 'I don't know,' she finally replied.

'But I want you to do it! You can't refuse this! I will pay you any price you ask.'

Suddenly Charlotte felt her head spin. Any price! She was very short of money. Maybe this was the answer to all her problems? 'Whom do you want me to sculpt?' she asked at last.

'Well... me of course. So you will do it?'

'All right. But a bust in marble will be extremely expensive.'

'That's of no importance. Can you start straightaway? Come with me now and I'll give you an advance...'

'Sorry,' protested Charlotte, 'not tonight.'

The woman insisted. 'You cannot come with me now?'

'That's not possible. I'll have to sort out all I need first, and I'm very tired.'

'All right... tomorrow then?'

As Charlotte nodded agreement, the woman continued, 'You know where I live. Come to my house at twelve exactly. I shall be waiting for you; I'll have everything ready to pay you.' Suddenly she lowered her voice. 'And don't tell anybody about this.' As she saw Charlotte's astounded look she explained, 'The bust is meant to be a present, and it must be a surprise.' Then she turned and went quickly up the dark street.

28

Julie wanted to do some shopping in Nerja the next morning and Charles offered to drive her. He hadn't been down to the sea for a while and was rather looking forward to getting out of Frigiliana and having a cup of coffee on the Balcón de Europa.

Julie was putting the last touches to her appearance, which would, she said, take no more than a minute. It was a lovely, sunny morning and Charles, who had already been hanging about for the last quarter of an hour, decided to go ahead and wait for her on one of the benches near the parking lot.

'Why are you so late?' he asked when she finally showed up twenty minutes later. 'You said you were nearly ready when I left you!'

'I was, but as I came out of the door I ran into Charlotte.'

'Was she carrying her suitcases?' asked Charles with clear sarcasm in his voice.

'No. Strangely enough, she's going to stay. She actually seemed quite pleased with herself.'

Charles shook his head. 'But she told me she was leaving! And didn't you say she was crying her heart out yesterday? How can her moods change so quickly? I think she's totally unbalanced.'

'Well… something new has cropped up. She has unexpectedly landed an extremely lucrative commission for a bust in marble. She has to go up the hill later in the morning – to that English woman's house – to take photographs of her.'

'What does she need photographs for if she's going to sculpt the woman?'

Julie lifted her eyes to the heavens. 'Surely, you cannot be as ignorant as that? Didn't you know people no longer sit for artists? The artist now takes photographs and works from them in his or her own workshop.'

'Well… it's her business,' commented Charles while starting the car. He sounded slightly put out.

He began the descent to Nerja but remained in a pensive mood. 'If you ask me, I find her whole attitude extremely suspicious,' he said after some time. 'So she wants us to believe that she went to an exhibition in Malaga?'

'Yes. And when she was there she found out about Edward as I told you last night. Why don't you believe her? You should have seen the poor girl.'

'I'm not surprised about that Edward. I tried to tell her he was a cheat. She wouldn't listen, but *I* knew it all along.'

Presently Charles began to concentrate on the hairpin bends until after a mile the road straightened somewhat and they suddenly saw the coastline and the white houses of Nerja. It was a beautiful view, but today Charles was not in the mood for appreciating scenic beauty. He had been thinking hard during the drive and suddenly said, 'I feel there's more to Charlotte than she's willing to divulge. She knew Fernando. And she also knew Meier. Remember the portrait? Why did she never tell us? We really don't know much about her, come to think of it. And do you recall how she tried to stop us finding out about the murderer when Angeles was doing the pendulum? She seems to have been very careful never to talk about the murder. But there was one moment when she was caught off guard. Didn't she say that Edward thought her poor but that she wasn't? That she was going to come into a lot of money? I really wonder what her exact relation with Meier was. I would be interested to find out who inherits from him.'

29

After Charles had dropped Julie and parked the car, he walked to the Balcón de Europa. It was filled with tourists, something quite unusual for a midweek day out of season. All the tables on the terraces were occupied and so Charles decided to sit down on one of the white marble benches situated around the Balcón, and wait there for a table to be free.

As he was looking around, a large group of tourists came into view. From the way they behaved and were dressed they could only be English. They had probably arrived that very day and were having their first look at the exotic south. Some stood staring in wonder at the tall palm trees and the magnificent views but most went straight towards the carriages with white horses that were standing at the side of the Balcón, waiting for customers. They didn't want a tour around Nerja though; they wanted a photograph of themselves in front of a horse and carriage, with the palm trees behind.

The voices of the people on the Balcón made a humming sound, rather like bees in some strange beehive, and the humming was punctuated by the click-click of the shears of a middle-aged workman who was trimming the low hedges around the big plane trees near the old whitewashed church. He handled his shears with dexterity but every now and then he stopped to take a deep drag from his cigarette.

Just then Charles noticed that a man who had been reading a newspaper on the terrace of the Mediterraneo, his favourite café, got up and he moved quickly forward to claim the table. The man had left his paper on a chair and after Charles had ordered a *café con leche*, he picked it up. It was *Bild Zeitung*, a popular German daily. On its front page it carried the usual articles under big titles about political corruption, scandals and celebrities – the staple food for sensation-hungry readers the world over.

A little blue-and-white tourist train pulling two miniature coaches loaded with people distracted him for a moment. It passed just in front of the terrace, ringing its bell madly. When it had gone he bent down again over the paper, turned to page two and looked absent-mindedly at a photograph under a large title: Heiress arrives out of the blue to claim a fortune! Then he was struck by the subtitle. It read: Meier had a daughter.

Suddenly his whole body began to tingle with excitement and he scanned quickly through the article. It said that Meier's daughter had turned up at his solicitor's office in Hamburg but that the solicitor had refused to accept her claim. There seemed to be some unsolved disagreement about the inheritance. Apparently Meier had phoned his solicitor a few days before he had been killed to tell him that he was going to send him a will. The solicitor hadn't received it but he had refused to do anything definite until he saw that will.

So there was a daughter! Charles had the clear foreboding that here was the key to the whole mystery, and he stared with undisguised curiosity at the snapshot of the heiress, taken as she left the solicitor's office. She must have been surprised by the photographer because her arm had been moving upwards as if she had tried to hide her face. It was half turned and slightly blurred, but even so it looked familiar to him... Then, suddenly, he recognised the face... it was her! He felt so agitated that he almost knocked his coffee cup off the table. That's why, when he had seen that drawing of Meier in Charlotte's house, he'd had the impression that, somehow, he knew the face! Why hadn't he thought of it before? Of course! If she was Meier's daughter, that explained everything. At once all the pieces of the puzzle fell into place: the murderer a woman... someone who lived in Frigiliana... Julie's reading of the character, it all fitted... yes, he knew... he knew!

All of a sudden a frightening thought flashed through his mind. He picked up the newspaper, threw a hundred-pesetas coin on the table, zigzagged between the surrounding tables under the surprised looks of the other customers, and ran off at top speed.

Within minutes he got to the place where Julie usually did her shopping and found her with a large basket, half full. 'Quick!' he cried. 'We haven't got a second to lose.'

'But...' Julie protested, 'I haven't finished yet.'

He pulled the basket out of her hand, dumped it on the floor, dragged her out of the shop and ran towards where the car was parked, pulling her along. By the time they got there Julie was completely out of breath and Charles had already started the car and was well on the main road before she was able to speak.

'What's the matter?' she gasped. 'Have you lost your mind?'

'It's got to do with Charlotte...' He overtook three cars and turned into the Frigiliana road. 'Can't explain now.' The car went into the first bends with screaming tyres. 'We must prevent another murder.' He negotiated two sharp bends at top speed.

'Please slow down,' pleaded Julie, holding on to the dashboard and the door, 'or you'll kill us.'

But his only reply was, 'I hope we're not too late.' And he tried to go even faster.

30

Charlotte was climbing up the hill trying to hurry, puffing with the effort. She was late as usual. When she had been ready to leave, she couldn't find her camera and had spent ten minutes frantically searching for it, cursing her disorder. And when she had finally located it under a pile of clothes, there was no film in it and she had wasted another ten minutes, first looking for a new roll, and then putting it in.

She hoped the woman wouldn't be too upset with her for being late. It would be ridiculous to lose such an expensive commission. Only once before had she been asked to do a bust in marble. It had been a challenge, but it had been very well paid. And today she needed both; she had felt so depressed lately, and when that woman contacted her yesterday it had seemed like a godsend. Even now she could hardly believe her luck.

She slowed down as she approached the woman's house. It looked new, impersonal, almost without style, in total contrast to Meier's property just above. She had passed the house before on her way to Meier, but had never stopped to look at it. Come to think of it, she didn't know much about the woman either, apart from the fact that she was English. Charlotte had seen her twice at Meier's. There was probably nothing strange about that; after all, they were neighbours. On both occasions, though, Meier had clearly shown that he preferred to be alone with Charlotte and his neighbour had left them after a short while, barely saying goodbye.

As Charlotte rang the bell she was worrying that the woman would no longer be in, but within seconds she heard sounds inside and the door was flung open. When Charlotte saw the woman she had a shock: her face seemed unreal, like a wax mask. She looks ghastly, Charlotte couldn't help thinking, and as the woman bade her come in she nearly stepped back. Then she followed her almost unwillingly through the hall and into the living room.

The woman now turned to her. 'You haven't told anyone that you've come to my house?'

'No; no one knows I'm here,' lied Charlotte, and the woman continued quickly, as if to draw attention away from her question, 'I see you've only brought a small bag. Is that all you need?'

Charlotte opened her bag and took out the camera. 'I shall need to take a series of photographs to do a preliminary study,' she heard herself say in a mechanical voice. 'Is there anything special you want to wear?' She sounded like an actress playing her role badly.

An idea seemed to flash through the woman's mind. 'Yes, there *is* something particular…' Her voice suddenly sounded challenging. 'A jewel. I'll change and put it on. Sit down,' she ordered.

While she was waiting on the divan for the woman to reappear, Charlotte felt strangely uneasy. There is something wrong here, she thought. I feel caught in a spider's web. I must get out of here. She half got up but hesitated. Come on girl, she tried to convince herself, this is all imagination. Put it out of your mind. Think of the commission.

She was startled by a sound behind her and as she turned around she shuddered. The woman stood there, dressed in black like a goddess of death, and around her neck she wore… *the jewel*, sparkling like dozens of bright stars!

A wave of panic struck Charlotte. Her throat was dry and her heart began to race like a stampeding horse. She tried to move but felt paralysed.

'I see you recognise it,' came the woman's voice, sharp like a cutting knife. 'Yes, *I* have got the jewel now.' She moved a step forward. 'So you thought you could lay your hands on *my* inheritance!' Then she hissed angrily, 'Miserable whores you are… all of you. Your sort thinks that you can get everything just because you are young. But this is what you'll get!' And she picked up a block of quartz that was lying on a sideboard, her fingers curling around it like snakes, her eyes filled with blind hatred.

31

Charles reached Frigiliana in record time, drove through the parking lot and stopped the car in front of El Darra Street. 'Park it!' he shouted to Julie and began rushing up.

Sam, who was lying in the sun outside *Locura*, looked up in surprise as Charles dashed by and began to follow him, curious to know what game he was playing and ready to join in. When Charles got to Charlotte's house he found the door locked as he had feared, and he carried on as fast as he could with Sam running at his side, looking as if he were asking, 'What's the game?' Just then Sven appeared around the corner higher up.

'Charlotte is up on the hill!' Charles cried out panting. 'Quick! She's in danger!'

Sven stared at him for a fraction of a second. Then he turned around and shot up the street like an arrow, followed by Sam who thought he had found a new playmate. By the time Charles rounded the corner he had lost sight of them and felt completely exhausted. Sweat was running down his face and his heart was thumping so loudly that he thought it was going to burst. The hilltop was now in view and as he looked up a young woman came fleeing down the path. She ran with difficulty, holding on to her shoulder: it was Charlotte! Close on her heels was a woman dressed entirely in black, her hand raised to strike. Sven was still twenty yards away.

Hurry, prayed Charles. Save her. Then, to his horror, he saw Charlotte stumble and fall, banging her head on a boulder! He stood there, gasping for breath, waiting for the blow that would put an end to her young life. Then he heard Sven yell, 'Attack!' and Sam, who was well ahead, shot forward. The dog leapt up at the woman's arm, trying to get at what he must have taken for a ball. She screamed with fright at the sudden attack of a big black dog and lost her balance while Sam fell on top of her. Sven, however, had no eyes for the woman but rushed to where Charlotte was lying unconscious, and bent over her. As he saw Sven lifting her up Sam ran towards them, wagging his tail as if asking to be invited into the game.

The woman now scrambled to her feet. She seemed to have collected her senses and began to flee down the path holding on to her right wrist, her face distorted with pain. Charles jumped in front of her trying to grab her arm, when suddenly the sun was reflected in a necklace she was wearing. Dazzling stars seemed to flash at him, blinding him for a second, and the woman managed to dodge him and continued dashing recklessly down the slope.

32

Bob Marvey was in a really foul mood. Nothing had gone right for him these days. Lesley had flown abroad promising to return with a lot of money, but she had come back empty handed! And when he reproached her for not keeping her promise, she had become positively horrid. Where did this leave him? A man from the bank was going to come to the restaurant this very afternoon to collect the arrears of the mortgage. What the hell was he going to tell him?

He hadn't felt like driving to Nerja at all today, yet for once Lesley wanted him to go! She had pestered him, nearly pushing him out of the house, till he had finally left. What was the point in opening the restaurant at twelve when there were no customers? Yesterday there hadn't been a single customer till seven at night. The atmosphere in the restaurant was frankly sinister. And Amanda hadn't turned up for two days now. Could it get any worse?

He went down dragging his feet, reached the parking lot and got into his Range Rover. As he began backing out, a lorry just passed behind. He hit the brake, but too late: he definitely felt a shock. He cut the engine and jumped out in a fury to see what had happened, leaving the driver's door wide open: his rear light was smashed! 'Not again!' he burst out. Then he looked at the lorry sticking up his fist but it just carried on and disappeared!

He strode to the nearby garage in a rage, only to find that the garage man wasn't in, and he nearly screamed. He waited for some time but as nobody turned up, he finally went to a nearby shop to inquire what that Vicente was doing.

33

Up on the hill Charlotte had regained consciousness and lay in Sven's arms, holding on to him. He was murmuring soothing words to her while Sam, having understood that no one wanted to play with him, just sat there looking bored. They don't need me, thought Charles, and he began to run back towards the village and the Guardia Civil post to inform the police about everything. As the parking lot came into view he saw a red car pull out and disappear into the *barrio nuevo*: it was the Range Rover with the woman at the steering wheel!

He rushed into the Guardia Civil post and, to his relief, bumped into Miguel, the inspector from Torrox who was standing there talking to a few policemen.

'Quick!' shouted Charles. 'Meier's murderer has just escaped in a car!'

Miguel recognised Charles as the man who had led him to the drug dealer, and for once he shot into action without asking questions. He began to yell orders and Charles jumped into a police car with him and another policeman. As the car started, Charles suddenly saw the R.R. man come running along, shouting, 'My car!' pointing down the *barrio nuevo*. And the man jumped into a second police car without so much as a "by your leave".

34

As she drove towards Nerja trying to steer with one hand, thoughts whirled through Lesley's mind like a dust devil spinning in the wind. Why had she lost her head again? But that shameless girl deserved my revenge, she thought angrily. My father had wanted to adopt her and leave her his fortune. The fortune that was rightly mine!

How she hated those young women who were trying to rob her of everything that was hers: that artist girl, and above all that red-haired schemer who had seduced Bob! What was there left for her now? She had lost the only two men she had ever really loved in her life: her father, who was dead, and Bob who was besotted with that little whore. And now they are going to put me in prison for the rest of my life, she panicked. Why should all this have happened to me? What have I done?

She had bought the house in Frigiliana to be nearer her father and had immediately presented Bob, but for some unknown reason her father had never been able to stand him – had felt nothing but contempt for him. That fateful evening had been no exception. He had continued to fiddle with that diamond necklace he had found during his diggings, saying he was busy and had no time to listen to her stupid sentimental affair. She had defended Bob as always, but this time her words had been more pressing. She had tried to justify his behaviour, not only to her father but maybe also to herself. It had all been to no avail; he had called Bob an egocentric opportunist and a sponger. When she heard her father put into words the doubts that had assailed her for weeks she had felt desperate but still, she refused to admit that he might be right and had continued pleading, 'Please help me. I need money urgently, otherwise I'll go bankrupt. And what's a bit of money to you? Don't you love me?'

Her father had looked exasperated. 'I'm fed up with you!' he had exclaimed. 'Wanting money to save your stupid sentimental affair!' Then he said that if she went bankrupt, she had been asking for it; that it was maybe the best thing that could happen to her because it would finally reveal the true character of that parasite who was scrounging on her. He had added that he would be willing to love her if she deserved it, but as matters stood he preferred to disinherit her rather than see his money wasted on a scrounger. And he had resolutely turned his back on her.

That had been just too much. She had been unable to control herself any longer. All the pent-up anger, the rage against life, against the injustices done to her, against that red-haired bitch, had suddenly exploded in a blind fury. She had picked up a poker that was hanging next to her on the chimney and hit her father hard on the back of his head. She had felt a certain satisfaction, as if justice had been done; then, with horror, she had realised that he was dead: she had killed her father! How could this have happened?

She hadn't been the same ever since. Guilt was gnawing her heart out, and the scenes of that fateful evening had begun to haunt her night after night, like a nightmare. She had tried to hide what she had done, even from Bob, hoping nobody would find out, and for a while nothing had happened. She had begun to relax somewhat, and had risked sneaking into her father's house to search for the address of his solicitor. And she had finally booked a flight to Hamburg to claim her inheritance. She needed the money urgently.

And then that drunken gardener had come along saying he knew who she was, and wanted money! And worse was to come. When she got to Hamburg, the solicitor informed her that she wasn't going to inherit because her father had phoned to tell him he was making a will in favour of that artist girl! It had enraged her beyond control!

Why had her life been plunged into insecurity and bitterness? She saw herself again as a young child, walking to the fairground between her mum and her dad, holding their hands, so happy, so confident. And then everything had broken up. She had seen little of her father after he had left her mother and gone back to Germany. Why had he rejected her? She had always wanted his love, his admiration, but he said she was just like her mother, superficial, only after money. But she wouldn't have been like that if only he had cared for her! Why hadn't her father given her love? She needed him so much now. Tears welled up from deep inside and streamed out of her eyes, half blinding her as she drove along. 'Oh Dad, Dad, please come back and help me out of this,' she cried. The pain was so great, it hurt so much... she couldn't stand it any more. She longed for the end, for the darkness that would settle over her... no more memories, no more suffering. Then a car appeared in a bend of the road and she wrenched the steering wheel abruptly with her one good hand...

35

The police cars drove through the narrow street of the *barrio nuevo* with howling sirens and began the descent towards Nerja in hot pursuit. Miguel had just reached the series of hairpin bends when his car nearly collided with a small car that had stopped in the middle of the road, its door wide open.

As Miguel got out in a rage, the driver, who was standing at the edge of the road looking white and shaky, began to yell, 'It's not my fault!' while pointing a trembling finger at the steep precipice. There, down below, lay the wreck of the Range Rover upside down, the wheels still turning. The policeman who accompanied Miguel was about to try and climb down when suddenly the wreck burst into flames.

At that moment the second police car appeared and as it stopped, the R.R. man jumped out shouting, 'What's happened? Where's my car?' Suddenly he saw the burning wreck and became frantic. 'My car!' he yelled. 'She's ruined my car, the old bitch! I'll kill her.'

Charles went towards the man clenching his fists, trying hard to keep calm. 'No need for that.' His voice was icy. 'She's in there. She's dead already.'

The man looked at him with empty eyes. Suddenly, he seemed to be overcome with distress.

There may be some decency left in that man after all, thought Charles, but then he heard him wail, 'What's going to become of me now?'

Charles couldn't believe his ears. 'Now that your wife is dead you'll have everything to yourself,' he said coldly. 'To enjoy it with your mistress!'

The man stared at Charles as if he had been stung. 'She wasn't my wife,' he hissed. 'I never married her. Everything was hers. The only thing that was mine was the Range Rover.'

36

'Look at this!' said Charles the next morning, showing Julie the regional newspaper he'd just bought.

The front page carried the headline: 'Torrox police scores another remarkable victory' followed by: 'Rich German murdered by his own daughter!' And Charles began to read aloud to Julie. 'Torrox police inspector Miguel Ortega, who already distinguished himself by putting the Nerja police on the track of an international organisation trafficking in drugs and young women, yesterday unmasked the perpetrator of the murder of Konrad Meier, the German who was killed in his house in Frigiliana several weeks ago. The murderer was the English woman who lived just below, and she was no other than his own daughter! It seems she also killed Fernando Lortez when he tried to blackmail her and then, yesterday, she attempted a third murder, but fortunately failed. While being chased down the Frigiliana-Nerja road by a police car driven by the valiant police inspector, the murderer lost control of her car and crashed into a ravine. She probably died instantly, and in spite of the efforts of the police who gave immediate assistance, the car burnt out completely.'

'There's not a word about you!' protested Julie. 'And without you there *would* have been a third murder. How you managed to find out! I just couldn't think what had come over you when you rushed me out of that shop in Nerja.'

Charles shrugged his shoulders. 'Never mind.' He pointed at a large photograph of the efficient sleuth. 'Look! There's promotion in the air. He's going to be appointed Chief Inspector.'

'Some people just have all the talent,' remarked Julie, shaking her head.

'I've also bought a German newspaper,' said Charles. 'I hope it will say less about the performance of Miguel, and more about Meier.' And he began to read. 'Yes, yes... of course,' he nodded. 'Listen: Meier married an English woman after the war and had a daughter with her, whom they christened Lesley.'

'How did he come to marry an English woman?'

'His plane was shot down over England, and he became a prisoner of war. He stayed on after the war because he was an engineer and found a good job there. Then he married but unfortunately the marriage didn't last and he went back to Germany where he made a fortune in real estate. He seems to have been an extremely successful businessman, but he withdrew from business when he was in his late fifties, and subsequently became interested in art and the protection of nature.'

They sat for a while in silence, looking at the gently sloping lines of the hills. 'So Meier came to the south of Spain because he wanted to turn his back on his old life. But what about his daughter?' asked Julie. 'What was her relationship with her father? And why did she come here? To be with him?'

'The article says that she saw very little of him once he had gone back to Germany, and by the time her mother died eight years ago, she and her father had become almost complete strangers. She had taken on her mother's surname and kept her late mother's English address, even after she had come to live out here. But the newspaper doesn't say what she came to Spain for.'

'Maybe she felt lonely after her mother had died. I bet you she wanted to be close to her father.' Julie nodded to herself. 'Why else would she have bought a property just below his?'

'Who knows?'

'So she might well have got away with the murder and collected the inheritance because there was no apparent connection between the R.R. woman of Frigiliana and the daughter of Herr Meier.'

'That's right. She flew from Malaga to Hamburg a few days ago to see her father's solicitor, presenting herself as Lesley Greenway of Torquay, England. And she had her birth certificate to support her claim on her father's inheritance. But unfortunately Meier seemed to have phoned his solicitor before his death to tell him he was making a will...'

Just then they heard steps in the staircase and there was a knock on the door: Alejandra had arrived for their lesson. When she saw the Spanish newspaper with Miguel's photograph on the front page she beamed. 'Isn't he clever! We are all so proud,' she said pointing at the photograph.

'It must be wonderful to have such a famous person in your family,' remarked Julie with barely hidden irony.

'Oh yes!' Alejandra seemed to have no inhibition about fame rubbing off on her. 'Everyone in the village keeps asking me questions. Do you realise that it took me a full hour to get here?'

'Can we ask you a few more questions?' enquired Charles.

Alejandra sat straight up. 'What is it you want to know?' She looked as if she were about to give a press interview.

'Is Charlotte going to inherit?' asked Julie. 'Have they found the will?'

'No. The police have searched the German's house methodically, but they didn't find anything.'

'How strange!' Julie shook her head. 'I just can't understand this. Didn't he make a will in her favour?'

Alejandra shrugged her shoulders. 'The police have done what they could, Julia.'

'Did your cousin's husband manage to interrogate the Englishman with the Range Rover?' interrupted Charles to change the subject. 'Well...' he corrected himself, '...without the Range Rover now.'

'That rude man! He refused to answer any questions without his lawyer being present, would you believe it! And he didn't show the slightest respect for the police. How dare he!'

'Maybe respect for authority wasn't instilled in him because he didn't grow up in Franco's Spain?' suggested Charles with a twinkle in his eyes.

'Well anyway, the police have searched their restaurant in Nerja – it's called *El Jardin de Roberto*. And guess what they discovered?'

'I have no idea.'

'They found that he had been cooking the books for years. He hadn't been paying any taxes, and the mortgage hadn't been paid for months either. The restaurant is now closed and the Englishman has been locked up. He may get five or even ten years.'

Suddenly she got up. 'I'm afraid I have to go now. I really only came to tell you that I won't have time for lessons this week. Too many people want to see me; I hope you understand.' And she said good-bye and left.

'Did you hear that?' remarked Julie after she had gone. 'Don't you think Alejandra is much more self-confident than when she first came?'

Charles suppressed a laugh. 'No wonder! She's a local celebrity now.'

'So they didn't find a will.' Julie shook her head and turned to Charles. 'Do you remember that night when we were up at Meier's house? And the person who was searching inside? I'm sure now it was the R.R. woman. She must have found the will and destroyed it!'

'I think she was rummaging through that drawer to find out about her father's solicitor,' objected Charles. 'Otherwise, how would she have known where to go to claim the inheritance?'

'But why then is there no will?'

'It wouldn't surprise me if Meier was killed before he had time to make it.'

They sat there for a while without speaking, their thoughts absorbed by the case, until Charles broke the silence. 'So that Lesley killed both her father and Fernando. And then she went for Charlotte. Once you've committed two murders, it's easy to commit a third; it's the psychology of the murderer. That woman had become a danger. She deserves to be dead.'

'Don't judge her too harshly,' countered Julie. 'I'm sure that poor woman must have suffered a lot. It wouldn't surprise me if she had killed herself.'

37

When Julie and Charles went to Charlotte's house the next morning, they found her sitting on the divan with her head bandaged and her arm in a sling. She was still weak but she seemed to have recovered from her traumatic experience and looked relaxed and even pleased. Sven was taking care of her like a first-class nurse, fussing all the time and enquiring whether she was all right, adding a cushion behind her back or under her legs... At last he left them alone; he was going to prepare tea and wanted to buy sponge cakes in one of the local grocer's shops.

'Charlotte,' asked Julie after he had gone out, 'there is something I do not understand. Why did you never tell us you knew Meier?'

At once the relaxed expression disappeared from Charlotte's face and she took some time to answer. 'I just couldn't talk about it,' she finally said, looking very sad. 'But I think I can now... you see, I was shattered when I heard he had been killed.'

'How did you meet him?'

'At an exhibition I gave last winter. We got on straightaway and I went up to his house several times afterwards. Konrad was such a refined man. He loved music and art.'

'Did you know that the woman who wanted to kill you was his daughter?' asked Charles.

'I thought she was just a neighbour. I had seen her a couple of times up at his house, but each time Konrad made it clear that he wanted her to leave.'

'So you had no idea that she planned to kill you?'

'Certainly not! She looked innocent enough the evening she knocked on my door, saying she wanted to have her bust done in marble. It was only when I was in her house yesterday and she returned wearing the jewel that I realised the danger I was in.'

'I don't understand, Charlotte,' interrupted Julie. 'What jewel are you talking about?'

'The diamond necklace Konrad found.'

'How could he have found a diamond necklace? You don't find diamond necklaces just like that.'

'Apparently Konrad had been searching for it a long time. He had been digging all over his property and even up on the hill.'

'You don't mean to say that he had been searching for the treasure of the Moors!' exclaimed Charles. 'And that he found it!'

'I don't know about a treasure... but if he had found anything else I would have known. Poor Konrad! He was always so eager to show me his prize possessions.'

'Did he find that necklace a long time ago?'

'No. Quite recently as a matter of fact. He had only just cleaned it when he showed it to me.'

'What did it look like?'

'It wasn't really a necklace. It was more like a breastplate, a thing to be worn by a high priest... or in this case an imam. It was plain, yet extraordinarily beautiful. It was made up of many larger and smaller diamonds set in silver. It represented a verse from the Koran – at least, that's what Konrad made of it.'

'Did you touch it?'

'I didn't want to, but Konrad put it around my neck while I stood in front of a mirror.'

'And did you feel something strange then?' asked Julie, almost holding her breath.

'Yes, it felt... how can I describe it... well, almost like a sacrilege. The power that emanated from it was so strong that I nearly dropped the necklace when I handed it back to Konrad. It felt like hot fire in my hands and the glow when the sun shone on it was so strong that it was blinding.'

'That's exactly what it did to me when I saw it around the woman's neck!' exclaimed Charles. 'It literally blinded me.'

'But how could that R.R. woman have had it?' wondered Julie.

'I suppose she took it after she killed her father.'

They sat there for a while. Then Charles remarked, 'You should count yourself lucky to be still alive Charlotte.'

'I still can't believe that I managed to escape,' she replied. 'I felt paralysed when the woman went for me with a block of quartz but somehow I managed to duck away in the last split second, and although she hit my shoulder I was able to open the door and rush out of that horrible house.'

'Even so, you would have been dead had it not been for Charles,' said Julie looking at him with undisguised pride.

'It wasn't me who saved her,' protested Charles. 'It was Sam.'

'Anyway…' Julie turned towards Charlotte, '…Charlotte thinks she wanted to kill you because of the inheritance. You said some time ago that you might become very rich. Did that have anything to do with Meier?'

'Yes… I thought I was going to become a multimillionaire! As both my parents have died, Konrad wanted to adopt me and leave his fortune to me. At least, that's what he told me the last time I saw him…'

'It seems he also phoned his solicitor in Hamburg to tell him he was going to make a will. When his daughter went to see the solicitor to claim the inheritance and heard that you were the one who was going to benefit, she must have been enraged. That's what must have decided her to act,' surmised Charles.

Charlotte nodded. 'When I was in her house she screamed in my face that I had stolen her inheritance!'

'But she made a mistake,' intervened Julie, 'because we've learned that no will has been found. I wonder why?' She looked questioningly at Charlotte.

'I think Konrad must have been killed before he had time to make the will.' Charlotte looked heartbroken. 'Poor Konrad.'

Suddenly Julie turned to Charles, exclaiming, 'So it was true after all, that story about the Curse! It has killed all those who touched that necklace. First Meier, and then his daughter. I hope it's not going to continue and kill Charlotte after all!'

'Of course not,' stated Charles calmly. 'The Curse is finished.'

'Why?' asked Julie and Charlotte as if with a single voice.

'Because the necklace has been destroyed.'

'But if that woman wore it the day she killed herself, it may still be in the car wreck; or else the police may have found it; or other people will. We must do something about that necklace. It brings nothing but death!' Julie seemed very agitated. 'It is evil.'

'That's not necessary. You remember that the car burned? The necklace has burned with it.'

'Silver and precious stones don't burn,' objected Julie. 'That necklace is still somewhere, ready to continue its malevolent action.'

'Precious stones don't burn but diamonds do,' corrected Charles. 'They are made of pure carbon. Of course, no one is ever going to use diamonds to make a bonfire, but in fact they burn very well. And the silver will have melted during the process.'

'What a relief!' exclaimed Charlotte. 'Maybe that's why I have been feeling so well since yesterday? The heavy cloud that oppressed me seems to have lifted.' Charlotte looked radiant indeed.

Julie turned to Charlotte. 'Still, it's a real shame you're not going to inherit. Wouldn't it have been fabulous if you had suddenly become very rich?'

'Yes,' sighed Charlotte. 'And now I will remain poor forever.'

Sven had just brought in tea and a tray laden with sponge cakes, and he had listened to the last part of the conversation with great interest. Suddenly he said, turning to Charlotte, 'My father died recently and I have inherited a substantial amount of money. I would gladly lay it at your feet.' His eyes shone. 'Would you come with me to Sweden? You can set up a studio there; I'm certain you'll become famous.'

Charlotte stared at him, surprised. 'I always thought I would live in the south. I'm not sure I want to live in Sweden.'

'Why not give it a try? The summers are beautiful there. And we can always return to Frigiliana for the winter...'

'Come on,' suggested Julie turning to Charles and pulling him by the sleeve. 'Time to go home.'

'Why did we have to leave so precipitously?' asked Charles as they were walking down Calle El Darra. 'I still wanted to ask a few more questions.'

Julie didn't answer but just said, 'I think they're going to be very happy.'

38

The Mediterranean can be misleadingly quiet. You may set sail in weather so calm that you wish for a stronger breeze, and hours later find yourself in the grip of a storm that has suddenly appeared out of nowhere. It is a treacherous sea, but that day it was as flat as a pond. The sun was warm and there wasn't a gust of wind. From the Balcón de Europa the sea was a blue expanse – the Mediterranean at its best. And a smattering of sun-worshippers were scattered over the beaches and coves, the forerunners of the millions who would inundate southern Europe within weeks.

Near the coast the water was almost transparent, and people were swimming around the rocks jutting into the sea. It was the beginning of May and the water was not very warm yet but it was better than the North Sea in August, especially in the sheltered, shallow bays where it heated up more quickly.

The Balcón de Europa had been taken over by couples with young children. The elderly and the retired, who had dominated the streets of Nerja through the winter months, had gone back north over the last few weeks like migrating birds returning to their summer nests. They had been replaced by a more mixed lot. You could see men in their late twenties wearing shorts, their milky-white legs showing their recent arrival. They were pushing prams while their young wives were busy licking ice creams with an expression of pure delight on their faces. And then there were grannies who had been brought to watch over young children, fussing and worrying while the parents were off on a sightseeing tour, freed at last for a few precious hours from the tyranny of their little darlings.

Sunbathers were sprawled on the beach trying to get some tan on their skins. They shared the available space with a few local fishermen who were leaning against a blue-and-red painted fishing boat, mending their nets only a few feet away from the provocative femininity of two young women who seemed completely unaware of the lustful stare in the fishermen's eyes. One of the women was lying on her back, the other on her stomach; they were topless and the bottoms consisted of no more than a tiny piece of cloth. They lay like lizards in the sand, the curves of their bodies, the voluptuous breasts, the round buttocks and well-filled thighs abandoned to their god and lover, the sun.

'Well, it's getting too busy and too hot for me,' observed Julie who was sitting on a bench next to Charles. 'I shall be pleased to return to the fresh air and green fields of the northern spring. No tourists there...' Then she added, 'and no murder cases to solve, which is a pity really. I must admit it was thrilling.'

'Who knows what we may run into next?' said Charles, laughing. 'By the way, there's something I still don't understand about this case. Why did Meier's daughter suddenly become so frantic? She didn't really need her father's money, did she? After all, she had her expensive restaurant here in Nerja.'

'Isn't that obvious?' Seeing that Charles looked at her as if he didn't think anything obvious, she explained. 'But don't you see? She was becoming desperate because her partner had an affair. And she thought she would win him back by becoming very rich. The only thing the R.R. man valued more than his pleasures was money. A lot of money.'

'Do you mean to say that three people died because of that pretty red-haired girl?'

'Yes. I'm not saying that girl was aware of the stir she was causing. She probably thinks only of herself. But she was the cause. She's a very dangerous girl!'

'I wonder what has become of her. Now that we're leaving we'll never know.'

They got up from their bench. A traffic jam had just formed in the narrow street that emerged into the Balcón de Europa behind a man who was unloading a van. As they strolled past the waiting cars Julie suddenly pulled Charles' sleeve.

'Look over there,' she whispered, pointing at a red-haired girl who was sitting in an open-top Mercedes sports car next to a handsome man of about forty. He had his arm around her and just as Charles looked up, the girl turned towards the man and kissed him on the lips.

'But... that's the girl friend of the R.R. man!'

'His ex-girl friend,' remarked Julie dryly.

'And... and that's the man we saw waiting for her in the *Jardin de Roberto*.'

'She hasn't wasted much time then. And I bet she hasn't finished stirring up trouble yet.'

39

Later that afternoon Charles and Julie were going for a stroll through Frigiliana. On normal days there were always some plastic bags, bits of paper or other small pieces of rubbish littering the streets, but today the pavements were impeccably clean. Charles loved those pavements. They were made of small cobblestones arranged in attractive patterns. There were S-shapes, lozenges, wings of windmills and petals, white set in a black background or black set in a white background. For the last few days, hordes of village women had been out, each sweeping the area in front of their own doorstep with long brooms. Many people had decorated their houses, and strings of flowers were hanging across the streets. It was the third of May, day of the Crosses.

As they left their house they saw a young man with dark wavy hair come out of *Locura*, kissing Peggy good-bye before going down the steps.

'I see you have an admirer,' remarked Julie.

'That's only one amongst many.' Peggy stuck up her nose and took on a blasé air.

'Well... anyway... this is a day to make a wish,' suggested Julie. 'Today anything is possible. Your wildest dreams may come true.'

'My wildest dreams?' Peggy chuckled. 'Good. I want ten admirers crawling up the steps of the street begging for my attention, with me saying, I don't want you... kicking one of them down the steps; not you... kicking another one down the steps, and so on, and they would roll down the street like balls.'

'All of them?' asked Charles, smiling.

'No, I would keep the one I fancied most. And he would be at my feet begging to be my slave.'

'That's going to be the balding man from higher up then because I'm sure he's the one you'd fancy most,' joked Charles. 'But somehow I can't imagine him lying at your feet begging to be your slave.'

'Him! He would already have rolled past the Guardia Civil post by the time I picked the one I fancied!'

They left Peggy to her fantasies and went up towards the top of the village. Crosses made of flowers had been erected in different places and garlands decorated the houses. There was a feeling of lightness – of celebration – in the air.

They met Sarah coming down with two women friends. 'Have you heard the latest news?' She was bubbling with satisfaction. 'The village Council has voted against the project! They were very upset that Sebastian got mixed up in a corruption scandal and feared that Frigiliana would get a bad reputation. They said they had been elected to protect Frigiliana and defend its reputation, and that they were not going to let themselves be manipulated by foreigners whose only interest was money.'

'Hurray!' exclaimed Julie. 'Frigiliana is saved.'

'And there's more. Remember the murdered German? I read that his nephew is going to inherit. He is active in Germany's Green Movement, and it seems that he wants to be involved in protecting the village!'

They continued along Calle Alta and then went down Calle Al Garra. A huge cross of red and white carnations stood straight in the middle of the steep narrow street. Tables had been put out in different corners loaded with food and wine, which the village people offered to anyone passing by. Charles was given a glass of Frigiliana wine and a sandwich.

'What a wonderful day,' sighed Julie.

'Yes. Blue sky, sunshine, free food and wine. What more can you wish for.'

'Look who's there!' Julie squeezed Charles' hand.

Charlotte and Sven were coming up towards them, arm in arm. He seemed transfigured; there was an expression of pure bliss on his face. And she looked prettier than they had ever seen her. Her hair was put up in a chignon, accentuating the classic features of her face, but what struck them most was the elegant way she had dressed: no more hanging baggy trousers and large pullovers but a chic flowery blouse and long skirt, which moulded her shape and moved attractively as she walked. For the first time they noticed that she had a body underneath her clothes, and a very pretty one too.

'I see that the Curse has definitely gone,' remarked Charles as they came level with them.

'Yes.' Charlotte smiled. 'And I don't ever want it to come back.'

As they continued on their way she turned around, saying, 'We're off to Sweden.' Then they vanished amongst the crowd further up the street.

'There's going to be love under the midnight sun,' remarked Julie, a large smile on her face. 'What a happy ending.'

They were walking slowly down the street when they bumped into Howard.

'Not too many people around for you?' enquired Charles.

'It doesn't matter.' He seemed relaxed. 'There's a strong concentration of positive energy right now. This is a time of great breakthroughs. The era of Aquarius is upon us. But I must be off. I have just discovered a new Uranus spot.' And Howard left them, walking away energetically, clouds of blue smoke coming out of his pipe.

'Yes,' agreed Charles. 'It does feel like a new era.'

40

A great commotion was going on in Church Square the next day. A pile of white sand had been dumped by a lorry in front of the church, leaving just enough room for cars to pass by. A man was shovelling the sand into plastic bags and then loading these onto a mule which stood with its head pressed against the wall of the church, waiting patiently for the man to finish. Two young boys, just back from school, were trying to get at the sand, grabbing handfuls of it and throwing it at each other. The man, of the wiry local type, dropped his spade every now and then, shouting at the boys and making a few menacing steps in their direction which made them flee, screaming with simulated fright, but the moment the thin man turned away and began to fill up another bag, they were back like flies.

After a while they tired of the game and began to splash each other with water from the white marble fountain in the middle of the square, drawing shrieks of disapproval from some older women who were passing by. The mule, which was now loaded, was led away up a steep street where a house was being renovated, the children ran home, and suddenly all was quiet. The square was empty but for two cats that lay dozing in the afternoon sun and a small white dog that walked by on short legs, ignoring the cats completely as if they were inferior beings.

Presently a couple of American tourists came along. They took pictures of each other in front of the old church and then began to photograph the orange trees and the brightly-coloured flowers lining the white walls while saying loudly what a picturesque, innocent village this was; they seemed to be totally unaware of the dramas that had taken place here so recently.

Everything had returned to normal. And somehow it seemed as if nothing had happened; as if nothing would, or could, ever happen here in Frigiliana.